Sand, Sea, & Second Chances

Sand, Sea, & Second Chances

A GULL ISLAND ROMANCE

GULL ISLAND
BOOK ONE

CATHERINE MICHAELS

Cover by Dena McMurdie

ISBN: 978-0-9983372-4-1

Library of Congress Control Number: 2024907492

Created with Vellum

To my husband, Jan Michael. You weathered every storm—from my writer's block blizzards to the tech-gremlin attacks during this book's creation. Here's proof our love story is truly epic, for more than three decades and counting.

May

GULL ISLAND NORTH CAROLINA

"May is the month of expectation, the month of wishes, the month of hope."

— EMILY BRONTE

Chapter One

KATE

Kate Fiore stepped up to the front porch of her rented bungalow. The relentless sun had bleached the once-bright red door to a pale rosy hue, while the heat danced off the white shell driveway. A gentle breeze brushed against her cheek, carrying the briny perfume of the ocean and the scent of jasmine from a nearby garden. Taped to the door, a note scrawled in black Sharpie swayed in the wind, its edges curled as if eager to reveal its secrets.

Kate shielded her eyes from the blinding sun with her hand, casting a shadow across the note she was trying to read. She squinted, her lips moving slightly as she deciphered the scribbled words:

Welcome to Gull Island!
Door's open. Make yourself at home.
Mae Gray

Five hundred miles of asphalt, then forty minutes of winding coast. Kate craved only two things: a frigid shower to chase away the highway dust and a bed that would swallow her whole. The unlocked 1930s bungalow, nestled behind Gray Cottage, promised both, a silent welcome that surpassed any Southern charm she'd imagined.

She had parked her Prius next to her rental's tidy yard secluded from beachgoers across the road. A red Bougainvillea vine flanked the small front porch, its fiery blooms twirling around a white lattice panel on one side and a terracotta pot stuffed with blood-red geraniums anchoring opposite. Cool air humming from the living room AC box greeted Kate when she sank into a plump chintz sofa. She fired off a safe-arrival text to her mother, and a classic Mom reply pinged instantly.

> Flad u made it. Get food night sleep.
> FaceTime us Subday.

Kate cracked a weary smile. FaceTiming with her family on Sunday was the perfect defense against encroaching homesickness. Her thumbs danced across the screen, sending a cascade of heart emojis in response.

The plush cushions welcomed Kate as she took in the beachy trinkets sprinkled around the room—sand dollar wreath, glass vase stuffed with seashells, and nautical maps. A driftwood plaque challenged her, *Life's better in flip-flops*. With a sigh, she slipped off her red Chucks as a sense of disconnect washed over her. *Clearly not in synch here,* she thought.

A grinning elderly woman and gentleman sporting a fedora and bowtie beamed with joy in the photograph resting on the color-washed side table. CeCe had mentioned that Mae had never married, but Kate wondered if love had found her later in life. The thought made Kate smile.

Her curiosity led her to the quaint kitchen, a desire to unravel the secrets of her summer home. On impulse, she bent under the antique farm sink and twisted the faucet. Cold water drenched her hair, running down her shoulders and soaking her white tank top. She didn't care if she looked like a participant in a wet T-shirt contest. The impromptu shower invigorated her.

She was tempted to explore more, but her practical side took over. Time to facc the scorching furnace to fetch her things from her car.

SWEAT STUNG KATE'S EYES AS SHE PACED ON THE porch, cursing her city-honed automatic reflex to lock the door behind her. The late afternoon sun beat down, mercilessly mirroring the inferno in her head. Eve Snow, her trusty Prius, waited patiently in the driveway, windows reflecting the heat like a bad omen. The five-hour drive after Baltimore had been a nightmare–air conditioning not working, hair whipping in the wind, skin burning. Now, stranded on Gull Island, her haven had become a fortress, with her keys, phone, and sanity held hostage inside.

Uncertainty gnawed at her. Mae Gray wasn't around to help, her return a mystery. Kate leaned against the weathered wood, each ragged breath a silent scream. She couldn't stand on the porch, watching her car, forever.

Sweat trickled down her face as she hopped barefoot through the shrubs to Gray Cottage, the main house where Mae lived. The stately home, a picture of island charm with its deep gray walls and white trim, offered no solace. The neat hedges and vibrant blooms only mocked her disarray. No one was around. Panic clawed at her throat, transforming her into a one-woman summer blues band: aching feet, pounding headache, and a chorus of buzzing mosquitoes for backup.

Back to the porch. The window, a cruel tease, mocked her with a glimpse of her phone, her lifeline. She pressed her face against the glass, frustration hardening her features. Then, a deep breath, the kind meant to calm, but instead inflated her chest with a frustrated huff.

It didn't work. The urge to scream, to release the pent-up months of upheaval, was overwhelming. This lock-out was another cruel twist, a metaphor for the divorce, the job loss, the whole mess. But then, a memory flickered–her teenage self, scaling a window after forgetting her key. She'd done it once. She could do it again.

Kate rattled the porch window, but it wouldn't budge. Undeterred, she followed the stone path, tugging at paint-stuck windows until one yielded. "Come on," she muttered, hoisting herself up on the siding. A yelp escaped her lips as a rough clapboard scraped her shins, but she pushed through the sting.

As she was about to throw herself inside, a deep voice boomed behind her, shattering her focus.

"Need help, ma'am? Maybe with your acrobatics routine?"

Kate twisted, losing her grip and landing on a bed of hostas with a thud that had her questioning her tailbone's integrity. Scrambling up, she dusted herself off, a torrent of Italian curses escaping her lips.

"No! I was fine until you startled me," she hissed, heart hammering against her ribs.

A man, his face shaded by a baseball cap, stood a few feet away, amusement dancing in his eyes. His polo shirt and work boots hinted at practicality, while his Ray-Bans reflected the disheveled cat burglar Kate must have appeared.

"No need to worry," he drawled, his voice laced with the laid-back cadence of the island. "I'm trying to be neighborly."

Kate crossed her arms, acutely aware of her damp shirt clinging to her skin. "Everything's fine," she lied, her voice betraying her vulnerability. "I'm renting the bungalow. You can be on your way."

He chuckled a low rumble that seemed to amuse him more than her discomfort. "I'm sure you can handle it, ma'am. But Mae asked me to see you're settled before she gets back from Wilmington."

He seemed kind, but the heat and her frustration had worn her patience thin. "Why the 'ma'am'? Do I look like your grandma?"

His grin widened and his eyes twinkled. "That's how my mama raised me."

Kate's sigh was a barely contained explosion.

"You should get inside and cool down," he said, his tone infuriatingly calm.

"D'uh! That's what I was doing when you interrupted me," she snapped, her voice a mix of anger and vulnerability. "I'm locked out."

He chuckled again. "Huh. Here I thought you were trying a new TikTok challenge."

Kate glared. "Got a better idea?"

He nodded, a mischievous glint in his eyes. “I might. Now, if you’ll step aside...”

Before she could protest, he was past her, shutting the window with an effortless thud. The earthy scent of mulch, familiar from her childhood days of helping Dad in the garden, filled her nose as he stepped away.

Another string of Italian expletives escaped her lips. “Why did you do that?” she demanded, stomping her bare foot in the hostas, instantly regretting it as pain shot up her ankle.

He chuckled again, the sound washing over her like the island breeze. “Don’t need you falling again. Miss Mae will have my head if you get hurt. You’re better off using the spare key under the flowerpot on the porch.”

Kate stared at him, unsure if he was joking. “So, not under the welcome mat?” she asked, trying to lighten the mood despite the throbbing in her ankle and butt.

He shrugged. “Nah. Too obvious.” He gestured for her to follow him to the porch, where he lifted the edge of the geranium pot to reveal the hidden key. “Easier than you attacking a window,” he said.

Relief flooded Kate, washing away the exhaustion. She grabbed the key, clutching it like she’d won the lottery. All she needed now was a shower and a vacation from reality.

“Thank you,” she said, hoping he’d get the hint and leave as she moved to unlock the door.

He studied her for a moment, then spoke, his voice softer now. “That’s how we do things on Gull Island. We watch out for each other. Not like city folk up North. Afternoon, ma’am.”

The cap dipped once, a curt farewell. Then he vanished into the emerald thicket, swallowed whole by the humid jungle.

She scoffed, shaking her head. The island's quirky charm, suffocating in this relentless heat, felt absurdly heavy. Spare key tucked back in its secret nook, she slumped onto the plump sofa. Phone already clutched, she fired off a text to CeCe, who pinged back in an instant, her signature exuberance blazing through the screen:

> HOORAY!
>
> Welcome to North Carolina! Lunch tomorrow. 1:00 our place xoxoxox

College memories of watching their favorite old movie stormed Kate's mind as she typed a reply to her bestie, a wry smile pulling at her lips: "As you wish."

Sinking deeper into the soft cushions, exhaustion finally dragged down her shoulders. Doubt, a persistent itch, wouldn't be ignored. The video interview nailed, CeCe's unwavering support secured, a nagging question still circled: had she chased a summer mirage, a colossal mistake disguised as an island escape?

Chapter Two

KATE

Dusk cast long shadows over the porch as Kate wrestled her suitcase through the doorway and across the old oak floors. This place felt strange, almost foreign, compared to the familiarity of her Connecticut home. This quaint bungalow on Gull Island was a temporary refuge, a fresh start after the emotional tsunami that had been her life lately.

Heaving the luggage onto the bed, she surveyed the room. It was a step up from "quaint," more of a luxurious Airbnb rental with its four-poster bed, plush linens, and a sitting nook framed by seascapes. Sunlight poured through double windows, revealing a patch of emerald lawn dotted with a picket fence and a small deck with an inviting red bistro set.

A bittersweet laugh escaped Kate's lips as she imagined herself spending the summer in this oasis. But the laughter quickly died, replaced by the echo of memories. Picnics in the park with Jon, cozy movie nights, European vacations, vintage treasure hunts... all shattered by the cruel wreckage of their marriage's demise.

Her fingers drifted to the silver locket on her neck, a relic from a bygone era of love and happiness. Jon had gifted it on their first anniversary, a heart-shaped pendant sparkling with diamonds, a symbol of their unwavering love. She twisted the delicate chain, taking in its familiar comfort as the cool metal scraped between her fingers.

She crossed the bathroom to wash away tears tracing hot paths down her cheeks. Leaning against the old sink, the cool ceramic was a comfort against the fire of heartbreak. Jon's mocking denials still echoed in her mind, mingling with the scent of Mae's citrus soap. With a trembling hand, she splashed more water onto her face. Cool water dripped off her chin, leaving trails of chill against the burning heat of her tears.

A stranger stared at her from her reflection in the mirror–pale skin stretched taut over cheekbones, haunted eyes staring back. This wasn't the woman who once walked through life with a smile like sunshine and confidence to knock on boardrooms. This was the face Gull Island would see, a face sculpted by loss.

A relentless tattoo of knocking drilled through Kate's thoughts. Someone at the door. With a sigh, she straightened, wiping the last smudges of tears. She hurried through the unfamiliar layout, toes protesting on what might have been a chair, might have been a rogue ottoman.

Reaching the door, she squinted against the night spilling through the open crack. A silhouette stood framed in the amber glow of the yard light, a tall woman wreathed in soft shadows. Short white hair, catching stray moonlight, danced around her face like a halo.

"Tired traveler, I presume? All those hours of solo highway driving!" The woman's voice boomed, warm and laced with amusement. A tray materialized in her hands, laden with the scent of warm pastries and something spicy and intoxicating.

Kate frowned, her sleep-deprived brain struggling to make sense of yet another stranger at her door.

The woman threw back her head, a laugh like wind chimes in a summer breeze. "Where's my manners? I'm your very own welcome wagon–Mae Gray."

Kate held the door as Mae stepped inside, expertly flipping on a lamp in the dark room. Then, with a flourish, Mae unveiled the bounty clustered on antique china serving ware. Chilled shrimp with dipping sauce. Warm biscuits alongside a cup of strawberry jam. Lemonade, the color of sunshine in a tall tumbler, ice cubes clinking. And a slice of strawberry pie that tickled Kate's nose with its sweet aroma.

"I hope you like strawberry pie," Mae beamed, leading Kate to the kitchen's small oak table. "I made some with fresh berries this morning for my SOS meeting and saved some for you."

SOS meeting? Was that something Kate should know about? It sounded dangerous.

"Bless your heart, Kate! You must be tuckered out," Mae prattled on. "Sit right here, and eat when you feel like it."

Mae opened the fridge and pantry, pointing out the stocked supplies. Caught between sleep and surprise, Kate struggled to find her voice. "Yes, thank you, ma'am."

Kate gave herself a mental head-slap. Now she was ma'am-ing somebody!

"Call me Mae, hon," her host chuckled, nudging a plate of golden biscuits and jam towards Kate. "Everybody does except for my former students, who still call me Miss Mae after all these years."

Kate bit into a biscuit and moaned as the sugary dough and buttermilk melted in her mouth.

"You must be parched from this heat, too. Have some lemonade."

Kate took a tentative sip. It slid down cool and velvety. She gulped another.

Before Kate could thank her, Mae nodded to a sheet of paper pinned to the refrigerator by a seagull-shaped magnet. "I jotted down things you'll need to settle. Harris Teeter and Food Lion are nearby for groceries. And there are nice shops on the island and over on the mainland in South Harbor. You know where the aquarium is located? Well, of course, you must."

Kate had no idea where anything was beyond her quick Google search.

Not waiting for an answer, Mae pointed to her list. "Best beaches are across the street, and at the Point, ten minutes down Island Drive for gorgeous sunsets. Need anything else, hon, besides a hot bath and good night's sleep?"

Kate yawned and rubbed her eyes, her sleep-deprived brain struggling to keep up with Mae.

Mae's gaze snagged on Kate's rumpled clothing and mussed hair. "CeCe tells me you've had a rough patch," she said, her blue eyes intelligent and kind.

Kate's throat tightened, an unexpected lump forming. The stranger's simple kindness had cracked a door she didn't even know was creaking. A single tear slid down her cheek, tracing a cool path through the warmth of her flushed skin. She fumbled for the silver heart pendant at her neck, its familiar weight grounding her even as her insides churned. A quick blink stemmed the tide of tears, replaced by a shaky nod and a forced smile. It wouldn't do to crumble here, not now.

"Glad you're here," Mae whispered, pulling her into a hug.

Kate melted into Mae's welcoming arms, her tears now tracing paths down her face. It wasn't only the divorce, but the sudden loss of her dream job and the uncertainty of the future. She came to Gull Island seeking refuge, a chance to start over, and Mae's kindness, like a warm summer breeze, had chased away the chill of her sorrow.

"It will be all right, hon," Mae whispered. "Gull Island has you now. Get some rest and call me if you need anything."

With those last words of reassurance, Mae Gray left as abruptly as she had arrived, leaving Kate alone again.

In the silence of the old bungalow, Kate felt the absence of her family echo hollow in the space. She missed the boisterous dinners with her extended family and the familiar warmth of her parents' hugs. Margaret and Michael Fiore, her pillars of strength, were miles away, and the ache of distance was a physical pull in her chest. They believed their only child would land on her feet, and she had almost succeeded.

But Viviane's startup offer hadn't worked out. And before that, the dream job in Stamford that had shimmered like a mirage in the desert had vanished in a single email, a hiring freeze swallowing her hopes whole. It felt like a lifetime ago.

Kate shook herself. The scent of strawberry filling the air was a sweet distraction. The quaint kitchen, with its overflowing cupboards and travel tips stuck to the fridge with a seagull magnet, felt like a scene from another world. This was her new reality, and Mae Gray, with her booming laughter and boundless kindness, felt like the perfect guide through this uncharted territory.

Chapter Three

KATE

Traffic was light on Saturday morning as Kate drove down Island Drive, a cup of coffee in hand and Mae's biscuits still on her breath. Her Prius hugged the curves as she made a test run towards the Gull Island aquarium, anticipation rising with every mile.

The ocean glistened in the sun, sprawling before her as if it were a sparkling jewel. She slowed down, transfixed by the vibrant water and breathtaking beach homes. What was it like to have such an incredible home with a view like this?

She swallowed the lump in her throat as she remembered the modest Cape Cod she once shared with Jon. It had been a walkable half-mile to the path along Saint-Mary's-by-the Sea along the harbor, and she thought that was a gift. She couldn't imagine oceanfront living.

A solitary jogger waved from the sidewalk that paralleled Island Drive, prompting a smile and a wave in return. This easygoing island vibe was pleasant, and she wanted to explore more.

But first, she had to locate the aquarium and buy a thank-you gift for CeCe before their lunch. Mae's note pinned to the refrigerator made it easy for Kate.

Gift and Garden on Bay Street in South Harbor. You must stop here! Tell Annie Lawson I sent you.

Kate nudged Eve Snow into the entrance of the aquarium. She should have known better than to be distracted, but the quirky metal sculpture of oversized fish swimming in a fountain was irresistible. And then a flower-drenched path led her to the wide bronze doors of the Visitors Center, drawing her in even more.

A jovial twenty-something woman with streaks of purple hair and a nose ring smiled from the kiosk. "Welcome to Gull Island Aquarium. Are you a visitor or member?"

"I–I'm Kate Fiore," she stammered, biting her bottom lip, "stepping in for CeCe Greenwood this summer… I wonder if–"

"Of course, Kate! You don't have your ID yet. No problem-o," the woman cut in, brandishing a visitor's pass with the gusto of a sommelier offering a rare wine. "Enjoy yourself!"

Soft lights glowed on the polished floor as Kate stepped into the cool, humid embrace of the aquarium. Schools of neon fish zipped through sun-drenched tanks, their scales catching the light like shimmering jewels. Jellyfish swayed like alien flowers, their tentacles floating in the water with a mesmerizing grace.

Voices of eager visitors echoed down the corridor as Kate's steps led to a room where a waist-high salt-water tank brimmed with sea creatures. A stingray, its diamond-shaped body cutting through the water with silent power, glided past. Beside Kate, a boy with a mop of sun-bleached hair and a gap-toothed grin chirped,

"They're like giant underwater pancakes! They wouldn't hurt a fly."

The boy showed how to pet the pancake with two soft touches on the ray's fins and said, without a clue about her avoidance reaction, "Or use one finger if you're scared."

Her pulse hammered against her ribs, drowning out the chatter of the crowd. This wasn't excitement, not even awe. It was pure, unadulterated dread.

Kate's hand hovered over the stingray's slick back, her fear an icy knot in her stomach. Two tentative touches, as the boy instructed, then a shaky retreat. Relief washed over her, but the triumph was short-lived. Across the tank, a spiky-domed carapace emerged from the sand. A horseshoe crab, the monster from her childhood nightmares, scuttled towards her. Panic clawed at her throat.

The boy, eager for a repeat performance, started chanting, "Do it! Do it!" Kate froze, her past clawing its way to the present. The boy's shrill chant escalated, attracting a swarm of wide-eyed toddlers. Panic welled in her throat, embarrassment flamed her cheeks as the echo of tiny tormentors filled the space. Kate's fingers, already clammy, found purchase on the cold metal rim.

A booming voice sliced through the Baby Shark cacophony. "Attention, miniature mariners!"

Kate's gaze landed on a name badge glinting amongst the sun-kissed wrinkles of a nearby volunteer. It read "Mansour," and the man himself, a twinkle dancing in his eye, gestured towards a vast, inviting space.

"Shark feeding time! Witness our fearless diver become a gourmet appetizer... maybe." His wink elicited shrieks and giggles as the children raced to the shark tank.

Kate's stomach churned. This wasn't the welcoming committee she'd envisioned. Yet Mansour's grin, infectious and genuine, somehow calmed her.

"Welcome aboard, Kate. Stage fright like that happens to the best of us."

"Wait, How do you know my name?"

Mansour grinned, his eyes sparkling. "Must be those coms buzzing with gossip... or I saw you check in earlier."

"And don't worry," he said, his voice dropping to a conspiratorial whisper, "touching the horseshoe crab isn't mandatory. But the sharks..." His voice dipped with playful menace.

Kate's heart sank. Kids jeering at her for bailing at the touch tank was not the first impression she wanted to make. She pasted on a grateful smile, mumbled her thanks, and fled past the shark tank.

KATE STEPPED INTO THE HUSHED IMMENSITY OF THE SEA turtle wing, her pulse finally settling into a steady rhythm. The space brimmed with an otherworldly serenity. Each cylindrical tank held a solitary turtle, adrift in its private saltwater oasis, leaving a gentle, rhythmic slap against the glass wall–their sole audience was the soft glow of fluorescent lights above.

She bent to read a sign attached to the closest tank:

. . .

JUVENILE LOGGERHEAD SEA TURTLE

Diagnosis: Boat strike. Injuries to the carapace and soft tissue.

Treatment: Injectable antibiotics and daily wound cleaning with antibiotic cream.

SUNLIGHT DAPPLED THE SHELL OF THE INJURED loggerhead, painting its weathered grooves with gold. Kate knelt beside the tank. The turtle blinked, its wise eyes mirroring the pain and resilience she knew so well.

Her heart tugged at the sight of the injured turtle, with its shell battered like a warrior's shield. She whispered, "Hey there, Flippy," with a single finger tracing its contours through the glass.

The turtle blinked again, a slow wink that lingered a beat too long. In that pause, Kate swore she saw a spark of mischief, a silent understanding. Then, with a flick of its flippers, it drifted away, leaving behind a trail of bubbles and the lingering scent of salt and freedom.

She tapped once more on the tank. "We'll get you back to the ocean, I promise."

"That's exactly right," a soft voice behind her confirmed.

She stood, drawn by a warmth radiating behind her from Mae Gray, blue eyes twinkling like the sun on the water. Blushing, Kate straightened her sundress. "Getting acquainted with the locals," she said, the turtle's mischievous wink replaying in her mind. "I didn't know you volunteered here."

Mae leaned closer, her voice a conspiratorial whisper. "Retired life wasn't all it was cracked up to be, hon. These little guys need all the help they can get." She glanced at the injured loggerhead. "Especially ones like Flippy there."

Before Kate could reply, Mae's gaze shifted to the ocean beyond the windows. "You know, we have a team who patrols the beaches for nests and injured turtles. Dedicated folks, like you. And we need another volunteer to fill in for a few weekends."

Kate's ears perked up. A way to fill the void, to channel her pain into something good. Her fingers clenched, anticipation fizzing beneath her skin. "Could someone like me…?"

Mae cut her off with a grin. "Absolutely! We'd be lucky to have you, Kate. And don't worry, you'll have the best teacher under the sun. He knows these shores like nobody else."

A jolt of adrenaline surged through Kate, igniting a spark of hope in her eyes. This was it. A new beginning. "When do I start?" she blurted, the question tumbling out like a wave.

Mae's smile widened. "Come by Gray Cottage at three tomorrow. Meet your team, take your first patrol, and get to know Gull Island up close and personal."

Sunday afternoon's FaceTime call loomed, family faces flickering on a screen. The prospect of joining Mae and the turtle team afterward offered a welcome anchor, a chance to trade loneliness for seashells and purpose.

She clasped the older woman's hand. "It's a deal, Mae. You have yourself a new turtle team member."

Family, FaceTime, and flippers, Kate thought, feeling like a woman reborn. Sunday was going to be epic.

Chapter Four

LUKE

The Gift and Garden in South Harbor buzzed with Saturday morning energy as coastal weekenders sought souvenirs. In the stockroom, Luke McAllister sorted through birdhouses—boats, cottages, and lighthouses–designed to catch shoppers' eyes.

His focus wavered until his sister Annie's voice jolted him. With her red-gold hair pinned up, she exuded confidence despite the challenges of single motherhood.

"Almost done, Luke?" she asked.

He raised his fist with a thumbs up. "Yep. Then one last delivery unless you need me."

Annie grinned, slipping out. "I always need you, Big Brother, not at the store right now. Speaking of need, how about a haircut?"

He laughed, running a hand through his overdue locks, making a mental note for a trim. Finishing touches in place, Luke heard a familiar voice. Peeking through the curtain, he saw the brunette from Gray Cottage, now refreshed in a red sundress that swirled around her like a sunrise. Freed from its slipshod ponytail, her chestnut brown hair, the color of baked earth, danced across her shoulders.

"How can I help?" his sister asked.

"I'm looking for Annie Lawson. Mae Gray says she'll help me find a gift for my friend."

"I'm Annie Lawson. Happy to help. What do you have in mind?"

"Not sure. She's renovating an older home in South Harbor."

Annie looked thoughtful. "Can't go wrong with summer annuals."

Luke shook his head, overhearing the woman's carefree giggle. This version was better than last night's hot, cranky encounter.

"She's expecting twins, so easy care," the woman explained.

"I have the perfect thing for a new mother," Annie said. "Come on, let's look!"

Luke imagined his mother's wistful expression hearing that news. She'd throw Luke what he called her "Hopeful Baby Look." One she'd directed his way often enough. Mom wasn't giving up hope for another grandchild, and her son was the top candidate.

When the women returned, his sister was talking in that chirpy, excited tone of hers when she made somebody happy. "Your friend will adore this, Kate."

First names already? It didn't surprise him. Annie Lawson could talk to a tree, and it would answer back. He moved the curtain, smiling as Annie showcased a rustic planter exploding with delicate emerald leaves. Baby's tears! She nailed it again.

His sister rang up the sale. "If your friend has questions about plant care, please tell her to see me. And come back soon!"

Kate vanished down the street, the monstrous potted plant casting a wobbly shadow behind her. Luke felt a phantom itch at his neck, where a bead of sweat threatened to break free. He couldn't shake that unexpected smile today. It was such a stark contrast to the woman he'd met at Gray Cottage yesterday, arms crossed and voice clipped. Now, he wondered which facade was real: the bristling warrior or this sun-kissed stranger.

Something tugged in his chest, a nameless ache that gnawed at the edges. Regret? Curiosity? A missed opportunity? He chided himself for leaving her so abruptly. Not stepping up to greet her today. Fists clenched, he made a silent promise: if there was a next time, he'd do more to get to know her.

But as he looked down at his worn boots, resentment flickered. What if she were just another transplant, another face blurring into the throng overrunning his beloved town in a tide of pastel cottages and McMansion wannabes? Her clipped Yankee vowels echoed in his head, a constant reminder of the widening cultural chasm. Would she be another oblivious newcomer, blind to the delicate fabric of life here? He hoped she'd find the beauty and vulnerability of this place he called home.

Salt wind whipped Luke's hair as he rolled down the truck windows, hungry for the open sky. The rumble of the bridge beneath his tires resonated with a familiar hum, a counterpoint to the late, great Jimmy Buffett's lyrics weaving from the speakers. It was a ritual, crossing this metal spine that stitched South Harbor to Gull Island, a gateway to his childhood haven. Every crossing held a memory, from childhood popsicle races to chasing the fiery dusk as it plunged below the salt marshes. His lungs drank in the air, an elixir of brine and sunshine, the essence of perfect spring.

But his bliss was shattered by the sight of a McMansion standing in place of the cozy cottage he remembered. The once-charming beach home was now reborn as a monstrosity of glass and chrome, a monument to the island's relentless gentrification. He longed for the simpler days of Gull Island he remembered, before the moneyed tide washed over his haven. Frustration gnawed at him as he parked and prepared for the promised delivery before returning to South Harbor to help his friend.

Hoisting a metal urn of flowering annuals, Luke climbed the steps to the deck. The tall blonde woman with violet eyes who waited there beamed.

"What a beauty," she crooned, gesturing at the flowers. "Perfect for punching up this place."

Luke swallowed, the bile rising in his throat. The place was punched up enough already. "Where do you want it?" he forced himself to ask with as much politeness as he could muster.

She pointed, then changed her mind, then changed it again. With each move, her voice became a grating melody of dissatisfaction. Luke's patience, already thin, began to fray. He wasn't delivering flowers. He was performing a ridiculous ballet for her amusement.

"That should do it, ma'am," he finally growled, wiping his sweaty face.

The blonde studied him, her brows knitting. Her designer

jeans and elegant blouse felt alien compared to his sunbaked skin and worn work jeans.

"Luke McAllister?" Her voice, saccharine and dripping with surprise, snagged on his name. Surprise morphed into amusement, the corner of her lips lifting in a suggestive smirk.

"Only a few gray threads but those eyes..." Her words trailed off, replaced by a lingering gaze that sent a shiver down his spine. A shiver tinged with...something. Recognition? Regret? Or simply the unsettling warmth of her unfiltered interest?

She pouted and clutched a manicured hand to her salon-styled blonde tresses. "I'm crushed you don't remember me. Is it my hair color?"

She arched a perfectly shaped brow and gave a flirty wink. Then he knew. Savannah Scott!

Memories, unwelcome and vivid, flooded him. A stolen kiss beneath the bridge, the sharp taste of salt on her lips, her intoxicating scent of jasmine. Then, the betrayal, a jagged shard of ice piercing his gut. The bitter months of picking up the pieces, the eventual relief of finally letting go.

But he had no bitterness now. Only the faintest memory of what once was. He smiled, a wry twist of his lips. Some storms leave rainbows.

He shifted and wiped his brow. "What are you doing back on the island, Savannah?" he asked. "That big house with your doctor husband in Chapel Hill not enough?"

Her pout deepened, a wrinkle marring the carefully curated facade. "Having myself a little beachside escape while I wait for divorce number two, darling. Care to join me for a drink? Between old friends, of course."

He stepped closer, his gaze narrowing. The cloying scent of

her perfume, once intoxicating, now clawed at his throat. "Savannah," he said, his voice low, each syllable precise, "we were many things once, but never friends."

He tipped his cap, the brim casting a cool shadow over his eyes, and turned on his heels. He had a friend to help and a life to live. Savannah Scott was no longer a part of either.

Chapter Five

KATE

The bridge to South Harbor loomed like a metal dragon, its shadow swallowing the morning sun. Kate's sundress, once a vibrant red, now clung to her like a wilted rose. The air was thick, a heavy blanket that choked her lungs and frizzed her hair into a rebellious halo. Even NPR's soothing drone couldn't drown out the rhythmic thuds of her car bouncing over the bridge's expansion joints.

Five miles across the waterways, Gift and Garden had been a haven, a riot of color and scent that soothed her jangled nerves. Mae's recommendation was a lifesaver—just the place for CeCe's gift—and Annie, bless her sweet soul, had been a dream to deal with!

With a gift secured and time to spare before lunch at the Greenwood's, she wandered down Front Street, her feet seeking the cool shade of a store awning. A coffee shop, nestled between a bookstore and a gelato stand, beckoned. An iced skinny mocha latte in hand, she found a weathered bench overlooking the marina. The gentle slap of waves against pilings, reminding her of strolls back home along the boardwalk at Saint-Mary's-by-the Sea.

Her fingers clenched on the cold mug. This time last year, Jon had gone for his run, no phone. She never pried, but with renovations looming, the ping of a new message had lured her in.

Jon, I'm lonely.

A string of texts, intimate selfies with a stranger, and words that carved canyons of betrayal had followed the message. Marriage meant forever, she'd believed, through good times and bad. Couple's counseling, even. But Jon had not spent those late nights at the office grinding reports. They were stolen moments of passion, shared with someone else.

Rage, hot and primal, had surged through her. His phone, shattered against the floor, echoing the breaking of their vows. Bags packed, his belongings dumped on the lawn, she'd sought refuge in the familiar warmth of her parents' kitchen, numb as they tried to mend her broken heart.

Now, the splintery bench mirrored her own jagged state. Each swallow of icy coffee was a slow thaw, a return from the numbness. Down the boardwalk, seagulls squawked and danced around a departing charter boat of excited tourists, their laughter ringing in her ears. She waved back at visitors, envying their carefree excitement.

One day, that lightness would be hers again. She had to make space for it—reclaim the life she put on hold for the past year of chaos. A fresh start beckoned, but it came with an undercurrent of fear. August loomed, the end of her contract, a return to an unknown future in Black Rock. What waited for her when September came?

The question hung heavy in the air, casting shadows on her next steps. But for now, she focused on the cool breeze, the salty tang of the sea, the promise of a latte's sweetness. One step at a time, she would rebuild her life.

Cobblestones crunched under Kate's sandals as she left Eve Snow, stepping into a world of quaint eighteenth- and nineteenth-century homes and gardens. Crimson ribbons adorned trees and porches, a jarring note in the historic district that left Kate wondering.

The white Victorian with its red-shuttered eyes, a familiar vision from countless bestie-gram photos, greeted Kate like an old friend. Sun-drenched steps led to the porch awash in sky-blue, each creak a welcome. Then, a sun-kissed bronze goddess greeted Kate in the doorway, her smile brighter than it had any right to be. Kate leaned in her hug, CeCe's lavender scent whispering of late-night talks and shared dreams. Years turned to moments, laughter echoing back to their carefree college roomie days.

"It's been too long," Kate murmured, her voice thick with affection.

Kate offered the basket of baby's tears, its greenery cascading over her outstretched hand. "For you and the little ones," she said, watching CeCe trace the delicate foliage.

Kate's breath caught in her throat. CeCe, finally face-to-face, was radiant. Motherhood bloomed on her, a new light in her eyes now rich with earthy wisdom. A pink-ruffle maternity jumper hugged her baby bump, and her eyes held a deeper, earthier intensity. "You're glowing," Kate whispered, a hint of longing laced in her voice.

CeCe blushed, hand resting on her expansive belly. "Well that plus tired and peeing constantly."

"We have that in common," Kate said, a laugh momentarily masking the pang in her heart. CeCe and David, years of trying, a ticking clock, and now, this miracle. "Everything okay otherwise?"

"Absolutely! And you taking over at the aquarium while I'm on leave is a lifesaver. But come in! Tour time!"

Kate stepped into the light-filled foyer as CeCe cradled the baby's tears in the walnut hall tree. "We can't believe we'll be parents soon," CeCe whispered, fingers stroking the delicate leaves.

Memories, unwelcome guests, flooded Kate's mind. *Not now, not when they were so happy! Don't ruin it!*

A shadow flickered across CeCe's face. "Oh, Kate! I'm so sorry."

Kate couldn't hide her sadness from her friend. CeCe knew all too well what lay beneath the surface of this moment. "It's okay, really... only my past sneaking up on me."

Kate forced a smile. She and Jon had longed for children. Had they gotten their chance, might things have turned out differently?

CeCe squeezed her friend's hand and asked one last time, "Sure you're all right?"

Kate let out a shaky breath. "Yeah, I'm getting there," she said, ready to turn the subject away from her bumpy past. "Anyway, your home looks ready for a magazine spread!"

CeCe beamed. "It was a fright when we bought it, but we saw

its potential. The garden and downstairs are mostly done, but David stopped everything to get the nursery ready."

"Did I hear my name?" David Greenwood shouted as he flew down the creaking oak staircase. "Katie-Kat Fiore, get ready for me to hug your neck!"

A paint-splattered giant, LeBron doppelgänger in jeans and a T-shirt, scooped Kate into a bear hug, his beard tickling her cheek.

David's playful tug at Kate's ponytail brought a burst of giggles. "How you been, Katie-Kat?"

"Better with the Greenwoods nearby," she said, already reaching for another hug.

CeCe rolled her eyes, but the glint in them betrayed her amusement. "David, don't squeeze the life out of our guest," she teased.

He released Kate, the warmth lingering, and pulled his wife close, a gentle kiss gracing the top of her head. "A few more minutes, Sweetness. Then, nursery reveal with Katie-Kate, promise?"

"Please! I can't stand the suspense. Kate and I will start lunch. Let us know when your masterpiece is ready."

Kate watched David sprint up the stairs, two steps at a time, a familiar mix of amusement and admiration washing over her. CeCe and David's meet-cute, a Carolina-Duke basketball clash where hunky history scholar met ambitious MBA student, still brought a smile to her face. She remembered CeCe's excited phone call, gushing about this "dreamboat in Tar Heel blue," like it was yesterday.

CeCe and David had an undeniable connection from the moment they met. It was energy that jumped between them like sparks of electricity. On their wedding day, Kate stood proudly as maid of honor while they said their vows and saw it magnified.

That same crackling connection still flamed between them after a decade. Theirs was an all-consuming, walking-on-air kind of love. The kind that made you feel you could do anything. They were best friends and lovers, all rolled into one. Kate once hoped for that kind of connection. Even though she thought she had it with Jon, but now she knew better. It wasn't meant to be for her.

Sensing her bestie's thoughts, CeCe put an arm around Kate. "There are good ones like David out there, Kate," she said. "Don't let one awful experience discourage you."

Kate shook her head. "Someday, but not now," she said with a rueful smile. "I'm renovating myself first. Honestly, CeCe, I'd rather stay single forever than fall into another disastrous relationship."

"You never know." CeCe winked, beckoning Kate to follow. "Just keep yourself open to possibilities."

THE GREENWOOD KITCHEN WAS A SEAMLESS BLEND OF old and new. Tall windows allowed sunlight to fill the room, while an oak table and French doors leading out to a small garden provided a cozy atmosphere. Kate glanced at the yard in awe, taking in the stone patio, carefully placed shrubs, and colorful flower beds that surrounded an emerald lawn.

"Your Insta Reels don't do the garden justice, CeCe!"

CeCe beamed at her friend. "David's friend is a landscape architect, so he helped us design it. David's even joined the South

Harbor Garden Club, and can you believe we're featured in South Harbor's open garden tour this month?"

Kate's smile widened as she pictured CeCe's giant husband, planting delicate flowers with hands used to tackling textbooks.

"But enough about us. Tell me about your trip. How's settling in? And what's this about Eve Snow and a missing air conditioning?"

As they transformed the oak table into a feast of salad and sandwiches, Kate filled CeCe on her adventures and the woes of her car's broken cooling system.

"We have a friend who's an excellent mechanic," CeCe offered. "He'll fix Eve Snow in no time."

Kate chewed her lip, considering. "Send me his contact information?"

CeCe was about to say more when David's voice crackled through the baby monitor resting on the counter. "We're ready, Sweetness. Come on up with Katie-Kat."

Kate's eyebrow quirked up. "You have a baby monitor already?"

"You know David. Always prepared."

A playful rumble cut through the monitor. "Hey, I heard that, you two. Can't deny my stellar planning skills. Now come and be dazzled by my baby room wizardry."

Chapter Six

KATE

CeCe and Kate waited in the upstairs hallway, giggling like the college roommates they once were. The old oak floors creaked under their feet as they shifted in their impatience at David's reveal. Although CeCe had shared ideas on her Pinterest baby board and directed the decorating, David insisted on finishing the nursery with a surprise.

CeCe clutched Kate's arm. "I'm so excited, I'm practically jumping out of my skin," she admitted. Unable to wait any longer, CeCe rapped on the door. "Let us in, David Greenwood. NOW!"

"Get ready!" he hollered back. "Close those big brown eyes, Sweetness, and don't look until I say. Katie-Kat, you can look, but please don't say a word."

CeCe squealed and obediently squeezed her eyes shut. The nursery door opened with a soft thud, and David met them, a wide grin stretching across his broad face. He winked conspiratorially at Kate and put a finger to his lips.

"I've got you," he told CeCe, holding her waist and maneuvering her gently into the nursery. "Katie-Kat, step easy. We touched up a few places and still have drop cloths on the floor."

Air escaped Kate's lungs in a surprised hiss, stifled by her hand. David had outdone himself. The room, bathed in Carolina blue, held two white cribs like welcoming boats, dressed in cheerful checkered bedding. Above them, fluffy clouds danced across the ceiling, shepherding a flock of smiling seagull plushies that floated down from the ceiling.

David coaxed CeCe through the doorway. "Open your eyes now, sweetheart."

CeCe's eyes fluttered open, widening as she took in the scene. They flew to her face, hands pressed against her lips in a silent gasp. "David," she breathed, her voice choked with wonder. "This is perfect. Perfect for our boys."

She approached one crib, reverence in her steps, and stroked the soft bedding. Her gaze drifted to the whimsical mural with its floating seagulls. David, an arm already around her, kissed the crown of her head. The world melted away, leaving only the two of them cradled in the promise of tiny fists and toothless grins.

Kate tip-toed back to give them a private moment, but her sandal caught on something hard. Her foot twisted as she jerked away, tangled in the drop cloth. Crying out, she bent down and clutched her ankle. She waited for another jolt of agony as she took a few steps. Her ankle had finally stopped throbbing after tumbling from Mae's window. And now this!

"I'm sorry, CeCe," Kate apologized, reaching for her friend. Knowing that she spoiled CeCe's surprise hurt worse than her foot.

"You made our moment more memorable," CeCe said, squeezing Kate's hand. "But I feel terrible you're hurt."

A grimace contorted Kate's face as she glared at the misplaced tray. Then her gaze landed on the rivers of blue paint cascading down its sides and forming puddles around her feet. "Oh, CeCe," she groaned, mortified. "Look what I did to your gorgeous floor."

David chuckled, brushing off her apology. "No worries, Katie-Kate. The drop cloth caught everything. You, on the other hand..."

He trailed off, gesturing to the paint marring her new sandals and creeping over her sundress. The vibrant outfit, carefully chosen for her island escape, was now sporting an unwelcome abstract pattern in splotchy shades of a morning sky. Kate's heart sank.

"I'm basically one of those blue tree people from *Avatar*, aren't I?" she grumbled, picturing the towering Na'vi.

A deep voice rumbled from across the room, tinged with amusement. "Nah, you're way too short for the tree people. Gotta be five feet taller for that club. But you rock the blue, that's for sure."

Kate whirled around and encountered the paint-spattered grin of the bungalow mystery man. He'd shed the baseball cap, revealing hair in desperate need of a trim, but there was something undeniably charming about his smile. It softened the harsh lines of his face, like sunshine melting frost. His eyes, once obscured by sunglasses, were the color of a summer storm brewing: a deep, enigmatic blue gray that seemed to pierce straight through her, as if he could read her every embarrassing thought.

"You're the bungalow guy!" Kate blurted, heart fluttering like a hummingbird with a caffeine addiction.

"That's me," he confirmed, giving her a slow, considering once-over.

"Kate," David said, "this is my friend, Luke McAllister. Luke, meet Kate Fiore."

Kate's jaw dropped. So, this was Luke McAllister, the enigmatic stranger who'd witnessed her humiliating moment of lockout yesterday?

Luke's gaze lingered on her for a beat longer than was strictly necessary before turning to David. "What do you think of the tree people? James Cameron fan, by any chance?"

David grinned. "Huge fan. Didn't peg you for the Avatar type."

Kate gritted her teeth as the two launched into a deep dive into cinematic lore, her frustration simmering. This was her second encounter with Luke in under twenty-four hours, and both had involved her looking less than graceful. Was that all he'd see? Clumsy Kate, tripped-up princess of Gull Island? She was determined to show him and everybody else the strong, capable woman beneath the paint splatters and hostage key fob.

CeCe's eyes sparkled with mischievous curiosity. "So, you two know each other?"

Luke flashed Kate a knowing smile. "Ran into her at Mae's guest house yesterday," he confirmed, leaving the juicy details mercifully unsaid. Kate cringed, reliving the memory of him discovering her hanging precariously out a window, drenched in a clinging T-shirt.

"Perfect timing!" CeCe declared, oblivious to the tension. "Since I'll be away for Founders Day, I was hoping you two could team up on the donor dinner. Kate's an event planning whiz, and with your board connections and island clout, Luke, we're guaranteed a smash hit."

Kate's brow furrowed. "Team up?"

CeCe beamed. "Absolutely! With your expertise and Luke's influence, we can make this dinner legendary."

"Wait, Luke's on the aquarium board?" Kate sputtered, trying to piece it all together. Dread coiled in her stomach. She wasn't here to play babysitter to some privileged insider.

"That's me," Luke drawled, his steely blue eyes narrowing as he took in her apprehension. "Funny how Mae's guest, David's Katie-Kat, and CeCe's summer replacement all happen to be the same person."

He held her gaze, leaving her wondering if he was joking or judging. But Kate had managed hundreds of complex events. A skeptical collaborator might be a challenge, but she wouldn't be derailed.

"Happy to help any way I can," Luke surprised her by saying, his voice unexpectedly warm. "Whether it's donors, logistics, or island intel, consider me your insider resource."

Kate offered a tight smile, her resolve hardening. "Thanks, I'll keep that in mind."

Leaving the room, she drew a deep breath. *Focus, Kate.* Show him you're a one-woman marketing machine, not a damsel in distress needing his islander tutelage.

Kate fidgeted in the Greenwood's kitchen after slipping out of her ruined dress and into CeCe's loaner cargo Bermudas. The shorts were hanging low on her petite frame, like a costume from one of her mother's Brit-coms. The borrowed gray tank top, emblazoned with a heart-struck seagull declaring love for Gull Island, strained charmingly across Kate's curves, hinting at the red lace bra beneath.

CeCe and David's animated chatter filled the air, punctuated by David's excited grin as he leaned forward. "Did we surprise you with the nursery?" he asked, like a kid awaiting a birthday cake.

CeCe blossomed. "Exceeded expectations, my love! The room, the clouds... everything's perfect. How did you manage?"

Pride puffed David's chest. "Luke, the artist, painted our Gull Island sky."

CeCe's eyes widened. "Of course! Thank you, Luke."

He nodded, a hint of a smile playing on his lips. "Anything for CeCe, and you, old man."

"Hey, watch the 'old man' stuff!" David chuckled. "You'll be catching up soon, hitting the big 4-0."

Luke winked. "Yeah, but you're already over that hill."

Kate stole a glance at Luke, surprised by the easy banter between yesterday's stranger and David. Today, a touch of blue paint in Luke's hair gave him an air of artistic whimsy. As she observed him, she noticed a charming chin dimple emerging when his face relaxed, a dimple that wouldn't be out of place on Tom Brady. *Wait, when did that become kinda sexy?*

CeCe's laughter cut through the men's sparring. "Before you two become ancient mariners, David, could you handle Kate's plant basket?"

Eager to contribute, Kate sat a little taller. "Speaking of greenery, I'm glad you like the baby's tears! Annie at Gift and Garden was a gem in helping me pick it out."

Luke arched a brow, amusement flickering in his eyes. "Annie, huh? Found her helpful, did you?"

Kate shifted slightly, a hint of self-consciousness pricking at her under his scrutiny. "Definitely." She met his gaze. "Friendly, patient, knew exactly what I needed."

A smile tugged at Luke's lips. "Good to hear. I'll let my sister know she gained another satisfied customer."

Duh. His sister.

Of course, in a small town, everyone had some kind of connection to everyone else. Kate huffed out a breath before stabbing a fork into her fruit salad. Her grip slipped, sending a grape flying across the table and skittering with a wet splat in front of Luke's plate. He eyed the grape with a smirk that made Kate wish the earth might swallow her up.

"Yes, please let Annie know," she said, smoothing over the incident.

CeCe, sensing the awkwardness, chimed in. "The McAllisters are Front Street royalty," she explained. "Luke's granddaddy started Gift and Garden back in the day, and his father expanded the landscaping in '97."

Pieces clicked into place, and Kate looked at Luke with newfound intrigue. Working with an entrepreneur with a creative spark might not be so bad after all.

"So, you design murals and gardens?" she asked, gesturing to the emerald expanse beyond the French doors.

Luke, ever the enigma, seemed to shrink under the spotlight. He gave a quick nod. "Yeah, I do. Murals are more of a side thing, though. Friends only."

"Luke's brilliant. Designs landscapes up and down the coast,"

David said, pointing his fork at his friend. "Would you like to see how he transformed our backyard?"

Kate would be delighted to see the backyard. And as soon as possible, she thought. Anything to escape from that grape she shot out earlier, taunting her from the tabletop near Luke, like an evil zombie eyeball.

Chapter Seven

KATE AND LUKE

Kate and CeCe waited contentedly on the shady bench after the garden tour, their smiles mirroring the tranquility of their surroundings. Across the yard, Luke and David huddled in deep conversation by a towering crape myrtle, their voices carried away by the gentle breeze.

Kate's eyes wandered over the yard, captivated by the garden. She stretched her legs and leaned back, relaxing for the first time in weeks. The hint of salty air drifting from up from Front Street kissed her senses and reminded her of home.

"This is your private heaven," Kate whispered, her voice filled with awe, her gaze lingering on a gurgling cherub fountain and the birds that darted among the boxwood hedge ringing the yard.

CeCe leaned into the smooth slats on the wooden bench. "Mmmm, that it is," she agreed. "We tuck away here when we want solitude, but when we're ready for neighborly chats, we settle into the rockers on the front porch."

Kate had to chuckle. "Is that a Southern thing?" she asked

playfully. "You fly a flag on your porch to signal you're ready for company?

CeCe's laughter rang out, startling a wren from finishing his bath in the nearby fountain. "Don't know about that," she admitted, giving her friend an affectionate nudge, "but porch etiquette is definitely a South Harbor thing."

Kate felt genuine happiness for her bestie. "Honestly, I'm thrilled you and David found a place you love. Great jobs, the boys on the way–it's all coming together for you."

CeCe hooked one arm through her friend's and leaned closer. "You'll find your special place, too, Kathleen Fiore," she said, her voice gentle and reassuring. "You've survived a miserable year. I don't know how you keep it together. If it were me, I'd pull the covers over my head and never get out of bed."

Kate's stomach churned as she drifted back to the challenges she'd faced: sleepless nights, endless days, frozen by indecision and depression as her marriage shattered and a job lost in a corporate takeover. The women in her divorce support group assured her the ache would lessen with time, but Kate wondered if it would always haunt her.

"I still have days like that," she admitted, reaching for CeCe's hand, finding solace in its cool, comforting touch.

CeCe squeezed her friend's hand. "Well, you're with us now," she said with a warm smile, "and we'll have the best summer together. Except," she added with a giggle, resting her hand on her baby bump, "I'm very pregnant."

Kate grinned at the baby bump with her heart full of love for her friend. "That you are," she agreed.

Even with the joy of reuniting with her friend after a long absence, Kate wondered how their friendship would change when the twins arrived. She hoped to remain part of the Greenwood's lives, offering her love and help with the little ones. If she'd never have children of her own, maybe she'd find some fulfillment in this way.

DAVID'S SHOUT INTERRUPTED THEM, SOUNDING AS excited as a kid who opened his dream birthday gift. "Luke says we can wait until fall to prune the crape myrtle!"

CeCe gave a thumbs up, and the two men moved on to David's prized Japanese maple. Kate noticed Luke relax as he moved around the garden, gesturing with excitement as he talked about shrubs and trees, while David hung on to every word.

"What's up with those two?" Kate asked, nodding toward the two men. "Do we have a bromance?"

CeCe chuckled. "You noticed? Ever since Luke did our garden, they've bonded like brothers."

"You and David hang out with Luke and his wife, too?" Kate asked, staring at her hands. She didn't know why she asked. Did it matter if Luke might be unattached?

When CeCe answered, her voice was deliberate and measured. "No. Luke's not married. He's dated lots of different women since we've known him, but no one seriously. And the ladies have tried! It's a shame he hasn't found someone. He's a great guy."

Kate narrowed her eyes, suddenly suspicious. "CeCe Greenwood, is this a setup?" she whispered, to make sure they couldn't overhear her across the yard.

Kate's friends' eagerness to help her in the dating world flattered her, but her hesitation to get out there again held her back.

Her experiences dating after the divorce had left her with a sour taste. Boring, self-centered, or individuals interested only in a one-night stand had driven her happily to give up trying.

"Never!" CeCe whispered back, but the twinkle in her eye gave her away.

"You need to remember I am not ready for a relationship," she scolded lightly, her tone laced with humor. "Especially with David's BFF over there, Mr. Southern Charm, who thinks I'm a bumbling, pint-sized blue Avatar."

"Luke's not that way," CeCe countered, her voice carrying her conviction, "though sometimes he takes longer to warm up to strangers. I'm sure he doesn't think that about you, especially after all the nice things David and I have told him about you."

Kate pushed her hair out of her face and watched Luke chatting non-stop with David with a natural ease. She was out of practice, but it seemed like he wasn't interested in anything outside of horticulture.

"Luke's a wonderful friend," CeCe went on. "He hasn't charged us for his work in our nursery. Insists it's his gift for our boys. Besides, he was coming today to help David. I thought having you two here at the same time was a good idea. This way, you'll be acquainted before our Monday team meeting."

Kate wagged a playful finger at her friend. "Okay, listen up, please," she said. "I know you mean well, but no matchmaking, please! I don't have time for it."

"If you're sure ..."

"Absolutely!"

"At least enjoy dessert," CeCe said, squeezing Kate's forearm. "Luke brought homemade banana pudding and I'm telling you... the man knows his way around the kitchen."

Kate threw up her hands in mock surrender and laughed. "You're impossible, CeCe Greenwood!"

LUKE WAS SHOWING DAVID HOW TO GRAFT A TREE when a chorus of giggles distracted them. Luke watched the two women, arms linked like schoolgirls. "What's the story with those two?" he asked.

"CeCe and Kate? They go way back. They were roommates at college in Connecticut," David said. "CeCe moved north for school. Didn't know anybody. Kate invited CeCe to her home for weekends and holidays, and the Fiores basically adopted her."

"And Kate's move to Gull Island for the summer? That's CeCe's way of paying back a friend?"

David considered for a moment. "Not really. Kate earned it by wowing the interview team. She's brilliant at leading projects like the donor event. CeCe won't worry with Kate taking over while we're on maternity leave."

Luke remembered something then. It was one of the few times he'd seen cool, composed CeCe Greenwood lose her chill. "Is Kate CeCe's friend from up north you always talk about? The friend whose husband cheated?"

"That would be Kate," David said, his face a mixture of affection and frustration. "We knew he wasn't right for her. She deserves someone who will treat her with kindness and respect her strength and intelligence."

Luke raised an eyebrow. There was more going on here than a casual lunch with friends. "You trying to set me up, old man?"

David raised his hands, palms up. "Don't know what you're

talking about," he protested. "Hey, Kate doesn't know anybody here and could use a friend. Plus, you two will work together this summer. At least sit through dessert and be sociable."

KATE'S SPOON CLINKED AGAINST THE GLASS, THE LAST creamy swirls swirling with a hint of rebellion. "Rum? In everyone's banana pudding but CeCe's?" She raised an eyebrow, her gaze meeting Luke's across the table.

His grin widened, blue-gray eyes twinkling. "Upgrade for grownups. CeCe gets full strength after the twins."

CeCe giggled. "My version is delish, but I'm holding you to that promise, Luke McAllister. Delivery of boozy pudding and twins are both expected later this summer."

"On my calendar," he said with a chuckle.

A comfortable quiet settled, the scrape of spoons against glass the only sound. Kate noticed the stark difference from the boisterous Fiore clan meals, where everyone spoke at once in a joyous cacophony, silence an invitation to add more. This genteel camaraderie was pleasant, but she craved a shift to a livelier rhythm. Taking a breath, she plunged in.

"Been meaning to ask," she began, "what's with the red ribbons? I see them all over town in town and on the Island."

The smile vanished from Luke's face, replaced by a flicker of raw vulnerability. "SOS," he muttered, knuckles rapping a staccato beat on the tabletop. "Save Our Shore."

His voice, rough with emotion, jolted Kate. She saw the fire in his eyes, a fierce protectiveness that mirrored her own, even if directed at different paths.

"The Point," Luke clarified, his tone thick with a passion she could almost feel, "isn't only sand and shells, Kate. It's the heart of Gull Island. Where my grandaddy taught me to fish. Where we built epic sandcastles as a kid. It's the rhythm of our lives."

"The Point is a magical beach on the western tip of Gull Island, Katie-Kat," David chimed in, punctuating his words with a wave of his spoon. "Folly River curves around one side before it pours into the Atlantic Ocean on the other. Brilliant for shelling. And sunsets there? Just wow!"

But Luke's jaw clenched. "They want to turn that magic into condos," he spat, bitterness lacing his words. "Luxury cages for tourists who wouldn't know a sunrise from a sequin. We can't let them."

Kate leaned forward, the marketing guru in her taking over. "Luxury condos? Sounds like progress to me. Jobs, revenue, a chance for a little island boom."

Luke scoffed, his eyes narrowing. "Oh, we'll be booming all right. Boomboxes on the beach, traffic jams longer than a sandbar at low tide. Tourists mistaking sand dollars for pizza toppings."

Kate pressed her lips together, considering. "But think of the possibilities, Luke! The new businesses, the tax revenue. Imagine a Gull Island buzzing with life, not clinging to the past."

His smile was a cold, humorless curve. "Sure, if you want to trade our unique coastal village for a Miami Beach knock-off. We'll have high-rises instead of dunes and traffic jams like your big city nightmares."

Kate's breath hitched. His words struck a chord, a flicker of doubt sparking in her eyes. There had to be a way for progress without such a sacrifice. She met his gaze, the challenge raw and real.

David's gentle clinking of his fork against a glass broke the tension. "Impressive arguments on both sides," he said with a wry smile. "How about you two debate before my contemporary American issues class? Are you available when school resumes in August?"

The question hung in the air, a bridge between two worlds, two perspectives. Kate met Luke's gaze, stormy yet hopeful, a flicker of something deeper hidden within it. The answer, she knew, wouldn't only be for David's class. The answer, she knew, might change them both.

Chapter Eight

KATE

The gray-haired stranger tipped his jaunty Panama hat as he ambled past Kate. "Evenin', ma'am," he said with a wide smile. "Lovely night to stroll the beach."

Taken by surprise, her gaze lingered on him for a moment before returning his greeting. She had been so immersed in the shore's beauty that she hadn't noticed him until he spoke. She'd finally made time to explore the pristine waters beyond Gray Cottage, and the sight took her breath away. No wonder people were moving here!

Dusk was blanketing the beach in shadows, chasing away the heat and crowds. Kate had kicked off her flip-flops and rolled up her cotton capris before ambling barefoot across the hard-packed sand to the water's edge. There were no rocks waiting to torture her feet like on beaches back home. Instead, creamy white sand stretched for miles ahead of her. And that warm southern Atlantic water! Its waves caressed her ankles instead of the cold punch New Englanders endured when they dipped their toes.

The ocean breeze, salty and clean, filled Kate's lungs as she gazed out at the vast canvas of blue. A sandpiper, a tiny shadow flitting against the shoreline, chased the retreating waves with frenetic energy. A smile, hesitant and tinged with worry, touched her lips. The Greenwoods had been a joy, familiar and comfortable, yet lunch with Luke McAllister left her uneasy. His tone, clipped and judgmental, reminded her of her ex-husband in the rocky waning days of their marriage.

She shook off those thoughts. She had been stuck, letting fear of failure rule her life because she'd dwell on past mistakes. Gull Island was her chance to start fresh. Taking a final breath of sea air, Kate set her jaw. She'd handle whatever situation the island threw at her—even if it meant working side by side with Luke McAllister on the donor fundraising in August.

Invigorated by her new resolve, Kate picked up her pace and turned toward her bungalow. Wet sand slapped beneath her feet and waves splashed her legs as she hurried, eager to find the path through the dunes before dark.

As she drew near to the walkway to her rental, she didn't notice the woman waving to her at first. Kate squinted into the gathering shadows. This time, there was no mistaking Mae Gray's white pixie cut and wiry frame.

"You're right on time, Kate!" Mae called out, a welcoming smile on her face. "Come join us."

Kate's heart dropped, and she racked her brain for an excuse. After her lunch debacle at the Greenwoods, all she wanted was a night alone to binge *Bridgerton* again and indulge in sunflower butter sandwiches made on Trader Joe's seven-grain bread she toted from Connecticut. But as Mae gestured to the blanket spread on the sand, Kate knew it would be futile to escape without offending her.

"This is my Law Law, Maxwell Lawson," Mae said with obvious affection, motioning towards the gentleman sitting next to her in a blue-striped beach chair.

"So, this is Kathleen Fiore," he said. He stood and removed his hat with an elegant flourish to reveal his thick head of gray hair that most men his age would envy. "At your service. I believe our paths crossed earlier this evening."

Kate's lips curved into a smile as she recognized the polite gentleman she met on her beach stroll. She now also knew the mystery man from the photograph in Mae's cottage.

Max chuckled as he sat down and settled his hat back on his head. "Mae is the only one who calls me Law Law," he said, with an affectionate smile at Mae. "See, my daddy was so nervous when I was born that he made an error on my birth certificate. He wrote 'Lawson' as both my middle and surname. Mama didn't have the heart to correct him. Besides, her family name was Lawson, so she was doubly happy."

"And he's been Maxwell Lawson Lawson, and my Law Law, ever since," Mae said, reaching across the to take his hand.

"Call me Max, Kate," he said with a grin. "But don't call me late for dinner."

Coming from anybody else, Kate would've grimaced, but Max, with his rolled-up linen trousers, white polo shirt, Huarache sandals and natty Panama hat, absolutely pulled it off.

"Sit a spell with us," Mae invited again.

Kate protested, but Mae shushed it away. "Nonsense. We love company! You must stay to catch the sunset."

"Gull Island has the most glorious sunsets," Max said. "They are not to be missed!"

Spending time with a senior couple wasn't Kate's idea of an exciting Saturday night. Still, it was probably better than sitting alone in her bungalow. She dropped to the blanket and took the plastic goblet of wine Mae poured for her.

"Here's to your first evening on the beach," Mae said, raising her glass, "and here's to many more to come."

Settling cross-legged, Kate stared at the tray. Mae had covered it with crackers, cheeses, and an orange dip she had never seen before. The tangy scents reminded Kate it had been a long time since lunch.

Kate picked up a cracker and dipped it in the chunky orange goo, swirling through with bits of something red that resembled the pimento part of a green olive. The flavors mixed on her taste buds, a party in her mouth! "This is delish, Miss Mae!" Kate said, licking her fingers. "What is it?"

"That, my dear, is Mae's famous Caviar of the Carolinas," Max said grandly.

"It's my mama's pimento cheese spread recipe," Mae chuckled. "You never had it before?"

Kate mentally clicked through past Fiore gatherings. Cream cheese with pepperoni. Goat cheese with sun-dried tomatoes. Mascarpone and Provolone with prosciutto. But never pimento. "Nope. Never anything like this," she admitted, reaching for more.

"Then this is indeed an occasion then," Max said. "Your first Gull Island sunset and your first pimento cheese. A monumental pairing indeed."

Mae and Max kept up the steady chatter of long-time friends, but Kate was content to sit in silence, savoring the moment. The beach seemed to embrace her, its cooling breezes caressing her face. She had to admit her second night on the island, in the company of this lively couple, on a pristine beach, while satiated with pimento cheese, was much better than her lonely first one.

Kate stretched her legs and leaned back on her elbows to watch people trickling to the shore. Armed with cameras or folding chairs, they turned toward the pier as if waiting for a parade to begin.

Max pointed to the enormous golden orb resting on the horizon, where water and waves collided. "Keep your eyes on the western sky, Kate."

As the sun dipped lower, streaks of flaming orange stretched on either side, turning clouds to fire in the fading blue sky. Right before the ocean swallowed it, the sun shot a final blood-red shaft to ignite the shore before soft darkness wrapped the beach.

"I'll never tire of our sunsets," Mae whispered as she leaned over to rest a hand on Kate's shoulder. "And they're here for you, Kate. All summer."

Laying back, Kate cupped her hands behind her head. She watched stars burst to life above her in the darkening sky and felt at peace.

Chapter Nine

KATE

Kate clicked FaceTime for the Sunday family chat and watched Margaret Fiore's worried face fill the screen. Her mother's hazel eyes, so like her own, searched Kate's face for signs that the 500-mile move from home had not damaged her only child.

"You're getting enough to eat, Kathleen? Sleeping okay?" Mom asked without preamble.

"It's good, Mom," Kate assured her. "CeCe and David are fifteen minutes away, and Mae Gray is helping me settle. And the mattress in my bedroom! It's almost as comfortable as the one at home. I even slept until 9:30 this morning!"

Her father's face leaned in next, squinting across the distance that separated him as if that would help him reach his daughter better. "How's the car, Kate? Still holding up?"

Kate's throat tightened. Dad, ever the pragmatist was ready to diagnose any car problem. Jon couldn't change a tire let alone troubleshoot an issue. Dad was her mechanic-in-chief, the one who'd taught her how to check tire pressure and decipher the cryptic language of warning lights. He loved fussing over the aging Prius and turning it into a testament to human ingenuity and duct tape.

She hated lying, but she hated worrying him more. Dad caught her hesitation.

"What's the trouble?" he asked.

"Nothing serious. Eve Snow's air conditioning went out."

"You need AC down South, Kate. Have the belt checked for coolant leaks," he suggested without skipping a beat. "Not a bank-breaker, and we can always..."

"Dad, I'm good." Kate interrupted, a touch too forcefully. "Mechanic's swamped, but I'm at the top of his wait list."

She chewed her bottom lip, a worry line creasing her forehead. "It feels like my fresh start is already sputtering."

"Give it time, sweetie," Mom soothed. "Two days isn't even long enough to unpack your boxes."

With a fanfare of bangles and scarves, Aunt Theresa, Dad's sister, inserted herself between her siblings, her voice a flamboyant explosion. "Hey, stranger! What's up on Gulliver's Island?"

Kate snorted. "It's Gull Island, Auntie. Gulliver's Island is in South Carolina."

Theresa gave her niece an exaggerated eye roll. "Of course. How silly of me! Anyway, we miss you. Michael, pass her around, so we can all say hello!"

She blew a kiss at the screen and sped away with a huge tray of Italian pastries from D'Annunzio's Bakery. Kate's mouth watered. She doubted there was an Italian bakery within 100 miles. She'd have to wait for four months to savor that kind of dessert again.

Dad shouted after his sister as he followed her outside.

"Theresa, save me a chocolate clam shell before the cousins eat them."

The screen was a shaky blur as Michael carried the phone through the house. When he reached the patio, he passed Kate around to Fiore cousins, aunts, and uncles for hellos until tiny hands gripped the screen. The curly-headed pixie that was Kate's second cousin, Angie, was determined to get her turn to speak.

"Are you coming home for my birthday, Cousin Kate?" the little one wanted to know.

Kate swallowed away the lump in her throat. That innocent request made her miss her family even more. Kate couldn't wait to get back to Black Rock, though she didn't know what direction her life would take once she got there.

"I'll be there in September, Angie. Wouldn't miss your birthday for the world!" she said with more bravado than she felt.

"Goody! You give the best presents!" Satisfied, Angie nearly dropped the phone before handing it to Kate's mother and skipping off.

"No pressure to come up with a gift," Kate joked.

Laughter drowned her mother's answer. It was probably one uncle telling funny stories. "I'll let you get back to your company," Kate said, her voice trembling as a stab of loneliness set in.

Her mother's eyes softened. "We're so proud of you, Kate. You'll be great on your first day on the job tomorrow. Let us know how it goes. Love you, sweetie."

"Love you, too. Call if you need anything," Dad piped in, blowing her a last kiss.

"Or text us," Mom said.

"You're becoming a texting guru, Mom," Kate said, trying to sound light-hearted. She dreaded ending the chat and being alone.

"Love you both. We'll keep in touch. By phone, text, or carrier pigeon."

"Everybody, say goodbye to Kate," Dad instructed.

The call ended in a raucous chorus of farewells. Kate blinked away a stray tear, the phantom ache of missed Sunday family gatherings settling into her gut. Ignoring the knot, she checked the time. Two hours until she met Mae for the turtle patrol at Gray Cottage. A one-minute zip across her tiny yard and through the hedges separating her bungalow from the main house, and she'd be there.

For now, she found solace unpacking while listening to audiobooks. Whether it was Elin Hilderbrand's idyllic beach stories or Julia Quinn's charming regency romances, the soothing words transported her to another world. With her headphones tuned to feel-good fiction, even a temporary beach house felt like home. And after that? She had sea turtles to save.

Chapter Ten

KATE

Max Lawson greeted Kate from the porch of Gray Cottage, adorned in a turquoise T-shirt with a Gull Island Turtle Team logo. "Mae's finishing something for SOS," he said, gesturing to the red rocker next to him. "Come sit and keep me company."

"I'm early," Kate said, biting her lip.

"Nonsense!" Max waved her off. "Never too early for agreeable company and conversation."

Kate sank into the chair, her gaze drawn to Mae's pristine garden and walkway that wound through the dunes to the sea. "This is a beautiful home," she said, her voice soft with admiration.

"It's been in the Gray family for generations," Max said with pride. "Mae's great-granddaddy built the bungalow you're staying in back in the 1930s. And Gray Cottage? Built it for his bride after the Great Depression."

Kate raised an eyebrow, her eyes catching on the trio of palm trees tied with red ribbon. Max would have insights about SOS.

"What's the deal with this Point everyone keeps talking about?" she asked.

Max rubbed his chin thoughtfully before answering. "It's right complicated," he said. "Some people want to build the condominiums and make money from it, while others like Mae want to preserve the Point as is."

He pointed at the trees again, each with red ribbons around their trunk.

"Mae worries that developing the area will ruin its natural beauty and accessibility for everyone. Traffic, high rises—you name it."

"Any room for compromise?" she asked. "Maybe a smaller complex?"

Max shrugged. "Sure, anything's possible. But folks are set in their ways about this. Mae's leading the charge with the community action group, SOS, along with her co-chair who feels just as strongly. You can ask him yourself when you're on patrol with him today."

As if on cue, a red truck pulled into the driveway. Kate shaded her eyes to catch the lean figure, who stepped from the red truck to help a child out of a car seat.

Max waved. "Hey, Lucas! Delighted you brought your helper today!"

Kate's eyes widened as she watched Luke McAllister and the freckle-faced urchin from the touch tank bounding up the steps.

LUKE

"THANKS FOR TAKING DAWSON THIS AFTERNOON," Annie Lawson said, looking up at her brother from behind her oversized tortoise-shell glasses, her blue eyes, the color of the endless sky on a sunny day, shining in anticipation of her 'me' time.

"He's a handful, but he adores his Uncle Luke and minds what you say."

Luke leaned against the kitchen counter in his sister's South Harbor home. Across from him, Annie absently twisted the gold wedding band she still wore four years after Evan's death. Even now, there were times he caught the sadness in her eyes. She was coping well enough as a single mom, but it was hard enough raising an active six-year-old without the love of your life.

The weight of his sister's burden settled heavily on his shoulders. He wanted to do more, to lighten her load. Their mother doted on her only grandchild, and he pitched in whenever his schedule allowed. Yet, no one, no matter how loving, could replace the boy's father.

Reaching across the counter, Luke pressed one hand gently on the side of her face and smiled. "Hey, you're great with Dawson," he said, releasing her.

Annie poked him playfully on the shoulder. "I try, but you have a way with him. He's excited you're taking him this afternoon. Honestly, it gives me breathing space, too."

"Dawson and I do the fun stuff, Annie. You have the hard part being on Mom Duty 24/7."

A genuine smile, that mirror of pure joy she shared with their mother, bloomed on Annie's face. Luke wished some of that joy had rubbed off on him. Lately, he felt like an old CD player, stuck on the same repetitive track.

Annie's smile widened, realigning her freckles into a hodge-podge of uneven rows. "Speaking of fun, I hear you had some interesting... encounters yesterday."

Luke's eyebrow shot up, his eyes narrowing. "Oh?"

"Delivery to Savannah?"

Luke's grin was more grimace than amusement as he shook his head. No surprise there. Secrets had a short shelf life in their town. He wasn't some lovesick teenager anymore, and seeing Savannah again was...jarring. It kicked up memories he wanted to keep buried.

"How'd you find out?" he asked Annie, going for nonchalance.

His little sister tilted her head with a mischievous grin that reminded him of a leprechaun about to unleash mischief. "Savannah's neighbor, one of Mom's church pals, popped by the shop. Spotted your red truck. Anything you care to share?"

"Nope."

"Sure? You two were quite an item back in the day."

He shook his head, not wanting to delve into the past. He knew what had happened between him and Savannah was a chasm of incompatible desires. She craved the glitz and glamour of city life, fancy cars, and sprawling mansions. He yearned for something quieter, a cottage by the sea, far from the city's clamor.

"Savannah? Nah, too high maintenance. Needs a personal stylist for her yoga pants," Luke chuckled.

Annie's laughter echoed through the kitchen. "Okay, spill. You've cycled through more girlfriends than a library goes through romance novels. What's your type, then?"

"Ideal?" he scoffed. "You mean the one unicorn who doesn't exist? Someone who gets my need for quiet and understands the tyranny of deadlines? Someone who won't melt down if I don't respond to every ping within seconds, or throw a fit if work throws a wrench in our plans because, you know, I actually run a business?"

Annie snorted, a mischievous glint in her eye. "So, a blow-up doll with a pulse? Sure you're not afraid of commitment?"

Luke's smirk faltered for a beat, then stretched wider, his playful mask back in place. "Afraid? Nah, commitment's just... inconvenient. I'd rather spend any spare time with family and friends instead of wrangling a serious relationship."

He raised his glass in a mock toast, hoping to put an end to Annie's inquisition. "Besides, dating's like sampling exotic beers. You try a bunch, hoping one will blow your taste buds away. So far, it's all been lukewarm lagers and overly sweet stouts."

Annie laughed, but she wasn't done, her gaze now sharp and probing. "I bumped into CeCe, too," she said, her voice dropping to a conspiratorial whisper. "She tells me you were charming at lunch yesterday... until her friend asked about the Point."

Luke scratched at the prickle of frustration on his neck. He loved his small town, every weathered porch swing and salty breeze, but sometimes, it was like being trapped in a goldfish bowl, with everyone's lives on display. His outburst surprised him when he had challenged Kate about her views of the Point. She'd spoken with such certainty about Gull Island, cracking its code like a tourist with a guidebook, and it rubbed him raw.

Then a memory flashed with Kate at Mae's guesthouse, facing down a stranger in a dusty yard, miles from her comfort zone. She had lifted her chin and faced him head-on, like she had today.

Maybe there was more to the Greenwood's gilded girl than met the eye.

"Fine. I'll be my charming self next time and won't give her my Terminator death stare," he promised with a wink as he stood and slipped on his sunglasses. "Now, where's my turtle team partner?"

Annie let out a laugh, accepting defeat. Luke was a master at avoiding serious conversation. "He's in his room, probably rubbing off the sunscreen I made him put on."

"Dawson Lawson," Luke called to his nephew. "Get yourself down here. We have sea turtles that need tending."

Chapter Eleven

KATE

Kate wanted to disappear the instant she heard Luke's voice calling out to Max. She didn't want to face him or deal with the touch-tank terror from the aquarium. She pulled her cap low over her face, hoping the child wouldn't recognize her. Thankfully, Max reached for the boy, and he shot into Max's outstretched arms without noticing her.

Luke, all bronzed-limbed and toned in board shorts and flip-flops, froze mid-lean against the railing. Sunglasses slid down his nose, revealing eyes wide with surprise. Kate's jaw clenched. Had she actually thought she could sneak past him, invisible in the late afternoon sun?

"I didn't know you had company," Luke said, tilting his head toward Kate.

Max settled Dawson on his lap, the boy snuggling against him. "Apologies," Max said. "I was excited to see Dawson and forgot my manners. Kate Fiore is Mae's summer renter. Kate, meet Luke McAllister and my great-nephew, Dawson.

Kate cleared her throat, awkwardness settling around her like a heavy fog. "We're already acquainted through the Greenwoods," she said, shooting Luke a warning glance under her eyelashes.

Luke's quirked his eyebrows, wisely getting the message. "You know how it is on Gull Island, Max. We're a neighborly place," he drawled with a wicked grin. "Falling out a window is like another form of neighborly greeting here."

A groan escaped her lips before she could stop it. As she was about to retort, the screen door banged open, and Mae Gray exploded onto the porch.

"Sorry I'm late," she boomed. She adjusted her turquoise T-shirt stamped with the Gull Island Turtle Team logo–two turtles swimming head-to-head in a giant circle, looking for all the world like they were going for a synchronized kiss. "SOS got the better of me again. Let's get started."

Mae's smile faded as she noticed the distressed look on Kate's face. "Something wrong?" she asked.

Kate gripped her chair. This would not work, she thought to herself. No way she'd team up with Luke and the touch-tank terror.

"There's been a misunderstanding," Kate stammered. "I thought I'd pair up with someone, um... who was more like you or Max."

"Why no, hon," Mae said. "Luke and Dawson can teach you all about sea turtles in a heartbeat."

Mae shook a finger at Luke, who looked ready to protest the pairing next. "And you, young man, work too much and need time off. Your crew can manage a few hours without you. Besides, with Dawson to help, you three will be the best team on the island in no time."

Kate's mind raced, searching for another excuse, when she felt a small, sticky hand resting on her knee. Dawson stared up at her, his blue eyes wide with concern. "Don't worry, Scaredy Lady. You don't have to touch sea turtles like you do with rays and horseshoe crabs. We watch turtle nests and keep them safe."

Kate sighed. Of course, the little monster recognized her. Her eyes narrowed as she noticed Luke's shoulders shake with suppressed laughter.

"Dawson, is this the lady from the aquarium you told me about?" he asked, his eyes dancing. "The one you helped touch the rays?"

His nephew grinned, revealing two missing top teeth. "Yep. It's the Scaredy Lady. I'll help her again today."

Max was confused, his gaze darting between Kate and Dawson. "Kate, you know Dawson, too?"

"I don't really *know* Dawson," Kate said. "We sort of ran into each other yesterday when I stopped by the aquarium."

"I showed Scaredy Lady how to be brave at the touch tank," Dawson said proudly, beaming up at Kate. "I can't wait to show her more today."

"That's mighty fine of you, Dawson," Mae praised. "But you must call your new friend 'Miss Kate.'"

Dawson glanced at Great-Uncle Max for confirmation, who solemnly nodded his agreement.

Max stood and offered his arm to Mae. "Dawson Lawson has spoken, my dear. It's time we start this patrol."

The child slipped his warm hand into Kate's and tugged at her to stand.

"Come on, everybody and Miss Kate. Sea turtles need us," he said, pulling her toward the steps.

Kate tried to wiggle out of his grip, but Dawson wouldn't let go. As he passed his uncle, the boy's free hand latched onto Luke's. With Kate on one side and Luke on the other, he marched them to the path through the dunes and the beach beyond.

DAWSON MORPHED INTO A MINIATURE TOUR GUIDE AS he led Kate away, chattering about how to identify the sea turtle tracks and protect nests until the eggs hatched. His face glowed with excitement as he halted at the end of the walkway, threw off his flip-flops, and raced across the sand with Luke. Kate followed close behind with Mae and Max. Her Chucks squished across the hard-packed shoreline that spread before her like a sandy highway. A refreshing breeze lifted her tank top away from her skin, providing welcome relief from Gull Island's sun.

Kate was seeing another side of Luke today. She watched as he spun Dawson around in dizzying circles, the child's shrieks of delight filling the air. Luke was a natural at entertaining children, and it was so endearing. The opposite of the stubborn man she'd clashed with yesterday.

Mae sighed, her gaze lingering on Luke and Dawson. "That boy dotes on him, doesn't he," Mae said softly. "Luke's been a steady hand since Evan...." Her voice trailed off, heavy with unspoken grief.

Max squeezed her hand, his own eyes welling up. "I know, Mae," he murmured, leaning down to kiss her forehead. "It breaks my heart knowing Annie and Dawson are alone."

The weight of the tragedy settled on Kate. "I see." Her voice was a whisper over the lapping waves. "So, Luke's Dawson's uncle, and you're Dawson's great-uncle?"

Max nodded. His voice was thick. "His mother, Annie, married my sister's boy, Evan... He was taken in a car accident when Dawson was a baby."

Max smiled faintly, a ghost of a memory lingering in his eyes before he continued."Seems like there's always been a 'Dawson Lawson' in our family," he said. "That's why Evan chose the name for his son."

"The helpful woman at Gift and Garden... that was Annie, right?" Kate asked, piecing things together. "So, Annie is Luke's sister and Dawson's mom?

"McAllisters and Lawsons—always close," Mae said, a fond smile crinkling the corners of her eyes. "Annie and Evan's union cemented the bond. Growing up when Luke and Evan were best friends, Annie followed them around like a little shadow."

A soft chuckle escaped Max's lips. "Mostly, the boys put up with Annie tagging along," he said. "But high school? Luke finally finally told her to skedaddle."

Kate traced the complicated lineage in her mind.

Luke's sister, Annie, married Evan Lawson but was now a widow with their son, Dawson.

Luke's nephew, Dawson, was part Lawson, part McAllister.

And Max and Mae knew everyone!

She hoped to get people straight in the tangled Lawson/McAllister orbit.

Mae's voice cut through Kate's concentration. "Look there!" she said, pointing ahead. "They've spotted something already!"

Kate squinted her eyes against the glare to see Luke and Dawson crouched low, studying the sand.

Dawson waved his chubby arms in a flurry of excitement. "Hurry!" he called. "We found a mama turtle track!"

As she got closer, Kate made out a set of foot-wide depressions extending from the shallows up to the dunes. The tracks made by the 100-pound sea turtle twisted and curved, as if a drunken peg-leg pirate stamped them in the sand. Kate and the others followed the tracks until they ended abruptly where the animal had turned and flippered back to the sea.

Max shook his head. "No nest here today," he said.

Dawson's smile fell. He kicked at the sand, his excitement gone.

Without thinking, Kate placed a hand on his sagging shoulder. "Dawson, you showed me my first sea turtle track," she said. "You are amazing."

She watched Dawson's face flit from despair to satisfaction.

"It's early in the season," Luke added, bending down to eye level with the boy. "Sea turtles are picky about laying their eggs. This one decided it wasn't the right time or place."

Mae then stepped in, always knowing the right thing to say. "Dawson, let's keep looking for more tracks around the pier, and then we'll finish with my homemade lemonade at Gray Cottage," she said, with the skilled practice of someone who knew how to cheer up six-year-olds. "Come on, I'll race you to the pier!"

"Some days, I simply cannot keep up with her," Max lamented, as he held on to the brim of his Panama hat and traipsed after Dawson and Mae.

To Kate's surprise, Luke stayed behind and walked beside her.

Chapter Twelve

KATE

Kate matched his long strides, her sneakers sinking into the wet sand. She was used to walking fast, matching Jon's six-foot-two gait. Luke wasn't as tall, but he still towered over her. She craned her neck to see his face, but his blue-tinted sunglasses hid his expression.

"So, Dawson's your nephew," she began.

"Yep."

Kate waited for more, but he kept walking, watching the boy race with Mae. She couldn't endure weekends with a Mr. Monosyllable. She'd tell Mae something came up at work and bail from this turtle thing.

Luke took a long breath and stared straight ahead. "Thanks for your kindness to Dawson today."

Surprised, Kate waited for more, but Luke kept walking, looking straight ahead and avoiding her gaze. She wondered if this was his attempt at being friendly. She gave him the benefit of the doubt.

"I'm used to handling six-year-olds. My little cousin Angie back home in Connecticut is a handful."

He nodded curtly, a flicker of something unreadable crossing his features before his gaze returned to the path ahead.

The uncomfortable silence fell again as they walked. Kate listened to the crashing waves and screeching seagulls instead of the dead space between them.

Luke cleared his throat, his words tumbling out in a rush. "Look, about lunch at the Greenwood's. I wasn't assuming anything about your abilities. I didn't know how familiar you were with our local issues."

Beach stones crunched under Kate's Chucks as she kicked a shell out to sea. The memory of Luke's fiery gaze during their argument was hot on her cheek. "No offense taken," she said. "But please don't write me off as clueless because I'm new here."

Luke held up his hands in surrender. "Okay, I get it. You're a capable woman who can handle her own, except for when you lock yourself out of your house."

Kate ignored his dig. "That's not the point," she said, her voice tinged with steel. "If we're going to work together, I want us to be clear. I'm good at my job, good at managing people and projects. I'll do everything I can to make my aquarium gig a success, and I hope you can trust that."

Luke stopped, meeting her gaze head-on. His voice was flat, his jaw tight. "Just don't think we're backward provincials. We're not afraid of change, but not at the cost of destroying our home and what makes us who we are."

Kate held his stare, her resolve hardening. "I understand," she said, her voice steady. "But I also believe we can find a way forward that respects both the past and the future."

Just then, Dawson torpedoed into Luke's arms, cutting their exchange short. "It's time for Miss Mae's lemonade," he shouted breathlessly. "Let's go!"

He grabbed Luke's wrist and Kate's, pulling them both toward Gray Cottage as Max and Mae followed.

LUKE

LUKE'S FRUSTRATION COOLED AS HE WATCHED HIS nephew and Kate together on the porch steps. She had gotten to him with her stubborn insistence that she understood the issues. But he had to admit, it impressed him when she stood her ground.

He caught Dawson's non-stop chatter about today's patrol. The child was determined to tell Kate everything in his vast six years of experience about Gull Island sea turtles. She listened and smiled encouragingly between Dawson's loud slurps of Mae's lemonade. Luke didn't know why Dawson was so taken with his Scaredy Lady. He was even more astonished that the twitchy newcomer put up with the child. Most adults didn't have patience for the boy's squirmy body and motor mouth.

"Dawson's found a friend," Mae said from her rocker next to Luke's. She tilted her head toward the tousled-headed child, leaning close to Kate in animated conversation. "And a good turtle team partner."

Luke stopped rocking. It was hard to buck Mae Gray. He was glad she was on his side about the Point. Her idea of pairing him with the newcomer—not so much.

He rubbed a thumb along his chilled can of South Harbor

Brewery's latest IPA–a spectacular lime-flavored Gose–as moisture beads slipped cool down his wrist. Here he was, a grown man enjoying a beer, yet feeling like the boy he had once been in Mae's fifth-grade classroom. He was about to tell Mae to find somebody else for the turtle team when an excited Dawson bounced up to him.

"I want people to know I'm protecting sea turtles, Uncle Luke. Can we have one of those?" he asked, pointing to Mae's colorful turtle team T-shirt.

"Those are only for people on the turtle team," Luke said. "Sorry, Dawson. I won't have time for the team after today."

Dawson hopped up and down, undeterred. "Please? Mom said I can help. And Miss Kate needs me to show her about the nests."

Kate was standing now. "You're sweet to want to show me, Dawson, but it's okay that you and your uncle have other things to do. Honestly, with my new job, I am too busy for this, too."

Luke turned toward her, surprised. She seemed to want out of this doomed arrangement as much as he did. Usually, women were eager to be with him.

"That's too bad, buddy," Luke said, turning to Kate for backup.

Kate took the cue. "That's right, Dawson. I have stacks of papers on my desk to finish."

"But it doesn't take long," Dawson persisted, "And it will be so fun to show Miss Kate the babies when they hatch. And how we help them crawl to the ocean. Please, can we be a turtle team, Uncle Luke? Please!"

Dawson rested a hand on Luke's arm, looking hopeful, and

Luke felt his resistance slipping. He didn't want to disappoint his nephew.

"If Miss Kate agrees, we can see how it goes and fill in until the regulars return."

He turned to Kate, who gave him a reluctant shrug. Dawson yipped and launched himself at Kate, throwing lemonade-covered arms around her legs. "I can't wait to get my shirt and show the kids at school," he squealed.

Kate untangled Dawson and bent down to cup his chin in her hand. "As long as you and your Uncle Luke remember that if I get busy at work, Miss Mae will have to find somebody else."

Kate glared at Luke, daring him to disagree. He raised his hands in surrender.

"Good by you, Miss Mae?" he asked.

Mae pushed out of her rocking chair. "Of course! But I know y'all will love it. Now, excuse me while I fetch us some shirts to try on."

As Mae excused herself, Dawson paced impatiently on the porch, waiting for her to return. Max snatched the boy up to settle on his lap.

Kate locked her gaze on Luke. He imagined it would be easy to get lost in the deep pools of her hazel eyes. "Can we do this turtle team together without *agita* for the next four weeks?" she asked.

"Agita?" he asked, confused.

"Sorry. My Aunt Theresa says that all the time. It means major aggravation."

He teased her down from being so high-strung. "Is that Yankee talk?"

She side-eyed him, and he broke into a grin.

"Okay, I get what you mean." He chuckled. "Not thrilled

about this arrangement myself, but no agita on my part. If it makes Dawson happy, I'm willing to try."

Kate crossed her arms and tapped her foot impatiently. "Well, I need rules if we're doing this."

He gave a sardonic eyebrow raise. The commitment ended in July when the full-timers took over. It was a beach walk. Not the NBA playoffs. Why complicate it with rules?

"Like what?" he asked cautiously.

"No discussion about the Point. Or any work talk. None! Pleasant, uncontentious conversation now and then would be nice."

He rubbed his temples and sighed. Luke savored his solitude, and he didn't understand why Kate couldn't enjoy the peace of walking the beach. He was around noise and people all the time. Speaking with clients. Barking instructions to his crew. Garnering support for SOS. He needed quiet time. Why couldn't she get that and relax?

But he also knew that he had been a jerk to her at the Greenwoods, and he owed her.

Kate fidgeted. "Well?"

"Okay, no work talk. What would we talk about?"

Kate rolled her eyes. "How about the weather? Or the price of coffee beans on the world market? Maybe fill me in about Gull Island sea turtles?"

Luke smiled to himself. Kate could annoy him, but he had to admit her quirky comebacks were entertaining. Then he noticed Dawson straining to hear their conversation, his little boy body still and a frown crossing his freckled face. He gave his nephew a reassuring wave, and Dawson snuggled back against Max.

Luke lowered his voice and moved closer to Kate, so Dawson

wouldn't overhear and worry. The slight citrusy scent of her hair distracted him. He shook it off and focused.

"And what do I get out of your rules?"

She shook her index finger at him, jabbing it into the air to emphasize her point. "You get quality time with your nephew. Like Dawson wants. Agree, or I'm out of here."

A corner of Luke's mouth turned up as the petite brunette fireball threatened him. He wanted to let her know what he thought of her ridiculous demands when Dawson's excited cries caught his attention. Mae had returned with shirts and found one for Dawson, who preened with his prize once he tried it on. Mae tossed one to Luke next.

Shaking off his tank top, Luke slid into the shirt. He smoothed the clingy fabric over his chest, pleased that his morning runs on the beach were keeping him trim. He wasn't the only one who appreciated the way he kept fit.

Kate turned away, blushing when he caught her admiring his hard stomach. Flustered, she grabbed the closest shirt from Mae's stash and struggled to pull it over her tank top. Made for a child, the garment cut into her arm and reached above her belly button. She tried to yank it off and over her head, but this made her shirts bunch up around her rib cage, revealing a smooth strip of pale stomach.

"Maybe a bigger size?" Luke suggested, grinning at her plight.

Kate tugged off the garment with Mae's help and snatched another. This time, the top swallowed her, reaching down to her thighs. Determined, Kate spread the hem, knotting two sections at her waist and cuffing the sleeves up on her slender shoulders. When she finished, the shirt accentuated her curves like a fashionable crop top.

Petite and with an hourglass figure, Kate was an interesting combination. Luke supposed he could talk about T-shirt sizes with her when on patrol, and how she looked good in tighter-fitting tops. But he didn't think that was the type of conversation she was after.

Mae flashed a grin, pleased with the recruits. "Y'all look nice in your team shirts! I must get a photo," she said, whipping out her phone.

Max helped Mae set up the shot, placing Dawson on the top step and directing Kate and Luke to sit one step lower.

"Lean closer to Dawson, so I can get everybody in," Mae said as she fiddled with her mobile.

"And big smiles!" Max added to the stage directions.

Luke's long legs brushed against Kate's knee, and she jerked away as if she stepped in a nest of fire ants.

A grimace flickered across Luke's face, the brief flash of annoyance quickly replaced by a sigh. Why was she so uptight about an accidental touch? Was this what the summer was going to be like? If it weren't for Dawson wanting the turtle patrol....

"Remember, we're testing this," Luke called out to Mae as she positioned herself at the best angle. "No promising we'll stay."

"And only if you agree to my ground rules," Kate hissed as Mae finally framed the shot.

Luke spoke low through his pasted-on camera smile as the camera clicked. "As you wish."

When Luke found Mae's photo on the aquarium webpage, it showed a rapturous Dawson with his cheerful uncle. And instead of looking at the lens, an open-mouthed Kate Fiore was staring at Luke McAllister.

Chapter Thirteen

KATE

Through her office window, Kate glimpsed the tall marsh grasses rippling in an unending parade to the bay. She arrived early for her first day, appreciating the comfort of Mae's pillow-top bed. Everyone she had met at the HR orientation that morning put her at ease. Before long, she was alone in her office, taking a moment to relax before CeCe arrived.

Kicking off her heels, she thought back to her days in corporate when dark-colored pant suits and dressier dresses were her go-to outfits. At least business casual was the norm behind the scenes here, while those on the floor sported jeans with the aquarium logo–not bad after all.

Yesterday's turtle team patrol with Luke hadn't ended as badly either, despite the accidental brush of their skin that made her yank away as if she were a schoolgirl. It surprised and scared her a bit that she enjoyed that nano-second of physical contact with Luke, the first she'd had with anyone since Jon.

She looked up as Liz Wilson, the HR rep from orientation,

hesitantly knocked on the open door and entered. Kate had seen an expression before, like the one on Liz's face now. Nothing good ever followed it.

"Everything all right?" Kate asked, despite her rising fear.

Liz perched on a chair and whispered. "David Greenwood called. CeCe started premature labor, and he took her to hospital."

Kate's stomach lurched, and she clenched into fists. Please, let CeCe and her babies be okay, she silently prayed.

"The doctors have her condition under control," Liz reassured her. "Multiples are more delicate. My daughter went through the same with her twins, and everything turned out fine."

Kate let out a shaky breath. "So, she's okay? The twins are okay?"

"Yes," Liz nodded. She hesitated, tapping a finger on the thick manilla file folded against her knees. "Except the doctor is putting CeCe on bed rest."

A wave of relief replaced Kate's worries. CeCe was okay. It didn't matter that the plans for shadowing CeCe during Kate's first week wouldn't happen after all.

"No worries, Liz," she said, a hand to her chest to calm her racing heart.

The blue notebook on her desk drew Kate's attention. "CeCe keeps detailed files and notes. I'll study them and ask questions if I get stuck."

Liz shifted the folders to her arms, her white curls bobbing. "Of course! Ask as many questions as you need! Perhaps I can brief you now on your meeting this afternoon with the board member?"

Kate nodded, feeling a stab of dread about meeting with Luke McAllister without CeCe. But then the familiar adrenaline rush returned. She was back in the game! Kate swiped closed her calendar and cleared her desk.

"Let's get started, Liz."

KATE WAS FLIPPING THROUGH CECE'S NOTES WHEN SHE heard the docent from the visitors' desk buzzing. "Got a minute to talk to a donor?" the volunteer asked. "Clayton Pruitt is asking to meet you."

"I'll be right there," Kate said, hanging up and checking her reflection in the compact mirror in her desk drawer.

After taming her frizzy bangs, she hurried to the lobby. The friendly docent gestured towards a well-dressed man in his early forties. His style caught her eye right away: clipped blonde hair, crisp white shirt, gray-checked blazer, neatly pressed navy slacks, and polished black tassel loafers.

She thought of her own comfortable slingback kitten heels as she made her way through the crowds, grateful for snagging them on sale at Nordstrom Rack.

She reached the man, extended her hand, and said, "Mr. Pruitt?"

He turned slowly, his smile wary and his handshake firm.

"Yes. Call me Clayton, Miss Fiore," he drawled in his southern accent, rolling *Miss* across his tongue as if they made the word for her. She didn't need to tell him she had kept her family name when she married Jon. or that she went by *Ms.* Fiore.

She beamed her best client-friendly smile. "And I'm Kate. How can I help you today?"

"I have a few ideas about our fund-raising projects I'd like to share. Might we have a quick chat?"

Her antennae went up. She wondered what ideas he had. As charming as he was, he had the directness of someone used to getting his way. She wasn't one to be steamrolled, even by a wealthy donor.

Pruitt flashed a wide, benevolent smile, revealing brilliant white teeth. It was the same smile–and dental work––that Jon used to charm a room.

"I realize how busy you are," Pruitt added, "but I hope you can spare a few minutes. Perhaps I can treat you to something from the snack bar while we chat?"

She shook off the unpleasant feeling in her stomach and knew she should keep donors happy. "No need to treat, but I'm happy to join you for a few minutes."

IT WAS COOL UNDER THE BROAD GREEN-AND-WHITE striped canopy shading the aquarium's outdoor snack bar. The smell of fried food and hot dogs filled the air, making her stomach rumble. She scanned the whiteboard menu and decided on an iced tea from the selection written in an elegant, curving script.

"Unsweet or sweet?" the friendly attendant asked, catching Kate by surprise. "Lemon?"

Kate blinked, confused before realizing that ordering iced tea in the South was a time-honored ritual requiring attention to detail. She chose unsweet with lemon and gripped the cold glass as they made their way to a shady picnic table next to a dolphin-spouted water fountain. Clayton followed with his basket of french fries and beverage, sliding onto the bench across from her.

She stared at his drink choice and wrinkled her nose. "Cheerwine? Is that a Southern thing? Having wine and fries together?"

He chuckled and pointed to the label. "Definitely part of our culture, but it's not wine, Kate. Cheerwine is a delicious cherry-flavored soda. Try a sip?"

The last thing Kate wanted was to share anything with this stranger, even if he was a rich benefactor. She waved a hand and flashed him an apologetic smile. "Thanks, but I'm not a fan of sugary drinks."

He took a long swig and gestured toward the golden-brown strips from his fry basket. "The snack bar here makes the best french fries on the island. People come here for the fries. You must try one."

It was hard for Kate to resist the offer this time. After pizza, fries were her guilty pleasure. She reached into his basket to grab one of the hot fries. She nibbled through the warm exterior until getting to the potato's pillowy soft center and let out a gasp of surprise. "This is bliss," she said as she licked a potato speck off her finger.

Clayton smiled knowingly. "Told you."

The fry was salty, but not overpowering, with a kick of something she couldn't identify. "What makes these so good?" she asked, savoring the last bite.

"It's a secret," he said solemnly. "Chef creates her special spice mix, and she's not telling."

Kate raised an eyebrow, turning over an idea in her mind. "If these are so popular, I wonder if Chef will share her secret. We could package the spices and sell them at our gift shop. Maybe stock them at local shops if they sell big."

Clayton set down his fries and looked at her with admiration. "I like your thinking, Kate Fiore. It's exactly what we need to excite the public and raise funds for the aquarium."

A deep baritone voice spoke up from behind Kate and quipped, "We know how you enjoy stirring up people and making money."

She whirled around to find Luke McAllister staring back at her through the sapphire lenses of his black Ray-Bans.

Chapter Fourteen

KATE

Chef's decadent french fries must have heightened her senses, making her hyper-aware of Luke's freshly shaven face, high cheekbones and alluring dimpled chin. He wore his navy denim deck shoes without socks, acid-washed jeans, and a pink polo that hugged his lean torso. Jon, her ex, would have scoffed at pink, claiming it was a "girl's" color, but Kate found Luke effortlessly stylish.

Kate's face flushed as she tore her eyes away from Luke as Clayton spoke. "Well, well, if it's not Luke McAllister, environmental Mighty Mouse. Saved any trees lately?"

Luke set his messenger bag on the bench next to Kate. "Yeah, plenty, Clayton. Destroyed any more natural habitats today?"

Kate watched the two men glare at each other, like rival seagulls squabbling over a french fry on the boardwalk. She wondered what had sparked their animosity.

Clayton took a slow sip of Cheerwine, his eyes never leaving Luke's face. "I'm here on business," he said with an exaggerated calm. "My business is all about improving our community, after all."

Luke snorted. "That's your perspective, not mine."

Sensing the need to intervene, she flashed Clayton her most dazzling smile and said, "Clayton, sorry to cut this short, but Luke and I have a meeting. We can chat again soon."

Clayton nodded gracefully, sliding his business card across the table. "I look forward to it, Kate. In the meantime, I have several fine properties available if you need a venue for events. Please let me know if I can be of service. I'm happy to help."

Luke cut in, his tone sharp. "A generous offer, but somehow I don't think charity is your motivation today." His steely eyes met Clayton's, revealing a hint of unresolved history.

Unfazed by the interruption, Clayton shrugged and reached for another fry, lazily popping it in his mouth. "No matter what you might think," he said smoothly, "I'm still offering my help."

"I'm always open to new ideas, Clayton," Kate said, standing to lead Luke away before his laser-like glare incinerated the picnic table.

TOSSING HIS SUNGLASSES CARELESSLY INTO HIS messenger bag, Luke settled across from Kate at her conference table. The muscles in his jaw flexed as he met her gaze for the first time since they left Pruitt. He hadn't said anything yet, but she could tell the encounter with Pruitt had irritated him. She needed to turn that around if they were going to accomplish anything for the donor event. She straightened and tented her hands in front of her.

"Thanks for coming," she started. "This news about CeCe has thrown us all off, but we'll make it work."

His shoulders eased, showing a hint of relief. It was a minor concession, but at least they found common ground. Neither of them wanted to disappoint CeCe Greenwood.

"Speaking of CeCe," Luke began slowly, "I heard from David."

Kate sat up, instantly alert. "What?"

Luke nodded, his eyes softening. "It's fine and CeCe is stable, but she feels she let you down on your first day."

"I can't believe she's in the hospital and worrying about me," Kate said, her hand fluttering to her throat.

"That's CeCe for you," he said, a brief smile crossing his face.

Kate's heart pounded in her chest, her mind already racing with how she'd split her time between work and caring for her friend. "What can I do?"

Luke shook his head. "Nothing. Her mother is coming from Wilmington. She'll stay as long as CeCe needs her."

Kate sat back, relieved, and her heart stopped hammering. CeCe's mother was a force of nature who'd make sure her daughter and future grandsons would get the best care.

Now, it was time to tackle the elephant in the room: Luke's feud with one of her donors. Clearing her throat, she fixed him with a patient smile and unflinching gaze. "Is there anything I should know about you and Clayton Pruitt before we get started?"

He leaned forward, his fingers laced tightly together. His eyes flashed with frustration as he spoke. "Pruitt is trouble, and you should be careful around him."

Kate raised an eyebrow, waiting for more. "Trouble? How so?"

His expression darkened. His tone became more urgent. "You don't know about Clay and the Point?"

Her stomach tightened at the implication behind his words. She straightened, feeling a mix of weariness and defiance at his insinuations.

"In the fifteen minutes I've known Clayton Pruitt since arriving on Gull Island, I've seen him as a generous benefactor who likes french fries and is eager to support the aquarium."

Luke ran his hand through his unkempt hair, pulling at the strands absentmindedly. "Pruitt's heading up the condo project on the Point," he explained, pushing back his chair with an annoying scrape against the carpet that reminded Kate of fingernails on a chalkboard.

Kate frowned, her patience thinning. "Luke, why should your rivalry with Clayton stop me from accepting his help for the aquarium?"

Luke's fingertips drummed on the table, each tap punctuating his words. "Pruitt is a user, Kate. He wants to turn Gull Island into his personal profit machine, with no regard for the environment or the people living here."

Kate studied him, trying to understand his perspective. In her Connecticut hometown, an advocacy group like SOS had formed, and her Aunt Theresa was a dedicated member. Kate had attended a few meetings and heard about protecting fragile ecosystems from developers like Pruitt.

"What about state and local regulations?" Kate said, her voice steady. "Can't they offer some protection?"

"It's not enough, Kate," Luke said, his voice gaining urgency as he leaned forward. "That's why Mae and I started SOS. We can't let people like Pruitt exploit the environment for personal gain. He'll steamroll anyone who gets in his way, even you."

Kate felt a prickle of annoyance. She wasn't some naive newcomer who needed protecting. She took a deep breath, her words carefully chosen. "If we have to work together, you need to trust that I know what I'm doing."

Luke's tone sharpened as his patience waned. "It's not as simple as that, Kate."

She met his gaze head-on and answered. Her voice was level. "I appreciate your concern. Pruitt's a weasel. I'll keep that in mind. Now, can we focus on the donor event?"

Luke's brows knitted "Fine, forget Pruitt. Think of Founders Day. Sixty thousand visitors, that's our lifeblood. Carries us through the winter, every single dime. And your fancy donor dinner? Smack dab in the middle? It's the aquarium's biggest haul all year."

Kate drew a slow breath, counting to ten in her head. "Look, I'm not blind. I get how much these events matter. But I'm not some rookie thrown in the deep end. I can handle Pruitt, and I can handle the dinner. So instead of the side-eye, how about a little trust? I know what I'm doing."

Luke kneaded his palm, knuckles cracking like tiny seashells. "What if you find yourself in over your head?"

Kate's jaw tightened, the smile she'd plastered on fading. "Honestly," she said, her voice clipped, "I don't mind being challenged. And I'm no stranger to deep water." She raised an eyebrow, a flicker of defiance in her eyes. "Don't worry, Luke. If I get in over my head, I'll ask for help."

He studied her for a moment before delivering a blunt assessment. "So, you want me out of your way at the donor event?"

It was more of a statement than a question, and it suggested he had her figured out.

"That's not exactly what I meant," she lied smoothly, trying to defuse the tension. "CeCe and the board expect us to work together, so that's what we'll do."

She watched him carefully, expecting resistance, or more questions, but he stayed quiet. She knew she had to set boundaries with him now to avoid chaos this summer. On top of her already chaotic life, that was the last thing she needed.

"All right," he finally said, giving a curt nod. "We'll stick to our sandboxes for the donor event. But I insist we continue with briefings to coordinate with my Founders Day team."

Kate's lips curled into a triumphant smile. She had won him over... for now. "It's a deal," she said, her voice steady and firm. "You focus on your tasks, and I'll handle mine. If I need help, I'll reach out."

Kate watched as Luke rummaged for his tablet, her eyes narrowing as she caught the hint of a grin flitting across his lips. Was he secretly pleased about working independently? Had he been planning this all along?

Kate cracked open CeCe's notebook and placed it on the table between them. "Let's dive in." A confident smile crossed her lips. "We know the basics, but let's analyze what clicked before–"

"–And what needs sprucing up," Luke chimed in, interrupting her. He seemed up for a challenge.

Kate eyed him for a moment. He had experience with the donor event. Ignoring him completely would be foolish. Maybe he'd come up with some good ideas after all.

She took a deep breath and looked him in the eye. "Sure, let's hear your take on last year's event."

Luke shared his insights from vendor management to guest activities, even emphasizing the importance of extra napkins. His keen attention to detail and business acumen impressed Kate. An hour later, they had drafted a comprehensive event timeline and roadmap leading up to the big day in August. They even carved out roles and responsibilities by task to avoid overlap.

By the end of the meeting, Kate felt satisfied. Despite their rocky start, Luke's input had seamlessly complemented her plans. She smiled to herself as she watched him gather his belongings and head for the door. He turned back to her with a casual grin.

"Not a bad start, Kate Fiore," he said, slinging his messenger bag over his shoulder. "CeCe knew what she was doing, pairing us."

Kate gave a small nod in agreement, but the moment Luke was out of sight, she pumped her fist into the air and let out a triumphant squeal. She was going to ace this project. Luke McAllister and everybody else would see her shine.

Chapter Fifteen

LUKE

Luke swatted the mosquito circling him, distracting the creature with his dirt-smeared glove. "David, it's time to quit."

David stood, tipping back his blue Carolina baseball cap to dab sweat off his forehead. He stared across the lawn at the diamond-paned windows near the patio. Lamplight from inside arced into the garden on an ivory stream. He shook his head. "Not yet," he countered.

"Can't stay out here forever," Luke said, spreading the last shovel of mulch onto the garden bed.

His friend straightened, eyes darting back to the windows. "I don't know about that. With Mother Nichols taking charge, I'm always in the way. And with CeCe, nothing I do for her is right."

"Didn't all those baby books clue you in about what to expect?"

David rolled his shoulders. "It did. But *reading* it and *living* it are totally different things."

Luke set down his shovel and gripped his friend's shoulder. "Only a few more weeks, and then overactive hormones and hovering mother-in-law will be gone."

"You sure that's how it works?"

No, it was only the beginning, but he wouldn't tell his friend that. David needed a little sugar-coating right now. "Yep," Luke fibbed. "It was like this before my sister's due date."

He waited for another excuse from David when a burst of high-pitched giggles cascaded into the dusk.

David listened, shaking his head. "How does Katie-Kat do that? Make CeCe laugh? Lord knows I try, but CeCe isn't having any of it."

"It's a girlfriend thing. If they're laughing, it's safe to go inside."

LUKE LEFT HIS WORK BOOTS ON THE PATIO BEFORE padding after David across the oak-wood hallway. The faint hum of a television grew louder as he neared the study David converted into CeCe's temporary living quarters.

The room was David's pride, an airy space overlooking the back garden. Yesterday, he and David stashed most of the furniture before hauling in a queen-sized bed, so CeCe would spend her confinement surrounded by books, garden views, and a nearby bathroom.

David poked his head inside, unsure of his welcome. "Sweetness, we finished the garden for the tour this weekend."

"Wonderful, David!" CeCe sang out. "Luke, I can't thank you

enough. Please come in, but don't mind me looking like a beached whale."

Layered in baggy sweats ballooning over her twin-sized stomach, CeCe leaned against an army of pillows, her toes spread apart by strips of cotton from the pedicure Kate had just finished.

David bounded to his wife. "Never a beached whale, CeCe! You're a magnificent, um, magnificent...." He trailed off, as if he were searching for words that wouldn't send CeCe into a snit.

Kate, who was capping red nail polish, paused the movie they were watching and finished for him. "Like a beautiful blossom, ready to burst. Except this beautiful Greenwood Blossom can't burst for another few weeks."

Luke thought David might need resuscitation until he heard CeCe's laugh.

David eagerly accepted Kate's lifeline. "Exactly, my lovely blossom!" he said, pressing his wife's hand to his lips with a tender kiss.

CeCe rolled her eyes, but she rested her hand in his. David cradled it like the most precious thing in the world, and CeCe closed her eyes, melting into his touch.

Luke felt like an intruder, his feet itching to walk away when a cough, crisp as a freshly starched tablecloth, snagged him back.

He turned to see Mrs. Nichols, a vision of cool efficiency in a sleeveless linen dress. In one hand, she juggled a tray piled with four crystal glasses filled with red liquid, a sugar bowl, and a plate of sliced lemons. Colorful beach towels draped over her shoulder.

"Evening, Lucas," CeCe's mother said. Her brisk alto voice still carried the low-country rhythm of her girlhood.

"Mrs. Nichols," Luke said, tilting his head at the stately older woman.

Mrs. Nichols set down the silver tray on the mahogany side table and held out the towels. "Gentleman, if you'll kindly each take one of these, so you don't stain the furniture."

Obediently, David spread a towel under his six-foot-three frame before settling on the Victorian side chair next to CeCe's bed.

Luke made one more attempt to excuse himself. "Thank you, Mrs. Nichols, but I really must be going,"

"Nonsense! You need a little refreshment after working hard."

He gave in. There was no resisting CeCe's mother. "Thank you, ma'am. Mighty fine of you to go to all this trouble."

"No trouble. I brewed CeCe's favorite red zinger iced tea. Perfect with a lemon slice and no caffeine to keep her up at night. Y'all must try some."

"Thank you, Mama," CeCe said, cradling her glass and snuggling contentedly against her husband.

The grandmother-to-be surveyed the room like a sentinel guarding a citadel. Convinced her daughter had what she needed, she turned her attention to Luke. He stood awkwardly, clutching a beach towel in one hand and a glass of Red Zinger in the other.

"Lucas, make yourself comfortable," she commanded, gesturing toward Kate, who perched on an antique loveseat.

Kate turned to Luke, her smile wide and radiant. Tonight, her hair was loose and flowing, her face relaxed. She looked more vibrant and alive than he'd ever seen her before. His gaze involuntarily flickered to her legs, encased in tight turquoise bike shorts that stressed shapely curves. He reined in his gaze and sat down on the loveseat next to her.

Satisfied everything was in order, Mrs. Nichols motioned to

the long-handled silver bell by her daughter's bedside. "Ring if you need me."

"We will, Mother Nichols," David promised, as CeCe's mother took one last look around before retreating.

Kate moved to make room for Luke on the settee. As he settled on the cushion, it tilted downward abruptly under his weight, and Kate slid into his thigh. In an instant, the glass he held slipped, sloshing Red Zinger through his fingers and down his arm.

"I'm so sorry," Kate gasped.

He shifted slowly to level the cushion and prevent damaging the antique piece. "Hey, my fault. I should've been more careful," he said, sticky iced tea covering him.

Kate grabbed a corner of Luke's towel to soak up the sugary liquid spill with a brisk, gentle efficiency. As she bent to her task, he caught her faint citrusy scent and hoped the smell of fresh mulch overpowered the chicken manure he had added to the garden earlier.

With a final slow, lazy circuit over his arm, she pulled away. "Thanks, Kate," he said, wishing she had stayed closer longer.

"All good now. You're dry and CeCe's loveseat is safe," Kate said, suddenly busying her fingers with the hem of her shirt and avoiding his gaze.

CeCe waved her hand dismissively. "I'm glad our two favorite people are here tonight," she said. "And knowing you're working together to keep my projects running while I'm on leave eases my mind."

"And for that, we are most grateful," David added, brushing his lips across CeCe's forehead.

"We're your go-to team, CeCe," Kate said, her face looking eager and earnest. "No worries while we're on the job."

Luke matched her enthusiasm, raising his hand to Kate for a high five. "That's us," he said, flashing her an exaggerated grin, daring her to respond.

Pursing her lips, she gave him a resounding hand slap. For someone so petite, she packed a wallop.

"Now back to movie night," CeCe said. "Kate, let's catch that scene where Dread Pirate Roberts tumbles down the hill and shouts 'Buttercup...'"

"'As you wiiiissssshhhh,'" CeCe and Kate called in unison, drawing out the last syllable to imitate the faux-pirate's famous declaration.

Luke frowned. The phrase sounded familiar, but the name of the movie escaped him. "What are we watching?" he asked.

David hooted, dropping CeCe's hand to slap his knee. "You're so lucky you don't know, my friend!" CeCe made a face and playfully swatted her husband.

Kate swiveled toward Luke with her eyes wide. "You've never seen *Princess Bride*?"

"Nope. Movies with 'princess' or 'bride' in the title aren't in my streaming queue."

Kate smacked her head. "Inconceivable!"

David's groan was drowned out by another round of infectious giggles from the women. Luke, still bewildered, watched Kate reach for the remote. A mischievous glint lit up her eyes.

"Well, Luke," she said with a teasing grin, "prepare to be dazzled."

As she leaned in to adjust the remote, the unexpected brush of her leg against his sent a jolt through him. It was a brief contact, a whisper of warmth against his skin, yet it felt like a spark had ignited in the air between them. Luke found himself inexplicably drawn to her, a strange energy crackling in the sudden silence. He couldn't quite explain it, but in that moment, something shifted within him.

Chapter Sixteen

LUKE

Silky ocean breezes cooled the night, and streetlights along the narrow cobblestone road wrapped the sidewalk in amber glows as Kate and Luke left the Greenwoods.

Luke strolled with an unhurried gait. He disliked desk work and wasn't looking forward to the towering stacks of invoices waiting for him at home. However, he enjoyed the evening with Kate and was looking forward to continuing that. As they walked, Luke noticed how the wind blew through Kate's hair, tousling its chestnut strands around her face. He loved she didn't realize how alluring that made her look. She smiled and kept walking, content to be with him, not obsessed with her appearance.

Kate absently pushed her hair from her face. "It was thoughtful of you to help David tonight," she said. "It's been hard enough on CeCe, but it's got to be stressful for him, too."

Luke deftly side-stepped a tree root that had punched through cement, buckling the sidewalk. "Yeah, he texted me and said he needed a friendly face."

Kate's laughter spun out, light and silver, like wind chimes dancing in a breeze. Luke caught himself wishing for more of it. He couldn't shake the image of her, alone on this island, not knowing her way around. He felt strangely protective of her, more than he had any right to be after their brief acquaintance.

Pruitt, with his oil-slick smile and eyes that held too many secrets, had been a warning flag. Kate, bless her, had brushed it aside, claiming independence with a tilt of her chin that made Luke both admire and worry. Sure, he'd respect her boundaries, let her handle things independently, but his guard would stay up.

A chirping chorus of crickets rose and fell as they walked, weaving through the South Harbor's historic heart. Luke watched Kate crane her neck, peering into the warmly lit windows, marveling at details he'd always taken for granted. He followed her gaze to a Craftsman bungalow, its plain curtains pulled back like a proud reveal, exposing the soul of the home within.

"I love the way the light bounces off beveled panels," she said, stopping to stare at the Prairie-style stained-glass. "I never imagined finding anything like that here."

Luke crossed his arms, his jaw tightening. "What did you expect?" he asked defensively, his voice sharper than he intended. He disliked her implication that his town was backward.

She puffed out her checks in frustration. "That's not what I meant," she said. "I didn't realize this cute little town would have such charm and character."

Luke clenched his jaw. "We're more than a cute little town," he said, unwilling to be patronized by an outsider.

Kate raised her palms in the air in mock surrender. "My bad. I meant it as a compliment. South Harbor reminds me of my cute little neighborhood in Black Rock. What's that expression I overheard at the aquarium the other day? No need to get yourself in a hissy fit," she teased.

His irritation deflated at her attempt at a Southern phrase. "Hissy fit, huh?" he said, breaking into a grin despite himself.

"I see why people like the island," she went on. "It's peaceful and beautiful. We have old houses in Connecticut, but this historic district is something else."

She stopped, unable to tear her eyes away from the whimsical dragonfly dancing inside the leaded glass panel of a 1900s bungalow. Her tone became distant, lost in memories. "I had a darling 1950s Cape Cod in Black Rock," she said, as they continued walking. "I wanted to install a panel like that somewhere, but never got around to it."

Her shoulders fell, the movement mirroring the quiet sadness in her voice. "The house just sold," she said, her tone laced with resignation. "I'll find a new place to fix up when I go home in September."

Luke's gut twisted at the raw resignation in her tone. He longed to offer empty reassurances, but the words felt hollow on his tongue. Instead, he met her gaze, his voice gruff but sincere. "I hope it happens soon for you, Kate."

"Thanks," she said, her voice brighter. "The timing was right when CeCe called about this summer contract. It'll all come together for me somehow."

They crossed the quiet cobblestone street, the streetlights casting soft shadows on Kate's face, her brows creased downward in a tiny V-shape. Was it worry? Concentration? Luke wasn't sure. He opened his mouth to ask what was troubling her when she spoke up.

"After I left my ex, I felt like my world had ended," she admitted. "I used to believe I could conquer anything life threw at me. Yet there I was, suddenly single, jobless, and bewildered. Nothing was certain. So here I am, starting from scratch and determined to do better. And that's why I can't fail this summer."

Luke was still reeling from her unexpected moment of vulnerability when she stopped and pointed to a late-model white Prius waiting at the curb. "But enough of my sad story," she said. "This is me and Eve."

He studied her curiously, wondering if her car was as unique as she was. "Eve?" he asked, his brow lifting in disbelief. "You named your car?"

"Of course!" she said, playfully placing her hands on her hips. "Meet Eve Snow. I bought her right before a fierce gale on Christmas Eve. She carried me home that night and everywhere else, like royalty since then."

Luke scratched his head, trying to understand.

"You didn't name your truck?" she asked.

"No, never occurred to me. And I wouldn't know what to call it if I did."

She watched him. "I can fix that."

"What are you thinking?" he asked, intrigued by what she might say.

Kate leaned against the car door, her face illuminated by the streetlight, biting the corner of her bottom lip in concentration. "Hmmm. Your truck is huge and red. Very manly."

"Wait, you think my truck is manly?" This was a promising beginning. What else was going on in that beautiful mind? he wondered.

"Are you kidding? Your truck screams rough, tough Southern testosterone!"

He rolled his eyes, but she ignored him, waving her fingers in the dark evening air as if writing on a whiteboard only she could see. This must be the marketing whiz CeCe told him about when he expressed doubts about hiring an outsider as her summer replacement.

"I got it!" She grabbed his arm in excitement.

He liked the way her fingers pressed into him, but she jerked them away to clap her hands in triumph.

"*Spike*! Your truck is *Spike*! First, I thought of *Berry*, because your truck's red and you're a garden geek," she continued in a rush. "But I don't see you motoring in any kind of berry, no matter its color. But then that smooshed-in fancy grill of yours reminded me of Cousin Jimmy's feisty bulldog, Spike. Nobody messes with Spike, but he's great with friends and family. And that's absolutely YOU!"

Luke threw back his head and roared so loud it roused a chorus of barking dogs across the street. He had to admit, it was the perfect name for his truck.

"Testosterone, huh? Well, I keep my truck in top condition, and no one who's ridden in it lately has complained."

She leaned against her car door, arms crossed and watching him with a bemused smile. "Hey, that was only brainstorming. You really liked it?"

"Absolutely! It fits. You blew me away with how fast you came up with that name. "

She tapped her forehead as she stepped inside Eve. "Idea person here, remember?"

Before Kate drove off, she rolled down the window and called to him. "I should charge you for my branding services."

"Send me the bill."

"Don't you want to know how much?"

"Nope. Whatever it is, it's worth it. You nailed that name!"

He watched the Prius tail lights bump over cobblestones before turning toward the bridge to Gull Island. Her soft touch lingered on his shoulder when he climbed into the newly christened Spike. Luke followed Kate at a distance across the bridge to Gull Island, wind whipping through his hair and Spike's engine roaring beneath him. He watched her turn east on Island Drive to Gray Cottage as he veered west.

The road unraveled deeper into the island, finally leading towards Luke's home. He pulled in, the engine ticking as it cooled. Stepping out, thoughts of Kate filled his mind as he walked onto the porch. She was an enigma, a kaleidoscope of facets. Tough professional, lonely soul, vibrant creative—who was the real woman? Or was she, like the island itself, a blend of all three and ever-changing around him?

His dog, a furry hurricane of wags and licks, greeted him at the door. Perhaps working with Kate this summer wouldn't be so bad after all. Maybe it would uncover something more profound than what either of them had expected. With a deep breath, Luke stepped inside, the unanswered questions about Kate swirling in his mind like the approaching summer storm brewing on the horizon.

Chapter Seventeen

KATE

Kate pulled away from Gray Cottage, Mae's voice ringing in her ears, *Can't miss the Point. Keep driving west until you run out of road.*

With her GPS ready and a cooler of snacks packed by Mae resting on the back seat, Kate set off. She lowered the car windows as she cruised down Island Drive, the evening breeze tickling knots of tension camped at the base of her neck.

"We did good our first week here, Eve Snow," Kate said, patting her dashboard with a free hand. "New home. New job. New everything."

The car hummed its acknowledgment.

"Yep," Kate continued. "Vendors, food trucks, and band confirmed. Ticket sales for the donor banquet going strong."

And here I am, five hundred miles away from home, alone, and talking to my car on a Friday night, she thought to herself.

But she had to admit it hadn't been too bad working with Luke McAllister. He listened without pushing his ideas or minimizing her role. Plus, he saved her time by introducing her to locals who'd help with the event.

As the road twisted west, she passed modest beach cottages hidden by stunted trees in the island's maritime forest. Unlike rows of look-at-me new construction on Gull Island's east side, long patches of dunes separated these older homes. Most sported the ubiquitous red SOS ribbons tied around mailboxes or trees. It made sense that people living close to the Point didn't want a condo complex spoiling their piece of paradise.

Eve's engine whined as Kate turned onto a narrow, winding road. The pavement ended abruptly at a grassy patch overlooking the Lockwood River, which meandered through the salt marsh. Kate parked the car facing the river, then hauled a blanket and Mae's cooler of snacks to the sand. Her eyes scanned the deserted beach, where a family of shell seekers and a lone explorer with a metal detector searched for hidden treasures.

Remembering Mae's warning about dangerous rip currents where the river and ocean merged, Kate had abandoned her swimsuit for a tattered neon pink tank top over old gray work-out shorts that cinched at the waist. She craved comfort over fashion tonight. Besides, who was around to see?

Kate kicked off her flip-flops and dug her toes in the sand, sliding the silky grains across her feet. Then she leaned back on her elbows, letting herself drift to other seaside Friday nights with Jon. They'd bring a picnic dinner to the waterfront park or scour yard sales and antique shops for hidden treasures on weekends. Their relationship had been good then. Before everything went wrong.

Her memories were sweet yet intense, still hurting like an open wound. She'd been so in love during those first few years of marriage. But Jon was her past, and now was her time to move on.

KATE WAS REACHING INTO THE COOLER FOR A PIMENTO cheese sandwich when she spotted a small dog crouched next to her blanket, watching. His short ivory coat blended with the sand, contrasting his compact body with oversized ears and paws that hinted at a mixed gene pool. She scanned the beach, but no one claimed the stray.

"Hello, doggie," she whispered while he licked her fingers in anticipation of a treat.

The animal yipped and curlicued his tail like a high-speed windshield wiper. He looked longingly at her sandwich.

"Look, cheese might not be good for you," she said.

The dog ignored her, looking hopeful. When he rested his wet nose against Kate's leg and regarded her with those wide eyes, she melted. Bribing him with specks of cheese, she reached for the ID tag on his collar. The cell number was unreadable, but she made out the dog's name and a nearby Island Drive address.

"Hey, Boo! Let's go home."

Boo licked her arm, and Kate could swear he winked at her.

BOO RODE SHOTGUN, STRETCHING HIS HIND LEGS TO soak in the breeze while resting his front paws and snout on the open window. Following her GPS directions, Kate pulled into a weathered, gray-shingled cottage near the Point. A generous porch spanned the first floor of the residence that nestled into the dunes. Only red ribbons flapping around a stand of palm trees jarred the natural landscape.

It was quiet except for the singing of a distant wind chime. The parking space was empty under the raised pilings. Bundling the dog in her arms and securing its lethal tail, she creaked up the steps to the porch. A riot of blooms spilled from oversized cobalt-blue pots, their bright colors popping against the house's weathered shingles. Three turquoise chairs rocked slowly in the wind as if they were waiting for someone to sit and enjoy the view.

Maybe the three rockers mean a nice Papa Bear, Mama Bear, and Baby Bear live here? Please, not Norman Bates! Norman wouldn't bother with flowers, would he?

A strip of sapphire ocean peeked between the wind-tossed dunes as a flock of brown pelicans swooped overhead. Kate wondered if the people who lived here ever tired of their front-row seat on nature. She'd never! Tearing her gaze away, Kate tapped the copper seahorse knocker.

And waited.

Nothing.

Kate peeked inside the nearest window, eager to hand off the squirming dog. She grimaced as tiny scratches reddened on her arm. "Hello? Anybody home?" she shouted, rapping on the pane.

Finally, Kate caught the sound of heavy footsteps sprinting to the door. "Be right there," a clear baritone called.

Her eyes darted up from the dog in her arms to the man standing before her. His feet were bare. He was clad only in nylon running shorts and a sweat-stained Henley that clung to his torso. She hadn't realized she was holding her breath until it spilled out in a slow exhale.

She held out the dog to its owner. "I found somebody who belongs to you."

He groaned. "Not again, Boo! You can't be sneaking out all the time!"

Ignoring his owner, the dog jumped from Kate's arms and scampered through the open door.

A flash of sandy-brown hair, a familiar dimpled chin. Before Kate could blink, Luke McAllister materialized from the porch shadows.

"Papa Bear?" she sputtered, surprise twisting her tongue.

He chuckled, rubbing his beard—more stubble than bear, honestly—and leaning against the frame. "Not Papa Bear, but I'll answer to Doggie Daddy."

KATE'S GAZE DISCREETLY SWEPT OVER HIM, TAKING IN the tanned skin, the sculpted legs, and the muscled thighs only hinted at under the long board shorts he wore on turtle patrol. But it wasn't only his physique that left her speechless.

It was the way he carried himself, the confidence radiating from his stance, the playful glint in his eyes. This wasn't the serious, focused businessman she'd observed. This Luke McAllister looked relaxed, approachable, and completely captivating. Her inner voice shrieked, *Get a grip, Girl!*

"Wow," she stammered, the word blurting out before she could edit it. "I didn't know you lived here,"

Luke gave an exaggerated bow. "This is me. Home, sweet home. David borrowed my truck to haul mulch, so no Spike outside to give you a clue. Where'd you find Boo, anyway?"

He dabbed his face with the towel tossed over his shoulder. Kate, recovering her composure, explained her dog encounter.

He leaned in, nodding as she spoke. "Thanks for bringing him home," he said when she finished. "I'm sorry Boo interrupted your evening."

Kate's heart tugged. Luke really looked contrite. "Well, I wouldn't say *interrupted*. I'm heading back to the Point, so it's more like an *intermission*."

"Still, my dog spoiled it. Can we make it up to you?" Luke pointed to a deck tucked between tall dunes. "I have the best view of the Point. Have time for a look? It's the least Boo and I can do for your troubles."

Kate hesitated. Her mind raced, weighing the options. Should she take him up on his offer and stay? Or keep things strictly to business outside the office and leave now? But before she decided, Boo pushed through the door and snuggled at her feet after licking a speck of spilled pimento cheese from her flip-flops. The dog's papery tongue tickled, and she giggled as she bent to pet him.

"Give this guy food, and you have a friend for life," Luke said. He nodded toward the door. "You like older homes, right? I'll throw in the nickel tour of my reno work inside."

The small voice inside her head whispered caution. *Leave now. Don't risk getting involved.* Yet, she was curious to see how Luke was transforming his cottage. She thought for a moment.

"Turtle team rules?"

"Huh?" He furrowed those dark eyebrows, looking genuinely perplexed.

Men have such short memories. "You know," she prompted. "The 'pleasant conversation' and 'no-work-talk' deal we made."

He snorted, a playful roll of his eyes. "Kinda hard not to talk about the Point when we're staring at it, don't you think?"

His playful jab brought a smile to Kate's lips. "Touché," she conceded, the warmth settling in her eyes. "New rule. Show me the Point from your deck. But no talk of Pruitt or SOS, so no need for that frowny-face, stormy-eye thing you do."

"So, you noticed my eyes?" he asked with an amused smile.

How could she let that slip? His blue-gray eyes were like a cool breeze on a summer day, refreshing and soothing, with a hint of mystery that made her wonder what he was thinking.

"Well, I noticed once or twice," she said. "Purely in a professional sense of gauging the best way to work with a colleague."

"Of course," he said, his eyes sparkling with humor and something else Kate couldn't identify. "Like I purely professionally picked up on that bite-y thing you do with your bottom lip when you're thinking or about to come up with an idea."

Kate's eyes widened. He was figuring out her quirks? She was embarrassed and flattered at the same time. "Now you know my superpower."

"Yep," he went on, "saw it last night when you were conjuring Spike's name. It impressed me. It's how you get your mojo."

Glancing toward the steps, she wondered again if she should leave, but something about Luke made her want to stay. Tonight, his eyes held kindness, and she sensed he understood how skittish she'd become after Jon. Before she decided, Boo trotted to her feet, begging for attention.

"Hey, Boo. Miss me already?" she cooed, reaching down to pet him.

"He likes you," Luke said. A smile curved up at the corners of his mouth. "You know, we might add another turtle team rule."

Intrigued, Kate looked up at him. "I'm listening."

Luke pointed to Boo, wagging his tail and content next to Kate. "Defer to the dog. Boo thinks you should stay."

"All right," she conceded with a smile. "New turtle team rule adopted: defer to the dog."

LUKE KICKED A PAIR OF WORN TENNIS SHOES UNDER A walnut console. "Wasn't expecting company," he apologized.

"No need," Kate said, as she stepped inside and gawked at the entryway. Gleaming pine floors stretched beneath her feet, while a white-washed staircase climbed to the second floor. Her fingers traced the horizontal planks of shiplap lining the walls, and she gasped at seeing he had whitewashed them, too.

"I always wanted to add shiplap to my Cape in Black Rock. What you've done here is genius."

A smile tugged at Luke's lips, his eyes glinting with pride. "You like it?"

She nodded, reluctant to move her hands from the smooth strips on the wall. "How long have you lived here?"

"The house has been in my family since my grandparents bought it from the original owners in the 1960s," he explained. "When my grandparents passed a few years ago, I bought it. Added central air and new plumbing, so I can stay here year-round."

Kate's attention returned to the white walls, and she said offhandedly, "Not too poor to paint or too proud to whitewash, I see."

Luke paused, his brow quirking up. "Is that an old Southern saying, too?"

"Don't know about *old,* but I saw it on a sign in Gift and Garden."

"Sure it's not a Yankee thing?" he teased.

"Wait a minute," she said, hands planted on hips, a playful frown forming. "Don't diss my attempt to embrace your Southern heritage, mister."

Luke's grin widened, his hands raising in mock surrender. "Point taken, and I am impressed by your knowledge of my culture."

A pleased smile bloomed on Kate's face. "So, what else is on this tour of yours?"

He offered a playful bow. "This way," he said, his smile genuine and warm.

His hand, a warm anchor on the small of her back, steered her into the living room. The touch lingered after he withdrew, a phantom warmth against her skin, as a cream area rug swallowed her bare feet. Her gaze snagged on the surfboard coffee table, sleek against matching coastal-blue sofas. Then, the walls, soft as beach sand, surrendered to a breathtaking view of dunes through the floor-to-ceiling windows. The gentle roar of the ocean echoed in the distance, a soothing melody that filled the space.

She walked around the space, her gaze lingering on each element with growing wonder. "You did all this?" she asked.

He tapped his forehead and grinned. "Creativity and muscle here."

"Huh. I'm not sure which one I'm more impressed by. And a reader, too?" she quipped, her attention turning to the overflowing bookcase lining one wall.

She had expected to find tomes on landscaping or oceanography—anything that matched Luke's smart, analytical mind. Instead, she found a mix of bestsellers and classics. Her fingers traced the spine of *To Kill a Mockingbird*, admiring its original cover.

"My grandmother loved that story, and we'd read it together," Luke said, pulling the book from the shelf and offering it to Kate.

"*Mockingbird* is one of my favorites, too," Kate said reverently.

She looked up and found him watching her, his eyes seeming to look into her soul. He stood so close that she caught the earthy scent of a pine forest mixed with a cool ocean breeze on a hot day. She wanted to inhale him. Instead, she asked, "You named your dog after Boo Radley?"

He shoved his hands in his pockets, pleased she understood the connection to his book. "I did. Calling him with 'Hey, Boo!' reminds me of Gram."

It touched Kate how he remembered his grandmother through such a thoughtful act. A smile crept onto her lips as she returned the book to Luke, the gentle brush of his fingers lingering against hers.

Luke started to the kitchen, passing a backward glance at the blizzard of papers covering a pine trestle table. "Ignore the chaos," he said. "We want to migrate the business to e-billing, but we're not there yet.

As Kate passed his laptop, she spotted a thick document with a title page strewn on his laptop. She stopped to examine it.

Landscaping and Conserving the Built Environments of Coastal North Carolina:

a History

by Lucas J. McAllister,

MLA, North Carolina State University

"This is you? A master's in liberal arts and an author?" she asked, her admiration for his accomplishments growing even more.

He laughed and shook his head. "Do I look like a liberal arts major? It's 'landscape architecture,' please! Yeah, I started writing the book a year ago, but I never have time to work on it."

Kate was about to ask more, but his phone trilled.

"Sorry," he apologized, glancing at the caller ID. "It's an anxious client."

Luke stepped into the kitchen to talk, so Kate wandered into a corridor branching off from the living area. She peeked past an open door.

It was a bedroom.

Luke's bedroom.

She gawked at the luxurious white coverlet draping the king-size shelter bed upholstered in a sumptuous navy fabric. The room was spacious and airy, with tall French doors opening to the deck and white wainscoting reaching up to the navy-colored walls.

Kate knew she shouldn't snoop around Luke's bedroom, but the small, framed drawing hanging over his bed drew her in. It featured a delicate watercolor of an indigo-feathered bird perched on a tree branch.

"Like it?" that familiar voice asked from behind her.

Startled, Kate straightened abruptly and stumbled against the bedrail. Luke's hands grasped her shoulders, preventing her from falling. He released her immediately, but that brief contact sent a pleasant warmth through her. She composed herself and shifted the conversation to safer ground.

"Did you draw this?" she asked, her tone calmer and more measured than she felt.

"I wish," he said, his voice laced with good humor. "It's by

Mark Catesby, a botanist who visited the Carolinas in the early 1700s."

Curious, Kate leaned forward to inspect the intricate watercolor strokes. "It's beautiful. And the bird's navy feathers match your enormous bed," she said with admiration.

Balancing on the balls of his feet, he rocked back, his cheeks puckering to suppress his laughter. "You like big beds?"

"Well, to be honest," she answered without thinking, still absorbed in the drawing and trying to forget the feeling of his hands on her shoulder. "I've never slept in a gigantic bed like this."

She bolted upright, realizing the implications of what she had blurted out. "And I'm certainly not thinking about this one," she added in a rush.

Of course, I'm thinking about his beautiful, gigantic bed.

Flustered, she hurried on. "A bed that size would be too big for me. If I were sleeping alone. And of course, I'd be sleeping alone."

"Kate Fiore," he drawled, looking delighted by her discomfort, "there is so much I could say about that."

She waved her palm, eager to move on. "No need. So, where's this amazing view you were bragging about?"

Chapter Eighteen

KATE

Kate leaned against the weathered bench by the sea, ignoring its bumpy wood pressing into her shins. The sky had deepened to a royal blue tinged with orange and pink as the sun dipped closer to the horizon, casting a warm glow over the deserted beach.

"We have visitors," Luke said, gesturing to the dolphin pod swimming beyond the breakers.

Kate's eyes widened as she followed Luke's outstretched finger. Though she grew up along Black Rock's salty coast, she had never seen dolphins frolicking in their harbor's cooler waters. But here they were, gleaming like silver in Gull Island's warmer embrace.

"It's like your own private magic show," she murmured, her eyes glued to the pod as it shimmered down the coastline.

Luke leaned against the deck railing. His hands clasped as he considered. His face softened, and she made out a hint of that chin dimple she'd seen earlier.

"You're right," he said, after a long pause. "Each day brings something different. The sky is a kaleidoscope of colors. Clouds morph into fantastical different shapes. Different waterfowl glide by. I come here every morning with my coffee, and I never know what I'll find."

The air hung heavy with a comfortable silence, punctuated only by the distant cries of the gulls. Kate felt a sense of peace, a tranquility she hadn't realized she craved until this moment. This little haven, tucked away from the hubbub of the world, felt like a secret shared between them, an oasis of beauty and serenity.

"It's perfect," she said, her voice barely a whisper. "Is that why you're writing your book?" she asked. "To help people understand why places like this are special?"

"Maybe," he said slowly before shaking his head. "Even if I had time to finish it, I'm not the best writer. I doubt my words would change what people think."

His words, laced with the raw fervor of a protector, ignited a spark within Kate. She saw in his fight for this land, his relentless push against the odds, a mirror of her own struggle. Both, warriors in different landscapes, she for a future and he for a legacy.

"You never know what your impact might be," she offered softly, her eyes locked on his face.

He quirked an eyebrow, a spark of hope behind the doubt. "You funning me, ma'am?"

Sensing his unspoken question, Kate knew she had to tread carefully. Their fragile partnership depended on it.

"Not at all, Luke. You can do this. I'd be proud to read your draft and help you with ideas for publishing it."

His eyes widened in surprise. "You'd do that?"

She nodded her encouragement. "You need to get your book into the world."

He looked away, shifting on his feet, as though embarrassed by her faith in him. Without thinking, she reached out and patted his forearm reassuringly. It was firm, solid. His eyes met hers, and she felt an unexpected flutter in her stomach at their connection.

"So, where's the view you keep bragging about?" she asked, moving her hand away and feeling a strong need to shift the conversation again.

Luke gestured toward the western sky. "Just there, over the dunes."

Kate stood on tiptoes, craning her neck to peer over the sand. "Can't see," she said, squinting into the distance.

"Dawson has the same problem," he said, nodding sympathetically. "We climb up here, so nothing blocks his sight line."

Luke leaped onto the bench and extended his hand. Kate slipped her hand into his, dwarfed by his own yet gently grasped. With an effortless tug, he pulled her up.

"Um, it's a long way down," Kate said, hit by a twinge of vertigo.

He moved behind her on the bench, the warmth of his chest against her back until only a whisper separated them. "Don't look down. Pretend this is the *Titanic*, with Jack and Rose flying on the bow together."

She shook her head. "You're kidding, right? That did not end well for them."

His chuckle breathed against her hairline. "Promise this will have a different ending." He placed his hands over hers on the deck railing and stepped even closer, so close that his chest brushed against her back, sending shivers through her body. "Now, hold on to the railing. You trust me?" he asked, in an intoxicating imitation of DiCaprio's Jack.

"I trust you," Kate answered breathlessly, playing along, "but I am not closing my eyes."

"Okay," he smiled, "but we're doing the flying scene."

Stretching out her arms, she felt him intertwine their fingers together with a light, exquisite touch. "It's all right," he whispered, bending low to her ear. "I've got you. Look straight ahead."

Kate's gaze focused on the horizon, her mind racing as she felt his chest pressing against her back.

"What am I looking for again?" she stammered, blinded by his closeness and the sun.

Luke dropped one hand and stepped aside enough to fish his Ray-Bans from a pocket and slip them around her neck. "These weren't in the movie, but they cut the glare," he said, un-Jack like.

The frames were too big for her face and slid down her nose.

"Let me help," he said, reaching around her to adjust the strap. His hands on her neck sent shockwaves down her neck and shoulders.

"Better?" he asked, returning to cradle her outstretched arms.

"Much," she murmured, settling comfortably against his chest.

He nodded to the horizon. "Good. Now look over the top of that dune."

She searched until she found where the sky and sea collided in a brilliance of blues, greens, and whites. The island disappeared in a riot of foam, waves cresting and swirling in a mad dance as the ocean embraced the river and carried it home. The unfolding beauty of the island took her breath away.

"Worth the climb?" His words broke her thoughts.

"Absolutely," she whispered, her voice barely audible over the wind.

Glancing sideways, she watched sunlight dance across Luke's face, casting coppery highlights in his hair. She fought the urge to touch the strand that curled across his forehead, wishing time would stop and keep her longer in this moment.

"You know," he drawled softly, sending her heart into backflips, "you could stay and watch the sunset with me."

Kate hesitated. Luke was her work partner and David's best friend. Despite herself, something compelled her to stay. Before she knew what she was doing, she melted into his arms. His lips brushed against her cheek, their warmth radiating through her body and awakening a want deep within her...

...until she felt a wet, papery tongue licking her toes.

Kate yelped and jerked away; the spell broken. Boo was staring at Kate with moist, adoring eyes.

Grateful for the interruption that might have led to something awkward, Kate slipped her hands from his and hopped down from the bench. With easy strides, he followed.

"Hey, Boo!" Luke said, scooping up his pet. "Don't be slurping on our guest like that."

"He's reminding you it's dinnertime," she said, giving the dog a slow pat. "Anyway, I've taken up enough of your Friday. I should go."

Luke's disappointment hung in the air. "You're not imposing, but I understand. Let me walk you to your car."

The air was thick with unspoken words as they walked to her car. Her pleasure at being with him had unsettled her. That happiness was a feeling she once knew, but it had long since disappeared from her heart.

He opened the car door for her, stoking waves of regret. If only she had the courage to stay.

"See you at turtle patrol tomorrow," he said, a soft smile gracing his face as he held Boo. "And thanks for your kind words about my book."

Kate's nod was hesitant, her mind a battleground of conflicting desires. The comfort and warmth she felt with Luke moments ago was intoxicating, a glimpse into a life she'd denied herself since her divorce. But the scars of past mistakes whispered warnings, urging her to retreat into the familiar isolation she'd built around herself. Alone was safer she told herself, and Luke was a challenge to the walls she'd constructed around her heart. Yet part of her yearned for the connection and vulnerability that came with letting someone else in.

She gave Boo a final scratch behind his ears, the simple gesture grounding her. Her heart tugged with a bittersweet pang as she turned to Luke. "Thank you," she said, her voice tinged with wistfulness. "I couldn't ask for a better way to end my first week on the island."

Luke gave a curt nod, his easy smile momentarily slipping. As their eyes met, a flicker of something deeper, something unspoken, passed between them. It was a subtle change, a crack in the façade he generally presented, and it stirred a curious warmth within her.

"Goodnight, Kate," he said, his voice low.

Her heart was heavy as she drove away watching Luke in the rearview mirror. He was petting Boo, his eyes lingering on her car. She replayed the evening in her mind. Her surprise at finding Luke. The pleasant heat of his body near hers. *What am I doing?*

She stopped herself from dreaming. She had too much to lose being distracted by a summer fling. It wasn't until she heard the familiar crunch of tires across her white shell driveway that she discovered Luke's sunglasses still wrapped around her neck.

Chapter Nineteen

LUKE

Morning light slipped through the kitchen window, painting long shadows across Annie's worn table. Luke, hunched over a mug of lukewarm coffee, ran a hand through his hair, the gesture more of a nervous tick than a styling attempt. Frustration gnawed at him, settling in his gut like a stubborn knot.

"I don't get it, Annie," he said. "One minute, we get along great. Next, Kate's taking off like the house is on fire."

Annie sipped from her mug and considered, her brow furrowing. "What happened before she left last night?"

Luke rubbed a hand over his chin, remembering. "Nothing much. I extended some Southern hospitality. She wanted to see her first Point sunset, and I asked if she wanted to stay and watch with me."

Annie put down her coffee and studied him. "I see. Do you like her?"

Luke threw up his hands. "What kind of question is that?"

Annie pursed her lips and stared. There was no way of getting around his sister once she was intent on something.

He hesitated before answering. "I don't know. Maybe. She's interested in old homes and asked about my book. Boo adores her. But she has this maddening big-city air that turns me off. Plus, she sides with Clayton Pruitt about the Point."

Annie chuckled, a soft rumble that warmed the cool air. "You know," she drawled, leaning back in her chair, "for someone who claims solitude, you wear protest like a badge."

Luke scoffed. The sound was too loud in the quiet kitchen. He ran a hand through his hair again, the gesture brushing against a phantom ache in his chest. He'd lost count of the women who fit between business meetings and SOS rallies. But somehow, the way this "twitchy Yankee" crinkled her nose when she argued with him, the fire that sparked in her hazel eyes when she spoke her mind got under his skin in a way he couldn't ignore.

"Would you like a female perspective?" Annie asked, her grin wide and playful.

And here it came. He prepared himself for the lecture ahead. "Please. Enlighten me."

Annie leaned forward. "From what CeCe says, Kate left an unhappy marriage several months ago. I think between that and starting a new job here, she's probably guarded, and rightly so. Your invitation likely scared her off, no matter how well-meaning it was."

Luke mulled over Annie's words. Perhaps his sister was right. He would take things slow and see what developed. But before he could say more, Dawson bounced into the kitchen, rubbing sunscreen into his cheeks. "It's how Miss Kate is, Uncle Luke," the boy said, after overhearing the adults' conversation. "She's the

Scaredy Lady. But don't worry. I'll help her on our turtle team, and she won't be scared."

If only it were that simple, Luke thought.

DAWSON RAN AHEAD OF LUKE, HIS LEGS PUMPING AS HE sprinted to the beach walkway. Luke locked his truck and followed, not nearly as excited as his nephew. He had a to-do list that seemed to grow each day, and this Saturday morning turtle patrol with Dawson and Kate was one more thing to tackle.

As he watched the boy charge ahead, a wave of nostalgia for simpler times hit Luke, for when all he had to do was play and help occasionally at Gift and Garden. Now, the family business was his responsibility, and it was consuming him.

Luke's eyes lit up as he spotted Kate waiting at the edge of the walkway. Today, she was rocking a baseball cap, her ponytail spilling out the back. He took in the classic red Chucks with her turtle team shirt tied around the waist and low-riding black running shorts that molded to her. Her look differed from the glammed-up style of most women he dated. She was comfortable in her own skin, and he couldn't deny how much that attracted him.

"Nice merch," Luke said with a teasing grin, nodding at the cap.

Kate stood, slapping sand from her legs. "I'm going for a native look," she said, a touch of pride in her voice.

"It's working for you," he quipped, earning a smile that zinged his heart.

At that moment, Dawson bulldozed into Kate, wrapping her

with chubby arms. "We'll find a nest today, Miss Kate. Follow me!"

The boy dashed away, looking for turtle tracks. Luke and Kate followed, an awkwardness between them. Remembering Annie's advice, Luke racked his brain for something to say, determined to put her at ease. "Dawson's convinced we'll spot a nest, he said," trying for friendly-casual. "I'm crossing my fingers he succeeds because a disappointed Dawson is a cranky Dawson."

Kate's eyes brightened, and she nodded. "I get that. My little cousin Angie is the same."

As they exchanged stories about their families, Luke felt the tension easing. Her warmth and openness drew him in, and he opened up as well. "Boo says 'Hey!' and promised not to wander off this morning," he said with a grin.

Her laughter was like music. "Well, 'Hey, Boo' back! He's got a big personality. Mixed breed?"

"Part chihuahua, part mystery mutt. I found him wandering Island Drive. Didn't have the heart to send him to the shelter, so I kept him."

"I think you're a big softie."

Now it was his turn to laugh. "Not usually, unless it comes to Boo and my family."

Kate's face widened with her warm smile. "I admire a man with heart."

His eyebrows lifted, and a hint of surprise danced in his eyes. "Really? I wasn't sure from the way you left last night."

She chewed her bottom lip, and her hand reached for the reassurance of her locket. "Sorry about that. It was late, and I was tired. In fact, I forgot to return your sunglasses."

He took the sunglasses she handed over, enjoying the soft

touch of her fingers against his palm. "Sorry again," she said, sounding genuinely apologetic.

"Not a problem. I'm glad you saw the Point from my place," he said, wondering how she'd react to his mention of their moment on the deck. And there *had* been a moment between them before she ran off. He was sure of that.

"Um, me, too," she said, looking up at him.

In the morning sun, it was hard to tell for sure, but he thought he caught a flicker of affection in Kate's eyes. They were a mesmerizing blend of warm honey and earthy amber, with gold flecks that danced in the light. As she looked at him, her eyes lit with excitement, Luke's pulse revved like Spike's engine.

They continued across the scorching sand, the space between them shifting to a comfortable silence. Luke felt a mix of anticipation and nervousness. He wanted to say more, to let her know he enjoyed being with her, but he didn't want to spook her. He knew she needed time.

Just then, Dawson called to them, his arms waving wildly and pointing to a patch of sand near the dunes.

"Uncle Luke! Miss Kate! Look what I found!"

LUKE KNELT BY THE UNASSUMING FLASK-SHAPED MOUND of sand where the sea turtle tracks ended against the base of a dune. He'd seen hundreds of nests but finding a new one never got old. He gave a thumbs up. "Our first of the season!"

Dawson yipped and circled the mound.

"Careful, buddy," Luke said, standing and putting a restraining hand on his nephew's shoulder.

Even though a foot of sand buried the eggs, they were still fragile. "Can't have you hurting the nest, even by accident."

Rolling onto his stomach, Dawson solemnly watched the two-foot-wide hump of sand as Kate crouched next to the boy. "Mama must not be particular where she leaves her eggs," Kate said, nodding towards the walkway that beachgoers would clog once the season kicked in.

Luke tilted his head to the nearby public access sign. "Sea turtles are picky about where to deposit their eggs. Unfortunately," he deadpanned, "turtles can't read."

Kate groaned and slapped her forehead with the heel of her hand. "Let's get cracking then."

Dawson bolted upright and rested a sweaty hand on Kate's shoulder. "No, Miss Kate. We don't crack the eggs. The babies crack open their eggs by themselves when they hatch. Then they dig up to the top of their nest."

Luke watched Kate stifle a laugh and arrange her face in a serious expression. "Thanks for reminding me," she said gravely. She bent closer and placed a hand on his shoulder. "You are a sea turtle whisperer, Dawson."

The boy beamed, and when Kate winked at Luke, his heart tugged.

THE SUN HAD CLIMBED HIGHER SINCE LUKE RETURNED from his truck with supplies to build a barrier around the nest. He swiped sweat from his forehead and pounded a nest alert sign into the sand. Around him, Dawson tied orange warning ribbons on stakes around the perimeter while Kate cut wire mesh to protect the site. When they finished, a knot of onlookers clapped.

"Come back in sixty days to see these eggs hatch," Luke called to them before they dispersed.

"I can't wait," Kate said, flipping her ponytail away from the back of her neck where it was pasted.

"You'll do more than watch," Luke said. "You'll help dozens of hatchlings crawl to the waves and guard them from seagulls and sand crabs, waiting to pick them off."

Kate's eyes widened. "I didn't realize there'd be so many hatchlings at once."

"It's hectic, but you'll never forget the miracle of those tiny sea turtles crawling to the sea."

"Such determination," Kate said, looking at the nest with new appreciation.

"There's a lot about our island that people don't know or take for granted," Luke said, his voice filled with passion. "They need to understand why it's so important to protect this place."

She nodded, but her eyes danced as she watched Dawson. The child was hopping up and down, holding onto the front of his shorts. "I get the message," she said. "But are you getting your nephew's message?"

Luke watched him and shrugged. "Ah, the downside of keeping hydrated on the beach—having to pee," he said matter-of-factly. "Time for a swim, Dawson."

"Swim?" Kate asked, puzzled.

"Well, no bathrooms or trees on the beach for when nature calls...." he trailed off.

Shucking off his shirt and sunglasses, Luke tossed them into his rucksack. He caught Kate's gasp, and her reaction to his toned chest pleased him. He didn't have six-pack abs or a perfect physique, but he worked at keeping in shape.

"Join us, Kate," he said, extending his hand to her.

She took a sudden interest in examining her shoes, shuffling her feet in the sand. "I didn't think to bring a swimsuit today."

"No need. You're fine as you are," he said, taking Dawson's hand instead and heading toward the water.

"I've been swimming since I was walking, but I don't do waves," she called after them.

Despite the sultry morning, Luke sucked in a breath when the first waves smacked into him. He pressed on with the boy, their bodies adjusting to the cooling temperature. Dawson hooted as they slipped past the breakers to the calm beyond the cresting waves.

"I can touch bottom," Dawson said proudly. He bounced on tiptoes against the sandy sea floor as water reached his neck.

Luke floated on his back next to his nephew while watching Kate. She waded a few yards away in the shallows, looking relaxed. A day at the beach will do that, he thought.

"Hey, Kate!" he shouted over the pounding surf. She raised her hand in an unhurried greeting.

Dawson dog-paddled to his side, a sea-sprite covered in mirth and salt water. "A roller's coming, Uncle Luke. Ready!"

They joined hands and ducked under the towering wave as it arced over them. Seconds later, they shot up, laughing and sputtering.

"Let's do another!" Dawson begged. "With Miss Kate."

"Don't think she's up for a roller, but we can ask."

Luke looked for Kate, spotting her flailing in the breakers. Her arms thrashed wildly and her lips formed words he couldn't hear over the waves. He didn't need to make out what she was saying from this distance—her fear was tangible.

His adrenaline kicked in as he tugged Dawson and fought the current to reach her. Just as a massive wave crashed into her, she went under. Pushing Dawson to safety, he gripped her shoulders and pulled her to the surface. She clung to him, her breath coming in ragged gasps, her body trembling. He felt the soft curves of her body pressing against him. Kate wasn't one to scare easily, but something had terrified her.

"Hey, now," he hushed, stoking her back. "I've got you. You're okay."

She wiped the salt water from her lips and pointed a trembling finger at the open sea beyond them. Her face was masked with fear.

"Shark!" she cried.

Luke spun around, searching the deeper waters until he spotted a blue-gray fin dipping into the surf.

"That's a dolphin, Miss Kate," Dawson said calmly, patting her quivering hand and waddling into the shallows as though nothing was amiss.

"A dolphin?" she groaned, burying her face in Luke's shoulder. "I didn't know. We don't have dolphins in Black Rock."

Luke held her close, his arms wrapped tightly around her trembling body. He was relieved that it wasn't a shark, but her reaction also amused him. "It's okay," he said soothingly.

It disappointed him when she straightened and pulled away. She had fit so right against him.

"I am beyond mortified," she said, shaking off the water dripping from her sodden cap.

Luke grinned. "Hey," he said, still trying to slow his racing pulse after fearing for Kate's safety. "You'll know next time you spot a fin in the water."

She looked up at him hesitantly, wringing water from her shorts. "It's not that," Kate said with a grimace. "I was so freaked about a shark attacking you and Dawson, I...I peed in the ocean before I went under."

Chapter Twenty

KATE

"I cannot believe you admitted to peeing in the ocean!" CeCe giggled, settling back into the pillows on her bed.

Kate stretched next to her friend. "I panicked!" she said ruefully. "Thought it was a shark. How was I supposed to know it was a harmless fin? I'm no marine biologist. I don't know one fin from another."

"So, this lovely man pulls you from the surf one-handed and then...?" CeCe trailed off.

"We finished looking for nests, and then I went home."

Kate remembered Luke's face after he plucked her from the surf. His dark brows were knit tight with concern, and he held her against his chest until he was sure she wasn't hurt. She wouldn't have minded staying in the strong arms longer.

CeCe rested a hand on her twin-sized stomach and tutted. "I can tell there's more. We're talking about Luke, the hunky conservationist with a heart of gold for his friends. It's not every day you get to swoon over someone like that."

"You mean how glorious it was to drape my arms around Luke's broad shoulders?" Kate asked, her grin teasing. "Or how his ripped chest glistening with salt water was absolutely amazing?"

"And?"

Kate tried to hide her face in the pillows, but her embarrassment was clear. "Oh, stop it, CeCe! Yes, if you must know, he looked swoon-worthy. And those eyes!"

CeCe nudged her friend, a mischievous glint in her eyes. "Uh-huh, intense eyes, huh? You're a goner, Kate! The Luke Effect strikes again! The man's got a superpower. David says the Garden Club ladies get positively giddy whenever he walks into a meeting."

"Shush, CeCe! You're making it worse!" Kate protested, but her smile betrayed her true feelings. "It's like I'm in high school again instead of a divorced thirty-three-year-old woman." Her playful facade slipped, and her voice carried the weight of old regrets.

CeCe clasped her friend's hand. "It's been more than a year since you and Jon split up. Sweetie, it's a good sign you're having these feelings again."

"Maybe. But let's face it. Happy endings don't wait around for me," she said, her hollow laughter giving away the emptiness in her heart. It was time to say it out loud. Kate swallowed.

"Apparently, Jon hasn't been waiting around. Mom told me his girlfriend's pregnant."

CeCe's voice softened with concern, and she brought her hand to her chest, as if Kate's pain were her own. "Oh, sweetie, I am so sorry."

Kate felt her eyes sting, and her fingers reached for her locket, twisting it as she said, "First, a corporate takeover makes my job redundant. Now, a twenty-something babe, who has the audacity to be a fertility goddess, makes me redundant as a life partner."

CeCe slipped an arm around her friend and drew her close. "Don't be so hard on yourself, Kate. It's natural to be overwhelmed after everything you've been through."

Kate wanted to sound light-hearted, but her voice cracked and gave her away. "I've lost a part of myself since all this happened, and I don't know if I'll ever find my way back."

"You will, Kate. I know you will!"

Kate rested her head on CeCe's shoulder as a stray tear fell. They stayed quiet, each wrapped in the comforting presence of the other, until David knocked on the door. He stood in the entry, shuffling his feet like a nervous teen waiting for his date.

"Don't want to intrude on your girlfriend time, Sweetness," he said. "Will you be okay if I head to the Garden Club meeting for an hour?"

"Go, have fun," CeCe waved him on. "The twins and I are fine, and Kate's on duty."

"Call if you need anything. Anything at all." David said, blowing a kiss to his wife. "And you, Katie Kat," he went on, pointing at her, "you'll get your happily ever after. If Luke McAllister isn't the one, he's an idiot."

The pillow Kate tossed at David flew over his head as he ducked and retreated, his chuckles echoing down the hall.

LATER THAT WEEK, KATE STRODE ACROSS THE sidewalk along Island Drive, unfazed by the evening drizzle. She'd taken to walking to work, finding it a welcome break in her day, even though she had repaired Eve Snow's AC.

The rustle of pines in the maritime forest and the rhythm of distant waves relaxed Kate as she passed by. She even recognized the same people: the jogging couple in matching jaunty shirts, the busy mom wheeling two tykes in a double stroller, and the friendly postal carrier, who always wished Kate a good afternoon.

It surprised Kate how much she looked forward to this part of her day. She was even enjoying her new role at the aquarium. Sure, there were deadlines, but people were friendly and low-key. There was no pressure to jockey for power or push to get ahead. She'd even led tours on the floor and recognized the friendliest stingray in the touch tank. But she had yet to stroke a horseshoe crab. Those knobby backs and pointy tails still made her cringe.

As Kate walked along, the once gentle rain morphed into fat splatters, pelting her from all angles. She picked up her pace and hoisted her carry bag overhead as an impromptu umbrella. The walkway became a cascade of water, forcing her to navigate around scattered puddles. She didn't notice the red truck through the gray curtain of rain until it slowed next to her.

"Looks like you need a ride," Luke shouted over a roll of thunder. He reached across the seat and pushed open the passenger door. Without hesitating, Kate threw her bag inside and tumbled after it as the sky unleashed a downpour.

"Thanks," she said gratefully, her wet clothes sticking to the bench seat. "It caught me by surprise."

"They do that this time of year," Luke said, waiting for a break in the traffic before merging onto Island Drive.

Kate brushed at the raindrops on her arms. "I'm dripping all over your truck," she apologized.

"Spike's been through worse," he said, his attention fixed on the road ahead. "You're heading home?"

She nodded, curious about his own destination. He was dressed for office work in gray slacks and a powder-blue collared shirt, and his messenger bag rested on the back seat.

"You, too?" she asked.

"Yeah. Just back from a client meeting," he said, his voice tinged with a touch of weariness. "They asked me to run an environmental impact study for an eco-friendly housing development along the Intracoastal, but I don't have time to take it on."

"You should go for it, Luke. Mae says you're brilliant at arguing against the Point development."

He shook his head. "Look where that got us. Pruitt shoots down every claim we make. Anyway, I thought turtle team rules forbid us talking about the Point."

"Well, this is different. It's allowed when it's a big career coup for you."

He took one hand off the wheel and landed it dramatically over his heart. "Grateful for this small favor," he said with mock seriousness.

"You should be," Kate said, flashing him a grin before turning serious. "A friend of mine needs beta testers for her small business software, and her app would free up time for you to take on jobs like that. I can forward her contact information."

The muscles in his jaw flexed during the long pause that followed. *Maybe we should stick to talking about the weather*, she thought, her playful mood ebbing.

"I'll think about it," he finally said, "and let you know."

The rest of the journey passed in silence as Luke focused on the road, and Kate winced as thunder grew louder and more ominous. By the time they arrived at her bungalow, the storm had picked up, flinging tree branches and empty flower pots across the yard.

"This storm is scary," she said, concerned for his safety. "Would you like to wait inside until it lets up?"

He turned to her, considering. "Boo doesn't care for storms, so I best get back to him."

A downed limb smacked the windshield with a wicked thud. Kate yelped and drew back.

"On second thought," he said, his frown matching her concern, "Boo can be on his own a while longer."

Chapter Twenty-One

KATE

Kate handed Luke the clean towel from her laundry basket on the sofa before tucking it away in a corner, careful to conceal her silky underwear at the bottom of the pile. As he dried the water on his shirt, jaw set in determination and rain clinging to his eyelashes like diamonds, he reminded her of the dashing lead from a Bridgerton novel.

"I have a dry shirt you can borrow if you like," she offered, trying to avoid staring at his muscular chest peeking through his wet top.

"You have something that fits?" Luke asked, his eyebrow raised in amusement. "We're not exactly the same size."

Kate pretended to be offended. "Of course!" she said, though she was secretly grateful that he made a pointed assessment of their differences.

She rummaged through her laundry basket for the oversized short-sleeved red V-neck from her college days. It served as a nightgown sometimes, but he didn't need to know that.

Kate tamped down her growing anticipation as Luke disappeared into the bathroom to change. Their unexpected encounter in the rain had sparked an excitement in her that made her attraction to him undeniable. Moments later, he emerged, wearing her shirt that clung to him with perfection.

Kate cringed as Luke settled on the couch and studied her living room. Unfolded laundry, legions of shoes scattered in the tiny entry, books and coffee-stained mugs littered the floor next to her reading chair, and an empty pizza box from two nights ago all greeted him.

"Quite the rustic charm vibe you've got going here, Kate," he said with a smile as he finished his inspection of her room.

Kate gestured around the space. "Is *rustic* a kind way of saying it's a mess?" she asked, a self-conscious laugh escaping her lips. Tidiness was not her strong suit.

He shook his head. "Nah, it's cozy and authentic."

"Not a fan of glam and trendy stuff?" She raised an eyebrow, intrigued.

He grinned. "Not my thing."

Taking a seat on an armchair across from him, she discreetly adjusted the slit in her wet pencil skirt. "Well, thanks, I guess. That's a compliment, right?"

"Absolutely," he said, his eyes briefly lingering on her exposed thigh.

Outside, the storm intensified, flickering the lights as a powerful gust rattled the roof. "Great," Kate groaned. "I better find some candles."

"I know where Mae keeps her stash in the pantry," Luke offered. "And you're soaked. Why don't you change into something dry?"

Shivering in the air conditioning and uncomfortable in her wet clothes, she didn't hesitate. "Dry clothes would be heavenly," she admitted, padding off to her bedroom.

As Kate pulled on her favorite red hoodie and black yoga pants, she heard the faint sounds of Luke rummaging in the kitchen, looking for candles. She thought back to a week ago, when he had lifted her from the surf, so worried about her safety. He might be stuck in his ways, but he was also kind in a manner that Jon rarely was. Jon would expect her to get candles and be quick about it, sometimes without a word of thanks. She wondered what it would be like to have someone like Luke by her side, someone who showed care and concern for her wellbeing without hesitation.

Kate shook off those thoughts. No sense in getting ahead of herself. Luke was a colleague and maybe a friend. She needed to remember that.

SHE RETURNED TO FIND LUKE HAD FINISHED COVERING a tea table with sleek battery-powered candles. Lightning flashed, and the lights snapped off, but the faux candlelight cast a welcome glint through the afternoon shadows.

A deafening thunderclap followed, and Kate covered her ears. She had hated thunderstorms since she was a little girl and lightning struck a tree, sending the old maple crashing onto their house. She fought the urge to dive next to Luke for comfort. Instead, she inched closer and tucked in at the opposite end of the sofa.

"That was close," she said, trying to sound nonchalant. She

was a grown woman. She would not let a thunderstorm scare her. At least, not too much.

Luke settled easily on the sofa, draping his arms over its back. "Thunderstorms here can be fierce, but we're safe," he assured her.

Kate took a deep breath and forced herself to relax. No worries, she told herself. Just trapped in a house during a raging storm with a colleague who gave her a ride home in the rain. But it was hard to deny how good Luke looked with candlelight flickering over his face, highlighting the strong angles of his jaw and the curve of his lips.

"I saw CeCe the other night," Kate finally said, figuring the Greenwoods would be a safe topic to discuss.

"David mentioned you were having a girls' night when I met him at the Garden Club."

"You do Garden Club, too?" Kate hoped that was the least of her conversation with CeCe that David had divulged.

"Yup. We install flower beds in downtown South Harbor for that quaint look tourists love. We're a fun group. You should join us, Kate."

"Even though I'm leaving at the end of the summer?" she asked.

"Hey, short-timers are welcome."

"I didn't think you liked summer people. Outsiders like me," she added.

"I've been known to change my mind," he said. He smiled, and his eyes crinkled at the corners. Despite the shadows of the darkened room, his eyes were so intense they seemed to look right through her.

"Good," she stammered. "I mean, good that you're flexible."

A familiar ringtone trilled, and Kate grabbed for her phone.

"It's my mother. She tracks the weather here, and she'll worry if I don't pick up. Do you mind?"

Luke waved her on and Kate accepted the video chat. Mom and Aunt Theresa's faces filled the screen.

"I got a storm alert," Mom said, her eyes wide with concern.

"What's going on?" Aunt Theresa asked, squinting into the screen. "It looks dark."

"A bit of wind and rain. Nothing to worry about."

As if on cue, thunder boomed, startling Kate out of her chair. "But the power has cut off."

Mom switched to high alert. "Do you have a flashlight? Stay away from the windows. And don't open the refrigerator!"

Aunt Theresa was more curious than worried. "Move the screen again, Kathleen," she said, straining beyond her niece to glimpse Luke. "You're not alone?"

"No. A colleague gave me a ride home, and he's staying until the weather lets up."

Kate shifted the phone toward Luke, and he gave the women a friendly wave.

"Thank you for looking after my daughter," Mom said.

"My pleasure, ma'am," he called in that charming Southern drawl that melted butter.

That got Aunt Theresa's attention. She tucked a curl behind her ear and scrutinized Luke. "Are you the hunk Kathleen told us about? The one on her turtle team with the cute dimple and nice abs who rescued her in the surf?"

Kate coughed and rocked the phone in her hand. "Can't hear you, Mom. Reception's breaking up. Gotta go. Love you. Bye."

Kate clicked off in an instant, her phone tapping against her forehead in slow circles. She lifted her gaze ever-so-slowly as if knowing what she'd find. Luke was stifling a laugh.

"Hunk?" he asked with a knowing smirk.

"I never said 'hunk,'" Kate protested.

"No?"

She groaned and rubbed her forehead with her hand. "No! That's my aunt's vivid imagination." Kate peeked out from between her fingers. "But the dimple and abs thing? I may have let that drop."

His eyes danced in delight at Kate's unwitting confession. "Well, I'm flattered," he said, with a hint of pleasure that made Kate blush.

"And I'm mortified. Again," she murmured.

Luke leaned closer to Kate and said, "Kate, you're adorable when you're flustered." His features softened until they almost seemed gentle. "You do this thing where you scrunch your nose and flap your hands around. It's quite endearing."

He reached across and brushed a stray strand of hair from her forehead. His fingers sent a shiver down her spine, and heat radiated through her skin where he touched her. When he moved away, her fingers stole to the thin silver chain on her locket, seeking reassurance in something familiar.

Before Kate could consider further, the lights flickered back to life with a soft oomph.

"Storm must be winding down," she said, feeling foolish babbling about the weather.

"Seems that way," he said with a nod, rising to make his way home now the storm was subsiding.

She didn't want him to leave. She liked his company but couldn't find the words to ask him to stay longer.

"Do you need to get back to Boo right away?" she blurted out. "Can you stay longer until it's safe to drive?" she asked with a shaky breath. She expected him to refuse while willing him to say 'yes,' so they could continue whatever this was that was happening between them.

Luke's head tilted, a flicker of confusion crossing his face. Then it clicked—this had to be a memory jog for him. Last week, when he'd asked her to stay for the sunset, she'd bolted. Back then, her jumbled feelings towards him had left her paralyzed, unsure of how to respond.

"Look, about the other night at your house," she began, "why I took off so fast."

He was watching her now, waiting for what she had to say. She took a deep breath and plunged ahead.

"Well, it's just that I ..."

Kate's mobile chirped, and she stopped to glance at the incoming text.

"Excuse me. It's David, and he rarely texts me."

Kate's eyes widened as she scanned the message. She looked up and found Luke staring at his mobile.

"David added you on the message thread?" he asked her, already knowing the answer.

She nodded. "The twins are ready. It's show time!"

June

GULL ISLAND

"June is busting out all over."

— RODGERS AND HAMMERSTEIN

Chapter Twenty-Two

LUKE

Luke's truck rumbled over the bridge towards South Harbor, his grin wide. It had been weeks since the twins stabilized, and he was finally going to meet David's boys.

Beside him, Kate stared out the window as they made their way to the Special Care Nursery Unit. He stole a sideways glance, taking in the delicate contours of her heart-shaped face and those captivating eyes.

Her voice sliced through his thoughts. "Do you think we're being too cutesy?" she asked, fiddling with her shirt. "Showing up in these matching turtle team shirts?"

He shook his head, a grin tugging at his lips. "Nah, it means we're rushing to a friend-saving mission and didn't stop for a wardrobe change after turtle patrol."

He was tempted to tell her how cute she looked, her turquoise toenail polish matching her shirt, but he held back, not wanting to ruin the easy banter between them.

"I don't know," she said, stretching in her seat. "Matching outfits scream 'couple,' right?"

He nodded, his mind racing as he tried to decode her words. Was she hinting at a connection beyond friendship?

"You think this is a couple thing?" he prodded gently.

Kate rolled her eyes impishly, but Luke detected a hint of vulnerability. His breath hitched as he sensed she was inviting him closer, only to draw back again. If only she'd let down her guard and allow him to glimpse something of the real Kate behind her defenses.

"You know what I mean," she said. "We're a good turtle team. Work partners. Anyway, do you have any insight into David's grand plan he wants us to pull off for CeCe?

"Not a clue," he said, disappointed as she pulled back once more.

The wistful tone colored her words. "David's been head-over-heels with CeCe since forever. He's always showing how he cares and respects her. It's nice seeing two people truly love each other. Not everybody is lucky enough to find their perfect match."

Luke's chest tightened at the thought of the ex-husband who had hurt this incredible woman. Part of Luke wanted to understand what had happened and to put it right. But he sensed Kate wasn't ready for a painful disclosure.

"Don't know about that," he countered gently. "I believe the universe finds ways of linking soulmates when the time is right."

Kate's smile lit up her face, reaching a sparkle in her eyes. "Awww, you're a romantic!"

"Maybe," he admitted with a shrug. "But what about you?"

She shook her head, her lips pursing before she spoke. "Definitely not me. The universe enjoys setting me up with disasters instead of soulmates. And you? More soulmates or more disasters in your life?"

His heart soared. She was asking about his experiences. *She wanted to know!* That had to be a good sign.

"I've had my share of disasters," he confessed, "but I haven't been seeking a soulmate for a long time. But you never know. Life has a way of surprising us."

Her hand briefly rested on his shoulder, setting off a comforting warmth that spread down his arm. Just as quickly, she shifted her attention to the window.

A BLEARY-EYED BUT ECSTATIC DAVID GREENWOOD greeted them in the special care nursery unit waiting room with a sleep-deprived grin that stretched from ear to ear. His arms shot out, enveloping Luke in a crushing hug. A mess of raven hair and beard couldn't hide the way his eyes lit up with pure joy.

Letting go of Luke, David snagged Kate in a tight embrace before whirling her around, a laugh escaping his lips. "Whoa there, tiger!" Kate squealed, breathless but delighted.

"Fatherhood is your thing," Luke chuckled, stepping back to admire his friend.

Kate, wiping a joyful tear from her eye, nudged him. "We almost brought cigars to celebrate," she teased, "but then we remembered you wouldn't be much of a cool dad if you smoked indoors."

David's booming laugh sliced through the tense hush of the waiting room. Startled heads turned, then a hesitant smile flickered across a young woman's face, followed by another, until a ripple of shared relief washed over the anxious group.

"Smoking would tempt me," David said, taking a deep breath and running a hand through his beard. "Leaving my wife and babies at the hospital these past few nights has gutted me. I couldn't stop worrying about them. But that's over. CeCe's coming home tomorrow! Doctors say the twins are doing well, so we can bring them home in a few days, too."

Luke slapped his friend on the back. "Great news! So, what's this surprise for CeCe you're planning?" Luke asked.

"I'll fill you in, but you gotta see my beautiful wife and boys first."

Kate and Luke followed David, their footsteps echoing through the sterile hallway. The scent of antiseptic and baby lotion mingled in the air. The rooms they passed resembled boutique hotel suites, save for their tiny occupants monitored by beeping machines. Wide windows allowed visitors to keep them company from the outside world.

Inside the SCN, soothing powder blue walls and gleaming tiles created a spotless, calming environment. Tiny infants rested in soft swaddles, tubes snaking from small bodies to watchful machines. Parents hovered nearby, their faces etched with love, hope, worry, and fear.

David stopped at the last room. He tapped on the window and waved to his wife seated on the other side of the glass. If David was bursting like a sunbeam doing Zumba, CeCe was glowing with the peaceful zen of soft moonlight. Dressed in a flowing caftan and relaxing on a cushioned recliner, her face was lit with a serene smile.

David's eyes softened as he pressed a palm against the glass. "Meet our Jacob."

CeCe drew back her caftan to reveal the sleeping infant tucked against her chest. She had wrapped him in a blue receiving blanket, and soft black curls spilled from his matching blue knit cap. His small hand gripped CeCe's pinky finger.

"He has your hair!" Luke said, draping his arm across his friend's shoulder.

David nodded, his face glowing with a huge grin. "Yep. He has his daddy's curls with his mama's gorgeous coppery skin."

David pointed to a second recliner hidden behind a phalanx of beeping machinery that monitored the infants. "There's Adam."

Luke craned his neck to see Mrs. Nichols holding her grandchild, already smitten by the tiny human as her face shone with love.

As David blew kisses to his family through the glass, a twinge of something poked at Luke's heart. He had given little thought to having kids of his own before because the right woman hadn't come along. Helping Annie raise Dawson, who was like a son to him, had seemed like enough. But now, seeing David with his boys, Luke wondered what it would be like to have a family of his own.

"That's one proud MeeMaw," Luke said, waving to David's mother-in-law. "Are you surviving having her around all the time?"

"Let's say we have our moments, but we're grateful for her help. And you can help, too, if you have time."

"Anything, old man. You in, Kate?" Luke asked, turning to Kate. She stood transfixed by the window as CeCe rocked her baby, an expression of sadness and wistfulness lingering on her face as Kate watched her friend.

"That precious little hand!" she whispered, dashing away a tear with her hand.

It puzzled Luke when David wrapped his arm around Kate and pulled her to him.

"I'm sorry, Katie-Kat," he whispered. "I got caught up in my daddy thing, and I didn't think."

Kate leaned into David's shoulder, a soft sob escaping her lips.

"It's okay. You and CeCe have a beautiful family, and I'm truly happy for you."

Luke didn't know what had triggered Kate's tears, but he recognized grief when he saw it. He'd seen that raw emotion with Annie when she lost Evan. And he felt it himself in high school when his father died. He caught David's eye, telegraphing a silent question to his friend. David shook his head slowly as if it wasn't his story to tell.

Kate straightened and took a long breath, struggling to regain her composure. Luke watched her, concerned about her reaction to seeing the babies. He realized she was still struggling and trying to put on a brave face.

"David, what's this plan of yours for CeCe?" she asked brightly. "And does it have something to do with your wedding anniversary Sunday?"

David smiled sheepishly. "Can't get anything by you, Kate. That's right. We'll be married seven years tomorrow!"

David's sheepish grin told the story before he even spoke.

"Congratulations!" Luke said, wondering about the wince that creased his friend's brow.

"Thanks, but I need to make amends. You might remember my big-time anniversary fail last year. Not proud."

Luke's wince deepened. Forgetting CeCe's anniversary with the date engraved on his wedding ring? Recipe for disaster. "Ouch, buddy," he muttered.

David chuckled, a hint of dread in his eyes. "Yeah, understatement. So, I'm planning a surprise romantic dinner at home tomorrow. Mother Nichols is leaving tonight and not back until the boys come home—our last shot at a peaceful evening."

Luke turned towards Kate, who responded with a quick nod. "We're in," he said. "What can we do to help?"

Taking a deep breath, David launched into his plan. "CeCe goes crazy for your banana pudding, Luke, and Kate—well, let's just say the Fiore baked ziti is legendary. Any chance you two could whip those up and drop them off at the house before CeCe gets home tomorrow? Maybe even spruce up the dining room a bit for a romantic ambiance, if you have the time?"

Luke found himself readily agreeing. He reached out and clapped David on the shoulder. "Consider it done."

"David, this dinner will be epic," Kate grinned, her excitement bubbling over. "Imagine CeCe's face when she's greeted by glowing candles and a spread that dreams are made of."

David closed his fist over his heart. "Can't tell you how much this means."

"Get back to your family and leave it to us," Luke said, already ticking off a mental list of what needed to be done.

Luke punched the button to the parking garage as he waited for the elevator with Kate. "We have twenty-four hours to pull this off. You ready?"

"Of course! I'll double-check with Mom about the sauce recipe. Oooh, and I'll do an antipasto. It's easy to make, and CeCe loves it. Any place to buy authentic Italian meats and cheeses here? And a loaf of fresh Italian bread? It'll be fun with your banana pudding."

The way her mind spun with possibilities intrigued him.

"Whoa, tiger! We're doing a Southern/Italian dinner theme?"

"Why not? It's an excellent combination."

The elevator dinged as Kate winked up at him. A whiff of citrus and something warm, distinctly Kate, invaded his senses as she leaned in conspiratorially. Her hand, cool and light, brushed his palm before confidently slipping into his. A jolt of electricity shot up his arm, momentarily stunning him.

They stepped inside, the heavy doors sliding shut with a metallic sigh. Encased in the confined space, the only sound he heard was the frantic hammering of his heart against his ribs. This summer, he realized with a sudden certainty, was going to be a lot more interesting than he could've imagined.

Chapter Twenty-Three

KATE

Kate squinted at the list she'd compiled for CeCe's dinner, spreading her phone screen to make the text bigger. She'd need reading glasses soon, but she wasn't ready to admit it yet. She bit her lip, double-checking the ingredients she and Luke had picked up together after leaving the hospital.

Luke sat across from her at his kitchen counter. He suggested using his house as a staging area for CeCe's dinner. It made sense. They had to move fast to pull off tomorrow's anniversary dinner, and Luke's spacious kitchen was a chef's paradise.

She watched him whirl around the five-burner gas range, pulling out gleaming stainless cooking pots and glass pans. She didn't recognize the catchy tune as he worked. Was it the Beach Boys? He was easy to be around when he wasn't spouting off about the Point or fretting about Founders Day.

"Got everything?" he asked.

"Think so. I'll make a quick call to Mom to be sure."

Kate wasn't a cook, but she'd spent hours watching her mother and aunt prepare Italian feasts. She usually dumped red sauce from a jar, so she had called for backup. She swiped open FaceTime.

"You look warm, Kathleen. What's the temperature there?" Mom asked without preamble.

"I'm fine, Mom. Just finished shopping for CeCe's dinner in ninety-degree heat."

"That's a furnace, Kathleen. Keep hydrated."

Aunt Theresa, who was visiting, leaned into the screen. "Did you find prosciutto and provolone? And sausage?"

Kate waved bulging packages of meat and cheese wrapped with butcher paper. "Luke knew an Italian deli that stocked them."

Aunt Theresa nodded approvingly. "Imagine. An Italian deli down South."

"It's not like I'm in the middle of nowhere," Kate protested with a giggle.

"Cousin Kate, Cousin Kate!" Angie inserted herself between Mom and Aunt Theresa, her pink princess outfit spilling around her like a cotton candy cloud. "I want to see your Hulk friend."

She baffled Kate. "Sweetie, I don't have a Hulk friend."

"You do," the child insisted. "Grandma says he's helping you cook."

Aunt Theresa hugged her granddaughter. "Not the Hulk, Angela Mia. You mean the Hunk, Cousin Kate's friend Luke."

"That's the one, Grandma! I want to see that one, Cousin Kate. Please?"

A soft chuckle from behind made Kate yank her ponytail tighter, momentarily wishing for the invisibility cloak she never got around to buying. Luke sidled up beside her, a playful smirk on his face as he leaned in to peek at her phone screen. Although the day was scorching, a shiver danced down Kate's arm as his shoulder grazed hers.

"Afternoon, ladies," he said, his voice dropping to a playful conspiratorial whisper near her ear. Kate could practically picture his dazzling "best behavior" smile. "Hey, Angie."

Mom's trademark mom-look, a mix of approval and scrutiny, lit up her face. It showed Luke was making a good impression, but judgment was still pending. Aunt Theresa's lips curled into a mischievous grin, her eyes widening, as she unabashedly admired the muscles beneath Luke's polo shirt.

But Angie folded her arms in disappointment. "You don't look like the Hulk," she said.

Luke mirrored her posture, a thoughtful expression on his face. Kate wanted to hug him for taking her little cousin seriously.

"Yeah, I'm feeling pretty good right now, but people say I can get grouchy like the Hulk."

"Okay, then you get to be the Hulk to beat the bad guys!" Satisfied, the child pranced away in a shimmer of pink tulle.

Kate was finding it hard to think straight with Luke next to her. She cleared her throat. "Back to the sauce, please. I want it to be perfect for CeCe."

With generations of Italian cooks in her DNA, Aunt Theresa got down to business. "The sauce is all about the meat. Slit the sausage so the juices run when you turn it over to brown. That adds the flavor. Without the meat, you have nothing."

"Add water to a small can of paste and mix it with Redpack crushed tomatoes," Mom added. She wasn't Italian-born, but she learned how to make a sauce after marrying into the Fiore clan. "And a pinch of sugar to cut the acidity."

Aunt Theresa looked horrified. "No, never sugar!"

"Trust me, Kathleen. It's better with a touch of sweetness," Mom said.

As the women debated the merits of sugar in red sauce, Kate slipped in her thanks and ended the chat.

Luke leaned against the butcher block kitchen island, his eyes dancing with mischief. "So, I'm a Hunk and a Hulk now? I'm flattered. And here I thought you saw me as more like a scruffy-looking plant nerd."

She shook a finger at him, remembering their frosty first encounters. "Oh, don't get too excited. You were like the Hulk when I first met you. Scary and surly."

He winced at the memory. "Ouch! I admit my behavior toward you was less than stellar. But since then, I've done my best to be the perfect work partner for you."

His manner toward her had softened lately—supporting her projects at the aquarium, offering her rides in the rain, even charming her on turtle patrol. She wasn't sure what to make of it.

"Points for effort, but I'm curious. What brought about this change?"

His brows knit together. "You want to know?"

Kate grabbed a wooden spoon and brandished it like a royal scepter. "Absolutely. I decree a new turtle team rule: honest responses are required to simple questions."

With a laugh, he grabbed the spoon and reeled her into him. His face was inches away, his eyes locked on hers so close that she could count the flecks of gold in his gray eyes, like sunlight ringing his pupils.

The heat from his body made her tingle in places Kate hadn't felt in months. Her senses suggested it was time for tingles again, but her brain reminded her that this was all happening too fast. She was both relieved and disappointed when Luke spun her away as suddenly as he had reached for her.

"Well, if it's a turtle team rule...," he trailed off, holding up his hands in surrender. "Here's the truth: even though we might disagree about some things, you're not quite the uptight Yankee invader I first met."

Oh no! Is that how I come across?

She tensed, her jaw tightening as she held back. Choosing her words carefully, not wanting to rant or be defensive, she said, "Thanks, I think?"

"I've seen too many newcomers who want to change our island to fit their lifestyle," he hurried on. "I figured you were like them. But you haven't been, and that snap judgment is on me." He ran a hand through his hair contritely, his eyes apologetic.

Kate couldn't remember the last time Jon had apologized. It was always her fault, and over time, his put-downs had eroded her self-esteem.

Without thinking, she reached across the counter to rest her hand on Luke's shoulder, touched by his apology. *The man had biceps!* She quickly pulled away, surprised by the warmth of his skin and unsure what to make of the pleasant sensation of touching him.

"I appreciate your honesty," Kate admitted. "I may have had a bit of an attitude when I arrived. Sorry about that."

He dipped his head in acknowledgment. "Now, your turn," he said, cocking an eyebrow as if daring her to say something outrageous. "Under your new turtle team rule..."

"Okay," she said, suddenly wary.

"When you saw the twins this morning, you had this look. I don't know, it was so sad." Luke's voice was gentle, but his words pierced Kate's heart.

She took a shaky breath and reached for the familiar comfort of her necklace. Luke was coming too near the truth.

"It's...it's complicated."

He hunched forward, waiting. His eyes were warm and full of kindness. She couldn't look at him. Instead, she stared at his long fingers laced together on the counter. Could he truly want to know why it was so hard for her to say?

He took her hand in his own, circling her thumb reassuringly with his before continuing in a gentle voice. "Didn't mean to upset you, Kate. Forget I brought it up."

He released her hand but stayed close enough that his warmth still encompassed her. She glanced at Boo, who had plopped at her feet, waiting patiently for attention.

"Hey, Boo! You're helping with CeCe's dinner too?"

The dog licked her ankles, and she rewarded him with a back rub. The tension left as she stroked the warm doggie body that squirmed with joy at her touch.

"That's enough loving on you for now, Boo." She giggled, straightening and moving to the sink to wash her hands.

"Back to the anniversary feast." She winked at Luke. "Sauce needs to simmer and sit overnight, so no distractions, Boo, or I'll never finish. And you can start your magic with the banana pudding, Luke."

He chuckled, mesmerized by the way she navigated the kitchen, a symphony of clinking spoons and rhythmic chopping. Her brows furrowed as she peered at her sauce notes, the picture of focused determination. If anyone was in danger of being distracted, it was him.

THE NEXT DAY, LATE AFTERNOON SUN STREAMED through the french doors of the Greenwood dining room and flitted across the walnut dining table. Luke tucked two white linen napkins alongside CeCe's silver charger plates and stepped back to examine his handiwork. The plates perfectly complemented the heirloom silver flatware, crystal goblets, and candelabra that David had unearthed for the occasion.

"My turn," Kate said, a mischievous glint in her eye as she elbowed Luke out of her way.

Kate sprinkled yellow rose petals from David's garden down the center of the table, winding them around the candles and crystal vases overflowing with white freesias from Gift and Garden. Luke fussed with glossy magnolia branches he draped on the sideboard, straightening the pillar candles laced among the greenery. He had to admit, it looked perfect for a romantic evening.

Luke checked the time, satisfied everything was on schedule. The bread was ready for slicing. Banana pudding and baked ziti awaited in the Greenwood refrigerator, along with Kate's antipasto tray of colorfully arranged meats and cheeses.

They had worked tirelessly yesterday to prepare this meal, texting each other late into the night with more ideas for David's dinner. Luke enjoyed Kate's company. She was becoming sassy and confident. He liked the way she bit her lip when she concentrated, the way she challenged his thinking, and her silvery laugh when she chased Boo around the kitchen for running off with a sausage.

"CeCe will love this," David said, bounding into the room and taking in the small touches Kate and Luke had styled for a romantic evening.

David pulled a white box from his pocket. Untying its velvet ribbon, he held it open. "What do you think about CeCe's anniversary gift?" he asked with a wide grin.

Kate gasped and stepped in for a closer look. Nestled in the box, rainbow colors sparkled from crystals inlaid on a burnished copper necklace.

"Copper. Good choice for a seventh anniversary, David," Luke said, slapping his friend's back.

"Does she suspect anything?" Kate asked, reluctantly pulling her gaze away from the necklace.

"Don't think so. She's worried about leaving the boys in the SCN, even with the nurses there. I had to think fast and talk her out of dinner at the hospital instead of coming home. In fact... " he trailed off, "You've already done so much, but do you have a few minutes for the twins at the hospital tonight?"

Kate watched Luke nod his silent assent and said, "Of course, David."

David let out a big breath and smiled. "It would ease CeCe's mind if she knew the boys had someone special looking in on them."

"You got it," Luke said, seeing the relief on his friend's face. "You and CeCe relax and enjoy the evening."

David's face brightened. "Thanks. You're are the best."

"Go bring your wife home from the hospital!" Kate said. "Everything's ready. We even paired a portable speaker to your phone and made a playlist of her favorites by Alicia Keys and Adele."

"Katie-Kat, I'm playing a special song when CeCe walks in that I swear they wrote for us."

David swiped the tune on his mobile, filling the room with the haunting refrain from Kane and Katelyn Brown's "Thank God."

"That part where I get to wake up by her side each morning? And how her hand fit perfectly in mine? That's my CeCe," David said, his eyes soft and filled with love.

"Hey, your evening hasn't started. Don't get emotional yet," Luke teased, although the lyrics had moved him, too.

Luke wondered if he'd find a love as complete as David's. He had a few close encounters, but no woman made the earth shake for him as CeCe did for his friend. Until Kate took his hand as they left the SCN yesterday. Her hand had been warm. Comforting. Had it been a perfect fit?

LUKE AND KATE WATCHED FROM BEHIND THE SCN window as a nurse checked the sleeping twins.

"They should be home by now," he said. It had been a short drive from the Greenwood's to the hospital, timed flawlessly for CeCe's surprise.

Kate nodded. Her eyes were drawn to the babies. "Can't wait to hear CeCe's reaction."

"Would you like to hold the boys?" the nurse asked after finishing her inspection. "We encourage physical contact."

Five minutes later, scrubbed and masked, Luke cradled the warm bundle that was Adam Greenwood. He remembered holding Dawson as a newborn. This child was more fragile, the tiny body barely larger than Luke's hand, but with that same sweet scent of baby lotion. Adam snuggled into his arms, his lips making suckling movements in sleep. Luke's heart melted when the boy's fingers curled around his pinky. He watched the child sleeping peacefully in his arms. *Could this be what my life is missing?*

He turned to Kate, who was rocking Jacob nearby. Her hazel eyes, usually bright and vibrant, pooled with tears, and her shoulders racked with silent sobs. His heart lurched at the sight of her pain.

"What's wrong, Kate? Please, tell me."

Kate held the baby close and whispered in a hitching voice that was barely audible over the bleating machinery.

"I never got to hold my baby."

Baby!

Luke's throat tightened. Was that what she couldn't tell me? He shifted Jacob to his other shoulder and reached for her.

"Kate, I'm so sorry. Do you want to talk over a coffee?"

Chapter Twenty-Four

KATE

The café on South Harbor's Riverwalk had been a five-minute stroll from the hospital. The twenty-something server greeted Kate and Luke with an infectious grin as they settled into the white bistro table.

"I'm Jerome, and I'm here to give you a coffee experience that is out of this world. What brew are we drinking this evening? Are we feeling caffeinated? Craving a cool java? Perchance a fruity taste sensation?"

Kate skimmed the menu. She was still raw from holding CeCe's baby. His solid warmth snuggled against her had opened a buried ache. By the time the nurse had returned, Kate pulled herself together. On the outside, anyway.

Luke's face was a mask of concern, but he hadn't asked questions. She was grateful he didn't press her. It was the grief, Kate knew. After three years, her anguish still attacked out of nowhere and gutted her. Holding that sweet child had triggered this attack. Kate rubbed a hand across her stomach, remembering.

It had been the Sunday starting her eighth week of pregnancy. After a year of trying, she and Jon were sharing their news with family over dinner that evening. The first cramp knifed Kate's stomach that afternoon although she thought nothing of it until she noticed spotting on her panties. And when a warm trickle of red oozed down her thigh, she knew.

"What can I bring you, ma'am?" Jerome asked, cutting into her fog.

She stared at the menu as Jerome, with his hipster man bun, board shorts, and Teva sandals, waited. She had no idea what to order.

Jerome cupped a hand under his chin and appraised her. "For you, I suggest our coffee affogato. It is a divine blend of vanilla ice cream drowned with hot espresso that will drown the sadness I see in your face."

Am I that obvious? Thanks for giving me away, runny mascara. Kate pursed her lips and nodded at the coffee ninja.

"Iced coffee for me," Luke said. "Decaf. Black. No sugar."

Jerome tapped the gold piercing on his lip with a finger. "Excellent choice, sir, but may I recommend our Thai iced coffee? It's a refreshing, exotic taste. Perfect for a warm spring evening."

"You positive, Jerome?"

"Absolutely, sir," the server said. "My coffee radar never fails."

"Then Iced Thai it is."

"I'll have them out right away." Jerome beamed and hurried off.

Luke sat across from her, his knee almost touching hers under the small bistro table. Beyond them, waves slapped against wooden pilings, where seagulls waited for discarded crumbs. Light breezes played with Kate's hair and tickled her face.

Luke leaned close, eyes locking on her. “New turtle team rule. You tell me what’s going on when the time is right. And I’m okay if you don’t want to say anything.”

It had been ages since a man outside her family had moved her with such kindness. She pressed her hand to her throat as a half-sob, half-laugh of relief slipped out as a hiccup. “Good rule. Accepted.”

Taking his lifeline to avoid a painful conversation, she plunged ahead. “I hope CeCe’s not too tired to enjoy her evening.”

As if on cue, Luke’s mobile pinged with an incoming text. Grinning at his screen, Luke slid his phone across the table. “See for yourself.”

The selfie David sent was grainy from the dim candlelight, but the glow in their faces was unmistakable. A giggling CeCe was spooning banana pudding into David’s mouth, his face smeared with the gooey dessert.

“OMG, is that Mr. Greenwood?” Jerome asked, peering over Kate’s shoulder as he set down their spoons and mugs. “He was my American History teacher my senior year. Best. Teacher EV-UH! You know him?”

“Yeah,” Luke said. “Good friend.”

Jerome stared at the image. “And is that Mrs. G?”

“It is. They’re celebrating the birth of their twin boys.”

Jerome clasped his hands over his heart. “Cannot believe it! You have made my night, wonderful people. This is a special occasion. Hold tight. I’ll be right back,” he said before hustling away.

Kate stirred the vanilla ice cream and took a tentative sip of her creamy affogato.

“Good?” asked Luke.

“Amazing! Try it.”

Grabbing her spoon, Kate filled it with a coffee drink and held it to his mouth. Luke wrinkled his nose.

"Come on. It's yum," she coaxed.

Steadying her hand with his, he brought the spoon to his mouth. Tingles shot through her fingers as he brushed against them for a moment.

Luke swallowed and darted his tongue over his mouth to catch a drip. "I'm convinced. The man's got coffee radar."

"Told you! My turn."

Kate dunked her spoon into Luke's coffee. "Mmm. Fruity and exotic. Like it?"

His eyes shifted to a teasing shade of blue. "Don't know. Too busy taste-tasting your drowning expresso."

Kate rolled her eyes and took another spoonful of his coffee.

"Try your drinks with this," Jerome said, returning with two plates covered with plump mini baguettes. "My treat for Mr. G's friends."

The yeasty aroma of bread, plus a hint of something sweet Kate couldn't identify, reminded her she hadn't eaten since breakfast. "What's in this?" she asked.

Jerome would be two feet off the ground with glee if it were possible to levitate. "Take a bite and guess."

She nibbled the baguette. It was out-of-the-oven warm and crunched with a buttery texture before a sugary, creamy mouthfeel slammed her taste buds.

"Is it chocolate?" she asked, her eyes growing wide. "But I don't see a brown filling in the bread."

"Exact-a-mento!" Jerome said, leaning close to Kate with childlike delight. "Chef tucks his to-die-for *white* chocolate inside the baguette. Enjoy!" With a small bow, Jerome scurried away.

Luke looked up from attacking his plate, his fingers already sticky from white chocolate. "This place is famous for its baguettes."

Kate had tasted nothing this decadent since Aunt Theresa's tiramisu. "I see why," she said between mouthfuls.

After a last bite of pastry, Luke leaned back and gestured to the horizon behind Kate. "Speaking of sweet, South Harbor sunsets are almost as good as ours on the Point."

Kate adjusted her chair, angling next to him to catch the view. Without a word, he draped his arm across the back of her seat. She relaxed against him as they watched the sky unfold in a brilliant display of pinks and crimsons.

With Luke near her, her painful memories ebbed away. Somehow, he had known exactly what she needed. Kate rested against the comfort of his arm and closed her eyes. It tempted her to open up to him, but she hesitated. Was she ready to trust someone she'd known for such a short time? Still, she felt an undeniable sense of security around Luke. And considering she'd be leaving at the end of August, would it matter anyway?

She unraveled the layers of her past—the trauma of her miscarriage and the heartbreak that followed. Luke listened, his thumb drawing gentle circles on her shoulder, offering without words.

Her voice cracked as she whispered, "I still think of the baby I never got to hold." A single tear escaped, tracing a glistening path down her cheek. She squeezed her eyes shut for a moment, silently grateful for Luke's quiet presence beside her. He didn't try to fill the silence, just offered a comforting hand on her shoulder.

Taking a shaky breath, she continued, "After that, Jon and I...we just drifted apart. He wanted to move on, start a family, but

I wasn't ready. The grief..." Her voice trailed off, a choked sob escaping her lips.

Tears welled up again, blurring her vision. She couldn't bring herself to say the words. How could she admit Jon's betrayal on top of everything else?

With a shaky hand, she wiped her cheeks and forced a smile. "We divorced. Then, well, life threw another curveball. Corporate takeover, you know the drill. Lost my job, sold the house..." Her voice trailed off again, the weight of it all threatening to pull her under.

Luke didn't need her to finish the sentence. His expression softened with empathy, and he shifted closer, offering silent comfort.

"Is that why you came to Gull Island?" he asked gently. "To escape?"

Kate massaged her temple, willing the throbbing headache to recede. "I wanted a fresh start. A way to escape feeling like a failure."

Luke's touch remained a comforting weight on her shoulder as he murmured, "I can't imagine dealing with all that, Kate. I'm truly sorry."

A wave of exhaustion washed over her, mixed with a strange sense of release. Without thinking, she leaned into him, the comforting scent of clean earth and pine filling her senses. The distant laughter from a passing tour boat shattered the quiet intimacy, jolting her back to reality.

Shame flooded her cheeks. What had she just done? Poured out her heart to a virtual stranger she'd known for a few short weeks? Ashamed, she met his gaze, expecting amusement or pity. But all she saw was genuine concern etched on his face.

"Those were tough times, Kate," Luke spoke softly, his voice a gentle rumble in her ear.

But you're here now, and that's what matters. You're healing."

She chewed on her bottom lip. "Yeah, maybe I am."

Taking a deep breath, Kate decided to lighten the mood. "Alright, enough baggage for one night," she said with a shaky grin. Reaching for a piece of baguette, she teased the persistent seagull hovering nearby. The bird swooped down, landing confidently in front of her, its beady black eyes locked on the prize.

She drew back in surprise, holding up her hands like a traffic cop. "Whoa, fella. Didn't intend for you to get quite so up close and personal."

Luke didn't look the least bit concerned. "Looks like you've got a new friend," he said.

Maybe Gull Islanders were on special terms with their avian namesake. The seagull gave Kate one last look before snatching the crumb in its beak and flying off.

Kate wrinkled her nose, a playful edge in her voice. "He's creeping me out. Reminds me of that scene in 'The Birds,' where seagulls go all Hitchcock on the townspeople."

"I'll have you know we have well-behaved gulls here," Luke said with a grin. "They know better than to peck our tourists to death."

"He likes you," Jerome said, who materialized with a tea towel to clean their table. "Our gulls have discerning tastes for choosing whom to grace their presence."

Savoring their coffees, Kate and Luke looked up as a smooth voice interrupted them.

"What a surprise seeing you here."

Clayton Pruitt stood behind them, impeccably dressed as usual. A woman in a lime green halter dress that clung to her like a second skin snagged Clayton's arm. The dress's daring slit traveled high up her toned thigh, a provocative flash of skin against the vibrant green. She mirrored Clayton's impeccable style but with a touch of undeniable heat.

Luke seemed unfazed by the interruption. "Clayton Pruitt and Savannah Scott," he said. "You two found each other. Makes sense. You're a perfect match."

The woman playfully swatted Luke's arm. "Now Lucas, don't get yourself in a hissy fit," she said in a sugary voice that made Kate grit her teeth. "I'm renting my home from Clayton's company, and he gave me a mighty generous deal, too."

The woman cocked her head toward Kate. "Who's your friend, Lucas?" she asked, eyeing him like he was a prized cut of sirloin.

As Luke introduced the women, Kate was painfully aware of her messy ponytail and clothing compared to Savannah's chic attire. How much history did Luke have with this woman? He was certainly in his stand-off mode, like their conversation over lunch at CeCe's a month ago.

"So, Kate, I hear you're at the aquarium this summer." Savannah purred. "How lucky to work alongside Lucas."

Kate's eyes flashed. *How'd she know?* Of course. Small town USA strikes again.

"That's right. Only the best for our aquarium," Kate quipped.

"Don't wish to intrude on your evening, Luke," Clayton said, "but you'll want to check with your attorney about my latest proposal for the Point. Get in touch if you have questions."

The muscle in Luke's jaw jumped at this. "Clayton," he replied evenly, "you can count on opposition to any proposal you make. There will never be condos on the Point."

But Clayton had a different resolution in mind. "We'll see about that."

Clayton took Savannah's arm, and they headed to a table in a far corner.

"I take it that was not good news?" Kate asked when they were alone.

Luke frowned. "It's a game for him. We block him. He finds loopholes. I know you disagree with me, but we won't let him win."

She bit her lip. Kate didn't want to argue about the Point and repay his kindness with contention. She had to admit that saving that pristine beach seemed like it was the right thing to do.

"You might find this hard to believe, Luke, but I hope you win."

He tilted his head and watched her. "You moving from the dark side?"

Before she could answer, Jerome was back to check on them. "Anything else for you lovely people?"

"Just the tab, please," Kate said.

"Absolutely not," Jerome insisted. "It's on the house tonight for friends of Mr. Greenwood. Y'all pay next visit."

As they thanked Jerome for his hospitality, an ear-piercing wail erupted behind them.

"Seriously? Not this not again!" Jerome groaned, hurrying to the aid of the distressed diner.

A delighted snort escaped Kate as Jerome shooed away the seagull that had decorated Savannah's halter dress with a glistening trail of poo.

Luke leaned close to Kate and shot her a devilish grin. "Other than a direct hit on Clayton Pruitt," he stage-whispered, not caring who overheard, "the universe could not have arranged for better cosmic justice."

Chapter Twenty-Five

LUKE

Sunlight dappled the aquarium courtyard, casting dancing reflections in the nearby dolphin fountain. Volunteers buzzed around, packing up after their successful planning meeting for summer's big events. Luke watched as Kate navigated the crowd, her coral blouse shimmering like a tropical fish in the fading light. A familiar warmth bloomed in his chest whenever she came into view. He had seen little of Kate since their coffee along the Riverwalk a week ago. The memory of her whispered goodbye, lips brushing his cheek, haunted him like a phantom kiss. He wanted more, but he didn't want to rush her.

Annie sidled next to him, a knowing glint in her eye. "What do you think, big brother?" she asked nudging him with her elbow, eyes fixed on Kate.

Luke shrugged, trying to appear nonchalant. "She's great, obviously."

"Obviously," Annie teased. "I mean, are you going to make a move, or just admire her from afar?"

His gaze drifted back to Kate, laughter echoing from her lips. "Annie, you know I care about her."

"Right." She sighed, rolling her eyes. "But there's a difference between respecting boundaries and letting opportunities float away."

His jaw clenched as his sister moved off to talk with other volunteers. He knew she was right, but it wasn't that simple.

Max's cheery voice pulled Luke from his worries. "Lucas! Excellent meeting," Max beamed before his smile gave way. "I wish we had the same success with our last SOS proposal."

Luke felt a stab of irritation. Pruitt's lawyers were adept at maneuvering around the challenges SOS set in their path.

"Never fear," Max continued with determination. "I have a lead on more research," he said, tipping his hat and making his way through the crowd.

A spark ignited on his bicep. Kate was beside him, her fingers whispering across his arm, a touch that lingered a beat too long. As she drew back, a phantom heat pulsed where her fingers had traced a map on his skin. He shook his head, trying to clear the fog of sensation.

"You crushed it this morning!" Kate's excitement bubbled over, but when her gaze found the storm brewing on his face, it faltered.

"Luke," she asked, her voice laced with concern, "what's wrong?"

He wanted to tell her. Spill the frustration gnawing at him, the sting of Clayton Pruitt's smug face across the table, and the growing threat to the Point. But the turtle team rule, an unspoken pact of their collaboration, hung heavy, a silent tether to their fragile trust.

Instead, he forced a playful smirk. "Let's say it has to do with that certain beach near my home."

"Understood," she began, the playful sparkle in her eyes replaced by a determined glint. "And I have a proposition for you that is not a turtle team violation."

His brow furrowed. "I'm listening."

"I hear you're short a shuttle driver for the garden tour this weekend, and I'm offering my services."

Luke blinked, surprised. "You? Garden tour driver?"

"Hey, I drive our golf cart back home like a champ," she said, a touch of self-consciousness edging her voice. "Plus, I could be green-thumbed for a day."

Her enthusiasm was infectious, her offer genuine. "Can you also keep visitors safe and happy?"

Her megawatt grin returned, lighting up the courtyard. "Consider me your newest chauffeur."

"Then you're in," he said, a newfound lightness filling his chest. "I'll text details."

A question lingered in his mind, though. "How did you know we needed a driver?"

Kate turned, waving across the courtyard to a woman with a mischievous glint in her eye. "That nice lady tipped me off. I've seen her before, but I didn't catch her name."

The distance couldn't dim Annie's triumphant smile. Luke, catching it, steered Kate towards her. "This is Annie," he said, a knowing glint in his eyes.

As they met, Kate's fingers snapped. "Dawson's mom! The Gift and Garden lady!"

"And I'm delighted to meet the woman who's caught my brother's attention," Annie said.

Kate swiveled toward Luke and grinned. "Really?"

"Annie's always joking," he said, hoping he sounded light and nonchalant. Few people could zing Luke like his sister.

"Interesting. He mentions me now and then?" Kate asked, with an impish lift of her brow.

Annie's grin widened, tinged with a knowing glint. "Oh, Kate, you have no idea." Her gaze shifted to Luke, a teasing lilt in her voice. "My dear brother here tends to become... overly eloquent when your name crosses his lips."

Busted. He didn't stand a chance against these two. Luke felt a blush creep up his neck. "Annie's... enthusiastic, but there's no need to overshare. I'm sure Kate's not interested."

"Oh, but I am," Kate said. "Luke doesn't say much about himself, so fill me in. What's he like?"

"Where to start? Did he tell you about the ex-girlfriend who was mad at him and had a pile of horse manure dumped in his yard? And he thanked her for the fertilizer."

"Horse manure fertilizer? That's... unique. Does he have many ex-girlfriends who surprise him like that?"

"Yep. That's my big brother, the heartbreaker. The ladies are eager for his attention, but he isn't interested these days. Too busy saving the planet and our business."

Luke groaned. This was agony. "My little sister is laying it on thick, as usual," he countered.

Annie's phone alarm hummed. She looked down and frowned. "Time to get Dawson at the sitter's," she said. "Kate, let's meet up for lunch or coffee soon."

The two women exchanged contacts before Annie dashed off. Luke could only hope they'd be kind when they met to dissect him.

Kate's eyes danced with amusement, not ready to let him off the hook. "So, Luke, do we need a turtle team rule for... unwanted fertilizer deliveries?"

He chuckled, feeling a blush creep up his neck. "The only manure I get these days is from my sister. No need to amend the bylaws."

He would so talk with Annie later.

KATE

"Lost, are we?" boomed a voice, startling Kate from studying her route map. She looked up to see a garden gnome in human form—towering, soil-smudged, and sporting a hat the size of a bird's nest.

He gestured towards a rambling Victorian house. "New driver, listen up," his voice rumbled, "my mulch is my kingdom. Last year, some bigfoot left craters like molehill mines. Keep those feet clean, you hear?"

Kate grinned. "Mulch Militia, at your service!" she declared, saluting with a mock flourish. The gnome-man chuckled, lumbering off.

A spark flickered in Kate's eyes as she brushed back her hair. The garden tour thrummed around her, a fragrant frenzy. Yet, her gaze held the faint glow of Luke's smile, a memory like sun on honeyed skin. Annie's teasing, *He talks about you,* echoed in her chest, a butterfly trapped in its sweetness. Loss still lingered. Divorce, miscarriage, and job loss, all left a sharp tang in the air, her past troubles dragging her down.

Then, Luke. Broad shoulders, infectious laughter, a life raft amidst the wreckage. But she was adrift, clutching the ruins of what was. Could she let go and trust the current, or was she chained to the phantom of what could have been?

A choice. A bridge across the chasm of her messy life. Breathe, Kate, breathe. One step at a time.

As if drawn by her thoughts, Luke materialized beside her cart, a flash of denim and Ray-Bans. "Hey, Kate," he greeted her.

His jeans hugged his legs, a subtle reminder of the way he effortlessly moved through the sun-drenched chaos. Two women strolled past, their lingering glances confirming Kate's secret observation. Warmth bloomed in Kate's chest, a flicker of something she hadn't felt in a long time.

"Ready to roll," she said, jazz hands waving in the air.

His walkie-talkie crackled, his smile flickering off like a dying flame. "Gotta run," he said, glancing towards the insistent device. "Catch you later?"

Kate felt a tug of disappointment, a slight shift in her heart. "Before you go..." she started, then swallowed the rest. Finally, she blurted out, "How about pizza and chilling at my place after all this garden madness?"

He raised an eyebrow, the smile returning full force. "Pizza? I'll be there at eight."

Watching him disappear, Kate felt her heart doing a gymnastics routine in her chest. The thought of creating a meal that rivaled Luke's culinary talent was daunting. However, one thing was clear—this invitation was just a way to see him again.

"Excuse me, dear," a voice trilled, saccharine and sharp at the same time.

A woman in her fifties, rocking cat-eye shades and a visor the color of Pepto-Bismol (it somehow worked with her tangerine shorts) sashayed up to Kate. "Transportation, please?"

She gestured to her friends in matching pink headgear. "We're eager to see these gardens."

Kate smiled, hiding her amusement at the matching headgear. "Absolutely! Hop in."

Visor Lady Number Two, clutching a chihuahua with a rhinestone collar, plopped down. "Pitt County Garden Club," she announced, the chihuahua yipping in agreement.

Her companion, Visor Lady Number Three, a plump figure in sensible shoes, tapped Kate's shoulder. "Will we be near that charming Point thing?" she asked.

"The Point is across the Intracoastal Waterway on Gull Island," Kate replied, her smile widening. "So, unless you're planning a long swim..."

Number Three chuckled, a nervous flutter. "Maybe another time, dear."

"How'd you hear about the Point?" Kate asked, eyes narrowed.

The chihuahua yipped again, its rhinestone collar glinting. "My niece told us," Number Two said. "Building condos there, she says. Sounds perfect for our second home."

Kate's smile faltered. "The council hasn't approved the project," she said, her voice tight, a storm brewing inside her.

"Only a matter of time," the woman chirped, oblivious of the impact of her words. "Savannah Scott, my friend's daughter, heard it straight from the developer."

Kate's grip tightened on the steering wheel. *Savannah!* The name echoed in her mind, a stark reminder of an escalating threat. She glanced at her watch—four o'clock. Eight pm for pizza with

Luke seemed like a lifetime away when she needed to warn him right now.

The question hammered in her mind. Would the Point, and with it, Luke's dream, be bulldozed before they could even mount a defense?

Chapter Twenty-Six

LUKE

Luke's hand swept over his damp hair, leaving a ruffled strand across his forehead. He straightened, taking a deep breath before raising his hand and rapping sharply against the weathered rose-colored wood.

Footsteps pattered from within. The door swung open, revealing Kate in a blouse of the deepest sapphire. The fabric shimmered with an inner light, catching the glint of emerald and gold in her eyes.

Her smile, a slow sunrise, shattered the walls he built around his heart. The playful lift of her lips sent a jolt through him, igniting a spark somewhere deep within. His focus drifted to the delicate line of her neck. A tiny birthmark peeked out from beneath her collarbone—a secret tucked in plain sight. Forbidden heat flared in his gut—the urge to reach out, to map the landscape of her skin with a feather-light touch, a desire he shouldn't want but couldn't deny.

"Luke!" Her voice, warm and welcoming, snapped him back

to reality. A wider smile stretched across her lips, chasing away the lingering tightness in his shoulders. Her eyes held a question, a flicker of amusement that made his own heart skip a beat.

"For you," he said, his breath hitching as his fingers brushed against hers as she took the pot from him. "Fresh basil from my kitchen garden. Just the thing for pizza lovers."

Her eyes lit with delight as she ran her fingers over the wine-colored leaf.

"Oh Luke, I love it! I have the perfect spot for this beauty. Please come in."

The warmth of her greeting lingered as he followed Kate into the kitchen, the quiet swish of her blouse and the delicate sway of her hips against her skirt inviting him. The way Kate talked to the plant as she set it on the windowsill tickled him. He wasn't the only one who talked to green things.

"Beer okay?" she asked, opening the fridge.

He'd been hankering for a cold brew all day after helping lost tourists and answering their million questions. She handed him a chilled bottle of South Harbor Brewery's latest IPA, the same brand he had enjoyed after their first turtle patrol weeks ago.

"Excellent memory," he said, tilting his head toward the label.

"How could I forget after that first awkward turtle patrol?" she said with a laugh. Kate sipped her tea and leaned against the butcher block island in her small kitchen.

"Two choices for dinner tonight," she said, her fingers fidgeting with the seams on her skirt, "and you get to pick. One familiar, and the other," she went on, her eyes sparkling, "is a bit more... adventurous."

He relaxed against the counter, his foot brushing against hers. The fabric of her skirt rustling for the briefest moment against his thigh sent a jolt through him, distracting him from the pizza choices.

"I'll take door number two, adventurous," he finally said.

She nodded. "That would be making my Nonna's fried pizza in my kitchen. And I have pizza dough and ingredients ready."

Luke rummaged through his memory. "Fried pizza? Never had it. Won't the dough need time to rise?"

A blush bloomed on her cheeks, as vibrant as spilled wine. "It's b-been rising since yesterday," she stammered, pointing to a bowl hidden by a towel.

He quirked an eyebrow, his voice playful as he teased, "Is this premeditated pizza?"

Kate grabbed a dish towel and flicked it at him with a teasing grin. "Maybe. I wanted to do something for you after you were so kind listening to me the other night."

He reached for her, his large hand swallowing hers. He cradled it, savoring the feel of her small, delicate fingers in his. "Kate, no need to repay me," he said, his voice low and reassuring. "I'm glad you could talk to me about what's on your mind."

Her hand squeezed his briefly, then retreated to fiddle with the buttons on her blouse. "And," she added softly, "you're not bad company."

Luke's grin widened, a wave of warmth washing over him. He tugged her a touch closer, their shoulders brushing. The question hovered between them, unspoken yet thick in the air. He swallowed, the room suddenly feeling too small. Finally, he met her gaze, a playful glint in his eyes. "Maybe," he teased, voice low, "you like me... a little?"

Her mouth opened slightly and Luke held his breath as silence settled between them. She looked so small standing there—barely reaching his shoulders. He imagined her fitting perfectly against him in the hollow of his chest.

She blinked, her fingers twisting the chain on her silver locket. "Maybe a little," she murmured, the words barely audible.

He cupped her chin, his thumb brushing away a stray tear. A fierce protectiveness surged within him, a promise to shield her from any future pain. "I'm glad, Kate," he whispered, his heart beating faster with each word. "Because I like you more than a little. We'll take it slow and see what happens."

The corners of Kate's mouth turned up in a small smile at his words. "Can we make a turtle team rule? Take things slow and see what happens?"

The tension seemed to ease from her face as he replied, "Absolutely. Taking things slow is now an official rule."

Her hand, hesitant at first, rose to rest on his chest. Her fingers traced the outline of his heart, and Luke felt anchored by her gentle touch. Their eyes met with a silent agreement passing between them. There was no rush, no pressure, only the quiet promise to explore this uncharted territory together.

"Pizza Nonna style?" he suggested, a mischievous glint in his eyes.

"Brilliant choice." Her voice was playful as she spoke but rippled with a gentle satisfaction. It held a hint of surprise, as though she hadn't expected him to agree to her suggestion. And then she gave him a shy smile, her eyes crinkling with joy and her cheeks warming with contentment. Her happiness was all the reward he needed.

They worked side-by-side at the island, flour dusting their hands as they kneaded the dough in a comfortable rhythm.

Laughter bubbled up, a melody weaving through the air with the earthy aroma of herbs and the baking dough.

Finally, Luke slid the pizza out of the oven, a golden wonder cradled in his hands. "Behold," he said with a wink. "The pizza of destiny!"

Kate's lips twitched as she tilted her head to get a better look. "So, a stop sign that skipped geometry class and lost two sides?"

"Hexagon, actually. Nature's masterpiece. Snowflakes, beehives, turtle shells—all hexagons. What do you think Nonna would say?"

A slow smile bloomed on her face, as bright as the red sauce on the pizza. Reaching out, she traced the edge of the unique crust with a fingertip. "Hers were always perfect ovals," she said with a soft laugh, "but I think Nonna would approve of your artistic freedom."

His hand shot up for a high five, but Kate surprised him again. Her fingers, light and cool against his calloused palm, slipped between his, seeking a deeper connection. A silent beat hung in the air, charged with shared amusement and a spark of something more. Their eyes met, a question lingering in the depths. Slowly, Kate's fingers trailed away, leaving a faint warmth on his palm.

With a reluctant smile, they both turned back to the marvel that was the hexagonal pizza.

Chapter Twenty-Seven

KATE

Twinkling fairy lights illuminated the patio as Kate and Luke settled at the small bistro table. The sweet scent of blooming beach roses and jasmine wafted through the breeze coming off the ocean. Kate nibbled her pizza with a contented sigh.

"I should spend more time on the deck," she said dreamily, admiring the tiny garden beyond the broad steps.

He shot her a satisfied grin. "You like it?"

Kate gestured with her fork around the yard. "It's magical! Did you have anything to do with it?"

He ran a hand through his hair, trying to keep it in place despite the wind. "I did the addition for Mae," he admitted.

"It's a gem, Luke! If you lived in Connecticut, people would knock down your door."

"No shortage of clients here. I can't keep up or take on the environmental projects I want."

And there it was.

The spark in Kate's eyes dimmed, replaced by a quiet sadness that settled over her. She would be gone in September, back to her family in Connecticut. Luke would be 500 miles away on Gull Island. But then she remembered the way he made her smile with his hexagonal pizza and brought her red basil from his garden. What was the harm of having a summer friend? She could handle a friendship.

"Work can be brutal if you don't love what you're doing," Kate said. "I wish you had more time for the work you're passionate about."

Luke shrugged. "It is what it is."

She knew a way to help if he'd accept it. "My friend still needs small business owners to beta test her software app," she said, swiping through her contacts. "I'm forwarding Viviane's contact information. Tell her I recommended you for the trial."

Kate set down her phone and steepled her fingers under her chin. "And I can update Gift and Garden's website to make it easier for customers to browse and order online. I can even design another website for your new career when you're ready."

He was staring at her, but he was impossible to read. Maybe she went too far. She squirmed and wished Luke would say something.

"I mean, if you want my help," she added, lowering her chin, her shoulders sagging slightly.

He shook his head. "That's not it. Your offer is generous. It's a lot to process."

"Of course. I get carried away sometimes. Don't mind me."

"Kate Fiore, you can get carried away on my behalf any time," he said. His eyes were liquid in the moonlight, and he watched her with such intensity that she had to look away.

Dinner finished, a logical point to end their evening, but the thought made her stomach clench. Luke's presence was oddly comforting, a stark contrast to her usual guardedness. Since leaving Jon, she'd held back, afraid of more heartbreak. Yet, Luke, with his patience and genuine warmth, had chipped away at her defenses, leaving her vulnerable, like a novice in the dating game.

Plus, she'd already burdened him enough with her emotional baggage. Yet, despite her hesitance, she searched for an excuse, any excuse, to keep him there a little longer.

"Ice cream?" Kate's eyes sparkled. "Mae keeps gushing about Island Scoops. Up for a walk?"

Luke's grin mirrored the moonlight's shimmer. "Lead the way."

The path through the dunes unfolded like a moonlit ribbon under their feet. Sand whispered with each step, the salty air a balm against the summer heat. Luke, his scent a heady mix of pine and sun-kissed skin, paused, his eyes sparkling like constellations.

Luke's excited shout, "Turtle hatchlings!" ripped Kate from her peaceful reverie. His hand shot out, warm and insistent, grabbing hers before pulling her towards a mesmerizing sight.

A line of crimson lights, like tiny fireflies, stretched from the dunes down to the water's edge. The air vibrated with a tangible energy, a mix of anticipation and the joyous squeals of children lining the sand. A thrill shot through Kate, and goosebumps erupted along her arms. She squeezed Luke's hand back, a silent question hanging in the sudden urgency of her grip.

"Nature's toughest obstacle course starts now!" Luke said, his voice buzzing with excitement. "These little champions are about to make a break for the ocean. It's a race against the clock. Every flipper kick is crucial for survival."

THEY JOINED THE CROWD RINGING A THREE-FOOT trench hollowed out in the sand, tamped down, and bordered by strips of garden edging by another turtle team. Onlookers camped on either side of the trench, like waiting for the start of a parade. Kate swiped the flashlight on her phone to get a better look, but Luke stopped her.

"Cut the light, Kate," he said. "It confuses the hatchlings. They think it's moonlight, and they'll crawl to you instead of the waves."

As she shut down her app, shouts rose from the nest site by the dunes. A blaze of crimson lit the turtle highway.

"Here they come!" Luke said, his voice as eager as the children jostling around him.

Kate felt Luke's hand on her shoulder, gently urging her closer to the trench for a better view. "Look there!" he whispered in her ear, making shivers tickle her neck where he had almost touched her.

Kate squinted to find the nest in the dark. Around its perimeter, dozens of tiny dark bodies popped up from the ground, a mass of movement like bubbles boiling up from a pot of water. Having spent hours pecking through their shells and digging up through a foot of sand, they turned toward the moonlight, spilling onto the smooth sandy trail volunteers had prepared for them.

The first hatchlings finally passed before them. Teeny flippers created a faint whispering sound as they moved, and sand covered their dark bodies from the ordeal of escaping the nest. One stopped inches in front of Kate, struggling to push itself over a bump of sand that any child could tackle with ease. It rested a moment before rising to attack the obstacle and then single-mindedly resumed its crawl.

"He's so small! He'd fit right in the palm of my hand," Kate said, marveling at the hatchling's determination to cross what must seem like miles of sand to a tiny marine creature.

"They won't quit until they reach the ocean," Luke said. "I'll show you."

They maneuvered past the crowds to wait as the first hatchlings approached the waves. People started cheering as the first hatchlings neared. Luke rested his hands on his hips, straining for a last glimpse as the surf swallowed the animals. Even in the moonlight, she saw the concern written on his face as if he were pleading with the sea to accept its newest inhabitant and keep them safe.

She understood with sudden clarity that this was his place. This was his element.

Then, her thoughts drifted to Flippy Junior and his fellow wounded sea turtles in the aquarium rehab tanks, each a testament to resilience and hope.

"These little ones are a miracle," she murmured as she wiped away a tear. She hadn't seen anything like this before, and their determination filled her with awe.

He nodded, his eyes still on the horizon.

"I get why you're passionate about sea turtles," she said, gently touching his forearm, the warm, solid feel of him lingering on her skin after she removed her fingers.

"Somebody needs to look out for them," he said. "If we're

lucky and don't let people like Pruitt stand in the way, we'll help even more."

Shoving his hands inside his pockets, he turned his gaze to her. She couldn't be sure because of the darkness, but she thought his eyes softened, grateful that she understood.

Chapter Twenty-Eight

KATE

Sunlight crept through Kate's office window, a shy visitor chasing away lingering thoughts of last night's laughter under a star-strewn sky.

Her mind swirled with the memory of sand, cool and gritty beneath her feet, as she watched the hatchling turtles. Beside her, Luke had laughed, a deep rumble that sent its own warmth through her. A quiet joy, a feeling born from their shared wonder, bloomed in her chest, a welcome counterpoint to the lingering sting left by Jon's betrayal. A faint hope, fragile yet persistent, raised its head and tugged at the darkness of her past.

The shrill phone shattered the quiet, and the coffee mug almost slipped from her hands. Liz's voice crackled through the receiver. "Tour leader's down. Morning slot's open if you want it."

Coffee forgotten, Kate sprinted towards the visitor center, glad to escape the tangled questions of her heart. Throwing a smile at the waiting crowd, she beckoned them forward.

"Welcome to the Gull Island Aquarium!" she announced, her

voice bubbling with practiced enthusiasm. "I'm Kate, and for the next hour, we'll dive into the amazing lives of creatures who call these waters home."

The tour snaked through the aquarium with Kate weaving tales of conservation and wonder. The shark tank erupted in shrieks of delight as a giant predator sliced through the water.

Still got it, she thought, basking in the infectious excitement.

Then, the otters. Sleek shadows flitting through their watery playground, the animals paused, watching with big, questioning eyes. One, bolder than the rest, launched itself onto a ledge, squeezing into a small plastic play tunnel. Gasps rippled through the crowd as only its dainty paws protruded, twitching like antennae.

"He's just playing," Kate reassured them, grinning as she had watched their antics many times before. "Otters are curious creatures, always up for a good time."

A tap on her shoulder, and a manicured hand brandishing a gleaming phone, broke Kate's concentration. "Aren't you going to help him?" the woman demanded, her frown as deep as her designer handbag.

Kate didn't falter. "He's fine," she assured her, eyes glued on the otter's antics. "They're notorious escape artists. He'll be back in the water in a jiffy." Her voice held a quiet confidence as she added, "If anything goes wrong, though, our caretakers are standing by."

The woman's lips pursed, but the phone remained glued to her face as she videoed the playful otter. Kate shrugged, her attention already shifting to the next curious face in the crowd. She led the group to the sea turtle hall next, discussing how displacement and pollution were shrinking their populations and urging people to do whatever they could to help.

While the visitors wandered the exhibit on their own, Kate checked the injured loggerhead she met the first day at the aquarium. "Hey, Flippy Junior," she cooed, tracing her fingers alongside its tank as the turtle bobbed contentedly inside.

Two girls holding hands, both with identical braids of long, dark hair, approached Kate. "Will he be okay?" the older one asked, her small face etched with worry.

Kate bent low and rested her hand on the little shoulder. "Absolutely," she said reassuringly. "We're taking good care of him, so he can return to the sea."

The sisters looked at each other, heads bobbing in relief before skipping off.

Kate ended the tour on the deck overlooking the bay. "Thanks for visiting," she said, smiling at her group, "and please come back. We're hosting a special dinner in a month right here during Founders Day. You won't get a better view of the bay's fireworks!"

After she wrapped up, the two sisters approached Kate again. "We'll never use plastic straws or leave open holes around our sandcastles," the older one promised shyly.

Kate crouched in front of the children. "Thank you," she said, shaking each little hand. "That means a lot to me and the sea turtles."

The girls' mother stepped forward, beaming. "You were a big hit with them. They are so excited about the sea turtles."

Kate thanked them again and waved goodbye. Checking her phone, she saw she had enough time to grab lunch at the café before her next meeting. She carried her unsweet tea and aquarium french fries to the shady table she favored, but someone had claimed it, his back turned to her. She stepped closer, hesitating before asking if she might join him.

The man swiveled around, and Kate's heart sank. Clayton Pruitt! He was here for lunch, too? What kind of coincidence was this? Then she forced a smile and sat.

"Clayton! What a surprise," Kate fibbed, swinging her legs over the bench to face him across the table. "I've been meaning to talk to you."

"Oh?" He tilted his head in curiosity and listened as Kate recounted her conversation with the garden tour visitors, who had asked about purchasing a condo on the Point.

"I get why people might know about your plans," she concluded firmly, "but I don't understand why anyone is talking about buying units when the city council hasn't approved the project."

"You know how it goes," he said, chewing his fry before he went on. "People hear things, and they make assumptions."

She set down her iced tea with a quiet clink, the ice cubes swirling in the condensation. Leaning forward, she steepled her fingers on the table, her gaze unwavering. "I'm concerned that information is circulating before a decision has been made. It might influence the outcome unfairly."

Pruitt flashed a gleaming smile. "No need to worry, Kate," he said, looking at the picture of innocence. "But let's be realistic. You can't stop progress."

Kate's jaw clenched so tight her teeth sang. Clayton's smug grin was a slap in the face, and the urge to scream "liar!" clawed at her throat. She dug her nails into her palms, swallowing the bitter taste of fury.

Before she finished her thought, Liz Wilson appeared at her

side, her brown curls bobbing in her haste. "We need you, Kate," she said breathlessly.

LUKE

THE SETTING SUN STREAKED THE SKY AS LUKE PULLED into his driveway, fatigue clinging to him like an unwelcome guest. Boo, his tail a blur, torpedoed through the open door, leaving a gust of excitement in his wake. The cold beer he grabbed from the fridge felt like an oasis in his parched throat.

Settling on the deck, he gazed at the shimmering water. The usual sounds of the waves seemed distant, replaced by echoes of Kate. His day had been a whirlwind, so he hadn't reached out since last night, but her moonlit face lingered in his mind—the sweetness, the vulnerability. Just being with her had sparked a warmth within him. Or perhaps it was the woman it revealed, her strength and determination shining through. Whatever it was, his connection to her deepened with every day.

He listened to the waves crashing into the shore, unwilling to get back to the piles of paperwork that awaited him tonight. Stalling, he checked his phone which he had silenced during client meetings. A barrage of texts from Annie urged him to check his news feeds, but it was David's message that alarmed him:

> Tempest in a teapot, but still trouble for Katie-Kat.

Luke followed David's link to find a photo of Kate, laughing before a group of visitors at the aquarium. In the background, a sea otter stretched inside a long, tubular plastic toy. Then his heart dropped when he scanned the comment under the photo:

> The way Kate treated the poor otter is outrageous. She laughed. Walked away without helping it! #GullIslandAquarium #OtterLove #FireKate

The post had gone viral, with thousands of views. Luke's breath caught as the screen flashed with Kate's laughing face, distorted by the grainy video into a look of cruelty. A roaring disbelief clawed at his throat. #FireKate. The hashtag burned into his retina. How could they twist her love and dedication into such cruelty? His fists clenched, knuckles white against the phone screen. He wouldn't let them hurt her. Not on his watch.

> I'm not saying Kate's a villain, but I wouldn't trust her with my goldfish. #GullIslandAquarium #OtterLove #FireKate

> I know! How could she leave that poor otter! #GullIslandAquarium #OtterLove #FireKate

> They say the truth will set you free, but in this case, I hope it gets Kate fired. #GullIslandAquarium #OtterLove #FireKate

> Agree. She has to GO! #FireKate

Luke's hands curled into fists. His knuckles were white against the phone screen. *No, no, no! This is all wrong!* The accusations were like acid, burning his throat. He scrolled through the comments, his eyes scanning for a lifeline, a spark of reason amidst the hatred.

Relief flooded him when he came to a photo of Kate before two children, graciously shaking their hands. The girls looked wide-eyed at Kate, enchanted by her attention. The comment caption gave Luke hope.

> No way! Otter was just playing. Never in danger. Staff was standing by. We returned later, and the otter was fine. Kate dazzled my girls with her love of animals. #GullIslandAquarium #WeLoveKate!

Luke sat up, ready to add his #WeLoveKate post, when another text from Annie pinged.

> Check out News 9 TV feed NOW!!

Luke opened her link, balling his hands into fists as he read the news crawl.

`Animal cruelty alleged at Gull Island Aquarium!`

He watched in disbelief as a camera zoomed in on Kate, and a reporter peppered her with questions. "Kate, can you explain the social media storm circulating about the otter incident?" the reporter asked.

Kate squared her shoulders, meeting the camera with a defiant glint in her eyes. "I'm here to set the record straight," she said, her voice steady despite the tremor in her hands. The lights seemed to magnify her every word as she recounted the events, her passion for the animals shining through.

Luke jumped up and cheered, his chest swelling with pride as Kate spoke with warmth and conviction. The reporter leaned in, her eyes gently probing.

"What about accusations of animal abuse? People say that your team mistreats animals in their care."

Kate shook her head. "Our animals receive top-notch attention from a dedicated team of professionals. But you can see for yourself. We welcome any examination of our practices," she declared.

The reporter pushed with more hard questions, but Kate handled each one with grace. Luke soared and fist-bumped the heavens, narrowly missing a Boo squash.

"Mic drop incoming!" he shouted. "Unleash the thunder!"

The camera turned to the reporter, an approving smile on her face. "And there you have it. An otter-ly reasonable explanation for what went on at Gull Island Aquarium today. Now, back to the studio for your local weather forecast."

Chapter Twenty-Nine

KATE

Kate stumbled into her bungalow, autopilot guiding her weary limbs. Clothes flung on the floor marked her escape route from the day's carnage. The Grumpy Woman's video. The viral firestorm. Humiliation simmered in her throat, a bitter aftertaste.

She sank onto the bed, the plush comforter offering little solace as thoughts of the meeting swirled in her mind. Liz's anxious whispers. The grim faces of the higher-ups. The cold, accusing prints of angry tweets. Her heart hammered a frantic staccato against her ribs.

What if she lost this job too? Another humiliation, another defeat. Her eyes, burning from unshed tears, sought solace in the familiar clutter of her rental. The discarded pizza box, the half-read book, the forgotten mug of coffee—all silent witnesses to her unraveling life.

A sob escaped her lips, a raw sound that echoed in the quiet room. She curled into a ball, burying her face in the pillow, the fabric damp with tears. CeCe's face, confident and trusting, flashed through her mind. She couldn't let her down.

Slowly, a flicker of defiance ignited in her chest. She wouldn't crumble. She would fight. But first, she needed a break from the craziness of the day. Dragging herself off the bed, Kate stumbled to the bathroom.

The mirror reflected a stranger—eyes red-rimmed, hair a tangled mess. Cold water splashed on her face, washing away the worst day since she lost her child. Comfort finally arrived in the familiar embrace of her favorite sweatshirt, whispered memories in its threads. Back on the bed, she huddled in a ball, the world shrinking to the fluffy cocoon of her blankets. Sleep, a welcome escape, claimed her, the storm receding as her eyelids drifted shut.

THE RELENTLESS POUNDING ON THE DOOR WAS A RUDE awakening from Kate's tearful slumber. She considered ignoring it, staying under the safety of her rumpled blankets, but the insistent rhythm wouldn't let her. With a sigh, she dragged herself out of bed, her heart plummeting when she saw Luke through the peephole. The rumor mill, she thought, a bitter taste filling her mouth. What must he think of her now?

Steeling herself, she opened the door. Luke's smile, the one that melted her like butter on toast, met her gaze. For a fleeting moment, she craved the warmth of his embrace. Instead, she stood there, exposed and raw.

"So," he said, his voice a playful lilt masking the concern in his eyes, "I hear you had a bit of a stir at work today."

Kate scrubbed her face with her hands, grateful for his attempt to lighten the mood. “Ya think?”

He stepped closer, his presence a comforting weight in the doorway. “Hey, it happens. Some people like to make trouble.” His hand reached out, a gentle touch tucking a stray hair behind her ear, and that gesture nearly brought fresh tears to her eyes.

“At least I still have a job,” she said ruefully, her voice thick with emotion.

“Never doubted you,” he said, his thumb brushing her jaw as he withdrew his hand. “How about we get you out of here and take your mind off things?” he asked, his eyes soft with concern.

She glanced at her rumpled clothes. Compared to Luke with his khaki shirt and windblown hair a picture of casual coolness, she was a hot mess.

“I don’t know, Luke. I’m a wreck, and you...” she trailed off, struggling for the right words.

He leaned closer, his gaze holding hers. “You look fine to me, Kate,” he said, his voice soft, reassuring. “Just like you are.”

Her heart gave a little oomph. How did he always know the right things to say?

“I know the perfect place to lift a bad day,” he continued with the playful lilt back in his voice. “Doesn’t matter what you’re wearing, but shoes might be helpful.”

She took a breath. Why should she care if he was oozing coolness like a popsicle on a hot day, and she looked like the mop left in the rain? Resistance was futile.

“Where are we going?” she asked, balancing on one foot to slip into her sandals.

“Someplace where taking a break from all your worries comes easy,” he said with a wink, “and yeah, where everyone knows your name." He flashed a mischievous grin. "Prepare yourself for seafood heaven."

WHEN THEY ARRIVED AT THE SHRIMP SHACK THIRTY minutes later, the eatery's unassuming exterior surprised Kate. The red shoebox of a building was a hole in the wall. Drab cylinder blocks fronted a boxy structure punctured by two screened windows serving as a walk-up counter for ordering. Outside, towering live oaks shaded picnic tables that were the restaurant's only sit-down dining option.

"Doesn't look like much, but wait until you try their shrimp-burger," Luke said. "Some say it's the best on the coast."

"What do you say?"

He nodded at the line of people waiting to order. "I agree, and I'm not the only one."

As they joined the queue, the smell of fresh-cooked seafood hit Kate's nose, and she realized she was hungry. She squinted at the cardboard sign above the ordering window: *Cash and Checks Only!* "Don't see that every day."

"Foodies find us, but their payment policy is one reason the Shack doesn't attract most tourists," Luke explained. "Plus, it isn't fancy enough for many."

"You must think outsiders are a pesky lot," Kate said, wondering if he'd ever change his opinion of off- islanders.

Or of her.

He considered her words. "Some can be, but I'm learning not to make assumptions. Thanks to you," he said, reaching around her shoulder to press his palm lightly on the small of her back.

Her heart soared with relief and pleasure, and she leaned into him, her body instinctively seeking a connection to his solid presence. It disappointed her when moments later he removed his hand as they reached the front of the line.

"What fresh delights to tempt your tastebuds can we bring you today, lovely seafood seekers?" the server asked as they stepped up to the counter. The man tilted his head and stared at Kate and Luke.

"OMG!" he cried. "It's my favorite couple from the Riverwalk Café!"

Kate gave a little wave as she recognized the man-bunned waiter who had served them at the café. "Jerome! You work here, too?"

"Filling in for a friend, but aren't I the lucky one to see you here tonight? And am I correct thinking we have a shrimpburger newbie here?" he asked, glancing at Kate.

"That would be me," she said, wondering what she'd gotten herself into.

Jerome flapped his hands in excitement. "Excellent-o!" He hooked a finger to his lip, thinking.

"Hmmm. For you, ma'am, I suggest our house shrimpburger. Hush puppies and mac and cheese for your sides as your Total Coastal Experience."

Kate paused, too brain-dead to decide.

"If you don't like it, we'll get you a regular burger," Luke offered.

She nodded, and Jerome shouted their order to the cooks.

The din of voices and laughter mixed with warm breezes off the bay as they sat across from each other on a wobbly picnic table. Kate lifted her steaming bun. Instead of a patty, it brimmed with fried shrimp topped with coleslaw and tartar sauce. "It's not a burger," she said, "but it smells divine."

Kate gripped the generous roll and struggled to open her mouth wide enough around the dense bread. She chewed slowly and closed her eyes for a moment to savor the aftertaste. "This. Is. Amazing!"

"Thought you'd like it," he said, looking pleased at her response.

She gave the shrimp a rest and dug into a heap of golden mac and cheese. "I could get used to island living, but you know what I miss the most about the city?" she asked between bites.

"The traffic? The noise? A drugstore on every corner?" he quipped.

"Hah! It's the anonymity of being part of a crowd. Here, everyone knows everyone's business. There's no such thing as privacy."

Luke nodded. "I know what you mean. But that's what makes Gull Island special, too. We know what's going on, and we take care of each other."

She thought of her home in Connecticut. Black Rock was a small coastal enclave surrounded by bigger cities along the I-95 corridor. It hadn't taken long before her neighbors knew she had left Jon. "That's true," she admitted. "I appreciate the sense of community, but it can be uncomfortable."

"Tell me about it." He grinned. "If my truck is spotted outside its usual route, my sister and mother know about it by the time I get home."

Kate shuddered, imagining an island-wide rumor mill kicking in after the few times he had parked his red truck by her porch. "Hmmm. When you're at my bungalow, is that considered part of your normal route?"

"Depends. You want it to become a routine stop, Kate?" he asked with a wicked smile.

She blanched and took a long sip of iced tea. "That's not what I meant."

"Relax, Kate. I'm at Gray Cottage all the time to talk SOS with Mae."

She nodded, feeling a wave of conflicting emotions: relieved something did not embroil her in another rumor, yet disappointed because she wished he'd stopped by more often to see her. At least he was here with her now. And that counted for a lot today.

The eatery's food and laid-back vibes were making her feel at ease... and so did being with Luke. She speared a hush puppy, savoring the sweet taste of fried cornmeal. "You were right," she said, with a contented sigh. "This is the perfect place. You come here often?"

"Growing up, we'd come all the time. Annie and I would stuff ourselves with shrimpburger and play on the lawn while our parents chilled." His eyes softened as he remembered.

"It sounds like it's been special to you for a long time."

A darkness passed across Luke's face, and his smile slipped. "After Dad died, this became our go-to spot. We'd come here with Mom to remember and feel close to him again."

Kate's eyes widened. She had no idea Luke had lost his father. His jaw tightened when he told her, and she knew that the loss was still real. She reached for his hand. "I'm sorry," she whispered. "I didn't know."

His thumb stroked hers gently. “It was a long time ago when I was in high school. It’s still hard sometimes. This place always helps me remember the good times we had together.”

She felt her heart ache for him. “I understand wanting to hold on to memories,” she said, seeing beyond the pain of why this place was important to him.

“It’s more than keeping memories of Dad alive,” he continued quietly, his eyes still distant. “It’s his legacy to our family. My granddaddy started Gift and Garden, and it’s up to me to keep it going.” He shrugged almost imperceptibly. “There’s always more to do and never enough time.”

She sensed there was something more to Luke’s dedication to the family business. Was it his father’s death driving him? Or was he trying to fill a void in his heart? Whatever it was, she knew that there was something deeper at play than what he let on.

Kate wanted to ask more, but an animated Jerome bounded from the kitchen holding a napkin and pen in his hand.

“You were killing it on camera today!” he said. His eyes shone with excitement and his feet were almost levitating off the ground. “Can I have your autograph?”

Chapter Thirty

KATE

By the time they finished dinner, evening shadows were creeping across their table at the Shrimp Shack, and the events of Kate's day were finally receding.

"I have a surprise for you," Luke said suddenly, breaking the comfortable silence between them.

Kate smiled at him, intrigued. "What is it?"

"Another special place from childhood. Come with me," he said, standing up and holding out his hand.

His hand was solid in hers as he led Kate down an overgrown path behind the restaurant. She stepped carefully as the narrow trail curved through a thicket of shrubs before ending on a rocky strip hugging the bay. A solitary wooden bench perched on the rocks overlooking the water.

"Have you seen a sunset over the bay?" he asked, leading her to the bench.

"Not yet," she said, surprised at her eagerness for the warmth of him next to her as they settled.

He gestured to the silhouetted skyline of South Harbor along the distant shore. "My sister Annie and I would sit here with our parents. When the sun set, it painted the town in a warm orange glow, like the town was on fire."

Kate shifted her body to get more comfortable, the grain of the bench rough against her exposed skin. She was hyper-aware that only a thin fabric was all that separated her thighs from Luke's.

"Feeling better?" he asked.

"Much."

His arm slipped gently around her shoulders with an impish spark in those blue-gray eyes. "Good. How about now?"

"Yep, better."

He tucked her in close. "And now?"

Kate rested her head on his chest, the roughness of his shirt tickling her neck. She inhaled his scent of soap and salt air. "Definitely," she whispered.

"Good," he said, gesturing towards the bay. "Mother Nature's show is about to start."

As the sun sank lower, its rays raked over the town in waves of crimson and oranges.

"You're right, Luke," she whispered in amazement as she watched.

"It's not over yet," he said, pointing across the bay.

As his voice grew more excited, Kate imagined the boy he'd once been, squirming on the old bench with his family, marveling at a sunset.

She stared into the inky night. Lights from homes and businesses in South Harbor began twinkling one by one, spreading their glow over the darkened water. Her miserable day was ending on a magical note. And Luke made it happen.

For her.

"It's gorgeous, Luke," she gasped, turning to face him with another soft kiss on his cheek,

In that split second, he had turned to look at her, and their lips met.

Kate's world stopped.

A wave of warmth and intimacy flooded her body. She melted into his kiss, his lips warm and salty from sweat and french fries.

But even as she got lost in his arms, reality intruded. Her feelings for Luke confused and frightened her. She thought about all the secrets she was keeping from him, things so hard to admit. But one thing was certain. She had to get her life back on track this summer. Kissing Luke was not part of the plan.

She drew back and his arms fell away, her body already missing his heat and regretting her decision. "Luke, I am so sorry. That was not supposed to happen." She hesitated, stumbling over her words as she tried to make sense of what had just passed between them.

He reached out and gently stroked her shoulder. "Believe me, it's not a problem." His voice sent chills through her body, and she fumbled with her hands to distract herself from how much she suddenly wanted him.

His grin made Kate both confused and drawn to him, a strange combination that she couldn't explain. "You're quite good already. You need practice to boost your confidence," he teased with a slow grin.

"That's it?"

"Absolutely. You know, I happen to be an excellent teacher, and I'm patient," he said as he tenderly pulled her towards him.

He watched her face, checking to be sure it was all right. She gave a slight nod.

"Lesson one: take a slow breath and loosen those tight shoulders," he instructed.

"Really?"

"Are you arguing with your teacher?"

She rolled her eyes in mock protest but followed his lead. When his hand brushed her shoulder blades, she felt a sudden calm wash over her like a gentle wave caressing the shore. Being with Luke differed from being with Jon in every way—even the way his fingertips brushed against her was like an intimate act all its own.

She savored the moment and gave in to the feelings that had been building inside her. It was a welcome respite from the chaos and confusion that had consumed her life.

"Good," he murmured, his voice soothing as he whispered in her ear. "Now close your eyes and relax."

Her shoulders slumped as she did what he said and gave in. His fingertips traced her features, cradling her face in a tender caress. She gasped as the feather-light brush of his lips on hers set off an explosion of sensation that took her breath away—heat, electricity, and pleasure all tumbling down on top of one another.

Luke's kiss was all-consuming, igniting her senses with a passion she had forgotten she possessed. He pulled her closer until she felt the beat of his heart thrumming against hers. She lost track of where she ended and he began, and for a moment, the world was only the two of them, spinning in a dizzying dance under the stars.

His lips pressed against hers, tasting like an addictive blend of honey and fire. He moved with a practiced ease and confidence that ignited her senses and left her wanting more. Her hands trembled with desire as they ran through his hair, pulling him closer. But underneath it all, there was a deep craving and yearning that jolted her, a raw passion that was a mix of fear and excitement, like standing on the edge of a cliff and not knowing if you'd fall or soar.

Finally, Luke drew away and searched her face. His voice was low, but his eyes still filled with a heat that made her knees tremble. "So, how was your practice session?"

This was it. This was the moment Kate had been dreading. Could she say more about her fear of disappointing him?

"Impressive," she murmured instead, even though her voice betrayed the nerves that coursed through her body. "You must have done this hundreds of times."

Luke chuckled, his thumb softly stroking her jaw as he watched her. "Let's say I'm a firm believer in practice makes perfect," he teased, giving her a hopeful smile. "What about you?"

Kate's throat tightened, and her palms sweat. She knew if she wanted to take a chance with Luke, now was the time. With a steadying breath for courage, she confessed in a barely audible whisper, "Not so much."

She paused, not wanting to say more, but knowing she owed him the truth.

"Of course, I was married," she said, struggling to find the right words. "But that was never anything, um, outstanding. And my experiences outside marriage are…"

Her voice faltered, her cheeks flushing with embarrassment. She didn't want him to see her weakness or think less of her. "Limited. Extremely limited," she said at last.

Time stood still as Luke studied her, his expression unreadable. Then he pulled her into him and placed a gentle kiss on the top of her head. “Nothing wrong with that,” he said reassuringly.

His unconditional acceptance washed over her, soothing her weary heart and making her feel like she had come home after a long journey. She shivered at his touch.

“Hey, you cold?”

“Maybe a little chilled,” she said, reaching up to twine her fingers in his. “But not from our practice session.”

Luke laughed, a joyful sound she felt rumbling through his chest. “Good to know,” he said. “We’ll have to schedule another session. Soon.”

She nodded and leaned in closer, a smile tugging at the corners of her lips. “I’d like that.”

But then she remembered tomorrow’s press conference. “Tonight’s been amazing, Luke, but I need to prep for a big press tour. And, well, I have to come across as the Queen of Caring to stop all doubts after that social media firestorm.”

He tucked a wandering strand of hair behind her ear. “You have to get up early tomorrow for your media show, and I need to drive to Wilmington for more client meetings,” he said. “Time to call it a night?”

Kate nodded, but she didn’t want to leave his arms. “Yeah, we should probably do that.”

They didn’t move. Instead, they sat in contented silence on the old bench, listening to the waves and watching the stars until finally, hand in hand, they made their way up the path together.

July

GULL ISLAND

"July is hot afternoons and sultry nights and mornings when its joy just to be alive. July is a picnic and a red canoe and a sunburned neck and a softball game and ice tinkling in a tall glass. July is a blind date with summer."

— HAL BORLAND

Chapter Thirty-One

KATE

"I can't believe we're doing this," Kate said, her voice a mix of excitement and nervousness as she waited on the Greenwood's porch with Luke. Kate and Luke were stepping in as babysitters when the Greenwoods' nanny became ill, and the grandparents had gone out of town.

"I know," Luke replied, flashing her a reassuring smile. "How hard can it be, right? It's just babysitting for a couple of hours."

Kate nodded, but she remained unconvinced that babysitting was easy. She knew from her limited experience of caring for her cousin that anything might happen.

David opened the door. Dressed in his Barack-tan suit and a patterned tie against a crisp white shirt, the big man was ready for a night on the town.

"Thanks for rescuing us," David said as Kate and Luke followed him to the kitchen. "CeCe will be down in a minute."

Kate took in the once-meticulous Greenwood kitchen. It had morphed into an explosion of bottles, binkies, and burp cloths. A whiteboard commanded the central wall, black marker outlining nap times, feedings, and a cryptic code Kate guessed was diaper duty—DWT.

"I'm ready," CeCe said, appearing in the doorway with a rustle of her dress. She was a vision in red silk and post-baby glow. Kate and Luke stood awkwardly, edging closer to each other like shields against the impending chaos. A whimper from the nursery broke the silence. Kate and Luke exchanged nervous glances, a silent pact forged in the face of drool and diaper duty.

She handed Kate and Luke each a folder filled with pages of baby care details. "All you need to know is on the whiteboard or in your folder. You'll find clean diapers in the nursery and extras in the library," she added. "Formula is in the fridge, and bottles are in the pantry."

"I texted you a link to a great YouTube video about baby formula and bottles," David said.

Kate's eyes glazed over as she skimmed the details laid out with the precision of a military exercise. Glancing at Luke, she noticed CeCe's instructions absorbed him.

"What's the DWT at seven pm?" Kate asked.

"Ah, yes. It's the boys' Desired Wake Time," CeCe explained. "You wake both boys at seven sharp for a diaper change, even if they're sleeping, and give them their bottle afterward."

"And the 7:45 to 10 DNT?" asked Luke, looking up from his folder, his eyebrows bunched in concentration.

"It's their desired nap time," David explained.

"So, they're only awake for forty-five minutes while we're here?" Luke asked.

"Sometimes it takes a little longer," David admitted. "But we'll be back by ten for their second feeding."

Kate was relieved. Surely, she and Luke could manage forty-five minutes with the twins.

"We dressed Adam in yellow and Jacob in green for you, so you can tell them apart," David said, "but my CeCe keeps them straight without color prompts."

"Yes, it's important for their language development to call the boys by their proper names," CeCe said.

"Remember, Adam's the milk monster. Jacob's the cuddle bug." David winked. "And their cries? Let's say they're...operatic."

CeCe smoothed her dress one last time. "Call or text with questions. We'll come home right away if you need us. Pediatrician's number is on the whiteboard."

"No worries. We got it," Kate assured her friend with all the confidence she could muster. "Enjoy your night on the town."

"Let's be off, Sweetness. We don't want to be late," David said, beaming. He took his wife's arm and led her away.

Kate waited for their car to drive off before bursting into a fit of giggles. "I've never seen CeCe in Mom Mode. I'm setting a timer, so we don't miss the DWT."

"Good idea," Luke said with a wry grin, punching up his phone with the YouTube tutorial on baby feedings. "We don't want any UST."

She studied the whiteboard for a moment, not seeing a UST designation. "I missed that. What's UST again?"

"Undesired screw-up time," he said his eyes still glued to the baby-feeding tutorial. "No epic meltdowns or projectile spaghetti. We can handle that much, right?"

KATE DROPPED THE MEASURING SCOOP ON THE counter as Luke stood behind her, nibbling her neck. She leaned into him with a soft moan as his butterfly kisses lingered and moved across her shoulder.

"I like it when you measure baby formula with that sexy, take-charge look," he said, his voice low and flirty.

It took a moment for Kate to catch her breath. "Though you're a delicious distraction, you're not helping." She turned to him, slipping her arms around his neck. "If we keep this up, we're endangering the Desired Wake Time."

"A few minutes off won't hurt," he said, pressing his body into hers with a fiery kiss that made Kate forget about baby formula...until she heard soft cries on the baby monitor.

They sprang apart. Kate checked the wall clock next to the schedule on the whiteboard. "They can't be awake."

"It's too early for their DWT!" she said in alarm.

"Maybe they'll fall back to sleep," Luke said hopefully.

A loud chorus of unhappy wails blared through the baby monitor.

"Or maybe not," he said, with a rueful smile.

They hurried upstairs to the nursery. Flicking on a light, they found the twins fussing and kicking at their crinkly diapers as though they couldn't get out of them fast enough.

Kate wrinkled her nose at the rancid odor of babies in full diaper explosion mode. "Well, we know what the problem is," she said, trying not to gag at the pungent aroma. "How about I change the yellow guy while you get the green one? Which one is which again? Is it Adam green and Jacob yellow?"

"Other way around. Adam yellow. Jake green," he said, walking to his little assignment and bending to the task.

She glanced at Luke, wondering how he looked so calm and unbothered by the odor. Perhaps it was his experience with smelly plants and composting things.

"Hey, little guy, I mean, Adam," Kate said, rubbing Adam's tiny yellow-clad chest as she peeked at his overflowing diaper. "Let's get you out of that stinky stuff and into dry clothes."

She slipped a waterproof changing cloth under his pint-sized bottom. Then, holding her breath to keep out the smell, she unsnapped his jammies, slipped off the diaper, and tossed it into a disposal bin.

"You are one very stinky, very cute fella," she cooed as she held her breath and cleaned the baby. Adam gave a gummy grin as he kicked his feet and rewarded her by shooting a stream of hot urine right into Kate's face with surprising accuracy.

"YEEEEEEUCK!" Kate screamed, jumping back and frantically wiping pee from her eyes.

"Did he get you?" Luke asked between snorts of laughter.

She grabbed a tissue, giggles breaking through her distress. "He got me good. On my face and even down my shirt."

"You're obviously not used to boys," Luke said, his hands moving swiftly to finish diapering Jacob. "I had practice when Dawson was in diapers. The secret is to keep them covered when they're exposed and always have something on hand for accidents."

Kate rolled her eyes and wiped away the last bit of pee from her forehead as Luke handed her another tissue. "Now you tell me," she moaned through a fit of laughter. "CeCe needs to add that to her baby manual!"

"Why don't you clean yourself up, Kate? I'll finish here."

Kate hurried to the bathroom and stuck her head under the

sink. Water splashed onto her face and down her shoulders, soaking her shirt. She met Luke with the twins in the library, a towel wrapped around her neck to catch water dripping from her hair.

"Better?" Luke asked, looking at ease juggling two little ones in his arms.

Grimacing, Kate pointed to her soaked shirt.

"Hey, I keep an extra shirt in my truck in case I need a clean one. If you'll watch them, I'll fetch it for you."

Changed, dry, and content in their bouncer chairs, the twins stretched and made happy gurgling noises. Despite the cheerful scene, Kate had a niggling feeling something was off with them, but she couldn't put her finger on what it was.

"Here you go," Luke said, returning with a white cotton shirt. "It'll be big on you. And no offense, it smells better than yours right now."

In the bathroom once more, Kate peeled off her pee-soaked top and slipped on Luke's collared shirt with long sleeves. He was right about its fit. She was swimming in his shirt which was like a mini dress on her, but she loved its softness against her flesh. Her skin prickled, imagining the same fabric that hugged Luke's skin was now wrapping hers.

She checked her reflection in the mirror and groaned. There was no missing her lacy black bra peeking through his white shirt. Perhaps he wouldn't notice? But then she felt a frisson of excitement and hoped that he would.

When she returned to the library, Luke stood in front of the bouncer chairs, staring at the boys, his gaze moving between them. "I messed up," he said, turning to Kate in confusion, worry etched on his face. "I'm not sure which twin is which."

Both now wore identical blue onesies instead of the distinctive yellow and green outfits. Luke's face was a study of misery. "I was rushing," he said, "so I grabbed the first things I found instead of CeCe's designated twin colors. How can we tell them apart?"

Kate scrubbed her eyes with her fists, trying to think. "We can't," she breathed out softly. "But CeCe knows her boys. We'll tell her about the mix-up and let her know we avoided calling them by name. Hey, it was an honest mistake."

"And then she'll kill us?"

Luke's shoulders, usually loose and broad, were knotted with worry. She stretched up to press a soft kiss to his forehead. "Not this time," she said with an easy laugh. "Our superior burping skills and schedule mastery will impress, and she'll spare us the firing squad."

Luke's nod held a hint of skepticism, but he pulled Kate back into him, his arms a warm embrace around her. She felt the reassuring weight of his chin on her head, his breath a tickle against her neck as she nestled deeper into him. The tension in his shoulders eased a fraction.

"We should probably get the bottles ready," he finally said, "before the twin chorus begins." He paused, then added with a playful smirk, "But I wouldn't mind a detour past that alluring black lace of yours for a few extra minutes."

Chapter Thirty-Two

KATE

Handing Kate the bottle for the twin they hoped was Adam, Luke sank next to her in the matching recliner, cradling the twin they hoped was Jacob. When Kate held the bottle to Adam's mouth, he eagerly latched on, his tiny hands wrapped around her pinky finger. Her breathing hitched as she held him. The familiar, sweet scent of his baby skin was more than a memory of holding Angie as a baby—this was the promise she'd ached for, warm and alive in her arms.

She watched Luke feeding the other twin. He was smiling at Jacob, whispering to him and rubbing the child's arm. Luke was great with kids. It was obvious he adored them.

Her heart pitched with a wave of regret. Luke needed someone who could give him a family. Why couldn't she be the one? She sighed. Even if they figured out every other challenge of a potential relationship, she'd never fix this one.

Luke caught her eye. "How are you doing over there, partner?" he asked.

She blinked, snapping back to the present. “Clean diapers and warm tummies make for a happy baby and me,” she said, forcing a light tone.

Then she bolted upright in her chair, startling the little one. “Oh no, Luke! I almost forgot about the burping. When is the desired burping time?”

He chuckled. “They just started feeding, so you’re okay.”

Her relief was palpable. At least Luke knew what he was doing. She allowed Adam a few more sips before prying the bottle from him. Cradling his head against her shoulder and patting his back. Luke did the same with his little one, and a series of loud belches soon filled the room.

Kate laughed. “We have us a band of burping brothers.”

As she cradled the baby close to her heart, a curtain of grief pressed down on her. Tears threatened to spill down her cheeks, but she fought them back. She remembered how Jon never understood the depth of her sorrow and wanted to try right away for another child. But what he didn’t realize was that she needed time to mourn before even considering it. The thought of losing another baby was too much to bear, and she wasn’t ready to risk that pain again.

Adam slept, his tiny fist clutching her shirt and soft sucking sounds filling the air. Kate glanced at Luke. He was gently rocking Jacob and humming softly to him. The sight of them together filled her with warmth and love. She shut her eyes for a moment to lock the details of this precious moment in her mind. Luke deserved a loving family, but she wasn’t sure if she’d ever be ready. This would have to be enough for her.

LUKE

KATE'S LAUGHTER FILLED THE ROOM, A BEAUTIFUL sound captivating Luke the moment he heard it. Her presence captivated him, and every amused glance she tossed his way made his heart leap like no one had before. As much as he wanted to keep her with him forever, he knew their time was ending.

As her laughter faded, he noticed a deep crease between her eyes, a shadow of something troubling her.

"What's on your mind?" he asked, his voice soft and inviting, hoping she would open up to him.

The corner of her lips turned up into a small smile, but there was still a shadow of something more complex hidden beneath her gaze. "Just thinking about how much I adore being with these boys," she said, her voice barely audible. Then she added, "And I can't stop thinking how I'll miss you when summer ends."

Luke reached across and took Kate's hand, lacing his fingers through hers. Her hand was icy, and he hoped this simple touch would bring her comfort. The words he'd held back for so long lingered, caught in his throat. He gazed into her sad eyes, searching for a way to say what he felt. After a steadying breath, he let words slip out.

"I'm falling for you, Kate," he said simply, his voice a whisper.

Kate's eyes widened, a flicker of surprise crossing her face. A soft smile graced her lips as she whispered, "Catch me, Luke, because I'm falling for you, too."

His heart felt like it would jump out of his chest as relief flooded him. "I'm glad I'm not the only one who feels this way," he confessed.

The urge to pull Kate into his arms was overwhelming, but he hesitated, mindful of the sleeping babies upstairs. Instead, he reached out, gently pressing a kiss to the back of her hand, a silent expression of his affection.

The timer jangled from the kitchen, reminding them it was the end of boys' desired sleep time. Reluctantly, Kate and Luke pulled apart, their eyes still locked. After tending to the boys' bedtime routine, they retreated to the library, snuggling together on the plush couch. Kate's body molded perfectly against his, her warmth radiating through his shirt as she leaned against his chest, his arms wrapping around her. She felt like she'd always belonged there, a missing piece finally found.

Luke's fingers instinctively threaded through her hair, the dark silky strands gliding effortlessly between his fingertips. A wave of desire washed over him, but he held back, respecting her boundaries and the delicate balance of their situation.

His heart ached with longing, a mixture of anticipation and restraint. He wanted to explore the depths of their connection, to lose himself in the intoxicating rhythm of her heartbeat. But he knew he had to be patient, to let their bond deepen naturally and in Kate's own time.

"So," he breathed out quietly, "what would you like to do for the rest of the evening?"

Her eyes twinkled with mischief as she locked her gaze on his. "What about a good old-fashioned make-out session on the couch?"

Laughing, Luke rested his forehead against hers. "Tempting, but we'd fail Babysitting 101."

"Spoilsport," she said, pretending to be devastated. "It'd be too much like teenagers making out on the couch, one ear listening for parents to come home. How about we pivot? Order pizza and watch *Princess Bride?*"

He groaned theatrically. "Not sure I can take that movie on a full stomach."

She jostled him, mischief in her eyes. "Hey, it's good for digestion. And it has the sweetest kiss scene."

He gave in to her as he knew he would. "You queue up the movie, and I'll call for delivery."

She sat up, her hands lingering on his chest, as if reluctant to break the contact. When she pulled away, her fingers left a trail of heat on his chest.

"Luke McAllister, you know the way to my heart is the perfect pizza order. Time to roll, or we'll miss our *Desired Pizza Time.*"

Her grin was infectious, a supernova grin that reached her eyes and tugged at the corners. In that moment, his heart was like the Grinch when those tight bands around the cartoon's heart snapped. And much like the Grinch, Luke was on a mission to snatch something precious...Kate's heart.

HOURS LATER, WHEN THE GREENWOODS ARRIVED HOME to a silent house, they hurried to the nursery. The new parents relaxed when the silver glow from the nightlight illuminated two little bodies cozying up in their crib.

When they checked their babysitters, David and CeCe found an empty pizza box on the coffee table in the library. Flickering blue light from the television showed Westley professing true love to Buttercup as Kate and Luke dozed side-by-side, peacefully sprawled on the couch, their arms and legs intertwined like a giant pretzel.

David whispered, “It’s about time those two figured out they should be together. I think we can leave them here.”

CeCe nodded and patted her husband’s broad shoulder. “I agree, David. Let’s give them a night together.”

She gathered her softest blanket to drape over the sleeping couple before the Greenwoods tiptoed out of the library and closed the door behind them.

Chapter Thirty-Three

LUKE

Carolina sun beat down on a beach choked with tourists. Luke shaded his eyes as he followed Dawson, who had raced ahead to a nest they'd cordoned off last week. Kate's laughter rang out as she watched the boy, sunlight catching the red in her hair. Island life suited her. The edgy newcomer he met months ago had slowly melted into this confident woman who was stealing his heart.

He remembered how light she always felt in his arms like she was made of sunshine and citrus. Her delicious scent lingered with him long after their embrace. Luke wanted nothing more than to keep her with him always. But he was a small-town guy on an island in the middle of nowhere, while she was a city girl, who'd be leaving for her place in a world far different from his.

"Is it always crowded like this?" Kate asked, breaking into the comfortable silence that fell between them.

"Once school lets out, it's non-stop," he said. "We're grateful for tourists but ready for quiet when summer ends."

Kate shot him a half-smile, reminding him, “Hey, I’m one of those people leaving at the end of summer.”

Squeezing her hand, he reminded her,-“We have weeks ahead of us still. Anyway, you’re not a tourist.”

“I’m not?”

“Nope. You’ve got the island vibe,” he said, scanning her attire with a playful grin. “Turtle team shirt, Gull Island cap. Flip-flops. You’ve got the whole look down.” He tallied points on his fingers.

Kate shrugged. “Anybody can shop the same look.”

“Ah, but they don’t look as good as you,” he countered, his gaze lingering on her for a beat too long.

She rolled her eyes, and a faint blush crept up her cheeks. “Thanks for the compliment, but I’m not exactly built for the beach volleyball team.”

“Disagree.” He leaned in a touch, and his voice dropped lower. “You’ve got the total package, Kate—the looks, the smile, the brains—you’re the real deal.”

“Huh. Good to know. Please continue with your list.”

Luke grinned and held up another finger. “You hang out with locals, always down for shrimpburgers and sunsets.”

A genuine laugh bubbled up from Kate, a melody that warmed Luke's heart. “Got me there, Obi-Wan.”

He chuckled and held up another finger. “Last, you walk to work in the heat of summer, despite fixing your car’s AC.”

She protested half-heartedly. “It reduces my carbon footprint, and honestly, I enjoy the exercise.”

“Well, if you like to walk, then join Boo and me sometime some evening for a run on the Point,” he asked casually, although his stomach did a nervous flip-flop.

Kate’s gaze caught his muscled calves and long legs, and a hint of amusement danced in her eyes. "Run? With you? And get left lagging behind? "

"Let's call it brisk walking then."

"Brisk walk I can do. Tomorrow?"

"Absolutely," he said, unable to control the rapid beating of his heart.

"Is this like a walking date with you?" she teased with an impish grin. "And perhaps organize practice sessions with my favorite teacher afterward?"

He nodded fervently, a genuine smile replacing his feigned nonchalance. Before he could say more, Dawson barreled into him, a 42-inch storm of little boy energy.

"Uncle Luke! Miss Kate!" the child called, out of breath from running. Dawson opened his palm to reveal a smooth, oval stone. "I found a pretend baby sea turtle egg. I'm going to take it home and take care of it until the real one hatches."

The corners of Luke's mouth hitched up into a grin as he examined his nephew's prize. "Nice, Dawson! You've got to keep it safe and protect the real eggs in our nest, too."

Dawson solemnly promised, tucking his treasure in a pocket. "Can I go to Gray Cottage by myself? Miss Mae says she'll have something special for me."

"Go for it, little man," Luke said, and the excited Dawson dashed away.

The feather-light touch of Kate's fingers on his forearm sent a jolt of heat through him. She knew how to get his attention.

"I feel foolish for forgetting," she said. "I bumped into Clayton Pruitt at work last week."

He stiffened, and his heart sank as he heard her words. Clayton Pruitt. Nothing about that could be good.

"What did he want?"

As Kate recounted Pruitt's denial of the condo leak, his frustration mounted, threatening to boil over. But Kate must've sensed his mood because she slowed her pace and brushed her fingers against his forearm. His anger slipped away as she soothed his worries without saying a word.

"Kate, I'm sorry I snapped. Pruitt shouldn't get to me, but he does."

"Still," she said gravely, "I know how much the Point means to you."

"It means a lot to everyone here. He can't win."

"He won't," Kate promised. "We'll stop him."

MAX CALLED TO THEM FROM HIS ROCKING CHAIR ON Mae's porch. "Lemonade?"

Kate poured a glass while Luke watched his nephew holding his prized rock and a small green object in the other.

"What do you have here, buddy?" Luke asked. He inspected the item, a toy sea turtle hatchling knitted with tiny stitches of green yarn. Its pillow-shaped body and teeny flippers fit snugly in the boy's hand.

"It's a baby turtle Miss Mae made for me," Dawson beamed, cradling the soft stuffed toy.

Mae smiled. "I made stuffies like that for my nieces when they helped with turtle patrol last summer. The girls absolutely adored them."

Kate studied the toy, biting her lip and furrowing her brow. Luke grinned, recognizing the signs of an incoming idea.

She rocked on her heels, her voice filled with enthusiasm, as she said, "We should do something with this! Luke's research and environmental studies combined with an adorable toy like this are exactly what we need to raise awareness."

Mae caught on immediately, shooting Luke a knowing look as Kate explained.

"What if we yarn bomb your SOS table at Founders Day?" Kate went on, her hands flying as she paced the porch. "An eye-catching display of little turtles will draw attention to endangered animals and get people caring about the Point."

Mae jumped onto the excitement. "My knitting circle can make hundreds of little turtles for Founders Day," she said, her hands moving by rote in a knit, purl dance.

"Think of it, Luke," Kate said, her eyes sparkling. "We can reach people who might never scroll past a petition. A cuddly turtle? That'll grab attention. And while they're taking selfies and posting online, they'll learn about the real issues. It's education in disguise!"

Luke couldn't deny the potential reach of social media. He still preferred data and research, but Kate's vision of an army of miniature turtles spreading awareness had a certain charm. Maybe it could work.

Kate continued pacing the porch, her hands waving non-stop. "Max, can we sell the toy turtles at Founders Day and encourage people to sign the SOS petition to halt Point construction at the same time?"

Max stopped rocking to consider. "Certainly, but only if you make the process transparent by clearly communicating the incentive and not using any misleading tactics. However, it's important to emphasize that the stuffed animal is a symbolic gesture rather than a direct exchange or inducement."

"Honey, in English, please," Mae said, patting his hand when she saw Kate's baffled stare.

"Yes, we can, Kate," Max amended, cutting to the chase.

Luke spoke up. He admired Kate's creativity and optimism, but this felt like a stretch. "I love your spirit, but isn't this a bit...cutesy for such a serious issue? Pruitt might spin it as trivializing the cause?"

Kate's smile faltered, but her eyes held their fire. "I understand," she said, her voice softer. "It's a little out there, but we need people to notice, Luke. We need them to care. Can't we be creative and still be ethical?"

Mae nodded. "What about selling the toys to educate people? Help them understand why it's important to protect sea turtles and the Point?"

Kate stopped pacing and snapped her fingers. "Brilliant, Mae! We'll sell the stuffies and donate profits to the Sea Turtle Rescue Foundation!"

"I can set up a station for kids with coloring sheets and sea turtle crafts," Mae said, the natural educator in her coming out.

"We can set ground rules," Max chimed in. "No pressure tactics. No guilt-tripping. We offer the toys, the information, and the opportunity to help. People choose to take part if they want to."

Kate beamed. "Exactly, Max! We're not selling salvation, just raising awareness, and, hopefully, some funds for the Sea Turtle Rescue Foundation."

Kate turned back to Luke, eyes sparkling with excitement.

"What do you think, Luke?" she asked, her hand brushing his forearm again in that gentle gesture of hers.

Luke felt a smile tug at his lips. This wasn't the approach he had in mind, but Kate had a point. Maybe a little creativity, a dash of cuteness, and a lot of transparency could be the key to saving the Point.

"I am clearly outnumbered," he said, raising his hands in surrender. "Let's do this!"

Chapter Thirty-Four

KATE

Needles clicked a steady rhythm in Gray Cottage, a symphony of purpose. Mae, a whirlwind in their midst, guided the creation of soft sea turtles with practiced ease. With four weeks until Founders Day, the knitters were working non-stop to finish 1,000 sea turtle stuffies.

Kate glanced at Annie Lawson, sitting next to her. Since neither of them knew how to knit, Mae had them add the pinhead-sized eyes to the toys with a simple French knot.

The black yarn, thick and stubborn, refused the oversized eye of the needle. Annie hummed, her wink a mischievous glint, as she finally coaxed it through.

"Dawson wanted to come tonight," Annie said, voice laced with a playful pout. "But Luke convinced him Boo needed company."

Kate, working on her miniature sea turtle, pretended to focus. But Annie's mention of Luke sent a jolt through her like a needle jab to her concentration.

Mae, surrounded by sea turtles, glanced up. "Annie Lawson, don't be distracting the help," she teased with a playful glint in her eye.

Kate's had faltered, caught mid-stitch, and she felt a blush creep up her neck. Maybe seeing Luke wasn't a secret after all.

Annie, leaning close, whispered, as if reading her mind. "I'm glad you two are together. Luke's been smiling more, working less, and I'm taking on more with the business."

The admission surprised Kate. Annie was following in her father's footsteps?

Before she could ask, Annie added, "And the big brother act? Gone. Can you believe he still blames Clayton for our split? I was the one who called it off."

Kate's jaw dropped. The Point rivalry, she always knew, went deeper than moats around a sandcastle.

A sly grin tugged at Annie's lips as she said, "Know what I miss about Clayton? He was fantastic at shagging!"

Startled, Kate's yarn slipped, as thoughts of Luke and Clayton unraveled in confusion. Her mind went straight to her British friends' outrageous "shagging" stories.

Annie continued, her eyes sparkling, "Luke's an even better shagger than Clayton."

Kate's face flamed as a barrage of Luke-related images bombarded her mind.

"Annie, my dear," Mae intervened, dipping her head toward Kate. "I believe our visitor from the North is confused."

"No!" Annie chortled as she caught on to Kate's misunderstanding. "Not that kind of shagging! In the Carolinas, the shag is a beach music dance. Like swing dancing's Carolina cousin. You know, Luke loves beach music. He'd be thrilled to show you the ways of the shag if you ask him."

Kate shook her head as she slipped a turtle eye knot. "Founders Day has him swamped, and he's working nights to get ready for the Point hearing."

Annie scoffed. "You're joking, right? I guarantee he'll make time for you."

"Well, my dears," Mae said, sliding her spectacles down her nose to peer at them, "it's time I open Gray Cottage for a night of beach music and shag dancing. What do you say, Kate? Up for a lesson from the master himself?"

LUKE

FRESH FROM THE SHOWER, LUKE STOOD IN A CLOUD OF steam. His Parrot Head shirt flapped wildly as he toweled off his hair. The pimento cheese he prepped, a beacon of cheesy goodness studded with mischievous crimson specks, was basking in the fridge light. Jimmy Buffett was crooning in the background, and mint-scented iced tea was chilling on the counter—all waiting for Kate.

The crunch of tires on the driveway signaled she was here. Boo, eager for his Kate fix, streaked for the door, his excited yaps competing with Buffett's lyrics. Luke flung open the door and found her already laughing. Boo's enthusiastic licks painted her face.

"Hey, you." She grinned, her leopard-print skirt swaying in

rhythm with her steps. The licorice crop top framed a smile brighter than the moonbeams filtering through the dunes.

Luke's heart did a little mamba. He took her hand, the cool touch grounding him even as her hazel eyes, wide and luminous, sent sparks dancing in his veins. The music from porch speakers pulsed a shared heartbeat with the night. This was it, the perfect Saturday night he'd spent the week orchestrating. And as Kate bit her lip in concentration, following his last shag move with an adorable clumsiness, he knew it was worth every detour for pimento cheese and every note of Buffett.

A misstep, a laugh, a graze of skin against skin. Kate's toe met his, a playful disruption in their dance. "Oops, wrong turn!"

Luke chuckled, his palm finding hers on her waist, a warm anchor in the rhythmic tides. "Shag's a duet, Kate, a mirrored dance in reverse." He guided her, and suddenly, it clicked. Her feet became whispers on the floor, echoing his every move. He spun her, a laugh escaping her lips like seabirds on the breeze.

The music faded, leaving them breathless in the moonlight. "One more spin?" she whispered, eyes like pools of melted gold.

"As you wish," he murmured.

The night air, laced with the scent of salt and her hair, swirled around them as he drew her close. Their bodies moved in silent conversation, a language only they understood. When the music stilled, he held her a moment longer, her warmth a secret he couldn't quite part with.

"I can now do you proud at Mae's," she whispered, her voice a shiver against his skin.

A wisp of sadness shadowed Kate's smile as she stepped back, one hand lingering in his. Her gaze drifted, something beyond the dance swirling in her eyes. He yearned to learn what clouded her mind. Turning her palm, he pressed a kiss to its center, his voice soft like wind through dunes.

"I'm always proud of you, Kate."

She hugged him close, her voice a whisper against his ear. "Thank you, Luke, for believing in me."

He kissed the crown of her head, holding her warmth, her hands tracing the curve of his neck. She was moonlight and magic, intoxicating in his arms. When she murmured his name, his breath hitched, husky with yearning. Never had a woman's voice held such power, tilting his world, revving his heart. He wanted to kiss her, to taste her, to claim her. But she wasn't there yet. He held her closer, savoring the quiet promise of this moment.

She pulled away and met his gaze. Her lips curled languidly, and a spark of mischief flitted across her face. "Considering how quickly I caught on tonight, don't you think I'm due some kind of reward?" she asked, her voice playful.

His grin widened at her boldness. "What sort of reward do you have in mind, Kate?" His voice was low and breathy.

Her gaze met his, her lips soft and needing to be kissed, a tempting invitation. "Let your imagination run wild," she whispered, taking his hand while keeping the curious dog at bay. "But make sure Boo is happy on the porch, so we won't be disturbed."

Luke took a steadying breath and closed the door. Inside, his fingertips drifted down her waist, pulling her closer until their lips grazed. The whisper of citrus on her skin sparked a hunger in him, the air thick with anticipation.

She melted against him, each curve finding its place. He lost himself in the feel of her fingers trailing fire down his spine, kneading his shoulders, gently sliding through his hair. Her breath mingled with his in a slow, hungry dance, their moans a counterpoint to the rhythm of their bodies. He wanted to drown in her, make her his own.

Outside, Boo settled on the porch, content to remain for a long night under the stars.

KATE

KATE SAVORED THE MORNING SUN LIKE A CAT WAKING from a dream, stretched out in her red Adirondack chair. Steam from her coffee danced in the golden light, the scent warming her face. Her eyes drifted closed, replaying the memory of last night's dance with Luke. The sway of the rhythm, the heat of his hand on her skin, the taste of salt on his lips—a delicious warmth bloomed in her chest, spreading outward like ripples in a sun-drenched pool.

Moonlight magic, she'd thought it then, the way the music had pulled her close, walls around her heart crumbling like sandcastles under the tide. Luke, patient and kind all summer, had been a steady hand as she navigated the choppy waters of her divorce. Memories flickered: him listening with soft eyes, holding her as silent tears escaped, reminding her she wasn't alone. A pang of regret struck her. How close she'd come to shutting him out, to locking herself back in the shadows. But she hadn't. And it was glorious.

Doubt had whispered then, a serpent in her ear, but he'd hushed it with gentle kisses and whispered reassurances. In the circle of his powerful arms, she knew. Trusting him, letting him in, wasn't merely a choice. It was the anchor she'd been craving in the storm. Her pulse echoed the certainty, a drumbeat in her veins.

A chime broke the reverie. Her phone buzzed in her pocket, and a rush of anticipation flooded her as she saw Luke's name. A smile bloomed on her lips as she read:

> Good morning! Boo and I miss you. <smiling dog face emoji>. Dinner at mine tonight? Your choice—grilled shrimp or steak?

She felt a flutter inside as she wrote a response:

> Steak AND shrimp? Yes, please! Perfect cure for a case of Luke-and-Boo withdrawal. See you soon.

A playful grin tugged at her lips as she added a sunshine-and-hearts emoji to her text. It felt cheesy, an overly optimistic symbol for the complicated knot of emotions churning in her stomach, but it captured a sliver of the happiness she wanted to share with him.

Settling deeper into the Adirondack chair, she curled her toes under her, the wood pleasantly warm against her bare feet. Each sip of coffee was a burst of flavor, a stark contrast to the blandness that had colored her world for so long. Now, bathed in the sun's soothing caress and the rhythmic whisper of the waves, everything felt vibrantly alive. It was as if she'd finally stepped out of the shadows, blinking in the sunlight, hand in hand with the man who had helped her find her way.

August

GULL ISLAND

"This morning, the sun endures past dawn. I realize that it is August: the summer's last stand."

— SARA BAUME

Chapter Thirty-Five

KATE

The makeshift dining area on the deck was a flurry of activity for Founders Day as Kate swept through, her eyes scanning every detail. Staff bustled around, carefully arranging crockery and cutlery, their movements swift and precise.

As Kate watched them, she felt a surge of determination and pride. Her heels clicked a nervous shuffle across the deck, each step echoing the months of meticulous to-do lists and late-night brainstorming sessions culminating in this evening. The success of this evening would reflect on her tenure as marketing director and boost her career. Missteps were not an option.

As Kate adjusted a centerpiece, a rogue petal fell onto her perfectly coiffed hair. "Great," she muttered to herself. "Just what I need–floral dandruff on the night I'm supposed to impress people."

A vision of cheesy catastrophe unfolded next in Kate's mind.

One misplaced stiletto and she'd be diving headfirst into a vibrantly orange abyss—a platter overflowing with pimento cheese. The image was so vivid, she could practically taste the tangy spread clinging to her designer gown. Clayton Pruitt, a shark in a tuxedo, would undoubtedly be hovering nearby, a smug smile plastered across his face and a champagne flute held aloft. “Seems you've developed a taste for the caviar of the Carolinas, Kate,” he'd likely drawl, his voice dripping with that saccharine charm.

Kate shuddered, the mental image making her cringe But then, her shoulders squared with steely determination. Tonight wasn't about Clayton or his cruel jabs. Tonight was about the aquarium, about all the passionate people who had poured their hearts into its success.

She took a deep breath and allowed herself a moment to reflect on Luke's contributions. His connections within the community had opened doors she never thought possible. With his advice, she had created an event to impress even the most discerning donors. The promise of a flawless night hung in the air, a whispered secret on the breeze.

She felt a rivulet of sweat trickle down her back, but she fought to maintain her composure. A hundred pairs of eyes flickered towards her, their unspoken trust a tangible weight on her shoulders.

Her phone pinged with a text from Luke, pulling her attention away from the room's anticipation.

Luke: Hectic there?

Kate: Crazy but ready to party.

Luke: Rocking here at the turtle toy table.

Kate: Awesome! See you later? <lady in red dance emoji>

Luke: If I can escape.

Kate: Try?

Luke: <heart emjoi> I'm a sucker for your charming pleading.

A smile curved Kate's lips as she slipped her phone into her pocket. Her gaze skimmed the bay to South Harbor. The Ferris wheel, a jewel against the twilight, beckoned her thoughts towards Luke, navigating the festival with his usual calm efficiency. Images of moonlit walks and cozy deck snuggles painted themselves across her daydreams.

But duty called. With a shake of her head, she refocused. Show time.

Pausing at a table, she straightened the centerpiece—a crystal vase cradling a single white magnolia blossom, its simplicity echoing the elegance she'd envisioned. Perfect.

"Kate?" Liz Wilson's voice, a tremor in its usual vibrancy, sent a prickle down Kate's spine. She pivoted, Liz's worried frown mirroring her rising dread.

"Don't panic, Liz," Kate said, forcing a confidence she didn't quite feel. "What's up?"

Liz hesitated, eyes darting around the room. "Band manager called," she blurted, wringing her hands. "Food poisoning. They're out."

The stress of the day finally slammed into Kate. She closed her eyes and massaged her temples, trying to ease the tension building there. "We'll figure it out, Liz. Don't worry."

Liz, however, wasn't done worrying. "Caterer called too. Same culprit and no show."

Kate squeezed her eyes shut, inhaling deeply. This couldn't be happening. *No music? No food? No way!* Tonight's gala was already teetering on disaster.

Liz's voice, a lifeline, cut through her panic. "I might have a solution for the music at least. My son's band plays beachy stuff, soft rock. Fits the summer theme we want, right?"

Kate exhaled, considering. A proud mother's bias aside, any music was better than none. Liz whipped out her phone, a YouTube link materializing on the screen.

Kate listened, eyebrows rising with each note. Liz's son's band was quite good.

"They're perfect, Liz. How soon can they get here?"

Relief washed over Kate as Liz dialed the number. She turned to mind towards Chef, but her phone buzzed, the caller ID sending a punch to her gut.

Clayton Pruitt!

She didn't want to answer, but generous donors didn't grow on trees. "Clayton," she said, her voice tight.

"Heard you're having a menu malfunction, Kate," he drawled. "Anything I can do to help?"

The island grapevine must be having a field day. Kate hated his knowing tone, the way he relished her discomfort. "Minor hiccups," she lied, her jaw clenched. "We're good."

"Well, I wouldn't want a lack of food to dampen the party

spirit," Clayton chuckled. "I have some prime oysters coming in. Consider them a donation."

Kate's stomach churned. Accepting felt like stepping into a spiderweb, but she pictured Chef's magic touch, donors slurping oysters with delight. The aquarium's needs outweighed her reservations.

"Thank you, Clayton," she said, her voice betraying none of her turmoil. "We'd be honored."

He cackled, the sound like pebbles on a tin roof. "Anytime, Kate. For the aquarium, of course."

The call ended, and Kate sagged against the wall. Tonight, she'd thank Clayton, swallow her pride, and keep the aquarium afloat. She could do this. She had to.

NAVY SILK SKIMMED KATE'S LEGS AS SHE SLIPPED INTO the midi dress, the white handkerchief hem flirting with her ankles. One final mirror check and a deep breath, and she was off to the makeshift stage, heels clicking on the polished floor.

The band's warm-up bloomed into a tropical groove, vibrant like Liz's parrot-print blouse and board shorts. "Liz, you're a genius!" Kate exclaimed. "This beach vibe is exactly what our fundraiser needs."

Liz, beaming, tilted her head towards the drummer, a tie-dye explosion topped with a day-glow orange shirt decorated with flamingos. "That's my son, Jerome."

The drummer erupted in a wild cymbal crash and a snappy salute with his sticks. "Mom!" he yelled over the music.

Kate's eyes widened. "Jerome? The... Jerome?"

"My eldest." Liz chuckled. "Big fan of yours."

Jerome's in charge of music! Relief washed over Kate like a piña colada. She pressed a hand to her chest, offering a grateful nod to the flamboyant drummer who bowed deeply in response.

"Lifesavers, both of you," she declared, squeezing Liz in a quick hug before dashing off to check on Chef.

The kitchen was a symphony of clinking oyster shells and whirring blenders. Kate's heart soared. Chef, a maestro in her white toque, orchestrated the chaos with practiced ease.

"You're a miracle, Chef!" Kate gasped, watching oysters transform into miniature jewels.

Chef winked, her gaze lingering on a fragrant dish she finished plating. "My specialty, Oysters Rockefeller."

Kate inhaled the buttery herbs, a smile blooming. Tonight, they weren't just serving food. They were serving a sensation.

Chapter Thirty-Six

KATE

Bay breezes tickled rows of linen-clad tables on the aquarium's spacious deck by the bay. Mason jars filled with tea candles and fairy lights strung over railings wrapped diners in a cozy glow as Jerome's band played in the background. The evening was coming together.

Kate's stomach growled when a waiter glided past with a tray of dinner entrees Chef pulled together–aquarium fries and crabmeat-topped all-beef hot dogs prepared in artisan brioche buns.

Kate took a sip of sparkling water, her throat drying with nerves. She couldn't eat. She'd have something later with Luke...if he finished in South Harbor in time. Maybe they'd even have a dance together.

CeCe glided over, looking stunning in white linen trousers and a matching sleeveless tunic. She slipped an arm through her friend's.

"Nicely done. We've already raised more money than from last year's dinner."

"Thank you for this chance," Kate said, leaning into her friend with a quick side hug. "I'm glad you could make it tonight. Grandparents on twin duty?"

"It wasn't hard to convince them. They even made it downtown with the boys in the stroller, but lines were too long for those adorable, plush sea turtles at the SOS table."

"No worries. I'll find two extra and deliver them personally," Kate said, making a mental note to ask Mae to knit more.

CeCe nodded and took a sip of her water, an eyebrow lifting as she watched Kate over the rim. "So, are you seeing that lovely man of yours tonight?"

"Stop it! He's not my lovely man."

"Uh-huh. And I'm supposed to believe there's not 'love' in the air between you two?"

"Don't know about love," Kate conceded, a rose blush creeping up her cheeks. "But falling hard for sure."

CeCe's fist pumped the air. "With all the time you two spend together and the way you swoon when I mention his name? It's about time you admit it."

"Hey, I'm on duty!" Kate protested, pretending dismay. "Don't distract me. I can't think about such things, or I'll get all melty and gooey like Mae's pimento cheese."

"It's about time you get melty and gooey, Kate. Both of you!"

Jerome's voice crackled with urgency. "Slow dances, last set! Grab your sweetheart or grab your courage and make it a night you won't forget!"

"Under the Boardwalk" by the Drifters melted through the

air, but Kate felt a different kind of melody—an anxious thrumming as she searched for Luke in the swaying crowd.

Suddenly, an unfamiliar hand on her shoulder. Clayton. His cologne announced his arrival before she even turned. "Up for a spin, Kate?" His voice, honeyed but sharp, cut through the music.

She forced a smile. Her body ached for escape, but her feet knew the practiced steps to satisfy a donor. "Of course."

"Those petitions about the Point," Clayton drawled, his voice a grating counterpoint to the music's velvet, "buzzing like angry bees, are they?"

"Thousands strong," she replied, lifting her chin, "and growing louder."

Surprise flickered across his face. "And yet you take my oysters for your fundraiser." A rich, baritone chuckle escaped his lips, a sound that lacked the warmth of his perfectly sun-kissed skin.

Despite the amusement in his voice, a flicker of unease sparked in her chest as his eyes hardened when he spoke. "Passion and pragmatism make for an interesting dance, don't they?"

"Some dances are worth the effort," she said, her gaze steady.

He offered a beguiling smile, revealing a set of gleaming white teeth. "Maybe. But even the most skilled dancer needs a strong partner." His gaze held hers, intense and unreadable.

"My door is always open to our patrons," she said, her voice cool as the bay breeze.

"Intriguing," he murmured, his hand lingering on hers as the music died. His smile, a mask slipping, never reached his eyes. "I'll remember that."

He melted back into the crowd, leaving Kate alone in the fading melody, the scent of his cologne a lingering reminder of the dance she couldn't escape.

The dance floor, a swirling sea of swaying bodies, held no appeal for Kate. The band's last song, a sultry slow groove, only amplified her growing anxiety. Luke wasn't coming, and disappointment tugged at her like a riptide. Just as she had given up hope, a voice, warm and close, broke through the din.

"Kate?"

The last sliver of sunlight sliced across the dance floor, illuminating his approaching figure. His dark T-shirt and charcoal jacket hung casually. His jeans hugged his legs as he moved with a dancer's ease. Yet, it was his eyes that stole her breath. Deep and stormy, they held a warmth that spread through her like a tide, washing away her defenses and leaving a strange mix of vulnerability and hope in their wake. A damp curl had escaped from the wind and clung to his forehead, framing his strong features. Her hand, drawn by an invisible force, reached out, and her fingertip traced a gentle path down the stray curl.

"You made it."

"Wouldn't miss this." The low timbre of his voice sent a delicious warmth through her.

He leaned in, closing the distance between them, as if their connection defied the crowded room. His hand, warm and solid, swallowed hers as he led her onto the dance floor. Breath hitched in her throat as his arm, a comforting firebrand, circled her waist. She closed her eyes, drowning in the intoxicating blend of ocean breeze and linen that was his scent.

"So glad you're here," she whispered, her voice barely audible above the music.

"Me too," he murmured, his fingers sending sparks dancing

across her back. Lost in his gaze, the beat of the music thrummed faintly against her skin, a backdrop to the rhythm of their clasped hands. He leaned in, his voice a velvet caress against her ear.

"Beautiful," he breathed.

Suddenly, a dizzying spin, the world tilting around her. He pulled her close, their bodies a perfect fit, the air electric with unspoken possibilities. His lips, tantalizingly close, sent a delicious ache and a current humming beneath her skin as their eyes locked.

She was about to succumb, to lose herself in this intoxicating dance, when a low rumble, not from the music, but from her traitorous stomach, shattered the moment.

"Buzz kill," she groaned, burying her face in Luke's chest.

A wry smile tugged at his lips, a flicker of something deeper igniting in his gaze as he leaned back to look at her. "Hungry?"

Kate closed her eyes for a moment, a contented smile gracing her lips as she leaned into his touch. "I don't eat when I work events like this," she confessed.

His voice softened."Why don't I whip us up something delicious at my place?"

She would have jumped into his lap if she were a cat and purred with pure pleasure.

Instead, she managed a breathy, "Yes, please."

Chapter Thirty-Seven

KATE

It was nearly midnight when Kate nudged her Prius into Luke's driveway. Crashing waves and rustling dune grass whispered in the warm night air as Kate walked toward his beach house. Meeting Luke for dinner seemed like a good idea when he had suggested it an hour ago. But now she was exhausted, and despite exchanging evening wear for shorts, a top, and her trusty Chuck's, her feet were killing her.

She'd lost touch with reality after dancing with Luke, his thumb moving in lazy circles across her back, the warmth of his solid body pressed against hers. She'd stay for a few minutes and then head back to Gray Cottage.

He waved to her from the porch, cradling Boo in one arm. Luke was barefoot and had slipped into shorts and a cotton T-shirt. After working non-stop since morning, he still had that effortlessly casual-cute vibe that made her toes curl.

An excited Boo intercepted her kiss meant for Luke's cheek.

"Good to see you again, Boo," she said, giggling as the dog licked her face.

As Luke gently nudged Boo aside, his hand brushed against hers. A spark, unexpected and sharp, surged through her. His gaze met, hers a silent question in his eyes.

He whispered, his voice husky with anticipation. "Let's try that again, Kate."

She wrapped her arms around his neck, the crisp fabric of his shirt grazing her cheek and sending his warmth through her body. Their kiss was soft, a combination of a sweet *hello* mixed with *it's-late-and-we're-both-exhausted-but-this-feels-too-good-to-quit.*

"Better?" She smiled, looking up from his chest.

"Much." He planted an affectionate kiss on her nose. "Still hungry? For dinner, I mean?"

"I am ravenous," she answered with a giggle, "so we better stick to dinner."

"WHEN DID YOU FIND TIME TO DO THIS?" KATE ASKED, her voice tinged with disbelief as she surveyed his dining room.

He grinned and looked pleased. "I prepped yesterday since today was absolute chaos."

Curiosity tugged at Kate, urging her forward to the tantalizing aroma wafting from an antique soup tureen in the center of the table.

"Peek?" she asked, unable to resist.

As he nodded, Kate carefully lifted the lid, a wisp of cool air carrying the scent of fresh vegetables tickling her nose. She gasped. Nestled within the chilled bowl, the gazpacho glowed a vibrant red, like a sunset captured in summer's heart. Her initial surprise melted into pure delight as she leaned closer, inhaling the intoxicating aroma of sun-ripened tomatoes, crisp cucumbers, and a hint of peppery spice.

Her voice was filled with awe. "Incredible."

A smile crinkled the corner of his mouth. "One of my clients brought me fresh tomatoes and cucs from his garden. We should dig in before the magic fades."

Luke held the chair as she tucked in before settling next to her. He ladled soup into her bowl and passed a basket of blueberry muffins. Kate sank into the bread, its taste sliding over her tongue and waking childhood memories. "Sweet and fruity! Like the panettone my Nonna used to make at Christmas."

A soft smile tugged at Kate's lips as the memory surfaced. "Nonna's panettone," she began, her voice softening with nostalgia, "was legendary. A tall, golden slice of heaven." Her eyes drifted upwards, lost in recollection. "But she never wrote down her recipe. Just tossed everything together until it was perfect."

Luke nodded. "Sounds like she was a discovery baker just like me." He leaned back in his chair and his eyes danced with excitement. "Creating something beautiful. Something to share. It's not just about the food, is it? It's the memories, the love, the tradition that gets passed down."

"That's exactly right!" Kate said, pausing to savor another taste of the muffin. It was like being transported back to her grandmother's kitchen, watching her Christmas baking.

"Mom and Aunt Theresa have come close to recreating Nonna's bread, but they've never captured the magic. Nonna's was truly special."

The flickering candlelight cast playful shadows across Luke's face, softening the sharp planes of his jawline and highlighting the inviting dimple in his chin. As his smile met hers, a knot of butterflies erupted in her stomach, their wings fluttering wildly as his gaze held hers. His generosity and understanding of her deep-rooted family ties were adding another layer to her growing affection for him.

"Why on earth are you still single?" The words slipped out before she could stop them.

He barked out a laugh, a rich, unexpected sound. "Panettone to my love life? Interesting transition."

She made a face. "Well, it's true, though. You're kind, you cook like a dream—you've got everything women want!"

He shrugged, a small imperceptible movement. "Many have tried," he admitted, his voice low. "But I never found one who wanted the same things I did. They always demanded more than I had to give."

Kate felt a pang of empathy, aware of the vulnerability in his words. "Well, then, we won't dwell on the old memories," she said gently, raising her glass. "Here's to a successful donor dinner and you, the perfect planning partner."

He met her gesture, his voice warm, as they clinked glasses. "You were a dynamo, Kate! To Founders Day and our collaboration."

"Speaking of collaboration," Kate said, ladling up her soup, "how'd the toy sea turtle sale turn out?"

He gave her a mock salute. "You were right. We sold out and added hundreds more names to the petition. That puts us in a solid position for the public hearing in two weeks."

Kate absently picked at the napkin folded on her lap. "I don't care so much about being right, but I am glad you had a great turnout," she said, chewing the bottom corner of her lip as she recalled her conversation with Clayton Pruitt.

"I know that look," he said, calling her out. "You do that bitey thing and stare into space, right before you say something difficult. Your turn to tell."

"It might be against turtle team rules. It involves he-who-must-not-be-named."

Luke put down his spoon and crossed his arms in mock seriousness. "We're beyond turtle team rules, so out with it."

She plunged ahead. "Okay. You heard our caterer canceled last minute?"

He nodded, his eyes locked on her, waiting. "Of course."

"And that Clayton donated the oysters?" she asked.

Even in the candlelight, she saw the flint returning to his eyes. "Yes. He stopped me at Founders Day to make sure I knew about his magnanimous gift. What else?" Luke asked, knowing there was more.

"When I talked to Clayton this evening, I got the impression he's hardening his stance on the Point after seeing the surge in petition activity. I think he's concerned that public opinion is shifting in your favor, and he's ready to play hardball."

She watched the muscles in Luke's jaws tensing as he considered her words. "Nothing Pruitt does surprises me," he started slowly. "We'll fight harder."

An idea had been percolating since Kate danced with Clayton, a way to beat him at his own game. Kate reached for Luke's hand, her grip firm. She watched him, looking for signs he was ready to listen.

"You are so talented!" she said earnestly. "No matter what Clayton tries, you can make the Point into something incredible that the city council can't resist. Imagine it—turning the Point into a place where people can come to reconnect with nature, relax, and experience something truly extraordinary."

Luke laced his fingers with hers, his eyes searching her face for understanding. "What are you suggesting?"

She leaned forward, her excitement growing. "I'm thinking something like…an incredible coastal nature park designed by you. One that would be safe from future development."

Luke's expression softened as he imagined the possibilities. "You know what? I think you might be onto something, Kate. We make the Point into a sanctuary for both the community and the environment. It will be a place where people can experience nature while we protect the coast at the same time."

She set down her spoon and leaned back in her chair, running out of ideas and energy after a long day. "I want to hear more of your ideas for a coastal park. But honestly, right now, my mind is fried, and my feet are killing me."

"Hmm. I might help. When's the last time you had a foot massage?"

She reached down to rub her ankle. "At least a million years ago," she said ruefully.

A sly grin rippled across his face. "In that case, finish your soup and meet me on the sofa."

KATE AWOKE TO THE SMELL OF DOGGIE BREATH AND small paws prancing on her stomach as sunlight flooded her face. "Ugh, Boo, you need a breath mint," she said, plopping the dog to the floor.

It took a moment before Kate remembered why she was sleeping on Luke's couch. Last night, Luke's sturdy fingertips had moved across her skin like gentle waves, slowly lapping against her foot and coaxing out tension. Her body sank into the plush cushions beneath her, and a wave of pleasure swept through her body with each stroke.

His tender caress was like nothing she'd ever felt. She had relaxed, her eyes flickering shut as he worked his way up her calf, gently kneading away stress with each stroke. His touch spoke of care, tenderness, and love as it lulled her into a state of bliss and deep, restful sleep.

Still relaxed and lazy, she snuggled under the blanket Luke had covered her with. It carried his scent of bergamot, sunshine...and waffles?

She followed the yeasty aroma to the kitchen, where Luke was at the waffle iron, pouring batter with a practiced twist. "Cooking breakfast for us now?" Kate asked, resting her head against his back and her palms rubbing his shoulders as he worked.

He turned to her. "Hey, sleepyhead. Of course."

"I quite like that," she said, turning and standing on tiptoes to kiss him. Their lips moved together gently as if they were always meant to be touching, and warmth floated through her body.

"Good morning," he murmured in her ear when their embrace ended.

"Mmmm. You're an angel not to mind my morning mouth," she teased, pressing butterfly kisses on his shoulders.

He nuzzled her neck. "I'll take your morning mouth any time you kiss me like that."

"Deal," she said with a laugh. "But I think your waffles are burning."

"You're such a distraction," he said good-naturedly, releasing her to save breakfast.

Moments later, carrying plates loaded with golden waffles, they settled next to each other on Luke's porch. Kate squinted at the morning sun as it winked over the dunes to heat the day. She stabbed her first forkful.

"You put chocolate chips in the batter!" she said, her eyes widening as she chewed.

"You like?"

"No, I *love* it! But we should outlaw them for causing strong women to swoon!"

Kate's heart melted as Luke broke into his lopsided grin. She loved the way he smiled when he was happy. She wanted to freeze this perfect moment and carry it in her heart always. But she knew she would leave Gull Island soon, and her heart shredded, thinking about missing moments like this.

Luke tilted his head, a glint of mischief in his eyes. "Maybe we should make this a regular weekend tradition for the rest of the summer." His voice lilted, teasing at the edges.

Her heart did cartwheels at the thought of spending more time with him. "Waffles and foot massages?"

His voice was gentle and inviting. "Yeah, why not? It could be our thing."

She leaned over and kissed him, a sweet and lingering kiss that made her forget all about leaving.

Chapter Thirty-Eight

KATE

The air in the high-school gym crackled with dissent, a cacophony of voices rising above the stale smell of adolescent sweat. Kate's heart echoed the escalating tension as she scanned the crowd, searching for Luke's calm presence. His proposal for the Point was about to begin, and its future hinged on his success.

"Mae, the gym's already packed!" Kate said, sweat prickling her neck as she navigated the bleachers, weaving through overflow chairs that spilled onto the court.

Decked out in Save Our Shore's signature red, Mae boomed over the din, her hands clasping Kate's shoulder. "SOS is here, and we're in it to win it."

A defiant chant ripped through the air. "SOS! SOS!" Cardboard fists, emblazoned with the words *Keep the Sand; Kick the Concrete* bobbled in the air as Kate squeezed through the throng.

Clayton Pruitt, all charm and gleaming teeth, reigned from the front and center of the overflow crowd, representing the antithesis of everything SOS stood for. Savannah Scott, shimmering like a Christmas ornament in a clinging lavender jumpsuit, draped herself next to him.

Kate's heart clenched until she spotted Luke, radiating composure, a few chairs away. His confidence seeped into her, unraveling the knots in her gut. She slipped beside him, drawing strength from his quiet certainty.

"Smart, handsome, and chill," she murmured, planting a playful kiss on his cheek. "You've got this, Lucas McAllister!"

He grinned, a warm, wide smile just for her. "Thanks. I feel good. Even better now that you're here." He squeezed her hand and turned to Mae.

"Max?" he asked, a furrow etching his brow, a silent question that Kate didn't understand.

Mae raised a hand, fingers crossed. "On his way."

Unable to contain her curiosity, Kate called over the roar. "What's up with Max?"

Mae's blue eyes flashed with mischief. "He's got a trick up his sleeve... if he makes it here in time. Be patient, hon, and don't fret."

Kate reached for Luke's hand, her fingers twisting into his like a vine seeking sunlight. The gentle pressure of his fingers against hers was a physical anchor, grounding her and quieting the storm roiling inside her.

Silence hushed the gym as Mayor Livingston and the council marched in. The crowd, a sea of expectant faces, buzzed with excitement as the hearing was about to begin. Kate's leg twitched under the hard steel chair, an outside manifestation of her churning stomach.

The mayor's procedural dronings faded the moment Clayton

Pruitt took the stage. Pruitt's voice, smooth as oiled gears, boomed, "The development at the Point unlocks our town's future!"

A video flickered to life, painting the gym with images of luxury condos nestled against a cerulean beach. Infinity pools shimmered, landscaped gardens and pickleball courts promised paradise. Kate swallowed the urge to ooh and ahh.

Pruitt's smile widened. "Concerned about the environment? We'll build green and partner with local agencies. Minimal impact, maximum benefit."

He paused, eyes scanning the red-clad SOS protesters, and then he rallied. "This project means jobs, tax revenue, and a revitalized economy. We will develop the Point responsibly, for the community, for the planet. Let's embrace this opportunity!"

Pruitt stiffened as a red tide of dissent rippled through the crowd. Battle lines were drawn, and the Point hung in the crosshairs.

The mayor's gavel rapped again, a summons for public comments. The air crackled with anticipation, divided between the fiery SOS supporters and the expectant glint of those keen for condos. Then Luke stood, his voice, a deep, clear baritone, cutting through the noise.

"I'm here for SOS, Save Our Shore," he said, a playful glint in his eyes. "Maybe you've seen our red ribbons around town?"

A chuckle, then a wave of laughter, broke the tension. Kate, seated near the back, pumped her fist in the air, a silent cheer for Luke.

"We believe the Point belongs to all of us, not a select few." His voice dipped, weaving a picture with each word. "For over a year, we've fought for this island treasure. Instead of luxury condominiums for the privileged, imagine a nature park and education center, teeming with life, where children can play on the sand, where families picnic, and where ocean waves and maritime life flourish undisturbed for generations."

He gestured, and the screen behind him flickered to life. An untouched beach, pristine and sun-drenched, gave way to families strolling along nature trails as vibrant marine animals danced on the screen. Then, a gasp. A 3-D model of the proposed park, lush and alive, filled the gym.

Applause erupted as Luke sat. Kate, tears brimming in her eyes, launched herself at him. "I'm so proud of you," she whispered into the depths of his chest.

"And I'm grateful to you," he murmured, his hand finding her cheek, tracing the curve of her jaw with a tenderness that sent another tremor through her. "You were the one who planted the seed for the park idea, remember?"

Mayor Livingston's gavel shattered their moment. "Final comments?"

Luke exchanged a silent look at Mae, her eyes wide with urgency.

"Madam Mayor," he said, his voice firm, "we're waiting on a vital piece of information that will impact our cause. We need a few more minutes."

Clayton sprang up, his face contorted with fury. "This is a stalling tactic," he roared over the growing murmur of the crowd. "I urge the council to vote now."

The gym tilted on its axis, a ripple of unease spreading through the rows. But Mae, unflinching, stood and met Pruitt's fire with a level gaze. Her calm voice sliced through the friction in the air.

"We're not stalling, Clayton. We're fighting for the future of our island. And we want to hear the truth."

Applause erupted again, punctuated with cheers and jeers as the room plunged into a riot of divided opinion. The noise dialed back abruptly as the doors flew open, Max Lawson striding in like a force of nature. Clutching documents, he sliced through the stunned silence, his voice a whip-crack of urgency.

"Madam Mayor," Max called out, "I have something that might guide the council's decision."

The room, jolted by the sudden shift, crackled with anticipation. Mae leaned towards Kate, a whisper curling from her lips. "Told you patience would be rewarded."

Max, mopping his brow with a white handkerchief, launched into his revelation.

"I just returned from the state archives in Raleigh," he said, his voice regaining its steady rhythm. "In a 1929 *Raleigh Herald* article, I discovered something about the original owner of the Point property and the area adjacent to its public beach."

Max strode to the council table, arms laden with copies of the article. He stepped to each of the seated members, one by one, setting papers in front of them before resuming.

"The owner of the land wanted to donate his land to Gull Island, for everyone in the community to enjoy in perpetuity. But he died before he made his wishes legally binding, so they were lost... until now."

Pruitt leaped to his feet, voice booming through the room like a thunderclap. "That doesn't mean a thing!" he said, stomping his foot on the floor. "It's an expression of will, not a proper contract. The condo project can still move forward!"

Luke met Pruitt's gaze, his face cool and unflustered. "You are correct, Clayton. This may not be a binding document, but it shows a commitment to uphold our town's tradition of keeping the Point open for everyone, as the original owner intended."

The room fell silent as the audience considered the implications of Luke's words. Finally, Mayor Livingston spoke.

"It appears we have a new angle to consider. Thank you, Mr. Lawson, for bringing it to our attention."

Kate perched on the edge of the creaky folding chair, her fingers digging into Luke's palm. Minutes stretched into an eternity as council members huddled over documents, their murmured exchanges muffled by the tension buzzing through the gym. Every rustle of paper, and every furrowed brow felt like a hammer blow to her already frayed nerves. Had they seen the photos of laughing children on the beach and learning in the education center? Had the passionate pleas of SOS resonated across the sweat-stained floors of the gymnasium?

Finally, the mayor cleared her throat, her gaze holding the weight of every hopeful whisper and silent prayer.

"We've heard your voices, weighed your arguments, and grappled with the future of this island. It's time to vote."

Kate's breath hitched, a silent plea escaping her lips. Everything hung in the balance, the fate of the Point teetering on the edge of a single vote.

The votes trickled in, an agonizingly slow drip-drop of approval and dissent. Three for the park, three for the condos. Despair gnawed at Kate's edges, but then, a ray of hope.

The mayor leaned forward in her chair, her gaze sweeping across the room. "After listening to all sides of this debate, I have reached a decision. I believe the original intent of the property owner was to preserve the Point for the community, and I cannot ignore that. Therefore, I am casting my tie-breaking vote in favor of exploring the Point as a nature park."

The room exploded. Cheers erupted like a tidal wave, washing over the stunned silence. SOS supporters, faces flushed with joy, leaped to their feet, their roar a victory anthem.

Relief washed over Kate. Tears of relief mingled with laughter as a sob escaped her lips, and she threw her arms around Luke, burying her face in his chest.

"You did it, Luke!"

"No," he said, raising his voice over the shouts of jubilation. "We did it. Mae, Max, the SOS team. And you, with your ideas for the park that inspired my design."

He was about to say more when well-wishers descended on him. Kate stepped aside, allowing him this moment of triumph. Her eyes darted through the crowd, landing on Max. A wide smile bloomed across her face when she reached him, her hands flying to his shoulders, squeezing tight.

"Max! You legend! That document... Wow. You're a lifesaver!"

His face lit up, bowtie askew, a casualty of the celebration. He patted her hand, a hint of awe in his voice. "The Point needed its voice, Kate. Just happy I could be a part of it."

Mae planted a jubilant kiss on Max's cheek next as he blushed, sending his bowtie twirling even more. Straightening, he nudged Mae playfully. "My dear, I believe a party is in order."

Mae's eyes twinkled. "A mere party? Bah! We're throwing us a good old-fashioned cookout and beach blast at Gray Cottage!"

Chapter Thirty-Nine

KATE

Days later, the Point victory shimmered like a miracle, but the looming tide of departure had drowned its triumph. The HR recruiter's conversation this morning, voice honeyed with words of "corner offices" and "Connecticut," still sang in Kate's ear. It was a siren call, sweet with the opportunity to return to her family and roots. But now it was choked by a conflicting longing.

Luke's face engrained into her memory, his laugh echoing in her dreams, the perfect fit of his hand in hers. Leaving had always been part of her plan, the finale haunting summer's end. But Gull Island, with its unexpected gift of friendship and connections, had woven roots around her heart. Now, the promises of her dream job had started the countdown clock.

Tonight, at Mae's moonlit celebration, she'd tell Luke. One last dance before the miles between them stretched, long and merciless.

BONFIRE SPARKS FROM THE BEACH SWIRLED LIKE fireflies against the twilight sky. Music thrummed, laughter fizzed like champagne, and the sunset bled its final lazy hues. But all Kate heard was the hollow whispers of goodbye protesting in her mind as she hurried over her small yard to Gray Cottage.

Across the patio, Luke's gaze caught hers, his Solo cup clenched in his hand. The intensity in his eyes was a lighthouse beam in the gathering dusk, pulling her in as thoughts of leaving pushed her away.

Around him, boisterous SOS volunteers were still buzzing with their Point victory. Steve Somebody (his last name a permanent mystery, but he had family in Kate's hometown) boomed the loudest. His voice, warm as Carolina molasses and thick with excitement, cut through the music and laughter.

"Hey, Kate! Just telling Luke how bigwigs are scooping up your talent," he said, clapping her on the back. His grin, brighter than the tiki lights, dimmed under Luke's intense stare. Steve, sensing a brewing disturbance, dissolved into the crowd, leaving Kate and Luke adrift in a sea of uncertainty.

The knot in Kate's stomach tightened as Luke's face crumpled. "A September start?" he rasped, his voice raw.

"Not official," she stammered. "No offer letter, but yes. I was going to tell you tonight, but—"

The catchy beat of "Carolina Girl" weaving through the speakers cut her off, calling everyone to dance.

The air, thick with unspoken fears and desires, threatened to choke them. Luke shifted. His hand, hesitant, reached out, bridging the chasm that had opened between them. With a tremor in her breath and a flicker of something raw in his eyes, their fingers entwined, a wordless offering between them.

"We need to talk, Kate," he said, his mouth set tight. "But first," he led her into the crush of dancers, "we celebrate like everyone expects."

Their steps were hesitant, mirroring doubts that lingered. But as they danced, a subtle shift occurred. Their bodies moved in sync with the music, as they had practiced, but Luke moved rigidly, a frown creasing his brow.

The warmth that usually filled his eyes was replaced by a flicker of sadness, then a spark of anger that died down almost as quickly. Was that acceptance, too, lurking beneath the surface? Kate ached with a similar mix of emotions—a cocktail of regret, defiance, and a sliver of hope clinging on for dear life.

THE SWEET SCENT OF THE OLEANDER AND A BRINY breeze filled the air by the time most guests said their goodbyes and Kate led Luke across the lawn. The moon shone down on them, its silvery glow highlighting the delicate fairy lights suspended above Kate's patio. Remnants of Mae's cookout, a mix of grilled seafood and fragrant herbs, wafted through from Gray Cottage.

Kate slipped off her shoes and settled across from him at her tiny bistro table. She picked at the hem of her dress, her breath catching in her throat as she struggled for words. While she yearned for familiar places and the closeness of family in Connecticut, she felt a sense of loss when she thought of leaving her found family on Gull Island. Mostly, though, it was Luke who made her heart ache with a mixture of joy and sadness. She'd only known him for a short time, but she already cared deeply for him.

"Luke, about the offer," she began. Her words tumbled out in a rush of excitement and worry, pleading with him to understand.

He watched her, curiosity and concern swirling in those cold blue-gray eyes.

"The call took me by surprise," she explained. "The interview happened months ago before CeCe called about the contract here. Honestly, I had forgotten all about it."

Laughter drifted by from guests lingering at Mae's party, but the peaceful moonlight seemed to crackle with sudden tension. Finally, he spoke, his hands tightened into fists at his side.

"What hurts, Kate..." he started, his voice raw and low. "What hurts is that I heard it from somebody else."

Kate winced, her eyes revealing the pain his words inflicted. She hadn't meant to hurt him. Fingers twisting the chain of her silver necklace, she took a long exhale before explaining, pleading with him to understand.

"Tonight was the first time we could talk," Kate confessed, her voice tinged with regret. "I never expected some guy bizarrely connected to the company would tell you before I could." Her gaze darted to Luke, searching his face for a flicker of anger, but finding only sadness. "I'm so sorry."

The metallic clang of his drumming fingers on the table echoed the frantic rhythm of Kate's heart. His eyes followed a moth's erratic dance among the fairy lights, its desperate ballet mirroring the conflict gnawing at her.

"So," he spoke at last, his voice a low rumble and his gaze locked on hers, "how do you feel about all this?" His question hung heavy in the air, a plea for honesty.

The corner office, a glittering symbol of success, shimmered in her mind. Visions of her family's proud smiles swam in and out, a stark contrast to the tears threatening to spill from her eyes. This opportunity was everything she'd ever strived for, the culmination of countless sacrifices. But the thought of leaving Luke, of this unexpected haven she found, sent a tsunami of despair slamming into her.

"I... I have to take it," she whispered, the words tasting flat on her tongue.

A wave of pain crossed his eyes before he masked it with a small smile and a nod. "I know how much it means to you," he said, his voice genuine, warm. "And if this is your dream...then I'm happy for you."

"Leaving this place..." Kate choked back a sob. "Leaving you..." Her words ripped the air, a confession in the quiet night.

Luke reached for a strand of her hair, caressing it between his fingertips. She leaned into the comfort of his touch. "I've never been happier than I have been with you this summer. But my life isn't here."

Across the wrought-iron table, Luke's silhouette was etched against the silvered light, his broad shoulders slumped. His voice, a fragile thread in the stillness, offered a lifeline. "Maybe... maybe we could find a way, even apart."

The words hung in the space, delicate notes against the chorus of crickets and frogs. But reality, harsh and unforgiving, gripped Kate. The miles stretched between them like an endless chasm, threatening to wash away any connection they built. A sob, choked and raw, escaped her lips. She wasn't sure if it was a lament for the future they might never have or a prayer for a miracle.

A ragged breath hitched in her throat. "Long distance..." she began, her voice rough with emotion. "Even living with Jon didn't work. How can this work?"

The last word came out in a shaky whisper, a tear tracing a path down her cheek as the weight of past failures pressed down on her.

Luke's smile, which had been hopeful moments ago, faltered. A muscle ticked in his jaw, and his hand, which had been tapping a nervous rhythm on the table, balled into a fist. His voice, when he spoke, was a rasp. "So...what does that mean, Kate?"

The corner of Kate's mouth twitched, a sad attempt at a smile. It never reached her eyes, which glistened with unshed tears. A choked sob escaped her throat as she forced the words out, each one scraping against the raw ache in her chest.

"We make the most of the time we have left." Her voice cracked, the future a daunting expanse stretching before her. "And then..." Closing her eyes, she steeled herself and whispered, "We get on with our lives."

Luke's jaw tensed even tighter. He listened, his body taut with unspoken emotion. "Is that what you want, Kate?"

His voice was a mere thread, the raw pain in his eyes matching the ache in her heart. She couldn't bring herself to meet the torment she saw on his face.

"Yes," she breathed, the word a surrender, her shoulders slumping under the weight of their inevitable goodbye.

The moon disappeared behind a blanket of clouds, dimming the darkness even more. He turned to Kate with a forced smile and swallowed hard, his voice breaking as he spoke.

"I get it," he whispered. "No forever promises, just a borrowed summer. I'll wish you the best, Kate, but I'm not good at goodbyes."

She leaned close, brushing a feather-light kiss against his cheek. It was a tacit acknowledgment that the end of summer was closing in. A tear escaped, streaking a salty path down her face. The thought of life without Luke was an ache she hadn't known existed. But the promise of new beginnings called to her, and it was time to let go.

Her fingers, restless with unspoken farewells, traced the freckles on his arm, a familiar constellation. His skin was cold against hers, the unexpected chill like the sadness hanging between them in the balmy night. His eyes, pools of molten gray, held hers as his hand covered hers, grounding her against the pain of goodbyes.

Moonlight painted the world in silver, erasing everything but their silhouettes and the looming shadow of her departure. In the hushed space between breaths, a single thread of hope flickered, defying the darkness. They had these last few weeks of summer, a bittersweet gift before their worlds parted.

Chapter Forty

KATE

Morning sun cast its golden light on the bay as Kate waited for Luke at the boat launch. A kayaker glided by, dipping an oar in greeting. It was early enough to beat the grueling August heat, but Gull Island humidity made the air feel like breathing through a cloud of cotton. Kate squinted at Carrot Island, a long stretch of stunted trees and shrubs lounging a quarter mile offshore. A flock of seagulls screeched overhead, eyeing the white chocolate baguette Kate had brought for the trip.

"Hah! No chance, birdies," she called out to them, clutching the bread tighter. "This is for Luke and me."

She heard the familiar rumble of an engine and spotted Luke pointing his truck to the launch ramp. He parked and embraced her with a tight hug, looking delicious in a rash guard shirt that rippled over his board shorts.

"Hey there," she said, leaning into him.

"I see you're ready," he said, popping the piece of bread she offered into his mouth.

She pointed to her stash. "Yep. Towel, water bottle, and bug spray. Plus, swimsuit underneath."

He gave a mock salute. "Let the adventure begin."

Kate settled into the back of the double kayak. "You realize we're paddling to an uninhabited island without running water or toilets," she said, as they pushed off into the pristine blue-green waters of the bay. "That's enough adventure for me."

He laughed, calling back to her over his shoulder. "No worries. It's a Kate-sized adventure. A mere ten-minute paddle to a beautiful natural area. No alligators or venomous snakes."

"Good to know," she said, distracted by his muscles rippling under his tight rash guard shirt as he dipped his paddle in the water.

As they drifted closer to Carrot Island, Kate spotted a trio of wild horses grazing contentedly in the grass. The animals were close enough to make out their golden coats and shaggy manes with a white blaze. They watched the kayak with mild curiosity before returning to graze.

"They're beautiful," Kate said, staring at the animals as they paddled past.

"We have a few here. More on Shackleford Banks over on Cape Lookout. If you had time, I'd take you there."

And there it was.

Kate was leaving Gull Island. Next week, she'd be in Black Rock with her family and starting her new job after Labor Day. Her stomach clenched. There wouldn't be more exploring special places with Luke. She felt the sorrow nestling in her chest like an unrelenting cold. She told herself it was better to part ways when summer ended. Her brain got the message. Why wasn't her heart getting the same message?

She wondered how Luke felt about their parting. Sometimes, she caught him gazing at her with the saddest expression on his face, but he'd said only that she should stick to her plans. Was he indifferent because theirs had only been a summer romance? Or was he freeing her up to follow her dreams? She wasn't sure. Anyway, he deserved to pursue his own life, too. But when she thought about being away from him, an unbearable pain threatened to strangle her insides.

Luke broke into her thoughts. "Here we are," he called, nodding towards an alcove of white creamy-colored sand.

"Ahhh, the Carrot Island welcoming committee!" Kate groaned, swatting at a mosquito buzzing around her head.

She hopped out of the kayak, the sand warm and inviting beneath her feet.

"This is incredible!" she said, taking in the pristine, sun-soaked beach they had all to themselves.

"Wait until you explore the trail," he said, gesturing to the narrow path meandering through the trees. "If we're lucky, we'll spot more wild horses along the way."

As the sun rose higher, they made their way along the island's meandering trail. They dodged prickly pear cactus and occasional piles of horse poo, evidence of equine residents. Crystal-clear waters sparkled in the sunlight, and a pod of dolphins played nearby. A flock of brown pelicans soared overhead. The only sounds were the lapping waves and their feet crunching on the gravel trail. Luke's face was lit with the wonder of nature surrounding him, and she sensed how much he loved it here—how much he loved sharing it with her.

Batting at the sweat on her neck, she turned to him. "Hey, where's that swimming hole you told me about?"

He pointed to the quiet waters in front of them. "Your private swimming pool awaits," he said, smiling with that chin dimple like an exquisite exclamation mark that made her stomach flip.

"Last one in and all that," she teased, racing him into the water.

LUKE

LUKE BRUSHED SAND OFF THE BLANKET, UNABLE TO tear his gaze away from Kate's sun-kissed skin and cascading dark hair. Like a classic old Mutabilis rose, she had unfurled this summer, shifting from soft pastels to vibrant hues, growing more beautiful and precious to him every day. She sat next to him, her voice soft and melodic as she talked about her childhood in Connecticut.

"Black Rock waters are always chilly. Nothing like the warm ocean here," she said. Her eyes danced as she recounted swimming at the city beach as kids with her cousin Jimmy. "We'd swim until our teeth chattered and our lips turned blue, but our parents still had to drag us out!"

Her hands moved in a constant dance as she spoke, and the soft staccato of her voice—a voice he once found grating—now underscored her vivacity and quick wit.

He noticed telltale patches of red on her back that preceded a sunburn, and he tossed Kate her T-shirt. "Better put this on. Sun's brutal."

She tugged on a shirt. "And you," she said, throwing him his rash guard.

"I'm tough," he protested, but he took the shirt on when she side-eyed him with a look that rivaled his mother's.

Luke snaked an arm around her waist, and she leaned into him, her head on his shoulder. They settled into a companionable silence, broken only by the slap of waves against the shoreline and the shrill cries of seagulls gliding overhead.

The sand beneath Luke's bare feet felt like a thousand tiny needles as he held Kate close, the warmth of her body a stark contrast to the icy dread that gripped his heart. Being with Kate was effortless, a haven he hadn't realized he needed. Their bond had grown deeper over the summer, and the thought of losing it, their private world dissolving, filled him with an unfamiliar dread.

He wouldn't only miss the way she ate his french fries, but the scent of her lemon-verbena shampoo and the way she loved to cuddle. Even the way she talked to Boo had become endearing in a way he couldn't explain. He cared for her deeply, more than he'd ever let on, and he felt like his heart might crack down the middle when their summer bubble ended.

The air was heavy with feelings left unsaid, clinging to them like the sand that sprinkled Kate's skin. Luke reached into the picnic basket, fingers brushing against the worn wicker in a nervous dance. He pulled out a slice of peach, its blush reflecting the morning light. His hand trembled slightly as he held it up to her.

"A last taste of summer," he said, his voice husky.

She smiled, a soft, bittersweet curve. "Spoiling me rotten, are you?" Her lips dipped into the fruit, juice dripping down her chin like a stolen kiss.

His gaze traced the arc of her jaw and then cupped her face, a grit of sand there a tactile reminder of the beach, of their stolen time. His thumb brushed away a tear, salt mingling with the sweetness of the peach on his skin.

"Every second," he whispered, the words tumbling out before he could hold them back. "I'll spoil you every second... for as long as you're here."

Those words hung between them, bridging the fragile gap between their silent wants and the reality ahead.

Her brows knit together and she grew serious, straightening to face him. "I'm torn. My family and job are in Connecticut, but my time on Gull Island with you..." she trailed off, unable to finish.

Luke stayed silent, giving her time, but he nodded in acknowledgment when she asked, "If I stayed, what kind of life would it be here for me?"

A spark of hope ignited in him. "There are good things about living here," he said. "The people in the community, the friends you've made, our lifestyle."

She took a long breath, her fingers twisting nervously in the sand. "And what about my family?" she asked, her voice barely above a whisper. The image of her parents and cousins at Sunday suppers flashed through her mind. "My career? All the long hours, the sacrifices I made...?"

Luke's mind traveled back to the times he sacrificed his dreams and ambitions to keep the family business afloat, and he understood. He also knew leaving Gull Island would never be an option for him. Just like staying here with him, giving up her career and her family in Black Rock wasn't an option for Kate.

"I get that," he whispered. His heart yearned for her to stay, but he couldn't ignore the truth of what she'd said.

"Maybe," she began, her voice trailing off as the sunlight glinted off the water. She hesitated, her gaze caught between the endless blue horizon and Luke's intense eyes. "Maybe it's better if we treat our time together like a summer fling."

Her words were heavy in the air. The only sound was the rhythmic crash of waves against the shore. Kate's words seemed to echo in the silence of the lapping waves, each syllable a blow to his heart. Luke's jaw clenched, his fingers tightening on the picnic basket strap. He averted his eyes, a tear threatening before he quickly blinked it away.

"Kate, this is not a fling," he said, his voice rough with emotion. "You know that." His heart twisted at her words, mirroring his doubts and fears.

Her hand hovered near his, fingers hesitant and trembling. She leaned in slightly, then pulled back, as if unable to bridge the gap. Her voice hitched, barely a whisper in the wind.

"No, not a fling, but then what? Goodbye is too final, and anything else feels like we're betraying ourselves."

She took a breath, each syllable measured. "I think it's best when we say goodbye ..." She stopped, swallowed by the vast unsaid future. "It's best when I leave to end things while we still have good memories. A clean break is easier."

He wanted to argue, to keep her with him against all odds. Instead, he simply rasped out, "I'll miss you, Kate."

His hand drifted up her arm, brushing against silky skin until it reached her shoulder. There, he paused, thumb caressing the delicate hollow beneath her collarbone, a silent plea to stop time.

Kate leaned into the touch, a single choked sob escaping her lips as she burrowed into his chest. "And I'll miss you."

The muscles in his jaw tensed and flexed as he struggled to

contain his emotions. “I wish you could stay, Kate, but I won’t hold you back.”

His usually calm gaze wavered with a mix of longing and resignation as he held her. A single bead of sweat trickled down his temple, catching the sunlight like a tiny teardrop.

Chapter Forty-One

KATE

The asphalt on Island Drive shimmered in the relentless morning sun, the air smelling of sunbaked sand and brine. The ocean breeze whipped around, but it couldn't cool the knot of grief in Kate's stomach as she walked along the familiar path to the aquarium for the last time.

Gull Island, once a blur of unfamiliar faces and oppressive heat, now called to her—sunsets over the ocean, children's laughter at the touch tank, and the fierce determination of sea turtle hatchlings' ocean quest. Each memory held a bittersweet ache, a reminder of what she was leaving behind.

She quickened her pace as she entered the aquarium, her footsteps echoing in the empty silence of the office. The smell of stale coffee hung heavy in the air. A lone chair creaked in the distance, a phantom echo of laughter that had once filled this space. Maybe she missed the staff meeting memo in the chaos of packing up. Setting down her bag, she made her way to the breakroom. When she opened the door, she discovered where everyone had gone.

Kate's smile stretched tight, a delicate shield against the warmth blooming in her chest. The break room, transformed into a festive wonderland with balloons and streamers, buzzed with joy. Her colleagues gathered around a table, proudly revealing a cake adorned with velvety icing topped with frosted dolphins and sea turtles, the words *Happy Farewell Day, Kate!* gracing its surface.

"You guys!" Tears burned behind her eyelids, contrasting with the warmth of embraces. "You're too much."

Laughter filled the sun-drenched room, tinged with bittersweet goodbyes. Familiar faces gathered around the towering chocolate and coconut cake, symbols of endings and new beginnings. Mae Gray, surrounded by volunteers who shared her passion for sea turtle rescue. Liz and Jerome Wilson, whose enthusiasm guided visitors through the island's secrets. Tour guides, visitor center staff, and Chef with her team were all woven into the fabric of the place. In that room, the island lived on through shared experiences and deep connections.

But one face was missing. Luke's absence left an ache in her soul.

Then, warmth engulfed her. CeCe's arms crushed Kate in a tight hug. "Thank you," Kate choked out, her voice thick with tears. "For everything." CeCe's response was a squeeze of her hand, a promise of unwavering friendship etched in the silent gesture.

But before questions about Luke's absence could surface, Liz Wilson stepped forward, a mischievous glint in her eyes. She held out a bulging gift bag, its white tissue paper cascading down. "We wanted to give you a few things," she said, her voice warm with affection, "to help you remember us."

Kate gingerly retrieved each item from the bottomless bag, her eyes widening in delight at each. The first was a sea-blue ceramic mug painted with a flock of seagulls and bearing the phrase *Dive into Marketing.*

"For your new marketing job," Liz said, clasping her hand on Kate's back.

Jerome pointed to the small white slip of paper tucked inside the mug. "And you have my special recipe for coffee affogato," he said, "so you can sip and think of us."

Kate laughed, a joyful sound tinged with an overtone of sadness. "As if I could ever forget any of you!"

Next, she held up an inflatable pool float shaped like a sea turtle. "To remember your days on the turtle team," Mae said, clapping her hands like the excited young-at-heart sexagenarian Kate loved. "And a sea turtle stuffy for your little cousin," Mae added, handing her another package.

"I'll wear the float next time I swim," Kate promised. "And Angie will adore her turtle toy."

Chef presented her with a large cloth sack tied with a ribbon filled with the aquarium's french fry seasoning. "I don't share my recipe with everybody," Chef said, smiling in her white jacket, her dark curls bobbing and free of their headband. "I hope it reminds you of the power of creativity and teamwork, like the time we saved the donor banquet."

Kate took the sack, feeling its true weight in her hands. She looked at Chef, eyes brimming and a wide smile forming as she nodded. "I'll sprinkle some of your magic on my new adventures."

The last gift was a pair of silver binoculars engraved with the Gull Island logo. Kate lifted the exquisite lenses to examine them, the metal cool against her palm. "For you to see your way back to us," CeCe said.

Kate held them to her eyes for a moment to mask her crying. "Geez, y'all." Kate's laugh came out as a hiccup as she gulped back tears. "Now you've got me saying 'y'all,' but really, you're the best. Thank you for an incredible summer."

CeCe slipped her arm through Kate's and led her to a quiet corner as the crew surged forward for cake. "One more from David and me," she said, handing Kate a small gift bag.

A pang of emotion swept through Kate as she discovered the framed photo of her and Luke at the donor banquet. In the picture, his arm wrapped around her back as they swayed on the dance floor, lost in their own world. She could almost feel the strength of Luke's hand on her waist, pulling her closer, and his warm breath on her neck as they danced together.

Kate looked up, eyes misting. "How?"

CeCe slipped an arm around her friend. "David and that new camera he got to photograph the twins. We hope a happy memory will bring you back to us from time to time."

Kate dabbed away a tear as she gazed at the photo. These people, this island, had helped to heal her heart. Though she was leaving, part of her heart would remain with them. And Luke... Could she ever come back? Could she even bear to see Luke, knowing she'd leave him all over again?

KATE VISITED THE AQUARIUM EXHIBITS ONE LAST TIME that afternoon before she left. Her first stop was at the sea turtle rehab unit, where she found Flippy Junior floating serenely in his tank.

"I've come to say goodbye, Flippy," she cooed, bending low to see him. She tapped lightly on the cool glass, and Flippy swam closer as if sensing that she was leaving.

"You're a brave turtle. I hope you'll return to the ocean soon."

As if understanding her, Flippy raised a flipper and slowly blinked at her before bobbing away.

Kate made her way to the touch tank, where she greeted Mansour, the volunteer she met months ago on her first trip to the aquarium.

"Where's your biggest horseshoe crab?" she asked, glancing at the touch tank full of sea creatures.

Mansour pointed to the enormous lump lazing on the surface inside the glass enclosure. "That would be Boris."

Kate stared at the creature, and she could swear it winked as if daring her. Sucking in a breath, she stepped to the edge of the tank and slowly extended her index finger into the water by Boris' knobby shell.

Gritting her teeth, she brushed the top of the hard, clammy body for a full ten seconds before jerking her hand away and fist-pumping the air.

"Who's the bad boss lady now, Boris?" she crowed as Mansour congratulated her.

After facing Boris, Kate shut her office door, the marsh wind sighing like a goodbye. Sunlight glinted off the bay, like her first day, when she'd been a big-city know-it-all, secretly terrified of failing. The wind whispered of salt and adventure. Flip-flops replaced her heels, and her pockets brimmed with memories and a newfound love for this small corner of the world. As she gathered her things and turned towards her bungalow, the rhythm of the marsh was her farewell song.

She squared her shoulders and blinked back tears as she walked home, but her resolve plummeted when she found a small brown package waiting on the porch. Even before she ripped off the paper, she knew it was from Luke. He wouldn't be coming to see her. Not now, or in the morning—or ever again.

She couldn't stop the tears when she saw the small watercolor painting inside. Her eyes widened at the artist's signature. Luke had painted this? She knew he was talented, but this was something else. This was breathtaking.

The painting captivated her. The emerald ocean shimmered under dancing sunlight, each wave carved onto the canvas with such lifelike precision she could almost feel the sea-scented breeze on her skin. But then, her gaze snagged on a familiar form. *Boo!*

The dog sprawled on the walkway in his signature "waiting for Luke" pose, ears perked, tail hammering the deck like a joyous metronome. In that moment, the canvas dissolved, and she was there on the sun-drenched beach, Luke's hand warm in hers as Boo bounced between them, a furry ambassador of their shared joy.

She choked back sobs as she read the note inside written in Luke's familiar handwriting.

Kate, I'm not good with goodbyes, but I know I have to say it.

This summer has been one of the best times of my life, and it's all thanks to you. You made me laugh, you made me think in new ways, and you made me feel things I never thought I'd feel.

I know you'll be amazing at your new job.

You're smart, talented, and hardworking. I'm so proud of you!

I'll miss you, Kate. Thank you for our summer.

Take care of you.

Yours, Luke

Fresh tears welled up, blurring his words. But through them, a tiny knot loosened in her chest. The painting wasn't just a goodbye, it was a promise—a promise to hold onto the magic, the laughter, and the lazy afternoons spent with Luke. It was a reminder that even as she left, a piece of Gull Island, a piece of him, would travel with her.

With a shaky breath, she clutched the painting to her heart. The journey home might be laced with sadness, but the future stretched before her, a canvas waiting to be painted with new memories, ones tinged with the gentle light of Gull Island and the love she had found there.

October & November

500 MILES APART

"And all at once, summer collapsed into fall."

— OSCAR WILDE

Chapter Forty-Two

KATE

Crisp autumn air tickled Kate's face as her rake skittered over maple leaves in Dad's yard. There was nothing like an October in Connecticut. It was the perfect blend of blue sky and patchwork of crimson, gold, and auburn maple leaves.

Kate's thoughts swirled like the autumn wind, a mix of regret and longing. Two months had passed since she left Gull Island. CeCe FaceTimed about the twins, Mae wrote about the aquarium, and Annie sent notes from Dawson.

But Luke remained silent, and despite her best efforts, she couldn't shake him from her thoughts. Work kept her occupied during the day, but nights were the worst. He haunted her dreams, leaving her feeling empty when she woke.

Now, as she worked alongside her father, a small smile tugged at the corners of her lips. Their camaraderie was familiar, comforting. It was in the shared moments of family that she put aside her doubts and let her mind rest, just as she had when she was a child.

A breeze stirred, and she zipped up her vest against the chill. "Remember when Cousin Jimmy and I used to jump off the porch into those huge leaf piles?" she asked, her voice carrying a hint of nostalgia.

Her father's chuckle was a warm echo of the past. "You were fearless, always keeping up with him."

His look faded to one of concern, and she saw worry etched in his eyes. "Are you happy here, Kate?" he asked, as he rubbed his beard thoughtfully.

She grasped his arm reassuringly. "Dad, I've got everything I need. My family, my work—it's everything I ever wanted. Don't worry about me."

"It's my job to worry about you," he said, slipping his arm around his daughter. "Why don't we head inside for lunch and home-made chili? But be prepared for your mother to ask you to make a Halloween candy run. She knows you love Halloween and thinks getting out will be good for you."

"Trying to sweeten me up?"

"Perhaps. But definitely trying to get you to smile."

She flashed him an exaggerated grin and pointed to her face. "Look, Dad. I'm smiling already. See?"

Dad's laughter warmed Kate's heart as they headed to the kitchen, and his steady presence gave her peace. Yet, his words lingered. Did she have everything she wanted? His question tugged at her heart and lingered in the crisp autumn air.

A FEW HOURS LATER, KATE WAS AT BLACK ROCK

Market, making her way around pumpkins and excited kids selecting Halloween costumes.

The pregnant woman standing beside Kate in the candy aisle gave a cheery smile as she brushed her fingers through her dazzling blonde curls. The shopper had tucked her cardigan tight around her burgeoning baby bump as she scrutinized mountains of Halloween treats in the never-ending candy aisle. Kate didn't recognize the striking stranger, but there was something about her, a certain confidence in the way she moved, that made it seem she was planning the coolest Halloween house on the block.

"I recently moved here," the stranger admitted, her eyes roaming over the assortment of sweets. "and I don't know what kids like for Halloween."

"Can't go wrong with Sour Patch Kids or mini chocolates," Kate said, standing and retrieving three jumbo bags for Mom. "Or, if you want to impress, stock up on full-sized candy bars."

The woman brightened. "Thanks. I'll try that," she said, straining to reach the display on the top shelf.

"How many do you want?" Kate asked, moving again to the display to reach for more.

"Six full-sized should do it. That's so kind of you!" the woman said, looking pleased as she took the candy from Kate. "It's exciting," she went on, settling the bags in her cart. "Halloween in a new home and a baby on the way."

"Welcome to the neighborhood," Kate said. "We're a friendly lot. You can sit back and enjoy the trick-or-treaters. I'm Kate, by the way.

The woman's lips curled into a wide smile that revealed perfect white teeth. "Thank you. I'm Hanna, and my partner is around somewhere."

"Did you find what we need, honey?" a familiar voice boomed from behind Kate.

Hanna's smile widened, and she held out her hand toward the man. "I found the perfect treats! This nice lady helped me, Jon."

Kate's heart pounded in her chest when she saw her ex-husband approaching. She hadn't seen him in months, but he was still the same handsome man she had fallen for a decade ago.

Jon's mouth twisted into a smug smile when he recognized her. "Kate's always been the helpful type," he said, his voice dripping with condescension. Beside him, Hanna stiffened and stared wide-eyed.

Kate's jaw clenched. She wanted to say something, anything, to put him in his place. She met his gaze and said with a sardonic grin. "I'm just spreading my charm around. It's a public service, really."

His eyes narrowed as he scrutinized her. "Seeing you again brings back memories. Not necessarily good ones, but memories all the same."

At his words, Hanna tugged at his arm, worry crossing her face. "Please, Jon," she implored softly, "we should go now."

He patted Hanna's hand dismissively. "You're right, my darling," he said, his eyes flicking to Kate. "We have a lot to do to prepare for our new family."

Kate took a deep breath and steeled herself. He was trying to hurt her, but she wouldn't let him. She wasn't the woman he once knew. She wasn't following him around, helping him climb the corporate ladder. His attention had once blinded her, but now she saw him for who he really was. He'd never again gaslight her or make her feel small. Those days were long gone.

She narrowed her eyes and stepped closer, her voice dropping to a conspiratorial tone. "The best thing I ever did was get away from you."

Jon's eyes widened in surprise, but before he could retort. Kate turned to Hanna and tilted her head towards Jon's expanding waist.

"Hanna, you really need to keep those chocolate bars away from him."

Jon's face flushed, his cocky demeanor crumbling. "Kate, that's not"—he protested.

But Kate cut him off again. "Oh, spare me. I've got a cart full of candy and a life full of happiness waiting for me. Enjoy your Halloween."

With that, Kate turned on her heels and walked away.

KATE'S BESTIE LOOKED RADIANT ON THEIR VIDEO CHAT that evening, despite a burp cloth clinging to one shoulder. CeCe laughed and raised a fist pump. "You did *not* say that to Jon!"

The adrenaline rush from confronting Jon still fueled Kate. "Yep. I kept my cool and walked away."

But seeing Jon had been a shock, and Kate's stomach churned with disbelief and hurt along with triumph.

Kate groaned. "How could I have been so naive?"

She shook her head as memories poured in of those first years of their relationship, filled with love and excitement. "He made me feel special at the beginning," she admitted sadly, recalling his romantic gestures back then. "I guess his true nature blinded me."

"There's nothing wrong with supporting the man you love,

Kate," CeCe said, "but in your case, it was one-sided. You were the giver, and Jon was the taker."

Kate's chest tightened as she recalled how she had poured her love into their marriage. CeCe always seemed to know when Kate was hiding her pain. "And how are you after seeing Hanna pregnant?"

Kate had longed for a child of her own, but Jon had already achieved his dream of a family without her. This time, Kate wouldn't suppress her tears. She let her grief wash over her, and as sorrow gave way to acceptance and relief, she allowed herself to cry.

CeCe waited quietly. Her eyes were soft with concern for her friend.

Kate's voice was raspy from crying, but still determined as she admitted, "It hurt. A lot. But I'll be okay."

CeCe whispered fiercely, her face shining with conviction, "You will be more than okay, Kate Fiore,"

Oblivious to the intense conversation, David's face slid into view before CeCe could say more. "Katie-Kat!" he called out with his big grin. "How's my girl? When are you coming to see us?"

Kate straightened, glad to see David and his infectious optimism. "Next summer," she rallied. "As soon as I get vacation time."

David waved and ducked away. "Don't stay away too long," he called over his shoulder. "The twins will be walking by then. And Luke misses you."

Confused, Kate dabbed away the last of her tears. "Why did David say Luke misses me?" she asked when they were alone.

CeCe sighed. "Why wouldn't he? You broke Luke's heart when you left."

Kate shook her head. "That's not true. When I took my new job, Luke was happy for me."

CeCe's tone turned serious. "You're partly right, Kate. He was happy for you. But he wouldn't ask you to stay because he's not like Jon. Luke loves you enough to let you go, even if it hurts him, because it's what you wanted."

Kate replayed her last conversations with Luke in her mind. What had she missed? "Luke loves me? I... How do you know that?" she asked. "Did he say anything?"

"Sweetie, he doesn't need to say anything for us to see how much he cares," CeCe said patiently. "He lit up like a firefly when you were around. He designed the park based on your idea. He's using software from Viviane's firm that you suggested, so he can cut back at Gift and Garden to concentrate on his career—all because of your inspiration. We'd never seen him so happy. Lately, though, it seems he's merely going through the motions. His heart is missing because you're missing.

Kate massaged her forehead to ease the throbbing blossoming there. "I thought it was a good idea. You know, a clean break. No false hopes or unnecessary pain."

"Kate, Luke is not like Jon. Luke will honor what you ask of him."

CeCe's eyes softened as she leaned closer to the screen, her expression conveying a desire to comfort Kate through the miles that separated them. "Were you holding back with him because you were afraid of being hurt?"

Kate sighed and sank into the pillows on her bed, her eyes welling up. CeCe was right. She had run from the possibility of love, and when she let herself care too much, she let her fears push her away. Instead, she set her life on the safer path of chasing her career.

A baby cried in the background, and CeCe morphed into Mom Mode.

"My turn for twin duty. We'll talk more later. I know you'll figure it out. Just use your heart instead of your brilliant brain."

Kate clenched her fists and swallowed the lump in her throat as the call ended. She hadn't considered how her actions would affect Luke, and she regretted any hurt she caused him. Closing her eyes, she conjured images of special moments with him—his dimpled grin, his laugh that filled the room, his heavenly foot rubs–and she ached for what she had lost.

Luke was the other half of her heart, but how would they make it work when they lived 500 miles apart? And what if she couldn't give him the family he deserved?

Her head spun with questions and worries. A future with Luke might not be possible, but one thing was certain. Without him, her life would never be whole.

Kate sat up and ran her fingers over the silver necklace Jon had bought her years ago. It had always comforted her, but now it felt like a burden. Slowly, she unhooked the chain from around her neck and cupped it in her palm. She'd drop off the pendant tomorrow at the Congregational Church's Christmas rummage sale.

Chapter Forty-Three

LUKE

Crape myrtles blanketed South Harbor with autumn golds and reds as Luke turned Spike onto the Greenwood's street.

He shook his head ruefully. Kate had been gone for two months, and here he was, still thinking of his truck by the outlandish name she had christened it. Luke shook off thoughts of Kate Fiore. She was out of his life. No sense dwelling on the past. If only he had a switch to turn off his feelings for her.

David was juggling two babies, one on each arm, as he greeted Luke at the door.

"Thanks for coming, man," David said, grinning. "The twins and I are ready for guy time while CeCe is shopping for Halloween."

"No problem," Luke said, tickling each boy's foot. "It won't take long to plant your Japanese maple, and then I can hang out with you and the little Greenwood guys."

As Luke hauled the tree to the backyard, he thought of Kate again.

He had met her for the first time at the Greenwood's—not counting the time she locked herself out of Mae Gray's rental. He lifted the tree from the wheelbarrow at the planting site and smiled at the memory. She'd been an uptight know-it-all then, but by the time she'd mellowed and he realized how much he cared for her, she was gone.

Too late.

He wouldn't think about her eyes, a blend of autumn leaves and early morning mist, or her soft sighs that made him wild with desire. He regretted not telling her what being with her this summer meant to him, but what was the point? She was leaving Gull Island all along to return to her family and her life.

Luke took out his frustration and attacked the garden soil with his shovel, digging a wide planting hole. His arms ached, and he was drained by the time he slid the tree in place. He washed up and joined David in his study, which was now filled with toys, baby blankets, and jumbo-sized packages of Pampers. Luke settled onto the couch, and David handed Luke a baby.

"Appreciate you planting that beauty for us," David said, shifting Jacob to the crook of his arm. "I don't get in the garden much these days since these two."

"Any time," Luke said as he jiggled Adam on his knee. "They're getting big."

David beamed. "Growing like weeds now! Next Halloween, CeCe will have them dressed in cute costumes, and I'll take them around the block for their first trick-or-treat."

Luke remembered when he and Kate visited the twins in the special care nursery. He could still see her sad, sweet face as she told him about her miscarriage and how she feared she would never have children.

Then Adam claimed his attention by flapping his chubby arms and giving Luke a drooly giggle and toothless smile.

"He likes his Uncle Luke," David said, adjusting Jacob on his shoulder for a back rub.

Luke made a silly face, and Adam giggled harder, his little chest hic-cupping with glee.

"You're good with them," David said. "Babies can sense who's comfortable with them."

As much as Luke loved kids, he'd be fine without them, too, if it meant being with Kate. There were other ways to have children. They could adopt or become the best aunt and uncle on the planet. But all that was beside the point. Kate was gone.

"So, what are you hearing from Kate these days?" David asked, as if he sensed where Luke's thoughts had gone.

"Not much," Luke said. "How's she doing?"

David's brow shot up. "You don't know?"

"She thought it was best if we didn't stay in touch," Luke said with a shrug. "So that's what we're doing."

It was Jacob's turn to giggle as David sucked in a breath and blew raspberries for his squirming son. "CeCe keeps up with her," David said. "Kate loves her job, and she's got her own apartment in Black Rock near work."

Luke listened intently, his heart aching with each tidbit of her life without him. He didn't want to know, but he had to ask. He took a long breath and plunged ahead. "Is she seeing anyone?"

"CeCe says Kate doesn't want to see anybody. You're a hard act to follow."

"Yeah, right," Luke said with a snort.

"And how about you?" David asked. "Are you seeing anyone?"

"No time," Luke said, making a face at the thought of dating anybody. He also grimaced at the pungent smell emanating from Adam. He lifted the baby to examine him.

"Whoa. What's that?" he asked.

"Wait for it," David said.

There was a moment of silence followed by loud farty rumbles before the boys kicked and cooed contentedly in unison.

Luke wrinkled his nose. "Ugh. How can two sweet little things produce such a stink?"

"Synchronicity, my friend," David explained, reaching for a diaper. "Double farting. Followed by double pooping."

"I've never seen a kid so excited about being an ear of corn," Luke said, twisting the last strand of beige raffia around a brown headband of the faux tassels before securing it on his nephew's head.

Pirouetting around the kitchen island, Dawson corrected his uncle. "Not corn. I'm the *maize* in our school Thanksgiving play, Uncle Luke," he said.

Annie reached out to prevent her son from circling the island again. "Dawson Lawson, stop sassing your uncle and hold still, so I can see how your costume fits."

Annie wrestled off her son's tassels to pull a green sweatshirt over his head. Then she tacked a yellow egg carton splayed open in the middle of his chest to serve as corn kernels.

"Here's your tassel, buddy," Luke said, placing the raffia-laced headband onto his nephew's head. Dawson tossed his head and made the fiber shake like real corn tassels.

"You look a-*maizing*, Dawson," Luke said, giving the boy a fist bump.

Annie rolled her eyes. "Lucas, don't stir him up any more than he already is."

"I'm a-*maizing*!" Dawson crowed, prancing away in a rustle of raffia to examine his costume in the bedroom mirror.

Annie rubbed the heel of her hands across her forehead. "He's been wild for the past week. I'll be glad when his performance is over tomorrow," she said. "You coming to see him?"

"Wouldn't miss it."

"You're tearing yourself away from work to watch a kindergarten Thanksgiving play?"

"And why wouldn't I?"

"You've been nose to the grind and miserable ever since Kate left."

Luke glared at his sister. He did not want to hear the lecture he knew was coming. "What do you mean?"

Annie gave him her you-need-to-hear-me look. "Kate is the best thing that ever happened to you. When she was around, you were like your old self before Dad died. Relaxed. Happy. You had a life."

A shadow crossed his face. He was tired of hearing the same unspoken accusation. "She decided to leave. Kate wanted that job and to get back to her family. How can I ask her to stay and give that up, Annie?"

"So, you let her go to make her happy, and now you're wretched?"

He threw up his hands in frustration. "That's it. No happily ever after, like in those movies she watches."

Annie's fingers tapped on the kitchen island. "I sent Kate a link to yesterday's post about the city council approving your proposal for Point Park and how it's a blueprint for conservation projects along our coast. It's taking social media by storm."

His jaw tightened, and he took a deep breath. "And why would you do that? She doesn't want to hear about me or the Point."

"Of course she does, Luke! You have blinders on when it comes to Kate. She texted me back right away, asking about the new park. And all kinds of questions about you," Annie added with a wink.

Was that even possible? Kate had made it clear it was over between them. Finito. Done.

"All I'm saying, Brother, is that you might want to reconsider your no-contact protocol. What's the worst that could happen if you reached out to her?"

He gave Annie a rueful smile. The worst thing had already happened.

Kate had broken his heart.

THAT EVENING, LUKE RUBBED LAZY CIRCLES ACROSS Boo's haunch, and the dog squirmed contentedly. "What do you think, Boo?" he asked. "Should we get in touch with Kate?"

The dog yipped and slurped Luke's fingers with a wet tongue.

Annie's words had haunted him all evening. Maybe he had blinders, but he feared the worst about contacting her: Kate wouldn't answer. Then he'd be back to the old pain that had knifed through him for months after she left.

He had been getting better lately. The gut punch that hit him when anyone mentioned her name had lessened, and he could even watch a sunset without his heart seizing. But those soft nights when it had been the two of them, leaning into each other, whispering dreams into the night sky, would always be a painful reminder of what he lost.

The wind shifted, ushering a stiff November breeze onto his porch. He tightened his jacket and scooped Boo onto his lap, the warm doggie body offering comfort. The first stars popped out in the evening sky as he absently rubbed Boo's muzzle, considering what to do.

If he texted Kate, he didn't know what to write. Imagining Kate seeing his words, maybe even hearing from her after all these weeks, twisted his stomach in knots. His phone trilled with a FaceTime call from David, and Luke fumbled for his mobile to answer.

"What's up, David? Kids in bed?" he asked.

"Yep, finally! We're still putting the boys down at their desired sleep time," David said proudly. "Helps us get a few hours of quality shut-eye now that we're both working."

CeCe's face slipped onto the screen next to her husband's. "Hey, Luke, congratulations on the city council's accepting your nature park design for the Point! That's huge. You must be thrilled."

"Yeah, pretty excited. The sea turtle toys convinced people we need a park instead of luxury condos. But I can't take all the credit. Kate came up with the ideas."

CeCe's coppery eyes bore into him. "Does she know that?"

"Um, no. Didn't think she'd be interested."

CeCe groaned with a facepalm on her forehead. "You didn't tell her?"

"Annie sent Kate the link to the *Gull Island Gazette*," Luke said sheepishly. "Does that count?"

"It does not. Here's what you do, Lucas McAllister," CeCe said, wagging her finger at him. "You let Kate know how she helped you make Point Park a reality and how much that means to you. Call her. Text her. Send a carrier pigeon. But you tell that woman somehow. And do it sooner rather than later!"

Luke groaned inwardly. First, Annie urged him to talk to Kate. And now CeCe.

David squeezed his wife. "I love it when you get fired up, Sweetness, especially when it's not directed at me. You get these shoot-y lightning bolt things coming out of your eyes like a Wakanda warrior princess."

"I'll show you a Wakanda warrior if you sleep through your turn to get up with the boys tonight," CeCe said with mock severity.

She kissed David playfully on the cheek before turning back to Luke. "Clear?"

"Crystal," Luke said, wishing them good night and disconnecting.

Boo jumped up on his lap and licked his face, eager for his owner's attention. "That's enough loving on you tonight," Luke said. "I have a text to send."

Luke settled his dog on the deck and watched the moon rise. He imagined Kate 500 miles away, watching the same sky. Would she be thinking? Would she remember the time they gazed at the stars on the old bench at the Shrimp Shack?

He couldn't keep his feelings to himself any longer. He had to tell Kate, even if she never wanted to see him again. Swiping open his mobile, he began texting.

> Hey, Kate Can you believe it? City Council approved Point Park! It's a-maizing, right? (Pun intended, thanks to Dawson's role as an ear of corn in the school play.) I'll never forget how you came up with the idea and encouraged me to run with it. The park is truly special. Something for people to enjoy for generations, and you helped make it happen. I know the miles keep us apart, but I miss you, Kate. More than I thought was possible to miss anyone. I hope someday you'll return to Gull Island, and we'll see Park Point together.

He zipped his jacket against the cool evening air and re-read the text, making sure auto-correct hadn't done anything silly. There was more he wanted to say, but he didn't know if Kate would listen. It had been almost three months since she left, and she was maddeningly true to her word of cutting off things between them.

Yet his text was an invisible strand, wrapping around his heart and winding toward hers. He had to get it right. He gritted his teeth, finger poised on the send button, when he impulsively added a final thought.

> X, Luke

This time he hit send without hesitation. Then, he scooped up

Boo, and they headed inside.

Chapter Forty-Four

KATE

It was after midnight when Kate finally shut her laptop and leaned back on the couch in her apartment. She finished her report due on Friday, so she couldn't postpone bed any longer. A cup of chamomile tea might ease her into a dreamless sleep.

She padded to the galley kitchen to brew a cup, her eyes darting to the cell phone resting on the counter near the teapot. After agonizing for the hundredth time, she re-read Luke's text. It was time to be brave and write him back. At least an acknowledgment of his accomplishment would be polite. With a deep breath, she picked up the phone and began tapping her reply.

> Great news, Luke! Thanks for telling me about the Point. Your proposal for the park was brilliant. And congrats to Dawson, too, for his star turn in the school play!

She stopped, staring at the text. She hated that it sounded distant and cold. Before she could delete it, her fingers flew across the keyboard as if they had a mind of their own.

> Tell Boo I miss him…and I miss you, too. A lot.

She hit Send, and the words raced across cyberspace. No doubt Luke was already fast asleep with those early morning hours he kept. It'd be morning before she heard anything back—if he bothered to answer.

Kate drizzled honey and lemon into her tea and wandered down the hall into her bedroom. She sipped from her mug along the way, ignoring the fluttering in her stomach brought on by thoughts of Luke. As she pulled back the covers, a ping came from the kitchen. Was it Luke? What was he doing up so late?

Heart hammering against her chest, she raced to her phone and grinned when she saw Luke's name on the screen, along with a photo of Boo wearing a wide-brimmed black Pilgrim hat with a ruffled orange collar around his furry neck.

> Can't hold a phone with these paws! Busy supervising the annual Turkey Day Parade (chasing seagulls on the sand, obvs). Happy Thanksgiving, Kate! Woofingly yours, Gobbler Boo

> P.S. Extra ear scratches always appreciated (and Luke misses his snuggle buddy too!)

Kate's smile deepened and warmed as her eyes wandered over Luke's text. Maybe they'd be friends, she thought. Keep in touch now and then. That would be okay, wouldn't it?

She tapped back a heart emoji in response, turned out the lights, and fell asleep, dreaming of seagulls on the shore and snuggles with Boo.

North winds blew sharp off Black Rock Harbor, and slate clouds smothered the late-November sky as Kate finished walking off a calorie-laden Thanksgiving dinner with the Fiore clan. She darted inside her parent's house and unzipped her jacket, grateful to be out of the cold.

At the kitchen table, her mother and Aunt Theresa faced off like gladiators, each waving a bread knife over a plate heaped with left-over turkey.

"It's better to leave the cranberry sauce off the sandwich completely," Aunt Theresa said.

"Nonsense. Spreading the sauce on the bread is delicious, not to mention that you must add mayo. Otherwise, it's dry and flavorless," Mom countered.

"Margaret, that disgusting cranberry slime will never touch the inside of my sandwich," Aunt Theresa insisted with a playful eye roll.

Kate listened as the two women continued their good-natured bickering, a sign that all was right with the world. They'd been having the same argument every Thanksgiving for as long as she could remember, and there was never a winner.

Kate rubbed the heel of her hand across her forehand, her mind already turning from her family's Thanksgiving to the work she needed to finish before the office reopened Monday. She prided herself on her organizational skills, but her to-do list for the new job kept getting longer.

Her fingers instinctively reached for her phone, the screen illuminating with the text message from Luke, sent days ago. There had been no further communication from him, and Kate assumed he was busy over the holiday.

She didn't want to admit how much she missed Luke in his vintage cottage by the sea and the rhythm of her life on Gull Island. The memory of their lazy evening beach walks and morning sea turtle patrols tugged at her heartstrings, a bittersweet ache. And when she recalled the brilliance of his smiles and the warmth of his embraces, she had to sit down and remember to breathe.

What did his text mean when he wrote he missed her? Was he thinking of her like an old friend? Something more?

"Would you like a turkey sandwich?" Mom asked, interrupting Kate's thoughts. "I'll make it any way you want."

Kate's head snapped up.

"Oh, um, I'm not hungry right now," Kate said, biting the bottom corner of her lip.

Her mother and aunt exchanged glances. They'd always been able to read her like a book. "What's going on, Kathleen?" Aunt Theresa asked.

Kate hesitated, her mind racing. She couldn't tell her family the truth about how much she missed Luke and Gull Island. It thrilled them to have her in Black Rock, and she didn't want to disappoint them.

"Nothing really. Working hard and a bit tired," Kate said, hoping they'd drop the subject.

But Mom wasn't easily deterred. "Are you sure, Kathleen? You know you can always talk to us."

Kate took a deep breath, knowing she couldn't keep it bottled up forever. "Okay, fine. Something is bothering me. It's just... I got a text from Luke recently."

Her mother's eyebrows shot up, and Aunt Theresa leaned in, eagerly anticipating the story. "How's that hottie?" her aunt asked, a teasing grin on her face as a blush rose on Kate's cheeks.

"You know we ended things when I left Gull Island. I haven't heard from him until now and...it brought back many memories," she admitted, her voice teetering off as she absently picked at a piece of turkey.

Her mother and aunt nodded sympathetically like they wanted to ask more. Kate rushed on.

"I don't know what to do," she confessed, folding her arms over her chest. "If I should stay in touch or let it go. His life is on Gull Island. Mine is here. With my job and family. No way of us being together."

"Why don't you text him back and find out what's on his mind?" Mom suggested, a mischievous gleam in her eye.

Kate's cheeks grow hot. "I don't know. What if he doesn't answer? Or worse, what if he does but thinks of me as an old pal? Or what if we start up those feelings for each other?"

"Do you want to see him again?" Aunt Theresa asked, her voice gentle but firm.

Kate's pulse was now thunder in her ears. Thinking of Luke made her feel exposed. Did she have it in her to take a chance? Fear gnawed at her insides, and she bit her lip even harder, trying not to let it win.

Mom placed a comforting hand on Kate's arm. "Life is short,

sweetheart," she said softly, understanding in her voice. "You'll never know unless you try."

Kate thought for a moment more, looking deep into herself for an answer. She had too much baggage haunting her.

"If you still care for him, then you should give it a shot," Aunt Theresa added, reaching for a slice of turkey and popping it in her mouth.

Angie flitted into the kitchen and twirled before Kate. "Cousin Kate, read me a story like you promised. Please?"

"You got it, sweetie," Kate said. "We'll finish the one about the sad princess and the handsome prince."

"Projecting there, are we, Kathleen?" Aunt Theresa asked with a wink.

Kate rolled her eyes as she took Angie's hand, and they went in search of a good book that ended with a happily ever after.

December

BLACK ROCK, CONNECTICUT

"What good is the warmth of summer, without the cold of winter to give it sweetness."

— JOHN STEINBECK

Chapter Forty-Five

KATE

Kate sighed as she coaxed her white Prius through rush-hour traffic and past snow piled high alongside the Connecticut Turnpike. Welcome back to long nights and cold New England winter, she sighed to herself.

Mom's familiar ringtone cut through the gloom on Eve Snow's hands-free console. Kate kept the ringtone to differentiate her mom's calls from spam calls since Margaret Fiore called her daughter most evenings when Kate was stuck in traffic, making her a captive audience.

"Come for supper tonight?" Mom asked without preamble. "Dad made minestrone, and I picked up cannoli."

It tempted Kate. Her father's soups were to die for, and it was hard to turn down Italian pastry. "Save me some?" she asked. "I'm beat after a long week. I only want to grab a bite and curl on the couch in the slug position."

"Are you sure, Kathleen? You need to get out. Do something besides work. "

"I'm good, Mom. I'll be over Saturday night for the family holiday dinner."

"Listen, sweetie, Cousin Jimmy is dropping off a few things to help with your Christmas decorating."

Kate appreciated her mother's offer. Kate had donated the holiday stash she had accumulated with Jon, and she wasn't looking forward to shopping for replacements.

"Thanks, Mom. That will help a lot. Love you."

Kate ended the call. She rolled her shoulders to dispel knots of tension that were popping up with increasing frequency from weeks of twelve-hour days, deadlines, and pressure. At least traffic wasn't bad tonight. Most Fridays, it took an hour, but with people slipping away for the December holidays, tonight's commute was clocking in at half the time.

Kate maneuvered the Prius around the pothole she nicknamed Grand Canyon that lurked right before her exit, and she zigzagged the dark back roads to her apartment. By the time she reached home, cars jammed her small street for Mrs. Sirkin's Hanukkah celebration. Kate circled the block until she found a space cleared of enough snow to squeeze Eve into it.

Kate stepped warily onto the icy pavement, her feet sinking into the cold slush. She pulled her coat tight and wrapped her chunky wool scarf around her neck, taking comfort in its warmth. She kept her head down against the wind as her boots crunched across the sidewalk.

The homes she passed with windows lit by Christmas trees and holiday candles proudly displayed inside made her lonelier than ever. She promised herself she'd buy a tree tomorrow and invite Angie over to help decorate it. The child's infectious energy would be exactly what she needed to lift her spirits.

She braced herself against the frosty night air and tried to force away her gloomy thoughts. Life was good and yet here she was, tired and meh. Her job demanded so much from her—and while it paid well, it didn't provide the same sense of purpose she had found working with the aquarium team or trying to save the Point. And then there was Luke... Well, he had been the best part of it all.

Kate, lost in thought, nearly slipped on the frozen pavement as she approached her apartment in an old periwinkle blue Victorian. Recent owners had converted the grand dame into two rental units from the single-family home of 150 years ago.

Gingerly, she climbed the icy steps to the shared hallway. As she bent to slip off her boots, her downstairs neighbor cracked open her door.

"I hope you found a place for your car with my company taking up the street," Mrs. Sirkin said, her dark eyes anxious. She held out a steaming plate covered with wax paper over two humps of dough underneath. "I saved you cheese blintzes to make up for the inconvenience of walking a million miles on such a night."

Nestling the plate in her arm, Kate reached for the elderly woman and lightly touched her shoulder. "I'd walk a mile for your cooking in any weather, Mrs. Sirkin."

The elderly woman brightened. "I made an extra for your friend, too. Such a nice young man. He came looking for you. I told him you weren't home, and he said he'd come back later. I hope that's all right," she said, her anxious look returning.

"Of course," Kate assured her. "It was my cousin Jimmy. He'll be back. Thanks for these beautiful blintzes, and Happy Hanukkah, Mrs. Sirkin."

AFTER DEVOURING HER NEIGHBOR'S HEAVENLY blintzes (she ate Jimmy's, too. He'd never know!), Kate couldn't wait to shuck her work clothes. She searched the tiny closet for something comfortable with a holiday flair.

She picked out an oversized red wool sweater that provided plenty of warmth. Paired with black leggings and a white turtleneck with dancing candy canes scored on sale at Target, it would do for a solo Friday on a wintry night. She had slipped on her red alpaca leg warmers and favorite fuzzy red slippers when she heard the doorbell.

"Just a sec, Jimmy," she called to her cousin as she raced down the steps to the hallway of the old Victorian.

Her fingers fumbled against the lock's cold metal. Flinging open the door, she shivered as frigid New England air pummeled her. The tip of a Christmas tree poked through the door, followed by long blue-green branches barely restrained by netting. Kate giggled as an unexpected forest materialized in the tiny vestibule, blocking her view.

"Geez, Jimmy, I was not expecting a tree! You and Mom are too much. Bring it inside before we turn into icicles."

Her visitor heaved a six-foot conifer through the entry with two gloved hands and slammed the door shut behind him with a kick.

Plastered against the wall by a sea of pine needles, Kate sidled over to the staircase. "Let's get this beauty upstairs," she said, huffing on the way to her apartment.

The green giant trailed behind her, its branches saturating the air with its crisp, mountainy scent. She strained as she guided it to the minuscule landing outside her apartment.

"Set it here for now," Kate said, catching her breath and stepping inside to make room for the tree.

"Can you stay for a minute, Jimmy?" she asked. "At least get warm. I have beer, coffee, and hot chocolate."

Without waiting for an answer, Kate crossed to the small kitchen. She heard the door close, and her visitor stepped inside as she rummaged in the cupboard for glasses.

"What a beauty! A Fraser fir, right?" she prattled on. "I love it. Where'd you find it?"

"Cut fresh before I hit the road at dawn,"

Her heart slammed against her ribcage as Luke's mellow baritone and island drawl filled the room. She whipped around to see him standing in the doorway, his solid form filling the space. Her pulse hammered in her ears at the sight of him. His tousled sandy-brown hair. Those piercing blue-gray eyes she had missed so much. Nothing prepared her for how seeing him again would make her heart somersault with joy.

But now he was here, standing in front of her, and everything she had imagined, every conversation she had rehearsed in her head, all became real. She sucked in a breath as he took a step closer. He smiled a guarded smile.

"Kate."

His voice was raspy against the silence and held the weight of miles and months. It landed on her name like a caress, a whisper that spoke volumes of everything he couldn't say. It hung in the air like a fragile thread before wrapping itself around Kate's heart, squeezing tight.

Chapter Forty-Six

LUKE

It had been late afternoon when Luke reached for another energy bar as he crossed the border into Connecticut on I-95 in Greenwich. He was making good time, leaving Gull Island before dawn for the ten-hour trek north, pure adrenaline pushing him through.

This spur-of-the-moment trip was so unlike his usual well-thought-out decisions. He almost turned around in Baltimore, doubting his decision to show up at Kate's door unannounced.

What if she didn't want to see him? He knew delivering a Christmas tree was an insane plan. She might slam the door in his face, but he had to try.

His mobile rang. It was Annie. He punched it to the speaker.

"Hey, Brother. Where are you?" she asked, getting straight to the point.

"About forty minutes from Kate."

"How are you holding up?"

"Fine," he fibbed, imagining her eye roll.

Annie's voice crackled louder through the speaker. "Liar. It's going to be all right. She loves you."

"There's more to it than love, Annie," he countered.

"Luke! Talk to her. You're two creative, smart people, and you love each other, even though neither of you is smart enough to admit it. You'll find a way."

"You might be right."

"Of course, I'm right! Oh, and Boo is fine. Dawson hopes you'll be gone for a long time, so he can keep the dog through Christmas break."

"Could be back as soon as tomorrow."

"Stop that, Lucas McAllister!" Annie said, her voice playfully scolding across the miles. "We'll miss you at Christmas, but you'll be happily occupied elsewhere."

He laughed and disconnected the call, concentrating on the road in the growing darkness. The first time he pulled up at Kate's apartment in Black Rock, his heart pounded as he waited for the door to open. Then the sweet neighbor downstairs told him Kate wasn't home.

The delay was maddening. Luke found a nearby coffee shop. When he returned two cups later, he had unloaded the Fraser fir from his truck bed. He hoped she wouldn't turn down a tree for Christmas, even if she didn't want him around. Forcing back lingering doubts, he marched up to her porch. Heart hammering in his chest, he rang the bell and heard her footsteps as she scurried to answer. He held his breath as she opened the door.

Yet Luke couldn't bring himself to step forward from the doorway with his truth. He let Kate mistake him for someone else, holding onto the tree like it was a lifeline connecting them.

KATE

Kate struggled for words as Luke stood before her, his presence overwhelming. He locked his eyes on hers with a tenderness that torpedoed her heart.

His shy smile hit her first like a burst of sunshine in the apartment. His cheeks, flushed from the cold December night, mirrored the rosy pink blooming on her own. She could almost feel his warm skin under her fingertips, warming her from the inside out. Looking into his eyes filled Kate with longing for their laughter-filled days on Gull Island and for the whispered secrets beneath a sky dusted with stars.

"Luke," Kate gasped, still grappling with the fact that he was standing in her apartment. She wanted to reach out and touch his face, tell him how much she missed him. How every night before bed, she had ached for the comfort of his presence.

"I was in the neighborhood," he said, his eyes never leaving her face.

"So, passing through from 500 miles away with a Christmas tree?" she teased, a grin blooming.

He raked a hand through his hair with a sheepish grin. "I always wanted to spend a Christmas in Connecticut."

He took another step closer, so close she made out ice crystals clinging to his coat collar. "I missed you, Kate."

She almost forgot to breathe. "I missed you too," she said, her voice barely audible. "But you didn't call or text. You cut me out of your life."

Pain flickered over his face as he shoved his hands into his pockets. "That was what you wanted," he said, his voice raw.

And there it was. She had set this in motion. His words were a whiplash, jolting her back to the truth. "I- I...," she stammered. "I thought it would be easier if we didn't contact each other," she said, her voice breaking.

Kate's breath caught, a sharp hitch in her throat. Silence stretched between them, thick and heavy with unspoken words. His gaze, raw and searching, held hers captive. The space around them seemed to pulse with the frantic rhythm of her heart. Months. Miles. A lifetime of emotions condensed into a single, choked breath.

Then, with a quiet tremor, the world tilted back into focus. Luke. He was here!

His scent, a bracing cocktail of salt and pine, washed over her, shattering the walls she'd so carefully constructed. Tentative, almost reverent, his hand traced the curve of her neck, a wordless echo of all they'd lost and all they yearned for. His eyes, the stormy shades of a winter sky, were like the tempest raging inside her, a reflection of the pain they'd each endured alone.

No flowery pronouncements, no declarations. Just the raw ache of unspoken emotions, laid bare in the space between ragged breaths and trembling fingertips. In that stillness, a universe bloomed between them. A tapestry woven from longing and grief, punctuated by the faintest flicker of hope, a stubborn ember refusing to be extinguished.

Kate traced his lips with her finger, and shivers ran across her body from his nearness, his warmth.

"I'm sorry, Luke," she whispered. "The way I treated you and shut us down... It was wrong. I was scared. Afraid of getting hurt again."

She reached for his hand, the heat from his skin melting into her. "And I never saw it. I was blind to the love behind your decision to let me go," she murmured, her voice full of regret and sorrow. "So, I ran to what I thought I wanted."

She brushed a pine needle from his hair, and as he leaned into her, she felt the weight of their separation melt away, replaced by a fragile hope that dared to spark. His hand circled her wrist, drawing her closer until their foreheads were touching.

"But it wasn't right," Kate said, her voice a whisper. "Because you weren't here, and I—"

He silenced her with a finger to her lips, his touch feather-light. "Shhh," he rasped. "We'll talk later. But now, I just..." His voice trailed off, replaced by a hungry glint in his eyes. "Kate, I need to kiss you."

Kate sensed it, too—this desperate craving so like her own. Her breath hitched in a silent confirmation. He snaked an arm around her waist, pulling her close, the familiar heat of him searing into her soul. His hand cupped her face, his thumb brushing across her cheekbone, a quiet yearning in the touch.

His lips met hers, a hesitant first brush that exploded into a wildfire. It was a kiss that tasted of longing and regret, of shared dreams and lazy moments on a sun-drenched shore. When they finally broke apart, Kate felt the weight of months lift, replaced by a fragile contentment she'd forgotten existed.

"Merry Christmas, Kate," Luke murmured into her ear, his voice a low rumble against her cheek.

She laughed, a shaky exhale that melted into a smile. "Merry Christmas, Luke."

Their laughter mingled with the scent of pine and burning logs, a fleeting prelude to their lips meeting again. This time, it was a slow burn, a deliberate exploration of every curve and hollow. Kate's fingers twitched against his chest, a silent plea for him to stay, to erase the miles and months that had separated them. The kiss deepened, a tangle of limbs and ragged breaths, until they pulled apart, gasping for air.

"You're good at this," Kate whispered, her fingertips tracing the lines of his jaw.

He chuckled, his eyes smoldering. "Practice makes perfect, right?" His hands danced across her skin, leaving goosebumps in their wake.

Laughter, raw and honest, filled the room before their lips collided again. Each kiss was a promise of a future they dared to dream.

Chapter Forty-Seven

KATE

Kate yanked the brush through her hair, strands rebelling in a familiar tangle. A sigh escaped her lips as she glared at her reflection in the dusty mirror. Fairfield U sweat-shirt? Check. Black leggings (yesterday's, who's counting)? Check. Not exactly a vision to greet Luke after months apart.

"Well," she muttered, a nervous flutter rising in her stomach, "this is me."

She stopped fussing when the clanging of pots and pans distracted her. Crossing to the kitchen, she found Luke rummaging through the cabinets, lining up cooking utensils on her small counter. He looked up and beamed when he saw her.

"Good morning, sleepyhead," he said. "Didn't mean to wake you."

Kate felt a rush of happiness at his kindness. There was so much about this man that touched her heart. How had she not seen it before?

"Not at all. I didn't hear you stir," she admitted.

"You were sleeping like a stone." He flashed a wicked grin. "You must've had a late night."

"Maybe I did," she said, raising a cheeky eyebrow.

"And I worked up an appetite after last night," he teased with a devilish wink.

She gave him a playful swat on his shoulder. "I would love breakfast, but I only have expired yogurt and stale pretzels."

"I see you're into waffles now," he said, a playful smirk on his face as his gaze landed on the waffle iron on her counter.

She gave a tiny shrug. "Well, I did miss yours," she admitted, a hint of shyness in her voice, "so I invested. The results haven't been stellar. Mostly char or casualties of the sticky kind."

He chuckled, reaching for the shopping bag on the counter. "Don't worry, I ran to ShopRite and picked up a few things for waffles."

"Wait. You got up early to go grocery shopping?"

He pushed back a stray curl from her forehead, his fingers lingering on her cheek. "You were sleeping so peacefully, making the cutest little snores. Didn't have the heart to wake you."

She circled his wrist with her fingers, enjoying the warmth of his skin. "So, I snore?"

"More like you make these adorable puffs of air," he said, stepping closer to nuzzle her neck. "I find it charming."

Kate leaned into his touch. He was crisp December wind, rumpled sheets, and lazy Saturday mornings.

"You know, if you keep doing that, we'll never get to breakfast," she murmured, longing for more of him.

"Waffles keep for lunch, too," he whispered before nibbling her ear.

"They will?" she asked, a tiny moan escaping her as his fingers trailed slowly across her jaw.

"They absolutely do," he said, his voice husky.

When he kissed her, she lost all thoughts of waffles.

BREAKFAST HAD TURNED INTO LUNCH WHEN KATE ONCE again nestled behind Luke as he worked a new batch of batter.

"Mmmm. I enjoy having you in my kitchen."

He stopped mixing the batter and planted a kiss on the top of her head. "And I enjoy being in your kitchen," he said before turning back to his task.

Her stomach rumbled. "I'm starving, so I won't distract you. This time, anyway," she said with a sly grin before disentangling to set the table.

As she trotted around the kitchen, she felt his eyes tracing her body in a way that sent sparks shooting through her. She smiled to herself, enjoying his attention.

They settled at the walnut dining table, which nestled in an alcove overlooking the street below. As they dug into the waffles, Kate reached over to swipe at a small drip of syrup stuck to Luke's chin. "Tasty," she cooed, licking her fingers.

Luke's lips curled up into a smile. "You're welcome," he said.

He leaned over to pop a forkful of bacon into her mouth, and her giggle rewarded him as she hungrily took it.

"Now that's something you don't see much on Gull Island," he said, his voice filled with wonder as he pointed to the snow-crusted ledge outside the window.

"How about a walk after lunch?" Kate asked between a mouthful of bacon. "I'll show you our harbor and the rest of my town. Unless... unless you need to get back to North Carolina right away."

She held her breath. Wanting him to stay. Willing him to stay.

It had been too overwhelming seeing him last night to ask. She didn't think ahead about his leaving. But in the light of day, there was an elephant in her otherwise perfect room. They had to talk. To see if there was any way to carve a future together. Kate wanted him in her life, but she didn't know how to without one of them giving up too much for the other.

His eyes searched her face. "December is our slow season, so I have as much free time as you want to put up with me." He paused before adding in a hopeful tone, "I could stay for Christmas...if you want, Kate."

She nodded, not trusting herself to speak at first. "Yes, please," she finally managed, her voice shaky with emotion. "I'm off for the holidays, so yes, please spend Christmas with me."

"Then I'll stay," he said simply. "For this Christmas, and the one after that. For as many Christmases as you'll have me."

Her heart raced and fireworks went off in her ribcage. "I would love that, Luke!"

But then she straightened in her chair, suddenly serious as reality set in once more. "And after that? What will we do once you leave?"

The tight knot in her stomach unraveled as she saw how he watched her with such tenderness. She knew the answer. He wasn't going anywhere without her.

She reached out and took his hand, her fingers tracing the lines of his palm. "I don't want it to be like this," she breathed. "Living apart after you go back to Gull Island...it feels all wrong."

He leaned closer, his eyes meeting hers. His gaze was intense, filled with longing and hope. He gently covered her hand with his own, his touch warm and reassuring. "It's not ideal, Kate, but we can try," he whispered. "I could always come here when business slows in winter. You could come to Gull Island during your vacations or work remotely from my place. What do you think?"

Kate bit her lip and forced herself to look into his anxious eyes.

"I'd try geographical jumping jacks if it meant we could be together," she said slowly. "But I worry about being apart. I don't know if I can handle it."

He smiled tenderly and brushed a lock of hair from her face before speaking again: "We can make it work if we both put our minds to it. We'll FaceTime and text. Maybe have sexy late-night phone conversations," he added with a grin before turning serious.

"We'll figure out a way, Kate."

His words comforted her, and she allowed a small smile to tug at the corners of her lips. Still, she knew there was something else hanging in the air between them. She took a deep breath. The burden of what she wanted to say pressed down on her.

"If we become serious," she steadied herself before continuing, "I want you to understand that I might not be able to give you a child."

She closed her eyes, waiting for his response. Perhaps he would stand up and walk away. Instead, she felt his gentle touch against her cheek. His features softened, his eyes crinkled at the corners and his lips curved into a gentle smile when she opened her eyes.

His jaw clenched as their eyes met. "Listen, Kate. You are my family," he said fiercely. "If it's only the two of us forever, then that's more than enough for me."

Kate swallowed back the lump in her throat as she searched his face for signs of doubt or regret, but all she found there was love and acceptance.

"I love you, Luke McAllister, and I don't want you to give up anything," she whispered, choking back a sob.

"Don't you see, Kate? When we're together, I won't be giving up anything. I'll have everything I want because I love you too."

He tightened his grip on her hand. "Are we good, Kate?" he whispered, his eyes hopeful.

"Yeah," she said, her voice certain. "We're good, Luke."

She swiped at the moisture pooling in the corner of her eyes. "Well, you certainly know how to disrupt a girl's waffles," she teased.

Luke grinned, looking relieved that they had finally talked. "I'm also a magician, and I can make your waffles disappear," he said.

He pulled her plate toward him. "Come here," he said, beckoning her closer, "and I'll demonstrate."

"You think you can handle this much responsibility?" she asked, settling onto his lap.

"I'd move a Mt. Everest-high stack of waffles for you," he replied earnestly before offering her a bite.

The warmth in his eyes made her heart flutter, and she realized with a sudden clarity how much she loved him. She had been terrified to open herself up to anyone, but with Luke, it was different. He made her feel alive again, and she couldn't imagine a life without him.

"Are you up for trimming my amazing Christmas tree today?" she asked, nodding to the Fraser fir propped against her living room wall.

He bolted upright, almost dropping her.

"What is it?" she asked, alarmed.

He slapped the heel of his palm against his forehead. "Forgot to tell you. I found a box of ornaments and a Christmas tree stand outside your door this morning when I left for groceries."

"That would be what Cousin Jimmy dropped off last night. I better text Mom and let her know I got them, so she won't fret."

Kate slid off his lap to retrieve her mobile from the kitchen counter. When she opened her messages, she found a string of texts and phone calls she'd missed with her phone on silent mode.

Luke was watching the falling snow when she returned. "Are you okay, Kate?" he asked, as she curled against him.

"It depends," she said from the depths of his embrace.

She sat up and brushed her fingers through that stubborn lock of hair that insisted on flopping onto his forehead. "How do you feel about meeting the entire Fiore clan for dinner tonight?"

Chapter Forty-Eight

LUKE

Luke shivered and tightened his coat as he walked with Kate to the Fiore home. His warmest clothes, a cotton fisherman knit sweater Annie gifted him for the holidays ages ago and a rarely worn woolen peacoat, were no match for the frigid New England evening.

He took Kate's arm as they gingerly maneuvered around a patch of ice on the sidewalk. "Do you ever get used to this cold?" he asked.

Kate shivered and pulled her scarf tighter, her breath crystallizing into frosty puffs as she laughed. "Winters never bothered me until I came back from Gull Island, so now I'm having to readjust," she admitted.

Luke clutched the canvas Harris Teeter grocery bag in his free hand. He had brought it from home but forgot to give it to Kate in all the excitement last night. Now, he was glad. It would be better to share the contents at dinner tonight.

She wanted to peek inside, but he insisted it was a surprise.

“Give me a hint,” she pleaded. “Is it animal, vegetable, or mineral?”

“Could be a little of each.” He grinned, giving nothing away.

She gave up guessing as they reached the Fiore’s home. The two-story neo-colonial loomed ahead, painted a stark white that seemed to almost pulsate in the fading light. Yellow shutters flanked the tall windows, and a festive wreath, a proud riot of red and green cheer against the yellow door.

A thrill of anticipation shot through Luke, quickly dampened by a wave of nervousness. He stole a glance at Kate beside him. Her smile faltered slightly, a reflection of his own mixed emotions.

“Ready to meet the parents?” she asked.

“Wasn’t that a movie where it did not go well for the male suitor?”

The porch light cast a warm glow on Kate's face, highlighting the amusement dancing in her hazel eyes.

"You're right," she said with a light giggle, the sound tinkling like wind chimes. "How about meeting my Fiore clan?"

A wave of relief washed over Luke, loosening the knot of nerves in his stomach. "Ready as I'll ever be," he replied, a confident grin replacing his earlier apprehension.

"They'll love you, you know," she said, her voice soft. "Because I do."

He felt the whisper of her breath against his cheek as she leaned in, and then the warmth of her lips pressed softly against his skin, sending a delicious tingling down his spine.

“Say that again, please?”

“They’re going to love you.”

She was crisp December and waffles and happiness. His arm snaked around her waist. “Nope. The other part.”

Her dark eyes shone in the moonlight, and her lips parted in a genuine smile that made his heart flutter.

"Because *I* love you, silly," she said, her voice giddy and breathless.

He was about to say more when the door flew open to a cacophony of laughter and holiday cheer spilling over to greet them. Kate's mother, dressed in black silk pants and a scarlet tunic adorned with a Christmas tree pin, ushered them into the warm hallway. She spread her arms to embrace her daughter.

"So glad you're here," Mrs. Fiore exclaimed as the two women hugged.

When she pulled away, Kate's mother regarded Luke with warm hazel eyes and a friendly smile that were so like Kate's. Petite, like her daughter, she also carried herself with the same grace and confidence.

"So, we meet in person at last, Luke! Welcome to our home!" she said, giving him a warm hug, too.

"Thank you, Mrs. Fiore." He smiled back, grateful that Kate had warned him about her family's custom of hugging everyone, whether or not they'd ever met them before.

"Call me Margaret, Luke," she said. She stepped aside to reveal a man of average height and dark brown hair that was graying at the temples. "And this is Kate's dad, Michael."

"Thank you for inviting me into your home, sir," Luke said, extending his hand.

Michael Fiore's brown eyes were thoughtful and intelligent framed behind his silver-rimmed spectacles.

"Thank you, Luke, for looking after our Kathleen this summer," Kate's father said. Then ignoring the handshake, he wrapped Luke in a bear hug instead.

Michael reached for the coats and Luke's shopping bag. "Come in and make yourself comfortable," he said. "Then I want to hear all about the ocean park you're designing, Luke."

As her father retreated, a tall, middle-aged woman wearing a sleek red pantsuit and sporting a reindeer headpiece decorated with blinking string lights descended on them. Luke recognized her at once as Aunt Theresa.

"Kate, he's taller and even hotter in person," she said, eyeing Luke approvingly.

"And you're even younger-looking in real life," Luke quipped, raising an eyebrow.

She wagged a finger at him. "You're a smooth talker, aren't you?" she said, playfully swatting Luke on the arm.

Luke laughed. "I try my best, ma'am."

She turned to Kate. "So, when are you two getting married?" she asked without preamble.

Beside him, he heard Kate sputter out a cough while her mother tossed her hands in the air. "Theresa, please!" Mrs. Fiore admonished. "No need to rush them. They just got here! At least wait until dessert to ask."

"Well, they better start talking," Aunt Theresa said. "I don't want to be an old lady by the time they walk down the aisle."

Luke's head tilted back as he laughed loudly, mirth bubbling up inside of him. "Appreciate your concern, ma'am," he said, trying to contain himself. "That's something Kate and I will discuss when the time comes, but you'll be one of the first to know."

"I'll hold you to that, young man! Now, you haven't met my son Jimmy and his wife, Claire," Aunt Theresa said, motioning to a young couple dressed in matching ugly Christmas sweaters, each with a massive holiday tree that had twinkling lights.

Jimmy greeted Luke with a hearty slap on the back and a hint of mischief in his eyes. "Now I get why Kate didn't answer the door last night," he said with a conspiratorial wink. "It's about time she had some action."

Claire poked her husband. "Jimmy! Don't scare him away," she warned before planting an air kiss on Luke's face. "Ignore my husband. He's harmless."

Luke felt a tug on his sweater to find a pint-sized Disney princess in a shimmery blue Elsa gown, holding a familiar knitted sea turtle stuffy.

"I'm Angie. Are you Cousin Katie's Hulk?"

He glanced at Kate for help, and her wiggled eyebrows signaled an amused confirmation. He crouched before the dark-haired pixie, so they were eye-to-eye. "I am, and I'm happy to meet you in person, Angie."

"I love my toy sea turtle. Did you bring any real ones?"

He shook his head. "No, they don't travel well in the cold," he said solemnly. "But if you visit me on Gull Island, I'll find you some."

"Okay. Bye," she said, satisfied with his answer and skipping off to play with her young cousins.

As Luke stood, Claire explained, "She's been obsessed with sea turtles since Kate told her about them. Your work to preserve the animals is fascinating. We want to take Angie to Gull Island next summer to see them."

"And I need to try those shrimpburgers Kate has been raving about," Aunt Theresa added.

It surprised Luke they were interested in visiting, and it

pleased him that Kate had talked about the island. "I'd be happy to show you around," he said.

Kate nodded and tugged on his forearm. "Come on. I'll introduce you to the rest of the clan."

A blur of faces, young and old, greeted him with hugs that were warm enough to melt a snowman. Not the frosty reception he'd nervously imagined! (Okay, maybe he'd overthought things a bit.)

"Eggnog?" someone boomed, shoving a steaming mug into his hand.

He took a grateful sip as he surveyed the Fiore living room. Forget the den of icy disapproval he'd conjured in his head. This place was a full-on winter wonderland explosion! Poinsettia riots and miniature Christmas villages took over every surface. A towering tree, draped in enough ornaments to rival Santa's workshop, dominated the corner. A toy train chugged merrily around its base, circling a mountain of wrapped gifts. The air hung heavy with the sweet scent of freshly baked cookies. Luke felt the tension in his shoulders melt away. This wasn't what he'd expected at all, but somehow, it felt...like home.

Suddenly, Luke felt a familiar hand slip into his. He glanced down to see Kate gazing up at him with a mischievous glint in her eyes. "Looks like we're under the mistletoe," she whispered, a playful smile tugging at her lips.

A collective shout of "Kiss! Kiss!" erupted from behind them. Kate leaned in, her arms wrapping around his neck as he brushed his thumb across her cheek. Their kiss wasn't exactly epic—more like a family-friendly smooch with a touch of holiday cheer—but it did the trick. Howls of approval filled the room as they pulled apart, Kate's eyes sparkling and her breath catching in a delightful little hitch.

"On a scale of one to ten, how mortified are you by my family at this moment?" Kate asked, grinning up at him and still holding his hand.

"About a five," he said, his lips curling into a grin.

"I'll take that as a win. At least you're not running out the door."

"You knew somebody who wanted to escape this?" Luke asked, pretending to be outraged. He guessed who she meant.

She made a face. "Jon couldn't bear to be around a crowd where he wasn't the center of attention. It irritated him when he couldn't impress my family. But you," she said, tapping his heart gently with her fingers and beaming at him, "you're fitting in fine."

THE FAMILY SQUEEZED TOGETHER AT THE FIORE'S LONG dining table for a leisurely feast of antipasto and baked ziti with pork and meatballs. They ate with gusto as a constant buzz of animated conversations flowed around Luke. He listened attentively and did his best to chime in.

Afterward, as Kate helped her parents prepare coffee and dessert, Luke retrieved a package from his satchel, which he had brought from North Carolina, and joined them in the kitchen.

"I thought you might like this, Mrs. Fiore," he said, handing her a tall, round package wrapped in red tissue paper with a glitzy white bow on top.

"Why, Luke, thank you," she said, carefully unwrapping the gift.

Her eyes widened as she held up a majestic dome-shaped loaf of panettone. He had carefully experimented for weeks after Kate left, eager to try his hand at the sugary bread with raisins, candied fruit peels, and almonds that she had described to him months ago. It had been his way of keeping her close, keeping memories of her alive.

"Look, Michael!" Margaret said, grabbing her husband's arm in excitement. "It's the bread your mother used to make!"

Luke felt Kate's hand reach for his. "You made Nonna's bread?"

He didn't think it was a big deal, but the way Kate was looking at him with such tenderness made him reconsider. "I wanted to recreate your Christmas tradition, but I wasn't sure about adding the brandy—"

"Of course, you add the brandy!" Kate's parents said in unison.

Kate's father reverently took the bread and sliced it onto a festive platter, leaving slivers for himself, his wife, and his daughter to sample first.

Her dad's eyes were misty as he clasped Luke's shoulder. "It's exactly like my mother's. Thank you, son."

The way Michael Fiore intoned the word "son" stirred something in Luke. No one had called him that in years, not since his father passed away.

Michael carried the platter to the table, and Margaret followed with a tray of cookies. Kate stayed behind, licking breadcrumbs off her lips.

"You never cease to surprise me," she said, looking up at him with a panettone mustache. "This is exactly like Nonna's!"

Luke's heart swelled as Kate's eyes lit up as she tasted his recreation of her grandmother's recipe. All the hours he spent perfecting it were worth it.

"I'm glad you like it," he said, dabbing a small crumb from her lip with his finger.

Kate hugged him, and he wrapped his arms around her pliant body that molded just right with his. "You're amazing," she whispered in his ear. "I love you to the moon and back."

Luke held Kate close, savoring her words and the heat of her embrace. With a tender smile, he whispered, "You're amazing yourself. You know that? And loving you to the moon and back? Well, that's only the beginning of how I feel about you."

He leaned in, brushing his lips against her temple, a tender whisper of a kiss that spoke volumes about his affection. "I wish I had your way with words to let you know how much you mean to me."

Her hands caressed his face as she smiled up at him with shining eyes. "When you look at me like that, you don't need words to make me understand."

Someone cleared their throat from behind, and the blinking lights of the reindeer antlers that crossed his vision momentarily blinded him.

"It's about time!" Aunt Theresa harrumphed. "We've been waiting for you two to wake up and realize how much you mean to each other! Now one more kiss and then join us for dessert."

Chapter Forty-Nine

KATE

Luke's fingertips, careful as a butterfly's landing, guided the antique glass angel to its highest branch. The delicate wings, catching the soft glow from the fireplace, shimmered like frosted glass. Kate, arms pleasantly tired from hoisting ornaments, leaned back with a satisfied huff.

"Perfect," she said, a triumphant grin splitting her face. "Now it's a proper Christmas tree. Let's switch on the lights on the count of three."

A lopsided grin tugged at Luke's lips. "Wait a minute, isn't this a Hallmark movie moment?"

Kate swatted him playfully. "You watch Hallmark movies?"

"With Annie, enough to recognize the setup," he countered, winking. "Besides, you've got the cozy fireplace and hot cocoa ready to go."

With exchanged laughs, raising their mugs in mock salutes and chanting, "One...Two...Three!"

Warm light flooded the room as the tree burst to life with twinkling bulbs.

It wasn't just a tree anymore; it was a symbol of warmth and a keeper of memories. Kate's eyes misted as a shiny crystal star, a gift from her grandmother, caught the light. Luke, sensing her emotions, wrapped his arms around her, his chin resting on her shoulder. A surge of warmth and connection coursed through Kate as Luke held her close, anchoring them to each other.

His voice was a soft murmur. "Moments like these..."

His words trailed off, but Kate didn't need them. The silent understanding between them spoke volumes in itself. A smile tugged at her lips, mirrored by Luke's own.

"You were right," she whispered, turning into his arms. "It's like a movie scene, but better. Because it's real. It's ours."

"And our story is just beginning," he murmured, his voice a low rumble against her ear.

Snowflakes pirouetted outside the window, their delicate dance illuminated by the soft glow of streetlights. Inside, nestled together on the couch, Kate's plush throw, a cocoon of warmth, enveloped them both. The fire crackled merrily, casting flickering shadows on the wall. A wave of peppermint sweetness, mingling with the crisp, clean scent of the freshly cut Fraser fir, filled the air, a delightful reminder of the season.

"Thank you for the beautiful tree," she said, resting her head on his shoulder. "And you earned extra points for surviving the Fiore clan's dinner tonight."

"Your family isn't what I expected," he admitted, a hint of surprise lingering in his voice. "But in fact, I quite like them, and I'm finding myself warming up to city life too."

A blush crept up Kate's cheeks as Luke brushed his thumb across her knuckles, sending a jolt straight to her heart. The touch lingered, a silent promise. "And me," he continued, his voice low and husky, "I enjoy making you happy. That's a job I want to take on full-time."

The unexpected intensity of his words left Kate speechless for a moment. A kaleidoscope of emotions swirled within her—joy, disbelief, and a teeny flash of fear. Was this happening?

Then, a shy smile tugged at the corners of her lips, a silent confirmation. "You sure?"

Luke threaded their fingers together and pressed tender kisses on each fingertip. "Never been more sure of anything in my life. You good with that?"

A choked sob, more of a happy gasp, escaped Kate's lips. Tears welled up, sparkling like tiny diamonds in the firelight.

"Yes," she whispered, wrapping her arms around his neck and pulling him into a deep, slow kiss.

When they broke apart, a radiant smile graced her face. "I am exceedingly good with that," she said, her voice husky with happiness.

They settled into a comfortable silence, the crackling fire the only sound in the room. Luke traced patterns on her palm with his thumb. "I was thinking," he said, "we should get a dog to keep Boo company."

Kate let out a peal of laughter. "Another dog? Are you serious?"

"Absolutely," he said, a mischievous glint in his eyes. "Annie tells me there's the sweetest rescue pup, a little ball of fluff in desperate need of a loving home. What do you say?"

With a smile, she snuggled closer. “Alright. You convinced me. I’m in.”

THE END

Epilogue

18 MONTHS LATER—GULL ISLAND

"Mommy Kate!"

The dark-haired boy, a blur of brown eyes and Harry Potter glasses, tore across the sand with his sidekick, Dawson. A triumphant yell escaped his lips. "We found another nest!"

Kate's heart swelled with a quiet pride. A slow smile spread across her face, crinkling the corners of her eyes. "Let's see these master nest architects at work, shall we?" she said, her voice warm with amusement.

She rifled through her backpack and handed Ben and Dawson each a plastic shovel. "Off you go, boys. Keep the beach safe for sea turtles."

"We'll save them, Aunt Kate," Dawson said. "Let's go, Ben!"

Beside her, Mae watched the boys scurry away. "Can't hardly separate those boys these days," Mae said. "They stick together like two peas in a pod."

"They'll even start third grade together this fall!" Kate said, shaking her head. "I can't get over how far Ben has come since he came to us ."

Beach breezes whipped Ben's wild curls as he chased the retreating waves, his laughter echoing down the shoreline. Kate watched him, a bittersweet ache blooming in her chest. Just six months ago, this carefree joy seemed an impossible dream for a boy who'd bounced around the foster system after losing his family in a car accident.

Ben used to be a tightly wound coil of suspicion, his eyes guarded against a world that had failed him. Sleepless nights were a battlefield, haunted by the ghosts of his unspoken rage and the heavy cloak of grief. Kate remembered nights curled up in the bedroom Luke had designed with a Hogwarts theme, where she whispered reassurances until sleep pulled him away from his nightmares.

Now, math was no longer his nemesis, thanks to Luke's patient guidance. Dyslexia's burden eased with Kate's gentle support. Every night, they nestled under the warm glow of his Gryffindor bedside lamp. Ben's face lit up as she read him chapters from Harry Potter, the magic words weaving a world where they all belonged.

Yet, beneath the surface, a flicker of uncertainty remained. Ben's fear of loss, a constant companion from his time in the system, hadn't fully vanished. But Kate held onto a fragile hope that this joy the three of them found might be theirs forever.

"How's the adoption going?" Mae asked as she picked up a plastic straw and stuffed it into her litter bag.

"Paperwork's done, so we're waiting on the court. Luke and I haven't told Ben we're trying to keep him. We don't want to get his hopes up until the decree is final."

Mae gave Kate's shoulder an encouraging squeeze. "It will happen for you, and we'll celebrate when it does. Speaking of celebrations," Mae went on, with a twinkle in her eye, "what are you and Luke doing on your first wedding anniversary tonight?"

A delighted gasp escaped Kate's lips. "It's a surprise. All Luke told me was to dress comfy." A wide grin spread across her face, her eyes sparkling with anticipation.

Mae leaned in conspiratorially and nudged Kate playfully with her elbow. "That sounds mysterious and rather romantic. Any idea where he's taking you?"

Kate shook her head, a relieved smile replacing the surprise. "No clue. But Ben is spending the night with Annie and Dawson, so..." Kate trailed off, giggling like a schoolgirl, delighted that her husband had thought of everything.

Mae wagged her eyebrows. "Well, there you go. An evening on the town without parental supervision—what more could you ask for?"

Despite the wide grin still plastered on her face, Kate let out a tired sigh as Mae placed a hand on her shoulder. She leaned into the touch, her posture slumping slightly. "It's just that I've been dragging lately between Ben and my new marketing business. Even though I'm tired, I can't wait for tonight!"

"Hon," Mae's voice softened with concern, "you two have been through the wringer lately, but you're both fighters. I know you'll hear good news about Ben soon. In the meantime, get some rest. You deserve a fantastic anniversary night, and a little energy boost will make it even better."

Taking Mae's advice, Kate stepped out onto the porch of their beach house and settled onto a wicker chair. The sun filtered through the leaves of the nearby palm trees, dappling her face in the warm light.

She closed her eyes and let herself drift away into a peaceful sleep. Suddenly, her phone blared to signal CeCe's FaceTime call, jolting Kate awake.

"Are we good for next week's schedule?" CeCe asked as they wrapped their discussion.

Kate double-checked her calendar. "Yep. I'm at the aquarium Wednesday through Friday while you're getting ready for a birthday party for the world's cutest two-year-old twins."

A chuckle escaped Cece's lips. "David ordered a mountain of cupcakes for the twins' birthday! Can you imagine the sugar rush?"

"Frosting apocalypse at your place?" Kate's eyes widened at the thought of double the birthday mess.

Cece grinned. "David's embracing the chaos. Speaking of success, those Park Point and Riverwalk Reels are everywhere! You're a social media queen, Kate."

A tired smile tugged at Kate's lips. "Thanks, Cece. The cafe's traffic has exploded, and the Park Point website is taking off. It's insane!"

Excitement flickered in Kate's eyes as a new thought popped into her head. "And guess who just bought a lot in Luke's new eco-friendly development outside Wilmington?"

Cece's smile widened, and she leaned closer to the screen.

"Wait, really? That's amazing! Your parents will be right up the coast. But Kate..."

Cece's voice softened as she noticed the faint line of fatigue creasing Kate's brow. "You look exhausted. Running on fumes?"

Kate sighed, her shoulders drooping as if she could hardly hold them. "Honestly, yeah. Between family and getting my business off the ground, I'm wiped. And even with Luke doing more at home."

CeCe leaned closer to the screen, a small smile turning up the corners of her mouth. "How long have you been like this?"

Surprised by the question, Kate's chest tightened and her mind raced back to their recent weekend with Ben in the Blue Ridge Mountains.

She'd forgotten to pack her birth control pills. She felt a twinge of guilt as soon as she thought about it, but she'd doubled up on the pills as soon as she returned home. Her period had been late since then, but she brushed it off as stress and her gynecologist's words running through her head. *Spotty cycles are common for a woman of your age.*

Could it be possible that...? *No! It couldn't be!*

A nagging fear gripped Kate, shadowing her joy. The possibility of having a child with Luke thrilled her, but lingering anxiety cut her excitement as her mind flashed back to the loss in her last pregnancy. She tried to suppress her fears, but CeCe quickly sensed her friend's silence and sudden mood shift. Before Kate knew it, she heard her friend's comforting voice.

"Mmm-hmm...Don't you get that scary-eye look thing, Kate McAllister. This time might be different. It might even be amazing for you and Luke. Now, run to CVS, get yourself a pregnancy test, and FaceTime me when you're back home. I'll wait with you for the results. You might just have an unforgettable anniversary gift for your man tonight."

THAT EVENING, LUKE WATCHED KATE'S FACE LIGHT UP as she removed the blindfold under the shade of a towering oak.

"Shrimp Shack! You drove me to the Shrimp Shack for our anniversary!" she said, clapping her hands in delight.

He smiled and his entire world turned brighter, watching Kate's face shine with joy. "I'm glad you like it."

He led her to a secluded table covered with candles on a blue-and-white checked tablecloth. In its center, a bottle of champagne chilled in a bucket of ice.

"How'd you manage this? Wait, don't tell me. You had a friend arrange it."

"A bit of this and that," he said, giving her a quick kiss on the temple. "Plus, the magic of Jerome."

Kate smiled, imagining the effervescent Jerome, as Luke fetched the shrimpburgers and placed the platters on the table with a flourish. "Dinner is served, my wife."

"Do you remember where we were this time last year?" she asked between mouthfuls.

He smiled to himself, recalling their wedding day like it was yesterday instead of last year. He remembered the warmth of the sun on his face as they said their vows in front of an archway made of wildflowers and driftwood. His heart had nearly burst when he slid the delicate platinum band with its diamond chips onto her finger.

"I was waiting on the beach for your father to walk you down the path through the dunes," he whispered, slipping his arm around her waist. "You were a beautiful bride, Kate, and I couldn't believe how lucky I was. Still can't."

She snuggled into his side, leaning into his hug. "Ah, and you, my darling husband, were the poster boy for a handsome barefoot groom at a beach wedding."

Her expression became somber, and she took his hand, looking at him with such love that his heart melted. "We've had our challenges, but this has been the best year of my life. And you are the best part of it."

Anticipation bubbled in Luke's chest as he reached into his pocket. He'd planned this surprise for weeks, hoping it would capture the essence of their love story. Brushing a tender kiss against Kate's temple, a silent promise of forever, he produced a small blue velvet box.

Her eyes widened in curiosity as he slid it across the table. A nervous tremor ran through his hand, a stark contrast to the practiced ease with which he usually navigated presentations or design meetings. "I asked a local artist to make this for you," he said, his voice slightly rough with emotion.

Kate unwrapped the ribbon with a delicate touch, her breath catching in her throat as the box revealed a dainty sea turtle locket. A surge of relief washed over Luke as a gasp of delight escaped her lips. The white opals on the sea turtle's flippers glinted against the silver, their brilliance rivaled only by the larimar gemstone nestled in its center, mimicking the calming blue of the ocean.

"This is exquisite, Luke!" she said, her voice a delightful blend of awe and surprise. Her touch lingered on the cool stone, tracing its smooth surface with a reverence that spoke volumes. A warm smile bloomed on her face, crinkling the corners of her eyes in a way that sent a jolt straight to Luke's heart.

"It reminds me of our beach house and turtle team days. Thank you!"

The simple words held a universe of meaning for him. In that moment, the countless hours spent searching for the right artist and the meticulous planning, faded into insignificance. All that mattered was the love reflected on her face as he leaned in and gently clasped the silver chain around her neck.

The cool metal felt warm against his touch, a symbol of their enduring bond. He watched, mesmerized, as the locket nestled against her skin, a perfect complement to the woman who had stolen his heart.

She turned to him, her eyes brimming with love as she fingered the new locket. "This beauty merges our past with our today. Now I have something for you that might be our future."

Kate's hand lingered on her purse clasp, her smile teasing. With a mischievous flick of her wrist, she produced a small, red-wrapped box. The white ribbon, tied into a perfect bow, was a detail that snagged on Luke's attention, warming a spot deep in his chest.

"Happy anniversary, Luke," she said, her voice a shy whisper filled with an unspoken intimacy.

He took the box, his fingers brushing hers, and he felt a connection between them that was tied tighter than the bow on his gift. Anticipation buzzed through his veins as he carefully peeled away the foil. Each delicate fold revealed more of the small plastic object nestled inside. Confusion slammed into him, momentarily drowning out the world. Then, clarity struck like a bolt of lightning. Two red lines glared back, their message impossible to miss.

The universe tilted on its axis. Disbelief battled with a surge of raw, exhilarating joy that left him breathless. A choked laugh escaped his lips, a sound laced with wonder.

"So, we're having a baby?"

The question tumbled out, his gaze darting to Kate. Her smile, usually radiating confidence, flickered for a moment. A touch of fear, quickly masked by a hopeful glint, danced in her eyes.

His heart hammered against his ribs, a frantic drum solo of emotions. But a wave of concern hit him, a sudden awareness of the path Kate had walked. He remembered the heartache etched in her ever-present smile when she spoke of her last pregnancy. He didn't want to overwhelm her with his elation.

With a gentle touch, his thumb brushed across her cheek, a silent reassurance. Her face was a map of emotions—love, trepidation, and a glimmer of excitement peeking through the worry. He knew the thought of another loss terrified her.

"How do you feel about this?" he asked, his voice laced with a tenderness meant to chase away her anxieties.

Lips trembling, she answered in a rushed whisper, "Happy. Excited...but scared. And you?"

His response came without thought or hesitation. "Over the moon!"

A grin erupted on Luke's face as his hands found Kate's. He squeezed gently, his eyes sparkling with a playful glint. "You know," he said, "another boy to join Ben and Boo would be perfect."

She straightened, her eyes wide with a mock severity. "And what makes you think we'd have a boy, Mr. McAllister?"

Luke chuckled, one shoulder in a careless shrug. "Just a hunch. McAllister and Sons has a nice ring to it."

"Fiore and Daughter is better," she shot back, a grin teasing her faux frown.

He leaned in, nuzzling her hair, before placing a soft kiss on top of her head. Then, with a gentle arm around her shoulders, he pulled her close. "Seriously, though, Kate," he murmured against her ear, his voice softening, "you're okay with all of this? Adding a little one to our crew?"

Kate nestled into his embrace, and he felt her heart beating in sync with his. "We're good, Luke," she murmured, her voice filled with quiet confidence. "Because no matter what comes next, we'll face it together."

He trailed a line of soft kisses down her neck, his fingers absentmindedly tracing circles on her back. In a voice husky with tenderness, he whispered, "Always."

He swept the champagne aside, pouring from a carafe of bottled water instead, and then raised his glass in a toast. "To our family."

Kate's hand trembled as she clinked her flute against Luke's. A tear welled up in her eye, a single glistening droplet that she quickly blinked away. "To our family," she said, her voice soft but filled with a quiet strength.

Their gazes collided, igniting a spark of shared joy. As they drank, an electric current seemed to flow between them, a silent conversation brimming with their laughter and unspoken promises for the future.

He set down his glass, his hand reaching across the table. His fingers brushed against hers, sending a warmth blossoming in his chest. “Care to watch a sunset with me?”

Her simple answer held the weight of their future together. “I’d love to.”

Luke slipped his arm around her waist, and they strolled through the shadows of gathering dusk to watch the sunset from the old wooden bench along the bay.

THE END

Author's Note

AND BONUS CONTENT

Thanks for being a reader. I hope your Gull Island escape left you with a happy sigh.

If you enjoyed my story, please leave a review on Amazon, Goodreads, or with your favorite bookseller to help other romance lovers find their next read. (Reviews also make this author do a happy dance in PJs—it's a *thing.*)

The magic of Gull Island isn't over yet. I'm already crafting the next chapter in the series, so if you're yearning for more sunshine and unforgettable characters, stay connected and join me *Inside the Pages.*

My monthly newsletter offers exclusive updates, a peek behind the scenes of a writer's life, and curated book recommendations—all delivered straight to your inbox. Plus, you get a chance to shape the future of Gull Island by offering feedback on my work in progress.

As an Insider, you can also download a **FREE** Gull Island

prequel, *Before Sand & Sea.* This novelette reveals the backstory that starts Luke and Kate's romance in the four weeks before they meet. Though their worlds remain tantalizingly close, fate has yet to bring them face-to-face on Gull Island.

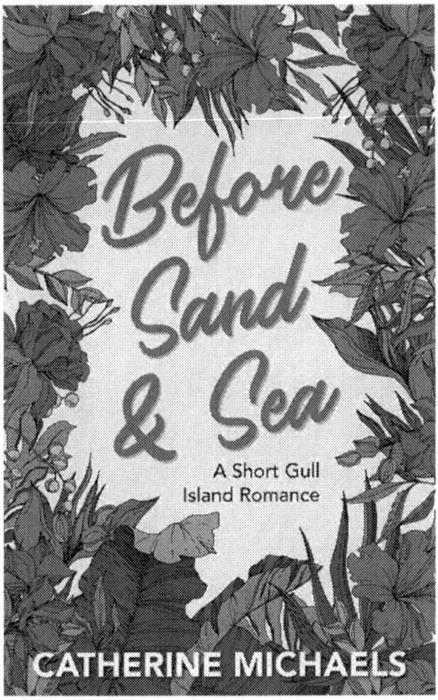

Visit catherinemichaelsauthor.com or click on the QR code below to become an Insider and download your prequel novelette.

Here's to happily ever afters, bookish adventures, and endless sunshiny days.

Warmly,

Catherine

A Note About the Settings

SUN, SAND, AND A TOUCH OF FICTION: INSPIRATION BEHIND GULL ISLAND

The ocean has always been my happy place, and its magic flows over these pages. **Black Rock,** a real town near where I grew up along Connecticut's Long Island Sound, sets the stage for Kate's world. **St. Mary's-by-the-Sea** waterfront park is a real-life gem. And the pizza and eateries around Black Rock are to die for.

However, when building dreamy North Carolina settings, I couldn't resist a touch of creative license. South Harbor and Gull Island are fictional mashups of my favorite beachy places, lovingly visited over the years.

Imagine the charm of **Manteo, Beaufort, and Southport**, with their historic waterfront homes, white picket fences, and vibrant Southern gardens. Then picture a network of bridges spider-webbing out from these towns over the waterways to the Atlantic Ocean. That's the essence of **South Harbor**.

Gull Island is a love letter to real beach communities, a mosaic pieced together from the Outer Banks' majesty to the Crystal Coast's laid-back vibes, and down to quaint Brunswick

County beaches. Here, Kate and Luke's romance unfolds against a backdrop of breathtaking beauty. And these beach town restaurants serve THE best shrimpburgers!

For the serene beauty of **the Point**, I drew on Oak Island's western edge, also called the Point. As a writer and nature lover, I can only hope its tranquility endures the challenges of coastal development.

The fictional **Gull Island Aquarium** might not exist, but North Carolina boasts a trifecta of real aquariums in Pine Knoll Shores, Roanoke Island, and Fort Fisher. These institutions dedicate themselves to education, coastal preservation, and, like the fictional Gull Island Aquarium, the vital work of sea turtle rehabilitation and rescue. They're all worth a visit!

This blend of real and imagined locations became the foundation of my Gull Island world, the perfect setting for a love story that wraps you like a starry summer night. I hope my tale whisks you away to a place where salty kisses and sweet dreams come true.

Readers' Guide

CALLING ALL BOOK CLUBS

For 15 years, my book club has been my haven for dissecting characters, debating plot twists, and celebrating the joy of great stories and friendship.

Imagine delving into Gull Island with *your* fellow bookworms and me. We can explore the complex characters, unpack the book's themes, its gorgeous coastal setting, and maybe even unearth some hidden details together.

If your book club is ready for a virtual adventure (no sunscreen required!), you can request a **30-minute author chat** through the "Contact Catherine" tab on my website: **catherine-michaelsauthor.com.**

I'd love to hear your thoughts and answer your burning questions about the story. In the meantime, you can spark lively discussions with your reading group with the questions suggested below.

Setting & Themes

- How did the author use sensory details to bring Gull Island and its challenges to life?
- Did any setting evoke a sense of nostalgia or yearning for a simpler life?
- How did the shift to the Christmas setting in Black Rock highlight the contrast between Kate's past and present life, and influence her emotional state?
- What details about Gull Island and Black Rock culture or traditions impacted the characters' interactions? Did any resonate with you and have you curious about a lesser-known place?

Characters

- We met Kate living in a bustling Northern metro area. She was at a low point and seeking a fresh start. Did her journey resonate with your own experiences of personal growth? How did her initial struggles shape your perception of her?
- How did Luke's initial resistance to change and his protectiveness of the island create both conflict and connection with Kate?
- Did Kate and Luke's personalities and backgrounds feel like a natural fit for a slow-burn romance, or were there aspects that stretched your believability?
- Which minor character surprised you with their role in the story? How did they challenge or support the main characters? Who was your favorite?

Plot & Romance

- How did the slow-burn approach build emotional tension and anticipation for Kate and Luke's relationship? Did it work for you?
- Were there moments when Kate or Luke's choices, based on their experiences or anxieties, felt frustratingly avoidable?
- The book doesn't shy away from difficult topics. What scenes stayed with you and why? Did it spark thoughts about a larger issue?
- How did CeCe and David Greenwood's friendship with Kate and Luke shape the main characters' emotional journey?
- The book explores the challenges of long-distance relationships. What did you think of Kate's reasons for cutting off her relationship with Luke when her contract ended in August? Were they believable?
- Discuss Luke's ultimate grand gesture. Did you find it romantic or unrealistic?
- The ending leaves room for the future. What are your hopes for Kate and Luke's future? How do you imagine them overcoming their challenges?

Themes

- The book explores several themes such as starting over, environmental responsibility, friendship, and found family. Which theme resonated most with you, and how did the author develop it?

- Did the book challenge your perspective on balancing tourism with environmental responsibility? How can travelers be more conscientious visitors?
- What are your thoughts about the scene with the sea turtle hatchlings? Did it evoke a sense of wonder or vulnerability about the natural world? If you witnessed a sea turtle hatch, was your experience like Kate's?
- How did the author weave the environmental concerns into the narrative without overshadowing the romance?

Writing Style & Story Structure

- How did the alternating points of view between Kate and Luke shape your understanding of their struggles and desires?
- What elements of the writing style (e.g., humor, vivid descriptions, emotionality) resonated with you and why?
- Beyond specific scenes, discuss the overall emotional arc of the story. Did it leave you feeling hopeful, melancholy, or something else?
- Did the ending feel emotionally satisfying? Were there any plot threads you wished were resolved more definitively?

Additional Discussion Prompts

- Did this book remind you of other slow-burn romances or second-chance stories?
- If you could visit Gull Island for a summer, what activity or place would you be most excited about?
- Imagine the book coming to life on the big screen! If you were casting the roles of Kate and Luke, which actors would best capture their personalities from the novel? Discuss why these actors fit the characters you've imagined.
- Of the many types of foods in this book, which have you already enjoyed? Which are you most eager to try?

Overall Thoughts

- Did the book's title and cover accurately convey what the novel was about?
- What was your favorite aspect of the story (characters, setting, plot, etc.)?
- This is the first book in the Gull Island Romance series. Based on the ending, what specific storylines and other characters would you like to see explored in a connected second book?
- Did the focus on emotional intimacy and character development ultimately enhance your enjoyment of this sweet romance?
- Would you recommend this book to others? Why or why not?

Acknowledgments

Big thanks to my critique partners, the champions of rough drafts! For the past two years, you waded through my story swamps and held onto hope when I was sure it was a lost cause. Your feedback has been a lifesaver (and sanity saver!).

Speaking of saving the day, a huge hooray to an incredible editing team, my *Jen duo*! Jen Milius, my awesome development editor got me out of the murky middle and encouraged me when I was stuck. Jen Boyes was a fantastic proofreader (and any errors are my own because, of course, I tweaked some after she finished).

Shout out to my beta and ARC readers, the story sharpeners! You helped me turn "meh" moments into "wow" moments. You're the secret weapon that makes this tale shine.

My reading circle, *Chapter and Chats*, is the joy squad! You remind me why I write: to create worlds for passionate readers like you. Thanks for the endless enthusiasm and bookish love over the past decades!

And how about that sunny, beachy cover? Friend and talented illustrator Dena McMurdie took my ideas for Kate, Luke (and Boo!) and made them come alive on the cover.

Special kudos to Laurie, the Emerald Isle, NC, sea turtle whisperer! Your insights on these magnificent creatures brought them to life on the page. (Some day, I'll be lucky enough to time my beach trip to catch a hatch.)

A huge thanks to Deb, the yarn wizard! You knitted up a batch of the cutest little sea turtle stuffies I've ever seen, and with ninja-like patience, showed me exactly how Mae and her knitters would get it done.

Captain Miriam Sutton, of Science by the Sea fame, ahoy! Thanks for the unforgettable boat trip to see the wild horses of Carrot Island off Beaufort. Inspiration definitely struck!

Family and friends, you're the ultimate cheerleaders. Thanks for putting up with this writer's rollercoaster over the past three years! You're the best! Forgive me for sprinkling your names among my minor characters?

And finally, the biggest shout out goes to YOU, awesome readers! This story was written with love, just for you. I'm beyond grateful for your support and hope you enjoyed the journey!

About the Author

Catherine Michaels whisks you away to charming small towns and sun-kissed shores in her swoon-worthy Gull Island sweet romances. Prepare to laugh, shed a happy tear, and fall for unforgettable characters.

A former educator with a passion for storytelling, Catherine brings her unique perspective to the page after years of nurturing young minds, publishing award-winning children's books as *Cat Michaels*, and leading in the corporate world.

Fueled by a desire for happily-ever-afters, she started her Gull Island series during the pandemic. Drawing inspiration from her coastal havens, Catherine weaves relatable characters and picturesque places into heartwarming escapes.

Catherine and her family live outside Raleigh, North Carolina, where she tends her fairy garden for neighborhood children and visits her happy places by the sea every chance she gets.

www.catherinemichaelsauthor.com

Made in the USA
Middletown, DE
19 July 2024

57476458R00214